"Theresa Scott's historical romances are tender, exciting, enjoyable, and satisfying!"
—*Romantic Times*

"Theresa Scott's stories are distinctive, well-plotted, and unforgettable."
—Debbie Macomber, Bestselling Author of *Dakota Born*

MARKED FOR LIFE

She lay on her back, staring up at the stars. They were clear white pinpoints on this summer night. She felt his arm go over her stomach, gently pinning her to the ground. She had known this moment would come. Had known ever since she'd first seen him. And now that it was here, her heart raced with excitement.

She reached up and stroked his face. He turned and kissed the palm of her hand. Shivers went through her at the touch of his lips. When he paused, she moved her hand up, up to his forehead and dared to touch the lock of hair that dangled over his forehead. "I have been wanting to do that for a long time," she whispered.

He kissed her then, and she knew he had been wanting to do more than that. He leaned over her, putting more of his weight on her now. She pulled his head down and they kissed, his lips warm on hers. She sighed happily and her toes curled. His skin felt smooth and warm. She ran a hand down one of his arms, over the black tattoo of the raven.

NORTHERN NIGHTS

THERESA SCOTT

LEISURE BOOKS   NEW YORK CITY

With sincere thanks to Drew Crooks of the Lacey Historical Museum, Lacey, Washington, for his help.

A LEISURE BOOK®

August 2000

Published by

Dorchester Publishing Co., Inc.
276 Fifth Avenue
New York, NY 10001

Cover art by John Ennis
www.ennisart.com

ISBN 0-8439-4748-9

Printed in the United States of America.

Although the historical incident in this novel is portrayed more or less accurately (as much as the passage of time and contradictory source material will allow), fact, speculation and fiction are freely mixed here; historical personages exist side by side with composite characters and wholly fictional ones—all of whom act and speak at the author's whim.

Prologue

Early Spring, 1854
Olympia, Washington Territory

Tsus-sy-uch, a youthful, tall, well-made Tsimshian Indian chief, wiped the sweat from his forehead. It was a hot day. Below him on the hillside were smoking, burning stumps and fallen trees that he, his friends and his slaves had labored to chop down over the past two weeks. Today they would be paid by Mr. John Butler, and then the Indians could return to their northern country in time for the berries to ripen and the salmon to fatten.

Tsus-sy-uch felt the grave responsibility of his position as leader. He and his men had ventured far south to O-lymp-ya, where they could earn more money in thirty days than they could in a year back at their village. While the white men paid well for the work, it was backbreaking labor

9

to clear the land. Fortunately, he was young and strong and his friends were too. They had cleared the land well, and sooner even than the time agreed upon with Mr. Butler. Mr. Butler would be pleased with the fine job they had done.

Tsus-sy-uch had known white men before. Back at his home, there was a fort, Fort Simpson. At that fort lived twenty or thirty white men, all eager and willing to trade with Indian people. On this visit to O-lymp-ya he had met and seen more white men than he had ever thought lived on the earth.

He was glad that this was the last day of their work. He felt anxious to get home to his people, to visit with his mother and father and uncle, and yes, to see his betrothed.

With a gesture, he told his men to stop working. They had already done more than agreed upon: cleared ten acres of hilly, rocky, treed land for Mr. Butler. It was enough.

The chief and his men put down their tools and picked up their personal things. Tsus-sy-uch took a drink of water from the deer bladder he carried with him. They walked the distance to the farmhouse where Mr. Butler lived. He hoped Mr. Burt was not there. He would rather receive his payment from Mr. Butler. Mr. Butler's helper, Mr. James Burt, had stopped by frequently to check on how the work was coming along. He was a crude, bossy man and Tsus-sy-uch did not like him. However, he hid his feelings because the white men paid so well.

But both white men were at the large wooden farmhouse when the Indians arrived. Mr. Burt came out, wiping his mouth as though he'd been eating. Mr. Butler stepped into the yard behind, hitching up his pants as though preparing for something. Tsus-sy-uch frowned. Both men walked toward him, and he noticed a belligerent attitude about them he had not seen before. His jaw tightened.

"I have come for our pay," he told Mr. Butler. Mr. Butler owned the farm. He was the chief. Tsus-sy-uch held out his hand for the money.

"So . . ." drawled Mr. Burt. "He's come for his pay. Whaddya wanna do about it, John?"

Tsus-sy-uch kept his eyes fastened on Mr. Butler, the chief, but inside, his heart burned with anger at the way Mr. Burt had spoken to him.

"What money?" demanded Mr. Butler in a loud and angry voice.

Tsus-sy-uch was puzzled. Had the white man forgotten their agreement? Fourteen days ago, Tsus-sy-uch and Mr. Butler, with Mr. Burt watching, had agreed upon a price, a very good price, for clearing a portion of Mr. Butler's land.

"We come for the money," said Tsus-sy-uch with the dignity that came naturally to him as a man who was a wealthy chief's heir and very honored in his own country. "We cleared land. We want our money."

"Money?" snorted Mr. Butler. "You'll get none of my money."

Tsus-sy-uch stared at Mr. Butler in confusion. "But we agree—"

"I agreed to nothing," snarled Mr. Butler. He looked very angry.

And now, Tsus-sy-uch could feel his own anger mounting. "My men and me work hard," he said, struggling to keep control of his anger, "and you agree to pay. Pay us now!"

11

Mr. Burt came up and glared at Tsus-sy-uch. "We don't owe you nothin'!"

Tsus-sy-uch raised both hands in a gesture of irritation. Mr. Butler ducked and cried out, "Shoot him, Burt!"

Mr. Burt pulled a pistol out of his shirt, cocked it at Tsus-sy-uch's chest. Tsus-sy-uch watched in disbelieving horror as Mr. Burt pulled the trigger. A terrible pain ripped through Tsus-sy-uch's heart. Then everything went black.

The young chief fell, dead before he hit the ground.

The stunned Indians gathered around their fallen chief. Bending over him, several of his men tried to pick him up, to awaken him. But finally the black blood pouring from the hole in his heart convinced them. He was dead.

Burt bolted for the woods.

Butler swung on the milling, distraught Indians. "Get outa here! Get the sam hill off'n my property or I'll shoot another one of you dirty Indians!" He menaced them with a pistol he pulled from under his shirt.

Confused and angry, two of the Indians picked up the dead man's feet. Another two picked up his arms, and they hurried down to the gravel beach where their canoe was moored. The other four Indians raced after them.

"And don't come back!" yelled Butler. He let out a triumphant whoop.

The Indians paddled swiftly north, to Fort Nisqually. They would tell the white chief there about the foul murder. Then the white men would kill these murderers.

Tsus-sy-uch would be avenged.

*   *   *

Olympia prosecuting attorney Donald Larson sat in his law office, feet upon his desk, staring out the window. He took out his pocket watch and glanced at it. Another half hour and he would meet John Swan. Mr. Swan wanted to purchase two acres of the Larson family land, and Donald badly wanted to sell it to him.

Donald was the sole support of his large family. Lately, it had seemed as if there just was not enough money to go around. Even though his hardworking wife made all the family's clothes, soap and butter and baked her own bread, it was still not enough. The truth was, a large household ate up money.

Donald looked at his watch again. He'd like to get out the door early today. That'd give him time to think about how much he should ask for the acreage. The price should be high enough to help out his family, and low enough that Swan would still want to purchase it. Maybe if he mentioned the timber on it . . .

His thoughts were interrupted when his law assistant poked his head in the door. "That case coming up this week. What do you want to do about it?"

Donald snapped back to the present. "Case? What case?"

His assistant eyed him. "That Northern Indian. The one killed out at Butler Cove—"

"That one," said Donald, swinging his feet to the floor. He hated it when his assistant acted as though Donald was aged and forgetful. He did it to feel important, and it irritated Donald. "Butler said it was self-defense. So did Burt. They feared for their lives . . ."

"The magistrate, Plumb, believes them," said the assistant.

"Hmmm," said Donald thoughtfully. "Those Indians were from where?" He rummaged through the foot-high stack of papers on his desk, trying to find the one about the case.

"From Fort Simpson," said his assistant crisply.

"Fort Simpson? Where is that?" Donald kept thumbing through the papers.

"A thousand miles north of here."

Donald sank back in his chair. "A thousand miles north—why, those Indians aren't even local." He pondered that one. "They won't be staying around to bother us about this . . ."

"No," agreed his assistant. "Besides," he chuckled, "Indians don't vote."

Donald shot his assistant an acidic glare. "I'm not up for reelection anytime soon."

He finally found the paper he was looking for. "It says here Burt and Butler are in custody. Staying where, I might ask? The big problem, as I see it, is that we have no county jail to keep them in. And I do not intend to build a jail for two men who killed in self-defense! Talk about expense! Why, the voters would never approve it."

"But—" said the assistant.

"Get out," said Donald, glancing at his watch one more time. "My mind is made up. As prosecuting attorney I see no reason to hold those men. Let them go. No sense wasting taxpayers' money. It would be an expense to the county to retain them in custody. Can't have that!" He did not want to be late to meet Swan. The man had been eager to buy the land, and Donald saw no reason to cool his enthusiasm for the acreage by being tardy.

"I'll be back in tomorrow," said Donald, shoving his hat on his head as he fled out the door. "I'm already late for an important appointment!"

His assistant stared at the closed door. "Let them go?" he muttered. Then he shook his head. "Very well, then. But I have a bad feeling about this. Real bad . . ."

Chapter One

Early Summer, 1855
The Town of Olympia, Washington Territory

The long, sleek, black canoe sliced like an obsidian knife through the smooth gray waters of Puget Sound. Low chanting echoed off green hills clad in cedar and fir and swirled across the water to where Elizabeth Desiree Powell stood on the gravel beach in her high-button boots.

"Who are those men?" she asked, shading her blue eyes with her hand. The sun was bright and the water sparkled.

"How should I know?" answered James Burt. At least he'd said that was his name. He'd come by her aunt's farm an hour ago, introduced himself, said he was a friend of Uncle John Butler's, then settled himself down on the grass without waiting for so much as a single word of invitation from Elizabeth.

She squinted at the passing canoe, then remembered Miss Cowperth's admonition about how squinting caused wrinkles. She deliberately relaxed her face. "There's quite a few of them. Must be at least ten," she observed. "How picturesque they look, rowing in rhythm like that, with the water dripping off their golden paddles and glinting in the bright sunlight." She sighed. "I wish Uncle John and Aunt Elizabeth were here to see this."

"You and me both," answered Burt. "Say, I sure could use a drink . . ."

"The water bucket is on the counter," stated Elizabeth. "Please help yourself."

"That's not the kind of drink I had in mind," he muttered. Grimacing, he rose and stalked across the yard, scattering chickens carelessly with each step. He entered the stoutly built, roomy farmhouse, leaving Elizabeth to watch the oncoming canoe. She supposed it was all right to let Mr. Burt go into the house. His clothes were neat and tidy enough, though his face had a scraggly, hard-living edge to it. And he *had* said he was a friend of Uncle John's . . .

Oh, why did Aunt Elizabeth and Uncle John have to pick today of all days to paddle the fifteen miles north to Fort Nisqually? If only her uncle had known Mr. Burt would be visiting, he surely would have stayed home.

From the barn she could hear the cow lowing. Elizabeth walked the well-worn dirt path across the yard and opened the barn door. She entered into the cool darkness and went over to the stall that housed the cow and calf. She led them out into the fenced part of the farmyard. "There you go, Esmerelda," she said. "You and your calf can munch on some of the grass here."

Time to go back into the house. She had chores to do before Aunt Elizabeth returned. The rising bread dough needed to be punched down, and there was thick cream waiting to be churned into butter, not to mention the hem she'd promised to sew on Aunt Elizabeth's best dress.

Elizabeth sighed. She wished she had gone with her aunt and uncle to Fort Nisqually, but her uncle had looked so angry when she'd suggested it that she hadn't dared utter another word. But if she'd gone with them, why, she could be asking some of the men and women at the fort if they had ever seen or heard of her father, Theodore Powell. Maybe if she could find her father, she would at last know who she was and what she was supposed to do with herself. As things stood now, she had a great hole in her heart, or soul, she didn't know which, and she didn't know how to fill it. Maybe if she found her father, she could become a whole human being, like everybody else. Of course, she would have to make inquiries outside of Auntie Elizabeth's keen hearing. Auntie went into a hissy fit at the mere mention of Theodore Powell's name.

Elizabeth glanced over once more to see what progress the black canoe had made. Usually a boatload of people waved as they swept past on the gray-green waters of Puget Sound. But this boatload of men—she could see them clearly now—were paddling determinedly. And they'd fallen silent.

She frowned. They'd been to town, she decided.

Across the water, at a distance of two miles or so, she could see the low, weathered buildings of the little town of Olympia. Uncle John's farm sat all by itself on the Sound, isolated from neighbors and surrounded by huge fir and cedar trees.

As she watched, the bow of the black canoe suddenly swung round and aimed directly for Uncle John's gray gravel beach.

"Mr. Burt," she called out. "Why, look! More visitors. Perhaps you should come and help me greet these people. They look like Indians. Mr. Burt?"

He came out of the door, a drink of water in one hand and a huge piece of chocolate cake in the other. She flushed, and opened her mouth, about to scold him for cutting into the cake she was saving as a surprise for Auntie Elizabeth and Uncle John. Then she snapped her mouth shut. In none of Miss Cowperth's etiquette books did it say that one should scold one's guest.

"Indians?" he inquired around a mouthful of cake. He stared at the newcomers, his eyes narrowing. "Yep. Look like Indians," he confirmed. "Aw, dammit!"

She really did not care for them to visit today either, though she cared even less for Mr. Burt and his rude words. She had chores to do. Well, no help for it now, she decided. Perhaps the Indians would leave soon, or perhaps she could convince them to return at a time when Auntie and Uncle John could better entertain them properly.

Indian visitors were rare. In the two months that Elizabeth had lived in Olympia, she'd seen the occasional Indian, from a distance of course, but mostly she'd seen the numerous white settlers that had arrived to populate the area.

19

"I suppose," said Elizabeth reluctantly, prodded by memories of Miss Cowperth's etiquette books, "that I should make them some tea."

Mr. Burt gave a snort. "Now why," he said, taking another bite of cake, then tossing it aside, "would you do that?"

Elizabeth straightened her spine. How rude! Throwing away the cake like that! It was Miss Cowperth's best recipe. "I," announced Elizabeth, drawing herself up to her full height of five-and-a-half feet, "have attended Miss Cowperth's Finishing School for Young Ladies, Mr. Burt."

She waited for some recognition, some glimmer that he understood the import of what she'd said. When he merely continued to stare at her, she explained with forced patience, "In San Francisco, Mr. Burt. Miss Cowperth taught each one of her young ladies how to behave and to be sensible of our manners when guests arrive, even uninvited guests."

"Uninvited guests? Oh, very good," he sneered. "Make *me* some tea while you're at it." He continued to watch the oncoming canoe. Long and narrow, with a raised prow, it cut through the water smoothly. A white design decorated the bow. "Girl, your uncle hide a rifle anywhere around here? Tell me quick, now."

"No, Mr. Burt," she answered sharply. "While Uncle John and Aunt Elizabeth always seem to be wary of the local Indians, I cannot recall that they have ever suggested shooting one."

He gave her a strange look.

Mr. Burt, she decided, was beginning to annoy her.

"These Indians ain't local," he said. "They look like Northern Indians."

"From Fort Nisqually?" she asked politely.

"Farther north."

"Well," she answered, trying to ignore the man's uncouth speech and lack of manners, "they will certainly appreciate a piece of cake and tea, then, won't they?"

"You gonna feed them?" he asked in amazement.

"Yes," she gritted. "I fed you, didn't I?" She dropped her gaze pointedly to the half-eaten piece of cake lying on the ground.

"You don't feed those Indians, miss. You run from them!" He looked worried.

She tightened her lips and marched toward the house. The man was truly beginning to annoy her.

"Girl!" called Mr. Burt.

She turned, slowly, ignoring the rudeness as well as the urgency in his tone. "Yes?"

"Wouldn't hurt for you to tell me where Butler hides his rifle. And tell me right quick, too. You go hide—up in the barn, or maybe in the cellar . . ."

Hands on hips, she marched back to face him. "Mr. Burt," she said as evenly as she could, "though I may not wish to entertain these Indians today, I assure you that I am not such a reprehensible hostess as to allow you to greet my guests with buckshot while I run off to hide in the barn!"

The man was decidedly odd, she told herself. She hoped that Uncle John and Aunt Elizabeth returned soon. To be trapped at the farm with this very odd man and a boatload of Indians would not make for a pleasant day.

"I won't use buckshot," Mr. Burt assured her. "I'll use bullets."

"Very well, Mr. Burt." Her lip almost curled into a sneer but she caught it in time. Miss Cowperth would never countenance a young woman sneering at a guest, however richly he deserved it. "I can see that I must be very forthcoming with you. I do not *know* where my uncle keeps his weapons, nor do I know where he hides his bullets." She whirled on her heel. "And now I will go and make some tea for my guests!"

"Well, girl, you do amaze me," Burt answered, shaking his head as he hurried after her to the house. "You look right fine enough with them blue eyes and all that brown hair knotted in a proper bun, and that pretty blue dress, but you don't have the sense God gave a goose!"

Elizabeth gritted her teeth. She'd heard his rude remarks, but she determinedly declined to answer. She would remember Miss Cowperth's training— she would!—and she would not lower herself to the level of her uncouth guest.

That decided, she marched to the house. Now, where had she put her white gloves? She would need those, too. When she peeked over one shoulder for a quick glance at Mr. Burt, he rushed past her, tore open the door and began rummaging among her uncle's things. "Mr. Burt!" she cried. "Stop throwing things!"

The way he was carrying on, it would take her the better part of the day to clean up after him! "Mr. Burt, that is my aunt's"—something whistled past her ear—"best tablecloth! What *are* you looking for?"

"No damn guns," he muttered and ran back out the door.

She watched him, her jaw gaping. Fortunately, she remembered in time that gaping jaws stretched facial skin, causing wrinkled jowls. She snapped her mouth shut.

Mr. Burt, meanwhile, was racing down to the beach to where his canoe lay. The black canoe was now only a little distance from shore.

"Mr. Burt? Mr. Burt? What are you up to now?"

He was bending over his canoe and rummaging ferociously through his things. He pulled out a musket and began loading it.

Miss Cowperth had never explained the loading of a weapon—it had not been necessary to explain such vulgar things to her young charges. Nonetheless, from her recent time on the frontier, Elizabeth recognized a man pouring black powder down the barrel of his musket in preparation for firing when she saw one.

And just whom would he be firing upon?

Why, her guests, the Northern Indians, that's whom. And they were, at this very moment, pulling their canoe into the shallow waters of Uncle John's beach.

She really must remonstrate with Mr. Burt! He had no idea, none whatsoever, of how to greet guests!

She forgot about the tea and her white gloves and marched back down to the beach. He must be told . . .

"Get back, get back!" Mr. Burt yelled at her, while he frantically pounded the ramrod up and down inside the barrel of his musket.

Three huge Indians jumped out of the canoe as

it ground into the gravel. They ran through the water toward Mr. Burt. The first one to reach him lunged for Mr. Burt's weapon. Mr. Burt had leveled his musket in preparation for firing, but the Indian seized the barrel and jerked it up before the gun fired. The gun's wild blast echoed over the quiet water. Startled, Elizabeth jumped.

Mr. Burt yelled ferociously, threw aside the weapon and sprang at the Indian. The two wrestled until finally the Indian dropped Mr. Burt to the beach, and flung himself atop him. Mr. Burt and the Indian rolled around, half in and half out of the water until the Indian got a choke hold on Mr. Burt's throat. Then Mr. Burt flopped around like a half-drowned fish trying to escape. His efforts proved futile, however, and his face turned purple before the Indian picked him up and effortlessly tossed him into the canoe. Two other Indians began tying Mr. Burt up.

Elizabeth froze in disbelief. Whatever was happening? Why were they doing this to Mr. Burt?

The Indian leader, between great breaths from his exertions, said something in his heathen tongue to the others, then turned to Elizabeth.

He was tall, bigger than any Indian she'd ever seen before, not that she'd seen very many. His straight black hair came to his broad shoulders, and his dark, bronze skin smoothly covered an expansive, muscular chest. Across the powerful muscles of his left arm was tattooed a huge black raven. He wore men's blue pants and his feet were bare. But it was to his face that her eyes were drawn. My, but he was a handsome man. Very handsome.

He had a straight nose with just the tiniest hook on the end; his lips were firm and his jaw square.

In fact, thought Elizabeth, her heart suddenly pounding loudly in her chest, he was probably the handsomest man she had ever seen. Even handsomer than Cyril B. Mandeville III, older brother of Mary Mandeville, a classmate of Elizabeth's at Miss Cowperth's school, a young man whom she'd foolishly mooned over though he'd never noticed her.

"What have you done to Mr. Burt?" she squeaked when she finally got her wits about her. The way the Indian stared at her made her feel funny inside. Kind of scared, but kind of excited and shivery.

"Lis-uh-buth?" he asked. His eyes were so dark a woman could get lost in them, and she saw a white flash of straight teeth.

"How—how did you know my name?"

He didn't answer her, just said a string of foreign words to his men and strode up to her. He put a hand on her arm and urged her toward the boat. She could smell him. He smelled of man, and salt and sun . . .

"Take your hands off me. I'm not going anywhere with you!"

But he didn't take his hands off her. He tugged on her wrist, urging her toward the canoe.

"No," she said, feeling alarmed. After all, it had not been pleasant, what he'd done to Mr. Burt. "I am not going with you!" She jerked her wrist free of his grasp.

He reached for her arm again, but she picked up her skirts and dashed for the farmhouse. If she could just get inside, she could lock the door and wait until these horrible Indians left her shores. . . .

She heard hoots and hollers from the Indians,

Theresa Scott

but she kept running. Footsteps pounded behind her. They were chasing her!

Faster! Faster! she panted to herself, but her legs moved with agonizing slowness. Fear coursed through her. She had to get away! She had to!

Bare feet thudded behind her. She put on a burst of speed. Only a few more feet to the door!

Tackled from behind, she tumbled into the dirt path, tripped to the ground by a wretched Indian. "No!" she cried. Her skirts tangled around her legs, and she couldn't get up.

"Let me go!" she cried, panicking. She kicked out at him and tried to scratch him, but he held her wrists together. She tried to bite him, but he just laughed. He lay half over her, crushing her. Deep brown eyes dared—yes dared—to laugh at her.

Desperate to get away, she struggled. "Let me go!" She twisted, managing to free her hands.

He caught her wild punch with one hand. Pity, because the blow would have landed squarely upon his jaw. She noted that he did not look quite so amused now.

He scrambled to his feet and yanked her up to hers.

"No!" she cried, for he kept an iron grip on her hands. Then, in one smooth motion, he picked her up and threw her across one brawny shoulder.

Elizabeth landed with a thump across his back in a bone-jarring thud that knocked the breath from her. It shook her body clear through to her teeth. She gasped several times, trying to recover her escaped breath. He said something in his heathen language, and indicated Mr. Burt's canoe with a wave of one hand.

"No!" cried Elizabeth when she could speak

26

again. "Put me down! Put me down this instant!" She kicked furiously.

He ignored her cries and walked back down the beach to the canoes.

Elizabeth's futile tears of rage fell with each step. Five Indian men walked slowly beside them, laughing.

"Put me down!" she tried again, kicking wildly and shrieking. No Indian was going to carry her off! "Put me down, I say!"

She thought she heard him laugh. But he did not put her down. "How—how dare you! Stop this, you—you heathen!" she cried. "Put—me—down!"

He laughed again, she was sure of it this time, and strode to the canoe, each step landing hard enough to jar her teeth.

When he got to the canoe, several of the Indians started gesticulating and pointing at the poor, unconscious Mr. Burt. "What have you done to him?" she cried. "Oh, no! What have you done?"

The Indian did not let her go, however, but kept her over one shoulder as if she were a sack of potatoes.

"Put me down, heathen!" Elizabeth spoke through gritted teeth.

They'd reached the water's edge by now, and the Indian did indeed put her down, but he kept a tight grip on her upper arm. Her legs wobbled as she tried to keep her footing on the beach, but her black boots slid on the wet gravel. She squirmed and attempted to free herself from his grip, but he tightened it, all the while gesturing from Mr. Burt to Mr. Burt's canoe. At last several of the Indians jumped out of the canoe and dragged the unconscious Mr. Burt with them over to his canoe.

Two of them pulled and prodded his canoe, a leaky-looking blue craft, into the water, and the other two threw Mr. Burt into the bottom of it.

Then one of them, a lanky Indian with a big belly, whose cheeks and forehead were covered in curling, dark green tattoos, strode over to where Elizabeth stood. He wrapped strong fingers around her free arm and gave a ferocious tug.

Elizabeth winced and looked from one man to the other. What was this?

The Indian who had claimed her first put a hand on the second Indian's shoulder and gave him a little push.

Tattoo-face grimaced and became angry. He said some words in a low voice, and even Elizabeth understood it was a warning.

But the Indian who'd carried her like a sack of potatoes ignored the warning. He pointed at Mr. Burt, said something, then pried the other man's grip off Elizabeth's arm.

Frowning, the tattooed man touched his thumb to his chest and said something. Whatever it was, the first Indian was not impressed, because he did not stop to talk; instead, he dragged Elizabeth over to the large black canoe.

He picked her up and lifted her into the canoe. She crumpled to the bottom of the craft and tried to get up, but he kept a strong hand on her shoulder, and she realized she could not rise in the tippy vessel.

Two other Indians pushed the large canoe further out into the water, then climbed aboard. Elizabeth gave a helpless wail as she watched the clear stretch of water widen between canoe and beach. "You can't do this!" she wailed in dismay.

The Indians stolidly ignored her distraught cry, speaking a few terse words among themselves. The one holding her shoulder released his grip and picked up his paddle. Then all five Indians resumed paddling in the same concentrated, rhythmic way she'd had the extreme misfortune to witness when they'd first paddled toward her uncle's beach.

Elizabeth huddled in the canoe and watched her aunt and uncle's farmhouse fade into the distance. How could this be happening to her? What would Aunt Elizabeth think? How would she know where to find her? Oh, no!

Where were they taking her? Why were they taking Mr. Burt, too? Oh, what would Aunt Elizabeth do when she returned home and found her gone?

Tears ran down Elizabeth's cheeks as she thought of dear Aunt Elizabeth. Would she ever see her aunt again?

She buried her face in her hands. At that moment, she suddenly remembered how her only concern, when she'd first seen these horrible heathens, had been to offer them tea and cake while wearing her white gloves. How foolish she had been! How foolish! And now she was paying for her foolishness . . . paying mightily.

Shakily, Elizabeth dragged a hand across her face, wiping away the wetness. She would not cry. What would Miss Cowperth say? But not a single one of Miss Cowperth's helpful rules of etiquette came to mind. Miss Cowperth had never mentioned what to do if one were seized by Indians.

Elizabeth shrank into herself, away from the large men who dominated the canoe and in particular from the one who eyed her, his face grim. How could she ever have thought him handsome?

And that she crouched at his feet helped not at all.

She forced herself to look away from him and back at the rapidly disappearing farmhouse. This could not be happening to her. It could not!

Chapter Two

Fights With Wealth, known to the white men of the Hudson's Bay Company as "Isaac Thompson," laughed to himself when he caught the white woman glaring at him through her tangled brown hair. She looks a mess like that, he thought. Looks like a slave.

He straightened at the somber thought and his mouth tightened; his humor fled.

Grimly, he paddled. He wanted to get away as quickly as they could from the town of O-lymp-ya, the white man's town. Both captives remained silent, although Isaac once glanced at the white man in the canoe with the Tsimshians. The white man lunged at the side of the canoe, trying to dive into the deep green waters. Fisher, the tattooed Tsimshian leader, grabbed his collar and pulled him back. Then he thwacked him on the cheek with a

31

paddle. Thereafter the white man lay moaning on the canoe floor.

Some of Isaac's satisfaction reasserted itself. He turned to Maggot, the Tsimshian slave. "Is this one of the men we seek?"

The slave hesitated. "Yes," he finally answered. "This white man is John Butler."

Isaac heard Chief Fisher's grunt of satisfaction as the Tsimshians talked among themselves. John Butler was the chief of the murderers.

Isaac already knew from inquiries in O-lymp-ya that the woman was Lis-uh-buth Butler, the wife. She kept quiet. Isaac saw her trembling once, but when she noticed him, she gritted her jaw and looked away, forcibly stilling the trembling. She did not want him to know she was frightened. She was brave. He liked that.

Isaac wondered to himself why he had not let the Tsimshian leader, Fisher, take the woman in his canoe. The tattooed man had wanted her. But something had kept Isaac from letting him have her. Perhaps it was the woman's youth—he was surprised to see Butler's wife was so young—that made him decide to keep her with him. And Isaac had seen the cruelty of the Tsimshian chief before.

Isaac and his men paddled silently past Fort Nisqually, careful to keep to the far side of the bay, away from the twinkling lights. The sounds of the fort at dusk told them the inhabitants were retiring inside for the night.

And nature helped the raiders when a low fog rolled in. Now no white man would ever find them. Soon the white man's longhouses were far behind.

Isaac smiled grimly. As he paddled, his thoughts drifted back to how he'd become involved in this raid. He had not wanted to visit the Tsimshians. But his uncle, his mother's brother, had for the first time in Isaac's twenty-five years acknowledged Isaac's existence by sending him an invitation to visit. It was actually a command. . . .

. . . Fights With Wealth, the Haida nobleman known to white people as Isaac Thompson, glared at the crowd of Tsimshian Indians awaiting him on the gravel beach. He stood in his blanket and cedar finery, bare legs braced in the bow of the black war canoe so he would not fall while his men paddled closer to the beach. Isaac and his ten Haida men were all wearing their best clothes for the Tsimshian feast his uncle had invited them to.

Over his shoulders Isaac wore the blanket called Cower From Me. It had been woven with great care by the women of his clan out of strips of cedar bark and white mountain goat's wool twisted together. The blanket bore a black rendition of his clan's crest: the great Haida Raven, its wings out-stretched to encompass the world.

Isaac stood unmoving as his men paddled the war canoe slowly and carefully so that he would not fall. Such a fall would humiliate not only Isaac, but his whole Haida house of nobles, the huge net of relatives that made up his family. The loyal men with him knew they must keep the craft balanced smoothly. They halted their paddling and chanting and let the canoe glide smoothly into shore. It was a perfect landing, and the young Haida chieftain stepped out of the canoe, coiled grace in his every move.

Only the hostile silence of the sullen Tsimshian

people greeted his arrival. It was as he had expected.

No Tsimshian chief came forward to sprinkle the white feathery down that indicated peace between their peoples. Isaac heard his men muttering under their breaths. He wondered if it had been a mistake to answer his Tsimshian uncle's invitation to the feast. His mother's brother had never shown any interest in him, and it had been a surprise when the Tsimshian messenger had arrived at Isaac's Haida village with the invitation to the feast. Now Isaac hoped he had not drawn his Haida relatives and friends into a trap.

Finally an old chief moved out of the crowd. Behind him walked two middle-aged men who appeared, from their elaborate dress, to be chiefs. On either side of the old chief came two young slave boys, each carrying a basket filled with white downy feathers. The old chief reached into a basket and took out a pinch of feathers and scattered them before him on the beach, then repeated the gesture over and over.

Isaac felt his tense muscles relax. The Tsimshians had intended no insult, then; it was merely that their welcoming chief was old and moved slowly. He wondered if this man was his uncle.

The old chief sang a Tsimshian welcoming song. Isaac and his men politely waited until the old man had finished, then followed him up to the biggest longhouse. People in the crowd parted to let them walk through, but despite the scattering of the white down, Isaac could feel their hostility. Perhaps he should have heeded his father's warning not to come.

Numerous canoes, small and large, were drawn

up in neat rows on the gray gravel beach. Behind the beach, ten cedar longhouses stood in a single row, out of reach of the winter's highest tide. The Tsimshian women of commoner status were easily identified by their brown, woven cedar bark cloaks and skin aprons and bare legs. Inverted cone-shaped woven cedar hats covered their long black hair. Here and there were flashes of red, green, yellow and white, the colors of the Hudson's Bay trading blankets doing double duty as shirts, jackets or cloaks for the Tsimshian Indian men in the crowd. The men, too, went bare-legged and bare-footed despite the chill of the early spring.

And of course there were the slaves, easy to pick out with their matted hair and ragged garments made of inferior marmot fur.

As the Haidas walked through the crowd, Isaac saw and heard the people whispering. He knew what they were saying, and he gritted his teeth against that knowledge.

"A fine welcoming party," joked William Kelp under his breath as he walked beside Isaac. "How I like to see friendly faces."

Some of the Haidas behind them chuckled.

Isaac said nothing, only stared straight ahead. His best friend was not going to be able to joke him out of the tension he felt.

He was glad he had brought strong, well-built men of the Haida nation with him. All healthy, hardworking men. All nobles or commoners. All of them free. Not a slave among them. Never a slave.

Isaac halted in mid stride and turned to his men. "Two of you stay with the canoe," he ordered, indicating two of his best fighters.

"Your father will not like it that you do not keep

all your men with you," objected William. "He sent these men along to protect you. They cannot do that if they are guarding the canoe."

"They guard our escape," answered Isaac shortly.

William grunted and surveyed the watching crowd. "These people do not seem to like us," he agreed.

They walked on, the old chief some distance ahead of them by now. From the obsequious behavior of the Tsimshian commoners, Isaac guessed the old chief was a man of the highest noble status; probably he was indeed his uncle.

"Why should they like us?" answered Isaac. "We are Haida, they are Tsimshian. Our people war and raid against each other. We have always done so."

"Look at their glares," answered William. "Do not try to tell me we are among friends, even if it is a feast we are invited to."

Isaac gave a snort. "I have seen some of these men at Fort Simpson, sitting around the fort, dressed like white men. And they know I am—"

"Do not say it," warned William.

Isaac smiled grimly. "You know what I am going to say before I speak now?"

But William would not be deterred. "It is not true, what you were going to say."

Isaac sneered inwardly. Even William, his closest friend, could not bring himself to say what these people surely were whispering to one another. "It *is* true. To these people."

William winced at his friend's harsh words. "No, no," he reminded quickly. "Your father washed your name clean. There is no taint. He gave great potlatches, two of them. They were the greatest potlatches our people have ever seen. He gave away many canoes, many blankets, fish beyond counting and baskets of berries, so many that our people had berries to eat for several seasons. No, you are a Haida nobleman, a great chief, and you do not need to be ashamed. Your name is cleared of any shame."

"The potlatch cleared my name among my father's people," answered Isaac bitterly. "These are my *mother's* people!"

Even William could find no answer to that. He subsided into silence.

The Haidas walked up the gravel beach until their way was barred by a barrel-chested, angry-looking man of about thirty winters. Even without the twisted cedar headdress and woven blanket cloak he wore, no one would mistake his status for less than a chief. His arrogant bearing indicated his membership in the noble class.

"I am Chief Blackfish, a great chief of the Tsimshian people. Who are you?" he demanded. "You, who dare come to our beach in a Haida war canoe. Do you not know I can have my men beat you?" He gestured at the two burly slaves on either side of him. The slaves moved closer to him, their hands reaching protectively for the big wooden fish clubs they carried at their sides.

"Remember what your father said," William whispered to Isaac. "Many Salmon, your father, said do not fight with these people. He does not want to have to make war on them."

"Call off your slaves, chief," said Isaac to the bristling Tsimshian nobleman. "We have been invited here. We are guests."

"Guests!" exclaimed the chief. "Whose guests are you?"

Isaac found his posturing amusing. The man knew very well that Isaac and his men were guests. This whole feast had been arranged by his uncle, with his clan's help. This chief knew they were guests.

"The great chief known as All Fear His Name invited us."

The young chief leaned forward and peered at Isaac. "You? I have seen you before. Somewhere."

"I would advise you to treat your great chief's guests graciously," interrupted William. "We are here to feast with him. And he is a great nobleman." *Unlike you*, said his silent sneer.

Chief Blackfish shrugged, not caring for this reminder of his lesser status, and of his poor manners.

"I am Isaac Thompson. I was invited to attend the potlatch given by All Fear His Name."

The young chief frowned. "That old chief thinks to get glory from this feast. It is my father who deserves the glory, the praise. It is my father who is wealthy, not the old chief."

Isaac shrugged. Rivalries were common among local chiefs. "We have no concern with your Tsimshian customs. We are but guests here. The white down of peace was scattered on the beach at our arrival. We come in peace."

The young chief gazed at Isaac. "I know where I have seen you." His curled lip made his face ugly. "At Fort Simpson. You are the slave. I have heard about you. Your mother—"

"Was All Fear His Name's precious sister," broke in William smoothly. "As the great chief's nephew,

38

my friend is to be honored. He is very important to the chief."

The young chief answered spitefully, "All nephews are important to their uncles. How else could a man have heirs? But no man wants a slave for a nephew." He recoiled disdainfully.

Isaac could feel the old familiar anger and shame rise. He tried to bite it back. His father had warned him not to fight with these people.

"He is not a slave," answered William loyally.

But Chief Blackfish had seen Isaac's flushed, shame-stained face. "He is. You tell this wretched slave"—the chief's voice dripped with contempt—"to get back in his leaky canoe with the other miserable slaves and paddle back to his dirty hovel!"

Isaac heard the collective intake of breath of his Haidas. He knew, too, they were reaching for the weapons hidden under their clothes.

"You tell him," continued the cocky young chief, "that I will spare his worthless life this once for daring to come and interrupt our great feast."

"We are guests," insisted William. "We have a personal invitation from All Fear His Name. My friend is a great chief among our people—"

"Let us leave," said Isaac, doing all he could to control his fury at the arrogant young chief's words. "I am not going to beg to attend their feast." He forced himself to turn back to the canoe.

"We have paddled for three days," reminded William. He faced the chief. "We bring gifts—"

"Slave gifts," said Chief Blackfish, waving a hand dismissively. "Give them to the dogs." There were titters and laughter from the watching crowd.

Isaac's blood throbbed in his ears. To have to

suffer the insults of this ignorant man was almost more than he could bear.

Only the thought of his father, Many Salmon, the man who had taught him, raised him, and who had stood by him through all the shame in his life, only the thought of his stern father stayed Isaac's hand from reaching for his knife. His father wanted no war. Therefore, Isaac would start no war.

"Come, William," ordered Isaac. "We will leave this land."

"You take orders from a slave?" hooted the chief at William. He laughed. "By your dress I thought you were a Haida nobleman. But now I see you are a cur, a dog who does whatever a slave tells him to do. Ha ha ha!"

To have the young chief sneer at Isaac was one thing. But to have him insult William Kelp, a Haida nobleman of fine character and good lineage, a friend who had stood by Isaac through many hardships, was too much.

Isaac whirled on the chief. "What did you say?"

"Tell your slave," sneered Chief Blackfish to William, "not to address me directly. I do not speak to slaves." He spat contemptuously at Isaac.

The spittle flew through the air and landed on Isaac's bare left foot.

A horrified gasp went up from the startled people. Even the Tsimshian onlookers were shocked at this new rudeness. To hit a man was demeaning. To spit on him was even more so. Tsimshian people craned forward eagerly to see how Isaac would receive this new insult. A little girl cried and her mother quickly hushed her.

Isaac could feel rage rising in him. Gone was his

intention to obey his father. All he could see was that this man had deliberately humiliated him.

Isaac seized the sneering chief by his neck and dragged him, head down, to the gravel. Muffled yelps came from the young chief.

William whipped out his knife. "Back!" he ordered the two slaves who had surged forward to protect their chief. "Get back or I will kill you!"

More muffled yells and oaths came from the chief. Isaac pushed his head down to the gravel. Then he dragged the chief's face across the stones.

"Lick up the spittle," Isaac ordered.

The Tsimshians were horrified. Some of the women were crying and wailing. The men looked grim at this insult to their chief. William waved his knife threateningly, keeping the crowd back.

The young chief struggled and yelled as he tried to evade Isaac's grasp. But Isaac had a sure grip. This chief had insulted him and he would pay for it. No self-respecting nobleman could accept what he had done. And Isaac was a nobleman, a Haida nobleman.

He pushed the protesting man's face into the sand and gravel. When the chief struggled and yelled, Isaac pressed his face farther into the gravel. "Lick up the spit or you die right here!" He pressed the tip of his knife against the exposed brown neck.

Soon he felt the warm tongue of the chief as he licked up the spittle. The chief was crying as he did so. Hot tears of humiliation dripped onto Isaac's foot.

Isaac pushed the man's nose further into his foot. "All of it!"

When the chief was done, Isaac threw him aside

on the gravel like he was a dead dog. Isaac was breathing as hard as if he had paddled in a canoe race. But there was none of the exhilaration of a race. "And do not call me slave again," he growled. "Ever!"

The humiliated young chieftain got up, clutching one side of his face. He watched Isaac out of black eyes filled with hate and fear. "I will kill you for this insult!"

He dropped his hand, and people gasped anew at the sight of his bruised face. To strike a man in the face was the highest insult.

"Get out of my sight, dog, or I will make you lick my other foot!"

The young chief ran back to the longhouse, screaming for his father. The Tsimshian crowd stared after him, muttering about this affront to their young chief.

Wearily, Isaac and his men got into the black canoe. William was just pushing them off when a man came running down the beach toward them.

"Fights with Wealth?" he called. "Are you the chief called Fights With Wealth?"

Isaac turned.

"Please," gasped the man, obviously a commoner by his cedar clothes. "Stay! The chief, All Fear His Name, knows of your arrival. He asks that you please stay and accept his hospitality."

Isaac glanced at William. Now that he was starting to cool down, things did not look so good for him at this Tsimshian village. He had just deeply insulted an important chief. "We should get back to our village and warn my father about the upcoming war with the Tsimshians."

William nodded reluctantly. "Yes. Your father

will not be happy about this." He glanced at the imploring messenger. "Unless we can stave off the war by staying and feasting," he suggested dubiously.

The messenger leaned forward confidentially. "The great chief, All Fear His Name, has told me to tell you that he does not fear that underling chief. He will give him one smoked salmon and he will go away, his honor appeased."

William laughed grimly. "Evidently your uncle does not care that you have offended that chief. One smoked salmon! Why, it would take hundreds of smoked salmon and hundreds of blankets and furs for me to forget something like that!"

Isaac privately thought it would take more than that to make up for the humiliation the chief had dealt him. He doubted Chief Blackfish would be so easily appeased, either. But how curious that his mother's brother had sent for him after twenty-five years of silence. And now to send this messenger to beg him to stay . . . and then to say that this humiliated chief was not important . . .

Something was very wrong about this.

Yet the thought of telling Many Salmon that the Haidas must now fight a war against the Tsimshians made Isaac's stomach clench in dread. Finally, he answered, "We will stay."

"Good," said the messenger, relieved. "Please follow me to the great chief's longhouse."

Wary, Isaac signaled the two men guarding the canoe to stay on duty. The other seven men he took with him. The muttering crowd fell back to let them through. Despite the assurances of his uncle's messenger that they would be safe, Isaac kept one hand on the hilt of his knife, as did William and each of the others.

They followed the messenger up the beach to the largest longhouse. They walked through the dark doorway space hollowed out between the legs of a tall human figure totem pole carved with his arms outstretched in welcome, and stepped down into the dark confines of his uncle's longhouse.

A fire burned on the hearth in the middle of the floor. Along the sides of the house were baskets, carved wooden boxes and plank beds. In each house lived about ten families, each with its own living space.

From the rafters hung racks of dried salmon. On a raised chair on a dais at the far end of the house, in the place of honor, sat the old chief who had done the greeting dance for Isaac and his men on the beach. He beckoned them to come closer.

Isaac studied his uncle by the flickering firelight. Though shriveled, the man had a familiar look to him. He wore the trappings of his status—twisted cedar headband and woven blanket cloak—and at his bare feet sat the two slave boys. Gathered on either side of the chief were the noblemen of all his house, and beside them, the important commoners. Women moved quietly about, carrying food to guests sitting on woven cedar mats on the dirt floor. Judging by the contents and well dressed occupants of his house, All Fear His Name was a wealthy chief indeed.

"Welcome to this funeral feast," said Isaac's uncle. "It has been one year since my beloved nephew, Tsus-sy-uch, was cruelly murdered."

Isaac nodded and went to sit where the old chief had indicated. He noted with some satisfaction

44

that it was an honorable place to sit. His men sat down behind him, but Isaac knew they were ready to spring to his defense should it become necessary.

The old chief signaled some of the women to serve the new guests, and William helped himself to smoked salmon. "Do not get too comfortable," Isaac warned William in an undertone.

After they had eaten, four dancers came out and danced a slow, sad dance. The old uncle did not eat, and when a woman pressed some berries on him, he turned away as though not interested in food. When the dancers were done, gifts were given to them and they left.

When a length of time had gone by, the old chief said, "My heart is sore." He tapped his chest. "My hate runs deep."

Did he mean his hate for Haidas? Beside him, Isaac felt William tense as he moved his hand to the hilt of his knife, at the ready.

"My hate for the men who murdered my heir will never lessen. Not until I have his murderers in my power!"

William relaxed. So did Isaac.

The old chief gave a long, grief-stricken wail, and several of the men seated beside him gave echoing cries. "Tsus-sy-uch was a good man. He was trained in the ways of the Tsimshian. He knew the dances. He knew the stories. He was a good man, an honorable man. He would have made a great chief."

Isaac found himself suddenly wishing he had known Tsus-sy-uch, his blood cousin. Perhaps they would have been friends had they grown up together, as they should have, if this old uncle had taken on his proper responsibility of raising Isaac, his sister's son, as an heir. A proper great Haida or Tsimshian chief was supposed to train his sisters' sons to be great chiefs.

"I will raise a memorial pole in honor of my nephew," continued the old chief. "A fine pole, carved to tell the story of my clan, of my great people."

His listeners all nodded approvingly.

"I will hire the best carvers. Only the best workmen will work on my nephew's memorial pole. It will be perfect."

Excitement swept through the listeners as they discussed what the pole would look like, and how wonderful the carvings on the pole would be.

"I want the men who murdered my nephew brought here!" thundered the old chief.

Isaac raised a brow. He doubted the murderers would want to come and look at the memorial pole.

"I want them brought to me! I want them to see the pole that will honor the man they murdered! And when they have looked upon the pole with their hated eyes, then I will kill them and raise the pole on top of their dead bodies. They will be buried at the base of it!

"I call upon all of you people here to witness my revenge. I will throw a great feast when I hold those murderers. And each one of you shall watch them die!"

Isaac nodded. It was fitting. It would honor the nephew, and it would shame and insult the murderers.

"Only then will the burning fires of anger and grief that rage in my heart be banked. Only then will they be reduced to glowing coals, and then to ashes. Only then will I be able to sleep." He touched his chest in the region of his heart.

Now the old man addressed Isaac. His gimlet eyes measured Isaac.

"I have brought guests here today, Haida guests," he told the people, and the large house grew silent. Isaac could feel the Tsimshians' bright eyes upon him and his men. "I have brought a man here called Fights With Wealth."

Isaac gritted his teeth as he heard the murmurs. The story of what he had done to the lesser chief swept over the crowd. And here and there he heard the dreaded word "slave."

"Fights With Wealth is a Haida chief. He is also my dead sister's son."

Isaac reached for his knife. Beside him, William tensed also. Isaac's mother had been sister to this old chief. But when she had been captured as a slave by Isaac's father, her Tsimshian family and clan, and this old chief, her brother, had disowned her. Even after Isaac's father had fallen in love with her and married her, the Tsimshians had refused to acknowledge her as one of their own. It was as if she were dead. Isaac sometimes wondered if her people's rejection of her had hastened her early death.

The shame of a noble daughter enslaved had been too great for the Tsimshians to face. And Isaac had lived with that heavy shame all his life, despite his father's attempts to banish the humiliation . . .

He heard more murmurs from the crowd around him.

"I invited him here for a special purpose," said All Fear His Name.

"Here it comes," whispered William. "Now we find out why he really wanted you here."

"I call upon every one of you to witness what I say." All Fear His Name stood up suddenly and walked straight out from the dais. He carried a wooden staff in one hand and leaned on it as he walked. He halted in front of the Haida delegation.

"Hear me, my people, when I say this. If this man, known as Fights With Wealth, brings back the murderers of my beloved nephew, I will give a great potlatch!"

The startled crowd began to murmur anew.

"I will give away many blankets, I will give away many canoes, I will kill many slaves—" Here several gasps from the audience could be heard at the promise of such lavish wealth to be distributed and destroyed. "I will give away baskets of berries and many smoked salmon, more than can be counted on the fingers and toes of everyone in this house."

The people leaned forward expectantly.

"I will clear this man's name. Everyone in the Tsimshian villages near and far will speak of this man as a great Tsimshian chief."

For the first time, hope leapt in Isaac's heart. To be accepted in his rightful status by his mother's people, to have people speak of him with respect and honor, to have the dreaded word "slave" banned from the throats of others, would surely be a feat worth accomplishing. Even his father would approve.

"Do you accept?" asked the old chief.

Isaac stared into the old man's eyes. They were

dark and unblinking and haunted by shadows. He wondered what secrets they held.

"I do," he said gravely.

"Good," grunted the chief. He held up a hand to silence the murmuring excitement of the crowd. "You are all witnesses to this. I will give a truly great potlatch. I will also arrange for this man to marry a noble Tsimshian princess."

More murmurs.

"In return, Fights With Wealth, you will bring back my nephew's murderers and throw them at my feet!"

Isaac rose and stood proudly before the old chief, towering over him. "I will," he answered solemnly.

The crowd murmured its approval, and for once he felt himself as kin to the Tsimshian people. How different it would have been if his mother's people had accepted him earlier in his life.

"There are two murderers," continued the old chief. "They are white men. They are named John Butler and James Burt. They are the men who killed my nephew."

The hushed angry tones of the crowd told Isaac how deep their feelings ran against the murderers.

"You will find them living in O-lymp-ya, a white man's village down the coast, south of Fort Victoria. It is in Boston man territory. My nephew was killed by those two when they would not pay him for the work he did." The old man's mouth worked, and Isaac saw that he still hurt from the death of his nephew. "My nephew's murder will be avenged! It will! I shall not sleep or visit my ancestors until those two are dead and buried at the base of my nephew's new memorial pole!"

The crowd murmured approvingly.

Isaac nodded and sat back down.

The chief said, "Take two of my noblemen with you. Fisher and Marten Fur are great chiefs of my household. They will go with you to help find the murderers."

Fisher was a tattooed, thin man with a full belly. His black eyes sparked angrily at Isaac. Isaac saw that he did not like being named to the raiding party. Marten Fur nodded respectfully, and Isaac thought perhaps he could work with the man. He nodded back.

Two male commoners were quickly chosen to serve and accompany their noble masters. Finally a ragged-clothed, mat-haired slave was pushed forward. "This slave will accompany you," announced All Fear His Name. "He was with my nephew when he was killed. He was there; he saw everything." The old chief pushed the slave to the floor in front of Isaac. "What is this insignificant slave's name?" the old chief asked a bystander.

"Maggot," spoke up one of the women.

"Take Maggot with you," ordered the old chief. "He will show you where the murderers live."

Maggot the slave remained crouched in front of Isaac, and Isaac could see him tremble. "Get up," said Isaac. "Get your things and come with us."

The slave scrambled to his feet and ran over to a drafty corner of the building to get his belongings.

"Bring in the dancers," ordered All Fear His Name. His business concluded, he went back to sit on his dais.

Isaac turned to William. "Will you come with me on this mission? I could use your help."

"Yes," answered his friend. "I will help you. But I must say that I do not quite trust your old uncle."

"Do you think he will not do as he says?" asked Isaac. "He has many witnesses to his promise of the reward if I fulfill the task."

"True," acknowledged William. "But there is something not quite right . . ."

"Huh," answered Isaac. "I think you are looking for trouble."

"Not me," said William. "But trouble finds you, my cousin. I have noticed this."

"Me?"

"Yes. It searches you out wherever you are and comes to you, running on swift feet."

Isaac chuckled at the picture William presented. "Like a naxnok of the forest," he agreed. The spirits of the forest could harm a person.

"Just like that," said William.

The Haida delegation stayed until after the dancing and other speeches were finished. A commoner sent by their host led them to their sleeping quarters for the night . . .

. . . Isaac shook himself from his reverie and lifted his paddle from the water. The black canoe shot into a small hidden cove and drifted up to the gravel shallows. The blue canoe lagged behind.

They would camp here for the night.

Chapter Three

Under cover of darkness the raiding party beached the canoes, dragging them well above the high-tide line. There were ashes in the firepit from the night before when Isaac's party had camped there.

After Isaac got the fire started, he glanced over at the captives. The white man was sitting on a log and staring sullenly at the fire. Fisher came along and kicked John Butler off his log. "Go get wood," ordered the Tsimshian nobleman.

John Butler cringed. Isaac smiled. Let the Tsimshian wreak his cruelty. Butler had killed Tsus-sy-uch.

But the white man did not understand the nobleman's language. "This white man is a cur," said Fisher in irritation after another healthy kick. To the Tsimshian slave, he ordered, "Tell him to get firewood."

"Yes, chief." Maggot, the slave, his tangled hair

and ragged clothes proclaiming his lowly social status, scurried hastily over to the white man. "Get up," he said carefully in the white man's tongue. "Go. Get branch."

Butler glared at the slave but stumbled to his feet. Fisher gave him another kick, and Butler moved away quickly from the tattooed man.

The white woman watched in silence.

"Branch," repeated the Tsimshian slave. The white man looked at him. Then with the same irritation his master had shown, the slave cried, "Branch!"

"I think he means for you to fetch wood," Elizabeth said.

Butler glared at her. "You can help me instead of sitting there like some high-and-mighty queen."

She rose and began searching the beach for driftwood.

She seems to be an obedient wife, thought Isaac. That is good.

The two captives and the slave each brought back six full armloads of wood while Fisher yelled himself hoarse at them.

As was their wont, the Tsimshians got out their blankets and slept on one side of the fire, while the Haidas and Isaac laid out their blankets on the other side. Thus had it been every night before the raid.

Isaac threw blankets at Butler and his woman and indicated they were to sleep farther away from the fire. Isaac was careful to keep between them and the Tsimshians.

Maggot settled down to lie at Fisher's feet. The nobleman kicked him. "Go sleep somewhere else," he snarled, and the slave obediently crept away.

Theresa Scott

"Haida!" snapped Fisher.

Isaac stared at him across the fire. "What do you want?" He deliberately left off the honorific title of "chief." He would not bow to this Tsimshian, no matter how high his family status was.

The second Tsimshian nobleman, Marten Fur, quickly scolded, "He did not call you 'chief.' These Haidas need better manners."

But Fisher ignored his fellow nobleman's comments. "Give me the woman to warm my feet," ordered Fisher imperiously.

"No." Isaac glared at the Tsimshian.

"I want the woman," said Fisher, sitting up.

Isaac thought for a time. "The great chief, All Fear His Name, will not approve," he reminded Fisher.

Fisher frowned. "He will not care. Give her to me."

Isaac shrugged. "Go and get her, then," he said with just the right touch of amusement in his voice. He glanced over at his friend, William Kelp, who had kept silent. "I believe," Isaac said conversationally to William, "that white people smell bad, like rotting meat. Have you noticed?"

"I have," agreed William, catching on.

"I would not want one of them warming *my* feet."

"Very true," agreed William with a chuckle.

Fisher stared at them, then with a grunt rolled over. No more was said about having the white woman warm his feet.

Isaac sighed. He looked at the whites; neither of them realized what Fisher's power could do to them, and he motioned for the woman to move closer to him. Isaac did not trust Fisher.

She shook her head.

Stubborn woman, thought Isaac. He wondered why he had bothered to protect the white woman. She was Butler's wife. He should have let the Tsimshians have her.

Isaac lay down and closed his eyes, but he felt restless. He opened his eyes, glancing over to where the woman lay at some distance from John Butler. Must have been an arranged marriage, Isaac decided. Either that, or she did not like her husband.

When dawn came, Isaac was on his feet. "Get up," he told William softly. They awoke the other two Haidas, both commoners, both faithful retainers of his father, Many Salmon. Only when his men were fully awake and armed did he walk over and awaken the Tsimshians.

Fisher sat up groggily and yelled at the two Tsimshian commoners who slept nearby. One of them crawled over and kicked the slave. Barely awake, the slave staggered over to the canoe and fetched some dried fish, then staggered to Fisher and gave it to the nobleman while he still lay abed. When the nobleman had eaten, he arose and the slave quickly folded his blankets for him, tidying up after the others as well.

Isaac gave his men some smoked fish, and they drank from bladders of water. He gave Butler one small piece of the fish, and to the young wife he gave a slightly larger piece.

She glared at him, then snatched the tasty morsel from his hand and gobbled it up. Like a squirrel she is, he thought. A little brown squirrel. He squashed the tender feeling that arose at the thought. She was Butler's wife. She was as bad as he was. And she would share his fate.

Finally all had broken their fast and it was time to leave.

While Isaac was putting his blanket in the canoe, the Tsimshian slave walked over to him and waited politely until, with a nod, Isaac acknowledged him.

"Chief?" As none of the other Tsimshians ever addressed Isaac by the higher status title, Isaac was curious. He waited.

"The chief called Fisher respectfully requests that the insignificant captive, John Butler, ride in our canoe."

Isaac thought about it. "William," he finally said in a loud voice, "if we let Butler ride with the Tsimshians, do you think they will paddle ahead and try to reach my uncle and take all the credit for Butler's capture? They would then get all the rewards, too."

"They certainly would," agreed William, equally loud. The Tsimshians glared at the Haidas. The Haidas glared back.

The slave bowed and hastily backed away. Fisher looked angry and kicked the retreating slave as he ran toward the canoe. Maggot tripped and fell.

Fisher walked over to glare at Isaac. Isaac's answering smile was more like a snarl. The Tsimshian nobleman looked unhappy at having his plan for glory quashed.

While Isaac and Fisher exchanged angry glares, the white woman helped the Tsimshian slave to his feet. Maggot shrugged away from her grasp as though bitten and climbed into the canoe, where he covered himself with a blanket, to hide his shame at tripping and being kicked.

Fisher's tattooed face looked pained. "If I cannot have Butler, I will take the white woman," he said.

Isaac's smile faded. "No."

"You already have Butler," complained Fisher. "The great chief All Fear His Name will give you all the rewards." His voice was bitter at Isaac's win.

But the white woman—should she ride in the same canoe as Fisher? Isaac glanced over at her. She was watching the two leaders, her bright blue eyes going back and forth. Though a blanket covered her shoulders, she shivered in the cool morning air.

Fisher could be cruel. Isaac had seen him strike his men during the time they had traveled together. What would he do to a captive woman?

Isaac was about to speak when William said, "Let her go with him. We have Butler. He is the one we came for."

Isaac looked at the man he was proud to call best friend. William rightly read the concern in Isaac's eyes, for he, too, had watched Fisher. William shook his head and mouthed, "Later," to Isaac.

Isaac shrugged. This was one time he did not agree with his friend. "Take Butler with you, then," he said carelessly to Fisher, again leaving off the "chief" title. "But be warned. If anything happens, I will demand payment for injury. We helped capture that murderer."

Fisher winced. He had a reputation for cheapness among his men, and Isaac knew it. Generosity was a highly prized virtue among the Haida and Tsimshian peoples. Cheapness was not. Fisher would not part with precious fish or blankets to pay for cheating Isaac if he could help it. And Isaac knew it.

They got into their canoes and pushed off from the beach, out into the deeper water. The white woman sat in Isaac's canoe, her back straight, a red and yellow and white striped blanket wrapped around her because the morning air was cool.

William lifted a quizzical brow, but that was his only response.

Isaac regarded the woman's straight, stiff back. She was proud, he decided. Prouder than her husband, who sat slumped on a seat in Isaac's canoe and glared at the water, muttering to himself now and then. He had shown little interest about where his wife was put. Isaac wondered at that. Most men protected their wives, or tried to. But this Butler was doing a poor job of it. He neither talked to nor comforted his young wife. Very strange, thought Isaac.

He urged his men to stay close to the Tsimshians' canoe and not let them paddle too far ahead. He did not trust the Tsimshian leader. Fisher might still try to paddle quickly ahead to reach the Tsimshian village first and thereby take the glory for capturing the killer.

The Haidas paddled northward to their next camping place. They plied their paddles stolidly in the Tsimshians' foaming wake, keeping a distance no greater than one gray whale length between the two canoes at any time.

No white men chased them. No whites even knew of their captive cargo.

And thus they made their way north to the place where they would camp for the night.

Chapter Four

At dusk, the raiding party paddled up to a gravel beach, hidden behind a small island. Tall fir and cedar trees loomed over the seaweed-lined tide mark. Deer trails led into the darkened forest. Gulls cried and wheeled overhead.

The men pulled the two canoes up on the beach and unloaded their scant supplies. Motivated by several kicks from Fisher, the Tsimshian slave built a fire, and soon a small blaze lit the evening. The woman and Butler helped the slave find wood.

There was a small creek running down to the beach, and Isaac and William and the other two Haidas went over to fill their sea lion bladders with fresh water for the next day.

When Isaac returned to the fire, Fisher walked over. "So," he said. They both watched as the two captives picked up driftwood. "I think you tricked me, Haida."

"Oh?" asked Isaac with interest. He straightened and faced the Tsimshian chief.

"White women do not smell like rotting meat."

Isaac shrugged and hid a grin.

"Tonight the woman will warm my feet!" Fisher sauntered away.

Warm his feet! Who was he trying to fool? It was summer; no one's feet were cold in the summer.

Isaac set his jaw. He did not like the idea of the white woman lying next to the Tsimshian chief. True, someone had to guard her from the forest spirits, but that was not why Fisher wanted her nearby. And Isaac did not like the lecherous way Fisher watched the woman. Warmed feet, indeed!

This day Isaac had had more time to study the two white people. It occurred to him that they did not act at all like husband and wife. Not like any of the Hudson's Bay Company white men he'd seen at Fort Simpson. Nor like any Haida husband and wife. These two kept apart, and the woman seemed to express a dislike for the man. Very interesting, thought Isaac.

The woman came over and laid an armload of sticks down beside the fire, then sank to the ground.

Isaac peeled off some pieces of smoked salmon and handed them around to his men. He gave a piece to the woman, who snatched it up and ate it hungrily. Then she held out her hand for more. Amused at her insistence, he gave her a second piece of the delicious fish.

He and William and the others ate in silence. The two whites, he noted, seemed hungrier this day. Evidently, the fish this morning had not been enough for them. He offered a second piece of fish to John Butler. Butler turned away. He had proven to be a surly man this day. But what did one expect of a murderer?

The white man suddenly turned back and glared at the Haidas and Tsimshians. "Why did you take me?" he demanded.

Isaac stared at him, surprised by the white man's sudden ferocity. To the Tsimshian slave he said, "Tell me what the white man says."

Maggot said to Butler, "Say again. Talk slow."

Butler repeated himself, surlier in tone and manner.

"He says that he wants to know why we captured him."

Isaac considered. "Tell him he should know."

The slave told the white man this.

Butler snarled, "What the hell nonsense is this? I don't know what the hell you Indians want. Tell me!"

The slave glanced fearfully at Isaac. "He say he respectfully ask the great chiefs to tell him why they steal him."

Isaac answered, "Tell him that he did something very bad and now he will suffer."

The slave said, "You bad man. You die."

The woman's mouth dropped open. "What did he do?" she squeaked.

Isaac looked at the slave. He did not answer.

"Tell me what the woman said," ordered Isaac.

"She is insignificant," protested the slave.

"Tell me," warned Isaac.

"She say, what did Butler do?" Maggot answered sullenly, obviously not liking to translate for her, too.

"Tell her that her husband killed our friend."

"Chief say your husband—" the slave began haughtily in English.

"—Husband? What husband?" She looked bewildered. She pointed at Butler. "This man? You think he's my husband?" Her voice rose incredulously.

Isaac waited.

The slave protested quickly, "This man Butler. I seen him!"

She fixed her bright blue eyes on him. "Butler? He's not Butler!" she cried scathingly. "He's Mr. Burt!"

The slave looked frightened suddenly. He glanced anxiously at Fisher, and Isaac remembered the slave had told them this was John Butler.

Isaac himself stared at the white man in astonishment. Not Butler? Who, then? Misterburt? Mister Burt? James Burt?

"What is the white woman saying?" demanded Fisher, drawn to the slave's fear like a circling shark to blood. "Tell me!"

The slave glanced around wildly.

"Tell me, you rotten string of sea cucumber!" Fisher shouted. He grabbed hold of the slave's ragged shirt and shook him.

Maggot cried out in pain. Fisher gave him a kick. "Speak up," he ordered, throwing the slave to the ground.

Maggot rolled on the gravel, then got painfully to his feet. "She say the white man is called Mister Burt," he murmured. He put his hands up to protect his head from the chief's blows.

"Mister Burt?" screamed Fisher. "Who is Mister Burt?" He grabbed the hapless slave and raised his fist to hit him.

"Burt is the other murderer," interjected Isaac. "James Burt. The great chief, All Fear His Name, told us *two* white men killed Tsus-sy-uch. Surely you remember, Chief? Their names were John Butler and James Burt."

Fisher lowered his fist and threw the slave aside. "So," he grunted. "We have *one* of the murderers. But not the one we thought."

"No," said Isaac. He tamped down his disappointment. From the story All Fear His Name had told, Butler was the main person responsible for the killing. Still, Burt was a murderer, too. They would just have to return to O-lymp-ya for the other murderer later. He tried to save the situation. "But All Fear His Name will still be pleased. Very pleased," he assured Fisher. "He will be able to assuage the pain of mourning the great loss of his nephew. He will be able to raise his memorial pole on this man's dead body."

Somewhat mollified, Fisher turned to glare at the white woman. "Then who is *she*?"

Isaac was wondering the same thing. "Ask her," he ordered the Tsimshian slave.

Frightened, the slave glanced at Fisher for permission.

The Tsimshian chief nodded curtly.

"What your name?" asked the slave in English.

She glared at him. "I do not have to tell you that," she said haughtily, turning away.

Isaac groaned. What a time for the woman to become stubborn!

"Hit her," ordered Fisher.

The slave glanced at the woman, then back at the Tsimshian chief. "I do not want to hit her, Great Chief," he said in a trembling voice.

"Hit her," ordered Fisher with a grin. "And keep hitting her until she tells you what she is named."

The slave hesitated.

"Hit her or I hit you," said Fisher, clearly enjoying himself.

As the slave lifted his fist to hit the white woman, Isaac grabbed his fist in midair.

"We already know the captive white woman's name," stated Isaac. "It is Lis-uh-buth Butler."

"Is it?" asked Fisher with a sly grin. "Or is it something else?"

"Ask her," Isaac ordered the slave.

The slave hesitated, looking fearfully at Fisher for permission. But Fisher said nothing, so the slave said to the woman, "Please. Please, please, tell name." His voice quavered.

The woman snorted. "I will not tell you Indians anything. I want to go home! Take me home! Now!"

Isaac gritted his teeth.

"She say she tell you soon," said the slave.

"How soon?" Fisher asked, his brown eyes glittering in the firelight.

"Very soon," assured Maggot.

Fisher glared at him.

"These damn Indians won't take you home," snarled James Burt. "All they'll do is kill you. Kill me. That's the way they think."

"What do you know?" the woman shot back. "It sounds to me like I'm in this trouble because of you!"

"I didn't do nothin'," Burt said sullenly.

"You did something," the woman accused. "That's why we're here. And they think I'm your wife!" She shook her head, eyes flashing. "I wouldn't be your wife for anything in the world!"

"That's fine with me, lady," snarled Burt.

"What did they say?" broke in Fisher. "Tell me," he ordered the slave.

The slave's lips moved, struggling to understand what he had heard. "They say you very fine chief," he said at last, helplessly. "They say they think you very great chief."

Fisher snorted. He glanced at the slave suspiciously, but Isaac thought the tattooed chief probably liked the flattery.

"Tell that woman to tell us her name," ordered Fisher. "I am tired of all their talk. Find out her name!"

The slave took a deep breath. "Great chief wants to know your name," he told the woman. "Say he be very kind to you if he know your name."

"Humph," said the woman. "He doesn't look kind. None of you people look kind. I want to go home!"

"Your name?" the slave begged. In the fire's light, Isaac could see beads of sweat glisten on his forehead.

She turned up her nose. "That," she said, "is private information."

The slave fell silent and bowed his head. "I do not know her name," he told the Tsimshian chief.

"What's the big deal?" Burt demanded. "Tell them your name, for God's sake!"

"I will not," she said. "And neither will you."

"Wanna bet?" sneered Burt. "I don't care what happens to you. You're nothing to me but a hard time." To the slave he said, "Her name is Elizabeth. Got that, Injun boy? Eeelizzzaaabethhhh," he drawled.

The slave brightened. "Lis-buth," he told Fisher quickly, as if the chief did not have ears of his own.

Isaac nodded. That confirmed what he had expected. She was Butler's wife.

"Oh, for heaven's sake," she exclaimed. She frowned at Burt.

"What did she say?" asked Fisher.

"She is counting," translated the slave blandly.

Isaac blinked.

Fisher said, "She does not make much sense. I suppose white women are like that."

"Yes," agreed the slave, nodding his head. His relief was palpable. Isaac felt the tension in his own shoulders lessen. He had expected a fight to come of this.

Realizing they did not have the man they thought, the Tsimshians shrugged and went about setting out their blankets on one side of the fire, while Isaac and the Haidas did the same on the other. Isaac shook out his Hudson's Bay blanket and laid it on the gravel.

Burt accepted the ragged blanket the slave threw at him, and Isaac saw that the woman still clutched the thick wool Hudson's Bay blanket. She would stay warm this night.

He signaled her to lie near him. He did not want Fisher bothering her. Nor did he want the forest spirits to steal her.

Just as he was drifting off to sleep, he heard Fisher say to the woman, "Come here and warm my feet."

Isaac's heart sank and he heard William Kelp swear under his breath. The uneasy peace between the Tsimshians and the Haidas was already weak, and Fisher was doing his best to make it weaker.

All Isaac wanted now was to get these captives back to his uncle and return to his own Haida village.

He opened his eyes, waiting for the woman's response.

Silence.

Fisher said to the slave, "Get her over here. My feet need warming."

The slave went over to the woman. "You come over and sleep with chief," he said.

"What?" she shrieked. "I will do nothing of the kind!"

She is faithful to her husband, thought Isaac approvingly.

"His feet cold," cajoled the slave. "You warm."

"I do not care if his feet freeze and fall off," she yelled. "I shall not sleep with him!"

The slave trotted obediently over to the Tsimshian chief and whispered to him. Evidently, he did not think it wise to embarrass his chief in front of the others by stating the woman's refusal aloud.

"You hit her or I hit you!" yelled Fisher in Tsimshian.

Isaac took a breath. The woman sat up, clutching the blanket around her and watching warily as the slave approached her.

"You come," the slave tried one more time. "Kind chief say you come."

"I will not!"

Before the slave could strike her, Isaac was on his feet. He pulled the slave away from her.

Fisher jumped up. "That's my slave," he cried. "You cannot touch my slave!"

He ran at Isaac and halted a mere hand's breadth

away. His brown eyes glowed in anger. "You keep your hands off my slave!"

"Keep your hands off the *woman*," said Isaac. "Chief All Fear His Name does not want a beaten woman for a captive."

"How do you know what the great chief wants?" sneered Fisher. "You who do not belong with good Tsimshians! We Tsimshians hate Haidas!" Anger sparked from his eyes.

William Kelp suddenly stood at Isaac's side. "Let us avoid a fight, if possible." He spoke calmly to Fisher. "We are here at All Fear His Name's invitation. He is a great chief. A wise chief. He asked us all to work together to bring back a murderer, not to fight with one another. Let us stop this.

"Your kinsman was killed by this bad white man, James Burt. Let us not add more deaths. Besides," William added innocently, "it would cost you much. This man whom the whites call Isaac Thompson is an honored Haida. He is Fights With Wealth, an important Haida chief."

"I do not think he is an important Haida chief," said Fisher with a sneer. "I think he is a sl—" Before he could complete the dreaded word "slave," the other Tsimshian nobleman, Marten Fur, put a warning hand on his arm. Fisher subsided into silence.

William Kelp's voice shook. He and the others knew the slur Fisher had been about to utter. "This man's father and family have given many potlatches and feasts to establish his good name! If you insult him or strike him, it will mean you and your house must give away many fine gifts to appease his father's pain."

"I am a wealthy man," boasted Fisher. "I come

from a very wealthy house. I can afford to insult a Haida sl—" He glanced at his fellow Tsimshian nobleman. "A Haida," he finished sullenly.

"That so?" said William Kelp. "I am glad you are a wealthy man. Because it would take all you have to ease this man's father's pain. Every blanket, every smoked fish, every carved spoon, every wooden box that you could find from every corner of your little house. This man's father is a great chief. Greater than you. Greater than your great chief."

Fisher bristled. Again, the other Tsimshian noble had to hold him back.

"And," continued William, "I can tell you that if you insult or injure this man, his father would be satisfied with nothing less than war with the Tsimshians!"

Fisher glared at William.

The Tsimshian nobleman Marten Fur said, "Let us do as this Haida chief suggests. We Tsimshians do not need to fight Haidas to know we are better than they are. We already have one of the murderers. Let us take him back to our great chief for punishment. Then we can leave these troublesome Haidas to themselves."

Isaac gritted his teeth, but at last Fisher listened to his fellow noble. "Very well," he said.

A fight narrowly averted once again, Isaac turned back to his blanket. He caught the woman's curious eyes watching him.

He met her glance. Her blue eyes narrowed, and he thought he saw a flicker in them. He stared at her, trying to read what she was thinking. Curiosity? Relief? Or a hunger? For what? His gaze held hers for a long moment; then he deliberately broke the glance, turning away.

He cared nothing for what the white woman thought. His duty was to deliver Burt to All Fear His Name for punishment. What the great chief would do with this woman, Isaac did not know, but he was suddenly beginning to feel uneasy about it.

And he knew she still did not realize how close she had come to danger from Fisher.

He motioned to the woman to roll up in her blanket and then he lay down on his own blanket, placing himself between her and the Tsimshians. He could feel her watching him in the dark; he felt as if a naqnox, a forest spirit, watched him.

It was a long time before he fell asleep.

At dawn, he awoke to the heat of another's body. With a start, he realized it was the white woman lying next to him. The skirt of her blue dress was hiked up, and her long, smooth legs were thrown across his own. Her lithe arms encircled his torso while she pressed herself against him.

Chapter Five

Elizabeth stared sleepily into shrewd brown eyes that watched her over one brown shoulder. She liked the way the light showed the depth of the dark color. She smiled lazily. *My, who are you?* she wondered as she yawned.

She had been dreaming about a strong man who . . . Suddenly she froze. Her legs, her arms, her whole body was pressed against . . . against this *man*! This wasn't a dream! This was real life!

Who is he? What does he want? Why am I here? Then memories of the previous days and her capture by the Indians flooded her mind. "Oooh, no," she groaned and tried to sit up, but her legs were entangled with his. With some struggling, she managed to pull her legs away from his and scoot backwards.

Her face burning, she seized the cream-colored red-and-green-striped blanket and wrapped it around herself though she was still clad in the same wrinkled dark blue dress she'd been wearing ever since her capture. She glanced down at herself, her body feeling cool where moments earlier she'd been curled up beside him. She felt suddenly bereft of his warmth.

Whatever was the matter with her? Whatever was happening to her?

She had been cold, that was all. It was still cold in the mornings, though it was summer. That was it. She'd been shivering and, in her sleep, had looked for a source of warmth. Nothing more. Perfectly natural, she told herself.

Elizabeth straightened her trembling frame. Her hands flew to her hot cheeks. Oh, what would Miss Cowperth say? Elizabeth frantically reviewed what she remembered of Miss Cowperth's *Authoritative Guide to Modern Etiquette*, but she could find nothing to quote to herself for consolation at this terribly awkward moment.

The Indian, however, seemed to suffer no such worries. He merely rolled gracefully to his feet and walked away. As she watched his proud, lithe form move away from her, she felt a strange compulsion to call him back—a compulsion she quickly quashed, thanks to Miss Cowperth. And now, just in time, when she needed it most, a quote from Miss Cowperth's book rose quickly to Elizabeth's mind.

"A lady is never forward around a gentleman. She always waits for him to express his manly interest and when he does, she answers him politely and with reserve."

Elizabeth flushed. She would not call this Indian a "gentleman," but she thought the rest of the quote fit the situation nicely. She would behave politely and with reserve. She touched her hair, feeling the tangled knots and wishing for the forty-fifth time that she had her hairbrush and combs with her.

The Indians broke their fast with more of the same dried fish from last night. When she looked up, there he was, handing her a small chunk of dried salmon. She could not meet his eyes as she took her fish from the man she'd come to think of as her foremost captor. Despite his shrewd brown eyes, he was a forbidding-looking man, and she thought now that he appeared rather unfriendly. Which was fine with her. She would be polite and reserved for the rest of the unfortunate time she was forced to spend with him and his miscreant friends. Which, if she had her way, would not be for long. She would escape.

She must escape. From what Mr. Burt had said, it sounded like he was in deep trouble with these Indians. Well, she had no intention of staying around to wait for them to pull her into deep trouble, too!

It was time to leave the beach. She saw Mr. Burt get into the same small sky-blue canoe that he'd ridden in yesterday. The leader of that canoe was the thin, pot-bellied, tattooed man she did not like. He was always hitting one of the other men and growling in whatever Indian language he spoke.

Elizabeth picked up a stick and pretended to linger over the fire, poking at it. She cast a quick glance at the trees. She could hear the Indians down at the water, arguing with one another, and the rasping sound of canoes scraping across gravel.

If she ran into the trees, she could escape. . . . The distance was not far, she assured herself. She could dash to the trees, run through the forest and find somewhere to hide, maybe behind an old log, and wait until the Indians gave up the search and left in their canoes.

Yet, what would she do if they left? She would be in the forest, on some island, in a place she didn't know. No food, no idea where she was, and no one to help her. She didn't even know what plants to eat. Why, she'd starve to death . . . and how would she ever find her way back to civilization? She had no boat, didn't even know what direction to go. . . .

"*Comshewanaa,*" she heard behind her. She whirled. It was the Indian she'd woken up with, though the thought made her blush now. He stared at her moodily, then gestured for her to go down to the black canoe. Unable to hold his eyes any longer, she hurried down to the water as quickly as her water-soaked black boots would let her. She felt most anxious to escape him. Where had he come from so silently? The last she knew, he'd been occupied with the canoes and arguing with the others. Instead, here he was, next to her.

Elizabeth stepped into the black canoe and sat down carefully on a middle seat, placing her legs straight out in front of her. She stared at her feet glumly. Her shoes . . . what a mess they were.

"*A proper lady is always correctly attired from the hat on the crown of her head to her daintily shod feet,*" she remembered. How fortunate that Miss Cowperth could not see the glimpse of pink skin peeking through the unraveling seams of Elizabeth's waterlogged leather boots.

She glanced up from her feet to see the Indian man watching her. He too glanced at her feet. She quickly folded her long legs under her so he could not see her wretched shoes.

"What are you staring at?" she demanded huffily.

The brown eyes turned on her showed no recognition that he understood anything of what she'd said. *Drat*. That matted-haired Indian, the one they all ordered about, was the only one who even remotely understood English.

She sighed. She couldn't even insult the man. He wouldn't understand. Then she smiled wickedly to herself. It might be interesting to *try* insulting him . . .

Two of the Indians waded out into knee-deep water as they pushed the canoe off from the beach. They clambered aboard.

The other canoe, the blue one carrying Mr. Burt, was already some distance ahead. The paddlers in her canoe pointed the prow of their boat in the same direction. She could hear the rhythmic singing in the other craft.

First there was some arguing, then finally the chanting began in her canoe, too, as the Indians took up the paddles, dipping them and lifting them at the same time. She had seen them do this for two days and had come to accept it as the way one traveled with Indians. She watched as the tall green trees where they'd camped receded into a gray mist. Their canoe headed for open water.

As they paddled, Elizabeth heard a splash off to the right. She glanced over just as a smooth, oblong head broke the water. It was a seal and it turned to watch them pass by, its big round brown eyes tracking them. Elizabeth smiled to herself at the sight.

The men continued paddling while she said to her tormentor, "I suppose you think you can just steal anyone you please." His blank look made her want to laugh, but she didn't quite dare. She had the impression that to laugh at these Indians was to gravely insult them. She didn't intend to *gravely* insult him, just *barely* insult him.

For a moment, she wondered at herself. The last two days had seemed to pass in a daze. She had been stunned to find herself captured. Never, ever had anything like that happened to her. Never, ever had she thought anything like that *could* happen to her. No one she knew had ever been captured. And Miss Cowperth's book had never mentioned it happening to anyone.

Now Elizabeth felt as if she were waking up a little bit.

"Where are you taking me?" she asked aloud. He merely sat there in the stern and stared at her. In frustration, she glanced around to see if the matted-haired Indian was in her canoe, the only one who seemed to know English. Yes, there he was, sitting in the stern of the canoe. Dare she ask him to translate?

The Indians continued to paddle, and the canoe shot along the water smoothly. There were no waves; the water was like gray glass. These Indians could paddle all day, she knew. They had done so yesterday.

It would make for a very long day. She huddled deeper inside the blanket, ignoring them all and pretending to sleep.

After a while, she gave up her pretense and contented herself with watching the shoreline pass by. There were tall evergreen trees that lined black, rocky beaches. Now and then she saw a bald eagle perched on a tree, watching them. Seals played in the water, and once she saw a black bear on the beach, turning over large rocks to get at the hiding crabs.

After a time, she ventured, "Where are we going?"

Her captor lifted an eyebrow. *Perhaps he is curious to know what I am saying,* she told herself. She turned to the translator. "Do you know where we are going?"

He said something to her captor, who was sitting in the bow. A slight nod was the only sign he gave to the translator that he'd heard what she said. Since he now stared off into the distance, she presumed his curiosity was meager.

"We go to village," said the translator.

"What village?" Not that it made any difference, she thought. But knowing something was better than knowing nothing.

He gave an unpronounceable name in the Indian language. "I see," she said with great dignity, as if she understood. She would not let these Indians know she knew so little about them.

She stared at the little green whirlpools the paddles made in the water with each dip. The gray depths now looked deep green, and she wondered if she should throw herself over the side and swim. But swim where? They were rapidly leaving the land behind. And she'd already missed her chance to escape this morning. The fog was gone. They would easily see her and follow her.

She should have escaped days ago, she scolded

herself, only she'd been too shocked to think of it. Only now was she beginning to think about her situation—and suddenly realized it was dire, indeed.

She was trapped in a canoe with five Indian men. In another canoe was a white man she barely knew, captive of four other Indian men. And where they were bound for, she knew not.

Every paddle stroke took her farther from the one place she knew.

And she had no food, no water, no weapon. She was completely dependent upon her captors for her survival.

She withdrew inside and closed the blanket up around herself at this thought. It did not feel good to be dependent on the very people who'd stolen you. Some part of her stirred restlessly, oddly grateful that she had not been killed. Yet.

Gone was her fleeting desire to insult the lead captor. In its place came fear, a gnawing, growing fear, and a strong desire to protect herself as best she could from the men surrounding her.

If only she knew what they wanted of her. That would tell her much. Yet, she wondered, even if she knew, would that not prompt her to do the one thing she knew she must do: escape?

As she sat there pondering, a little breeze sprang up. Then she began to notice that the canoe was beginning to wobble in the water. Soon there were waves on the water; the glassy smoothness was gone. They were far out to sea now; there was no longer a black, rocky shore within swimming distance.

The canoe shuddered suddenly, and she had to grab the sides for support. She glanced warily at the Indians to see if they were as concerned as she was about the waves. The men talked among themselves, but did not seem unduly worried. She continued to grip the sides. The wind grew, blowing harshly, and rain pelted against her cheeks.

The smaller, blue canoe that Mr. Burt rode in bounced on the top of a white-foaming wave. Spray splashed Mr. Burt.

The Indians with her laughed. The black canoe she rode in was long and lean and had high sides. It did not bounce every time a wave hit. A frisson of gratefulness shivered through her that she was riding in the better canoe.

She studied each Indian in the canoe with her. The matted-haired man bent down and picked up a cedar blanket that he wrapped around his head and shoulders for protection from the wind and rain. The other four men paddled steadily, ignoring the needles of rain against their naked chests and shoulders. The waves disrupted their paddling but little. The craft plowed on, the bow going up and then down in small troughs of waves.

Through the curtain of rain she could see the blue canoe as it continued to bounce. Over the distance, she could see Mr. Burt huddled over, and the Indians in the canoe paddling quickly. Once, the tattooed leader glanced in their direction and raised his arm in some sort of signal.

The translator, whom Elizabeth had privately named Jake, said to her with a chuckle, "He very mad we in better canoe. He say next time he ride in this one."

Elizabeth did not like the sound of that. She did not particularly want to share the good canoe with the bullying tattooed leader.

As the waves continued to roll under the craft, the Indians began to murmur. Then their voices rose, and she realized that two of them—her main captor and his friend—were disagreeing with the other two paddlers, who were pointing wildly at the blue canoe.

Elizabeth gripped the wooden sides until her hands hurt. She feared being dislodged from her seat and possibly flung into the water by the wild rocking of the canoe. Was it only this morning she'd been contemplating swimming as a means of escape? Nothing would get her into that water now. Not even a whole tribe of Indians!

She glanced around, looking for some sign of land, wondering when this rocking ordeal would be over. By now her stomach was starting to feel queasy from all the rolling. "How long before we reach land?" she squeaked at Jake.

He pointed into the distance. "Land over there," he said.

She peered into the distance, trying to focus in the direction he'd pointed, but the canoe went down into a trough, then up onto the crest of a wave and she lost her sense of where he'd pointed. She strained to see into the distance each time the canoe crested the top of a wave, but she could see nothing but rolling gray water.

Suddenly the canoe lurched and she was falling over headfirst toward the water. A strong hand on her shoulder pulled her back. She was sitting in the middle of the seat again. Safe.

It had all happened so fast she almost didn't know what had happened. Or if it had actually happened. Had she almost fallen overboard? The touch that had righted her was firm and reassuring. She glanced behind to see who had saved her.

Black eyes met hers. It was the man she'd awakened alongside this morning, which now seemed so long ago. He said something to her, softly. She did not understand, but she knew it was meant to be reassuring. Had he just saved her life? Or would she have righted herself with the next wave?

With an effort, she shrugged, trying to shake off her doubts. She stared stonily at the waves. She did not want to be beholden to him. Not for her life.

The Indians were talking, coming to some sort of decision. To distract herself, she glanced around for the blue canoe but couldn't see it. She wondered if it had overturned in the waves. Poor Mr. Burt. Awful as he was, she still would not have wished a drowning death upon him.

The canoe gave a great shudder, and she gripped the sides once more. All thoughts of Mr. Burt fled.

The Indians in the black canoe grew silent. Their faces were grim as they paddled, plunging the paddles down, sometimes into air when the canoe crested, sometimes deep into water when their craft hit a trough. The heavy rain pelted her face and hair. She put the blanket up over her head, trying to protect herself from the wet onslaught of spray and rain.

How long the nightmare continued, Elizabeth did not know. She shivered under the sodden blanket, hoping that this voyage would end. She didn't know how, she didn't care how, she just wanted it to end. Now.

But it went on and on—the dipping and swaying of the canoe, the grim faces of the men. Even Jake in the stern was helping. He bailed with a wooden scoop, trying to keep the canoe from sinking.

It was only when she heard the scraping of rock under the craft that she knew they'd reached some sort of beach. She blinked, coming out of her cold, fear-induced stupor. They were pulling up on a gravelly, sandy spit. About a half mile away were tall black trees looming up behind a wide expanse of gray gravel. Their huge branches shook with the wind.

The canoe glided onto the beach, and two of the men stepped out, pulling it in closer.

One of them helped Elizabeth out of the craft. On legs that trembled with every step, she staggered to the beach, then collapsed on the wet rocks. She kept the sodden blanket wrapped around her, though why, she could not have said.

The tall Indian came over and helped her to her feet. Exhausted from the strain of getting through the storm, she thanked him with her eyes. She allowed him to lead her to a log. Slowly she sank down, her legs unable to take another step.

The Indians talked and gesticulated among themselves. She guessed that they were discussing the missing blue canoe. The waves were huge, tossing driftwood about while seabirds rode down the troughs and channels. She peered into the rain, looking for some sign of the missing canoe, but she could see nothing but gray. Gray, heaving seas, gray skies, gray rain.

"Jake" came over and sat down beside her. "They argue," he said, indicating the men with his chin.

She nodded, shivering, not much interested in what he had to say.

After a while she ventured, "A-a-are th-th-they l-looking f-for the b-blue c-c-canoe?" Her shivering was uncontrollable. She could barely speak.

"Canoe? Yes," chortled Jake, vastly amused. "They lose big prize. Very unhappy."

"Wh-why are you l-laughing? It's your f-friends who are l-lost."

He turned a dark eye on her, his amusement lighting up his brown face. "Not my friends," he corrected. "I no like them. I hate."

She was puzzled. He'd come with them, hadn't he? Weren't they all one tribe?

He lowered his voice. "Me what you call slave," he said. He looked at her as though expecting her to suddenly jump up and run away. When she just sat there, shivering and clutching the wet blanket, he added, "They big chiefs. Me little slave."

Then he chuckled again.

None of this made sense to her. "Wh-why are you laughing? Sl-slavery isn't f-funny." The black slaves she'd seen in San Francisco had not looked amused. Nor did she think she would find being another person's slave amusing.

"Hee-hee," he said. "We in my people's place now. They catch these chiefs. Make them all slaves, too, hee-hee."

He was staring at the trees. She looked at the forest, too, trying to puzzle out what he meant. All she could see were swaying branches and pelting rain.

Meanwhile, the four Indians were arguing and pointing to the rolling seas every once in a while.

"They want lost canoe. But too late," said the slave. "It gone."

She nodded. She expected Mr. Burt was drowned by now. The thought troubled her.

"Tsimshians want look for them."

"They can't go out in that storm again!" she exclaimed.

The slave grinned. "Want prize. Want prize very much."

He glanced toward the forest again. "Maybe my people come. Take these chiefs. Take you. Make you slave."

She glared down her nose at him. "No one is taking me for a slave," she pronounced.

He shrugged. "Happens," he said.

She glanced at the forest uneasily. Were there other Indians hiding there? Waiting to pounce on her and these four Indians? She wondered nervously if she should mention it to the one who'd saved her—no, he had not saved her, merely righted her on the seat. Maybe she should mention to him about the hidden Indians.

Then she realized no one spoke English except this slave beside her. And he wouldn't tell the others, she thought. Not when he was so gleeful about their possibly being captured!

The four men down by the shore had fallen silent.

They trudged up the beach carrying the canoe as far as they could. One of them said something to the slave. With one final grin at Elizabeth, Jake hurried over to help lift the heavy craft.

The men staggered under the load, carrying the canoe to a pile of driftwood and placing wood over it here and there, obviously to hide it. Maybe they did know about the forest Indians, Elizabeth thought.

The seas continued to roil, and she guessed the storm would last for some time. The tall Indian came over to her and pointed at the forest. She rose and followed him and the others.

They walked back from the spit toward the forest to take shelter from the pelting rain.

When they reached the trees, the slave began looking for firewood. As he gathered wood, there was a little spring in his step and he hummed. He raced around, finding big pieces of wood for the fire. Still shivering, she looked around for wood and staggered over the wet sand, head bowed against the wind. She knew the trees offered shelter, but what threats did they also hide?

She carried an armful of sticks over to where the others were building a fire.

"Make big, big fire," said the slave happily.

Elizabeth frowned. He wanted a big fire, did he? No doubt so all his forest Indian friends would notice the smoke and come running to help him. And while *he* might be happy at the prospect of the forest Indians, she decidedly was *not*.

They sat beside the fire, and she began to feel warmer. The rain stopped and the sun came out. The wind died down. She spread her blanket over a bush near the fire so it would dry.

The Indians passed around dried fish, and Elizabeth ate some, surprised at how good it tasted. She felt the nourishment permeate her body. The men lay down and slept, all except the slave, who was supposed to wake them if anything happened. Elizabeth did not expect he would wake anyone if his forest Indians arrived, so she found herself surveying the forest and trees nervously every few minutes. It did not help that Jake would go off into the woods from time to time, no doubt looking for his friends. Each time he came back, he acted less energetic. Maybe his friends were not around, thought Elizabeth hopefully.

Toward late afternoon the four Indians awoke. They argued about something, pointing to the forest and to the sea, and finally it was decided to head back down to the shoreline.

Elizabeth noticed Jake slinking out of the forest and hurrying up to the fire with an armload of wood. She knew he was trying to look as if he'd been gathering firewood. One of the Indians cuffed him on the head, sending him and his wood sprawling. Elizabeth winced and turned away. A slave's lot did not seem to be an easy one. She tried to focus on the sea instead. The gray roiling seas had died down, and the water was calm.

Soon they were dragging the black canoe out of its hiding place, and the tall Indian signaled Elizabeth into the canoe. She dutifully climbed in and took her place on the middle seat once more.

She stole a glance at the man who had already pulled her back once from the sea. He met her eyes solemnly, and she felt as though they now shared a secret, that he had indeed saved her life and that he knew it and she knew it. It had all happened so fast. Perhaps none of the others had even noticed. Perhaps she could pretend it had not happened.

In another moment, the canoe moved, they pushed offshore and were on their way once more, paddling north.

Chapter Six

They found the blue canoe upside down on a beach on a large island. The canoe had a gaping hole in the bottom. A small fire burned, sending off smoke; that was the reason they'd found the canoe. Next to the forlorn craft stood the skinny, tattooed Indian leader, the other three Indians and Mr. Burt. The tattooed leader looked almost pleased to see them.

But Mr. Burt looked rather bedraggled, thought Elizabeth. He had jumped to his feet when the others spotted the black canoe, but he was not waving it in closer as they were. He looked rather unhappy that they'd been found, in fact.

When the black war canoe glided toward the beach, two of the Indians came out to help pull it ashore. Now all the Indians spoke excitedly among themselves, telling one another what had happened.

Realizing that Mr. Burt was not going to say anything, Elizabeth finally asked, "What happened? How did you come to be on this island?"

The white man shrugged carelessly. "We got lost in the storm. One of these stupid Indians headed the canoe for the rocks. That explains the damn hole in the bottom. Though, to tell the truth, I didn't think we were gonna make it. That storm . . . came out of nowhere." He shook his head, still in disbelief. "I see you're still with the party," he said snidely.

"It is not a party," said Elizabeth.

"You're right, it's not," he agreed.

Elizabeth frowned. "How can you make light of our desperate situation?"

"Easy," he answered. "I just been through a storm, woman! I had to swim through thirty-foot waves to get to this beach. I'm damn lucky to be alive. So are you. 'Course, you were in the better canoe," he accused, as if she had somehow had a choice.

She refused to respond to that petty comment.

They watched the Indians for a few minutes; then Mr. Burt said in a low voice, "I'm gonna escape from these here Indians. First chance I get. You just see if'n I don't!"

Elizabeth intended the same, but she found herself reluctant to confide in Mr. Burt.

"Trouble is," he continued, "now we all gotta ride in the same canoe. That'll make it more difficult. All of them Indians in one place, keepin' watch on us."

"What do they intend to do with us?" Elizabeth wanted to know.

The slave was walking toward them. "Uh-oh,"

said Mr. Burt. "Time for the wood-gathering part of the show." He hobbled off, bent double, as if actively searching for firewood, the big fake.

Elizabeth glanced around. It appeared the Indians were going to camp on the island for the night. The slave confirmed her observation. So she, too, set about looking for wood. Only she'd do a better job than Mr. Burt, she resolved.

She helped the slave gather wood, and he said to her, "The Tsimshian chiefs plenty happy they found."

"Yes," agreed Elizabeth. "They must have been worried."

The slave looked at her. "Too bad we found them." He grinned. "Better to leave them on this island, I think."

"So your forest people would find them?" asked Elizabeth. "And make them slaves?"

The slave looked sadly at her. "We past where my people live now," he said. "Do no good now."

"I'm so sorry," said Elizabeth. "I know you must be terribly disappointed."

The slave frowned. "Talk slow. Don't know all words you say . . ."

"What is your name?" asked Elizabeth to change the subject. She couldn't bring herself to express any more polite sympathy for the man. No doubt Miss Cowperth would not approve, but then, if his people *had* found them, Elizabeth would be the slave.

He eyed her suspiciously and then said something in the Indian language. She stared at him. His name was impossible to pronounce. "I will give you a new name," she said.

His eyes almost popped out of his head.

"Would you like that?" she asked brightly.

"Want powerful name!"

"A powerful name?" Elizabeth pondered this. She'd only meant to distract the man. "Yes, the name I'm going to give you is very powerful."

"What power in it?" demanded the slave. "To my people, names very important. Want power in my new name."

"Whatever do you mean?" asked Elizabeth, bewildered. "It is the name of the old janitor at Miss Cowperth's school," she added. "He was always very kind."

"Kind? What this 'kind' mean?" The slave looked almost angry.

"Oh," she hastily assured him, "it means a very good person, someone who does good things for other people." Really! How could a man carry on so about a mere name?

The slave was silent. At last he said, "You give me name. I do good things for good people." His frown grew heavier. "Just good people, you hear? I not help bad people."

"Yes, yes," agreed Elizabeth in relief. "I will give you the name now. It is 'Jake.'"

He pronounced it slowly. "Jake." He nodded. "I like."

It seemed to Elizabeth that he suddenly stood a little straighter. She found herself nodding back. "It *is* a lovely name," she agreed. "And one that is easy to pronounce."

"Is there dance go with name?" asked the newly named Jake.

But before she could answer, a deep voice interrupted them in a spate of Indian words. Jake jumped.

Elizabeth whirled to see the tall Indian. He actually had an amused look on his proud face. "What—what did he say?" she asked Jake.

Jake looked a little uncomfortable. "He want to know what *we* say."

"Well, tell him. I have nothing to hide."

Jake looked at her askance. "Him chief. Be careful what you say."

"I don't care what he is," said Elizabeth, though she had to admit she was intrigued to know the tall man was a chief. It fit him, somehow. She had already noticed that he always walked so straight and proud.

Jake translated to the chief. He nodded as if satisfied.

"What did you tell him?" asked Elizabeth curiously.

"I tell him you give me powerful name."

The chief said something.

"What did he say?" prodded Elizabeth when the slave did not translate.

"He say he give *you* name."

"Me? What name could he possibly give me? I am already well named! My name is Elizabeth!"

"He know that. He give Indian name."

"I do not want an Indian name!" Her stay with them would be short. Very short. She had no need of an Indian name.

"He is chief. Better listen," advised Jake. His brown eyes flicked over her face, and she suddenly had the strange notion that he was trying to warn her.

"Oh, very well. What name does he think he can give me?"

The two Indians talked for a time. Finally Jake

said, "He give you good Indian name. You like."

"Oh, will I?" she inquired archly. This heathen chief could never give her anything she would like!

"He call you Woman Who Fall Out of Canoe."

She gasped. "How dare he? I did not fall out of the canoe!"

"He think it a good story. He say he save your life."

"He did not!"

Jake shrugged. "I believe chief."

She tightened her lips. She could see that it would do no good to argue with the man. "Tell him I do not like the name!"

Jake sighed. "You like. If you smart."

"What do you mean?"

"He chief. He always give good name."

The chief was watching this exchange. His arms were folded across his naked chest as he watched her calmly. She thought she saw a gleam of laughter in his dark eyes. An idea suddenly occurred to her. "Tell him I have a name for *him*."

Jake glanced from her to the chief. "Better be good one," he advised.

"Oh, it is," she assured him. "Tell him I think this is a good name: 'Miserable Chief Who Steals Women.' We can call him 'Miserable' for short." There! That should fix him! He wouldn't know the meaning of the name, and she could secretly laugh at him every time she used it.

Jake raised a scraggly eyebrow.

"It is a verrry powerful name," she assured Jake.

The chief was frowning. So was the translator.

"Are you sure he does not speak English?" she asked, suddenly cautious.

"He no speak English. He need me. I know this,"

assured Jake. "What this name mean?" He flicked another glance at the silent chief. "Chief wants to know."

"Oh, it means very wise man," she said airily.

"You sure?" asked Jake.

"You are a suspicious man," she told Jake innocently. "Don't you trust people?"

He said something to the chief. The chief was suddenly looking grim.

"Here," she said. "I will tell him his new name, since you're afraid to tell him. He needs an English name, anyway." She faced the chief and took a deep breath. "You are called 'Miserable Chief Who Steals Women.' "

A storm was gathering on his handsome face.

"Is there a dance goes with name?" asked Jake. "Chief not look happy. Dance make him happy."

"Dance? Oh. Oh, yes. Yes, there is a dance," she assured Jake and the chief. She thought quickly. Then she tucked her hands under her arms like a chicken and proceeded to jump around and squawk. She craned her neck back and forth and high-stepped about. She did little hops. She squawked some more.

The chief frowned. The slave frowned.

Elizabeth stopped and straightened. "He doesn't like the dance?"

"No," agreed Jake.

"Too bad," she said with a sniff. "That's his name and that's his dance."

The chief looked furious. He said something to Jake.

Jake did not translate, but he did say, "Do not give me dance. I just take name."

Elizabeth pouted. The chief shook his head in disgust and walked away.

"Too bad he doesn't like his name," sneered Elizabeth.

"Too bad," agreed Jake. "Go get more wood."

The fire was burning low, and dark was settling across the island. It was night. Elizabeth could hear an owl hooting. She pulled her blanket around herself and crept closer to the fire. This was the time she dreaded. Night.

Mr. Burt had been silent for most of the time except for the occasional complaint about the dried fish. Elizabeth was so hungry for food that she would have eaten wooden canoe chips, so she did not see why he was complaining.

One by one, the others drifted away from the fire and rolled up into their blankets. Finally Elizabeth was the only one sitting at the hearth.

A deep voice called to her, and she turned. It was the tall, proud Miserable Chief Who Steals Women, whom she'd managed to avoid for most of the evening. She did not want to go with him, but she knew the skinny, tattooed chief with the big belly had been watching her all evening, and the hairs on the back of her neck had risen at his regard. She did not know where he was now, but she could still feel him watching her.

So this handsome chief did not seem quite so repellent. In fact, he seemed almost acceptable. She'd had a chance to study all the Indians this evening, assessing them and the possibility that one of them might help her escape. She knew that the tattooed chief would not help her, nor any of his friends. Deep in her heart, she knew that Mr.

Burt would not help her. That left the Miserable Chief Who Steals Women or his tall friend, or perhaps Jake. But Jake was powerless. And this chief was the one who'd captured her; he wouldn't help her. His tall friend seemed disinclined, too. So . . . she was on her own.

"So, Mr. Miserable," she said as brightly as she could. "What are your plans for the evening? Shall we dine, then perhaps attend a dance? Or would the theater be more to your liking?" She was smirking, but she truly could not help herself. She had to keep her spirits up somehow.

To her surprise, he reached for a curl of her hair that had strayed from the bun on the top of her head. He said something, which of course she did not understand. She swiftly reached up to move her hair out of his hand. It would not do to let him touch her, no matter how gentle he appeared. And he did appear gentle—at the moment. Gentle, and his dark eyes were curious. For a moment she found herself wishing they could speak to one another. Then she drove that impulse away.

He sighed and turned, motioning to her to follow him. She wondered briefly if he was as frustrated with their lack of a common language as she was.

She picked up her blanket and followed him over to where he'd spread his own blanket. For the first time, she began to get a little nervous. While it was true that she'd slept beside him last night, and the night before, this was becoming a little too much like a routine for her to feel comfortable. What if he expected her to lie beside him every night?

She glanced around, but everyone else was either snoring or sleeping. So she wrapped her blanket around herself and sat down on the ground. She would sit here for a while, she decided. She could stare at the stars; at the moon; at the tall, dark trees behind her; at the forest; at the white, phosphorescent waves tickling the shore; at anything that would keep her mind from centering on him.

She heard him lie down, heard his breathing. When he did not stir for a time, she realized he had fallen asleep. A wry smile curved her lips. Apparently, he did not find her irresistible. Not that he should, of course, she added hastily. After all, he was an Indian; she was a woman of the world, from San Francisco. Their worlds were very different. Very different.

She nodded off to sleep, the fire cracking now and then, smoke drifting in and out of her hair. She awoke for a moment and decided that if she lay down she would sleep better. When she felt an arm move around her and hold her firmly, she stiffened. But he kept breathing evenly, obviously still asleep. Well, she couldn't help what he did in his sleep. Besides, the warmth of his body, the firm clasp of his arm around her, all reassured her on this dark night, on this lonely island in the middle of who knew where.

She awoke to the humming of a mosquito in her ear. At least she thought it was a mosquito. Then she realized the little hairs on the back of her neck were raised like prickles. What—?

She lifted her head a little, listening. What was that sound?

She peeked out from under lowered lids and saw a dark shadow move. Then there was a glint of steel in the moonlight. A knife!

"Aaaaiiiieeee!" she screamed, and her thrashing and kicking awoke the man beside her. He lifted his arms to protect himself just as a dark shadow launched itself at him. Elizabeth lunged out of the way, crawling away from the two men as they struggled. At a safe distance, she turned and looked. She thought she recognized the assailant in the moonlight. It was one of the tattooed chief's friends.

She couldn't see much of the fight, just two dark figures rolling around on the ground. The other Indians had awakened, and were yelling encouragement to the combatants. She noticed they did not interfere. Then suddenly Elizabeth heard a long gasp, and one of the men went limp and still.

The other one got slowly to his feet, and she saw that the young chief was the victor. Relief shot through her.

She watched as he moved one of the man's limbs with his foot.

"Is—is he dead?" she muttered, afraid of the answer.

Several grunts were the only response she got, but as the man lay unmoving, she assumed the worst. It was difficult to believe. Everything had happened so fast. And now an Indian man, one of the men she'd traveled with for the last several days, lay dead on the beach. A quick, brutal death in a cold, brutal world.

Two of the young chief's friends came over and one took the dead man's feet, the other his arms, and they dragged him to the water. They were about to throw the body into the water when the tattooed chief and two of his friends rushed over and began shouting and gesticulating.

She heard movement behind her. It was Jake. "They throw dead body in sea like dead slave," he said contemptuously. "Other chief no like that. Want good burial for friend."

"That *friend* tried to kill the other chief," said Elizabeth archly. "Just how friendly are all these Indians?"

Jake chuckled. "Not friends," he admitted. "From two tribes. Haida and Tsimshian. Hate one another."

"Is that what they are?" asked Elizabeth. "Two different tribes?" It began to make sense to her. She realized now that they were always splitting into two groups: the young, arrogant chief and his tall, quiet friend with their two companions, and the tattooed chief and his friends. First they had fought over Mr. Burt, then over the canoes, then over her, and now this . . . this murder had happened.

"What is he?" she asked, pointing to the young chief, her protector, who was silently watching the others argue over the dead body.

"Him Haida chief."

"And him?" she pointed to the yelling tattooed leader.

"Him Tsimshian chief."

"And him?" she pointed to the dead man.

"Him Tsimshian."

"So, a Tsimshian tried to kill a Haida," she mused aloud.

"Yes," agreed Jake. "Instead, Haida kill Tsimshian." He laughed.

Elizabeth did not find this very amusing. After all, she could have been the one killed. A man sneaking around with a knife in the dead of night could easily mistake whom he was trying to kill. "Why did he try to kill the Haida chief?" she asked.

"Don't know. Maybe not like."

There was an outburst of Indian words from the tattooed chief. He spoke quickly and furiously. The young Haida chief glared at him.

"Hmmm," said Jake, listening to the tattooed chief.

"What is it?" asked Elizabeth.

"Tsimshian chief say that dead man tried to kill this Haida chief for revenge. He say this Haida chief insulted a Tsimshian middle chief and scraped his face."

This made little sense to Elizabeth, but it seemed to anger the Haida chief. She shrugged. What did she care about these Indians' squabbles? She just wanted to go home. "You just told me none of them like one another."

"Yes," said Jake.

"If they don't like one another, why are they all traveling together?" she asked reasonably.

"Great chief send them."

"Who is this great chief?"

"You see," said Jake, suddenly mysterious. Then Elizabeth noticed the young Haida chief staring in her direction. Evidently Jake noticed it too. "Uh-oh," said Jake. "I go now." He slipped away.

The young chief picked up Elizabeth's blanket and walked over to where she stood. He handed her the blanket, and she marveled that he thought of her comfort at a time when he'd almost been killed.

"Thank you," she said and wrapped the blanket around herself to stave off the night chill. She looked at the dead body and the men still arguing over it. Then she looked at the young chief. The moonlight was strong enough that she could see him fairly well. Even though she knew he could not speak English, she said, "I'm glad you weren't killed."

He stared at her, his brows close together in a thoughtful frown, and then with a sigh he went back to where they'd been sleeping. He sat down and patted the blanket beside him. She walked over, leaving the other Indians to their arguing, and sat down beside him. "I wish you spoke English," she said.

The fire had burned low, and she could see the orange embers reflected in his eyes. He smiled, and she stared at him, her mouth agape. He really was most attractive. She tried to squash the new feelings for him arising in her.

He had just killed a man. A man who was trying to kill him.

And, she suddenly realized, she had saved his life. "Now we're even," she told him. "You saved me from falling overboard in the canoe and my screams just saved you from being stabbed to death." She smiled ruefully. "Although you saved yourself by fighting," she admitted. She brightened. "Still, if I hadn't awakened you, you'd be a very dead man."

He merely watched her calmly.

She sighed. It was frustrating having a conversation with oneself. She looked up at the moon. Clouds drifted across its bright face. "I wonder if I'll ever get home," she breathed. Home. Strange, she did not truly think of Olympia as home. She hadn't been there long enough, she supposed. Still, it was better than where she was now, wherever that was. And she would be free. Not held against her will. "Auntie Elizabeth," she said longingly.

He still watched her, and she thought for a moment that his face grew sad, but then she knew it was the moonlight playing tricks on his face. She lay down, her back to him, and when he put his arm around her, she did not squirm or object. They had somehow become important to one another, she realized. They had saved each other's lives.

Chapter Seven

She had to stop thinking of him as her protector. But try as she might, the thought kept coming back to her. She needed someone willing to fight for her against the other men. Miss Cowperth would never approve, and there had never even been a lecture in her class about such things. Yet, Elizabeth sensed she needed some protection. It was as if the civilized, schooled woman from San Francisco had been suddenly stripped away and in her place was a frightened girl who was cunning and thinking only of her own survival. Whatever would Miss Cowperth say? Mercifully, Elizabeth decided Miss Cowperth would never need to know.

Elizabeth shifted a little on the seat and caught the tattooed chief watching her, a sneer on his lip. He made her skin feel unclean. He was a dangerous man. And already on this voyage one man had died. Did the tattooed chief have anything to do with that murder? wondered Elizabeth. A shiver went up her spine as she watched the green water swirl by. She hoped they weren't planning to kill her. Yes, she needed a protector.

The Indians had been paddling since early morning. The water made the canoe bounce, but she knew it was not dangerous. Certainly not like the storm yesterday. Was it only yesterday? So much had happened.

Suddenly the Indians began talking, and Elizabeth came out of her reverie and looked around. To her surprise, ahead she could see a long, low strip of land, with yellow cliffs. Behind the cliffs were blue hills. She straightened. Where were they?

Jake, sitting in the stern, stopped his paddling, pointed, and said to her, "Fort Victoria."

"What?" she exclaimed, then lowered her voice, fearing to draw attention to herself. Excitement rose in her. A fort! There would be people there, white people! She could escape!

For the first time since her capture, Elizabeth's spirits rose. But then a wily animal cunning swept over her. She had to keep the Indians from knowing how pleased she was. She shot a glance at Mr. Burt. He was asleep, snoring. Well, maybe she could make a plan with him. He'd want to escape, surely. Everyone knew he was destined for death at the end of this voyage.

She could barely contain her excitement over the next hour as they drew closer to Fort Victoria. Where before it seemed the black canoe flew across the waves, now it seemed to crawl along. But she must be patient; she must! Her whole life depended on it.

Her glance strayed to the handsome young chief. He was paddling steadily. A lock of black hair had fallen across his brow, making him look untamed. She almost lost her breath at how handsome he looked.

He seemed unaware of her excitement at nearing Fort Victoria. Good! Of all the Indians, he had the most ability to read what she was up to. Jake would know, too. But Jake was paddling determinedly, no doubt planning his own escape.

She straightened on her seat, noticing for the first time that the tops of her once-black leather shoes were totally white from the salt. Oh, how embarrassing. To have to enter the fort in discolored, tattered shoes. She glanced down at her dress, covered in sea-spray blotches and stains from carrying wood. She wanted to squirm in humiliation. Miss Cowperth would have a fit!

Elizabeth closed her eyes when she thought of what her hair must look like. She'd left it in a bun for the last four days, uncaring, too despondent to do anything with it.

But now, in the new Elizabeth, the newly discovered, cunning, animal part of her asserted itself. The condition of her shoes and clothes could not be helped. One could not expect to stay fashionably dressed when one was captured by Indians. Best to shrug it off. After all, it was just a pair of shoes and a dress.

It would be nice, though, to have a comb or brush for her hair. Looking as she did, she would probably scare her rescuers away! She wanted to laugh aloud at the thought. *This must stop*, she told herself sternly. *I'm getting positively giddy at the thought of arriving at Fort Victoria!*

They were entering a long, curving, rocky bay, forested on both sides.

Oh, she could see the buildings now. The fort was still some distance away, but she could see it! How high the wooden walls looked. Good, they could keep out Indians! But as they got closer, she could see tents and makeshift dwellings scattered outside the fort. A blue haze of smoke from many fires floated over the area. Tall trees rose behind the fort, and she was surprised to see how close the forest was to it. And how large the fort appeared.

Across the bay from the fort were more huts and tents. It looked like Indians lived there. The Indians in the canoe muttered among themselves, but she paid no attention until Jake whispered to her, "They beach canoe over in woods. They no want Mister Burt to escape."

She realized then that the canoe was heading away from the fort. Instead, it was veering to the side, toward a low, tree-covered point of land.

Alarm shot through her. "What about me?" she whispered. "Do they think I will try to escape?"

Jake shrugged. "You stay with canoe, too. No want white woman walking through Fort Victoria."

She stared at him. "What about you? Are you going to escape?"

He looked taken aback. "Why escape?" he asked. "I slave all my life. I go nowhere."

She subsided into silence. She wasn't going to be like that. Ever. She would escape. She would!

But how could she do it if she was stuck on some beach with a vast forest between her and the fort? Oh, what to do?

The canoe glided smoothly to the beach, and most of the men hopped out and pulled it in closer. She stayed where she was, thinking frantically. Civilization was so close. And people! White people. Men and women who, if they but knew she was here, would help her, surely.

Yes, yes, of course they would. How silly to doubt it, for even a moment.

Through narrowed eyes she watched as the Indians pulled the big canoe up over the gravel. She heard the scraping beneath the thick hull, felt the canoe jerk with each pull. Mr. Burt sat sullenly on his seat, slumped over as though weighted down by hopelessness. She had to admire him. Perhaps he would have been a thespian, under normal circumstances, though a picture of Mr. Burt treading the stage as an actor did seem far-fetched. Drat! She was so excited by the proximity of the fort that she couldn't think straight.

The Indians talked among themselves in a group. She sat as quiet as a mouse, hoping they'd forgotten her.

The young chief, Miserable Chief Who Steals Women, sauntered back to the landed canoe. She had to admit that "miserable" did not really describe such a man as he: a man who walked tall and proud, a man whose hair glistened so black, and whose body was so well muscled and broad shouldered. And a man to whom the other Indians listened. Maybe she should change his name to Handsome Chief Who Steals Women.

She had to stifle a giggle at the thought of brazenly calling him "Handsome."

He walked up to her side of the craft. She unwittingly leaned toward him as she met his dark eyes. "Yes?" she said.

He smiled, and her heart fluttered. Then he turned to Mr. Burt and motioned him to get out of the canoe. With a sigh, Mr. Burt heaved himself to his feet and clambered over the side of the canoe, letting out a few choice curse words as he waded through the water.

"Handsome" motioned her to come out of the canoe, too. She got to her feet, carefully, for the canoe was a little tippy. He reached out a hand to steady her, and she felt his warm clasp on her hand. Startled, she stared at him. His smile made her want to melt inside. She pulled her hand away. "I can walk by myself, thank you," she said, using her best Miss-Cowperth-trained diction.

She lifted her skirt a little, conscious of his gaze, and swung her leg over the side of the canoe away from him. She would not, would *not*, expose her ankles and limbs to the eyes of the likes of him!

But the side of the canoe was a little higher than she'd thought, and the water a little deeper. She struggled on the edge of the canoe, lost her balance, then collapsed in the water.

It was frigid! She jumped to her feet with a yelp.

Mr. Burt snorted. "I seen cows frolicking in the pasture that's more graceful than you."

"I will thank you," she said frostily, "to keep your opinions to yourself." She lifted her skirts just a bit and dragged herself out of the water.

Handsome, she noticed, when she finally regained her courage enough to glance at him—and merciful heavens, she'd say her prayers every night for the rest of her life if only he'd not seen her horrible fall—was staring solemnly at her. Evidently

Providence was not in a bargaining mood, for the twinkle in his eyes told her he'd seen everything.

With a sniff, she turned and marched up the beach to plunk herself down on a log. What did Indians know about the difficulties of debarking from a canoe when one was entangled in a long skirt and shoes that no longer fit? Nothing, that's what!

She sat there quietly, hoping they'd all walk away. But alas, her hopes were in vain. Two Indians remained, both big, strong-looking men: one of the tattooed chief's Tsimshian men and one of the Haidas. It did not help that one lingered close to where Elizabeth sat and the other, arms crossed, practically sat on Mr. Burt. Not really sat, but stayed very close to wherever the hapless Mr. Burt moved.

Well, it was obvious to Elizabeth that she would not be escaping on this fine day. She sighed and blew at the wisps of hair that hung in front of her face. At least the sun on her skin felt good, and her dress dried rather quickly. It seemed as though they waited a long time, perhaps three or four hours, before she heard twigs crackling and men's voices approaching along the forested path.

The Indians came into view. Whatever it was they'd stopped at the fort for must have been accomplished, because they were laughing and joking with one another.

How unusual for them all to get along so well, Elizabeth noted. And then she froze. A beautiful woman stepped from behind the single-file line of men. She was talking animatedly to the young chief, Handsome. How dare she!

Then Elizabeth caught herself. So what if he had

a wife? It was none of her concern. . . .

But she couldn't help watching them. The jealousy rising in her throat threatened to choke her. The woman was indeed beautiful, with long dark hair and sloe eyes. Her golden skin made Elizabeth feel pale and sickly, and her graceful movements—well, Elizabeth reddened at the thought of her recent debarking from the canoe.

Her heart sank to her shredded shoes. How could she hope to compete with a woman who looked like that? And, worse, who spoke his language? Which, Elizabeth could see, was exactly what they were doing this very moment, talking away to each other as though no other person existed.

She pretended not to watch them, but the whole time the fire was being lit and the dinner prepared, Elizabeth was achingly aware of the two, talking away. Once she caught a pitying glance from the other tall Haida, Handsome's good friend. With a frown, Elizabeth turned away. Now the Indians were pitying her. Her! A woman of the world, educated in San Francisco. A woman born to marry well, according to Aunt Elizabeth and Miss Cowperth. A woman who could read and do sums and even play parlor games. It wasn't to be borne that he would prefer that . . . that . . . beautiful woman. . . . My heavens! Now she was pitying herself!

In disgust, Elizabeth jumped up and went to fetch more firewood just to keep herself busy and her mind off Handsome and the lovely woman.

She and Jake gathered enough wood for the fire to burn all night. Mr. Burt had to be convinced to help them by vigorous kicks from the tattooed chief. Mr. Burt certainly does not make anything easy for himself, noted Elizabeth acidly, tempted to kick him herself. Oh, heavens! Now she was venting her spleen on Mr. Burt, of all people.

She would have been happy to sit there all evening complaining to herself, and would have, had not a young white man come paddling by in a canoe. When he saw their group on shore, he waved and called out to the Indians.

"Ho, the shore! That you, Thompson? That you, Kelp?"

Elizabeth sat up. Maybe he could help her escape these heathens. After all, he was white.

Several of the Indians walked down to the water to greet him, and there was much to-do and talking back and forth. All of a sudden, Elizabeth realized that part of what was being said was in the English language. She sat up straighter.

Then she stood up. That cad, that miserable chief, no longer Handsome, but Mr. Chief Who Steals And Deceives Women was speaking to the newcomer—in English!

Hands on hips, she looked around to see if anyone else had noticed. The slave, Jake, was watching too, and he took several steps back up the beach, a worried look upon his face. He knows, she thought. He knows now that Handsome can speak English. And he's afraid.

As for herself, she wasn't afraid, she thought, stomping back and forth in front of the log while the Indians had a merry old time chatting with the paddler. She was angry.

She cringed when she recalled the things she had said in front of that deceiving heathen chief. The cad! He'd been pretending all along. Couldn't speak English, indeed!

Furious, she continued to stomp up and down the beach. She didn't care that the Indian woman watched her curiously.

Finally, she realized she should be down at the water, too, telling the young white man of her plight. He would surely want to rescue her.

She marched down to the water. Mr. Burt, she noted, continued to sit on the sand, guarded carefully by two large Indian men. Well, he was old enough to take care of himself, she sniffed. She had to look out for herself.

When she reached the water's edge, she had to wait several minutes while the deceiving chief and his friend bantered back and forth with the newcomer. Finally there was a slight lull in the conversation, and Elizabeth spoke up. "Young man," she said, "I have been captured by these heathens!"

"That so, Isaac?" asked the white man, staring at the miserable, deceiving chief.

To Elizabeth's surprise, the chief nodded casually, as if it were of no import that he had stolen her away from home and hearth.

"He had no business to capture me! Help me leave these horrible heathens," she said at once.

The white man, his hair and eyes dark, but his skin pale, said to the two Indians, "Where'd you get her?"

"O-lymp-ya," answered the miserable deceiver.

The white man let out a low whistle. "Partner! You get caught with her and you're going to be in big trouble."

Elizabeth stamped her foot. "He is already in big trouble," she said. "He stole me, and he stole that white man up there." She pointed at Mr. Burt, sitting slumped on a log. "He plans to kill Mr. Burt."

111

"That so?" mused the young white man.

Elizabeth wished he would get on with rescuing her instead of doing all this infernal talking.

"What are you killing him for?" he asked.

The miserable chief answered, "He murdered Tsus-sy-uch."

The white man's face changed to an ugly snarl. "Kill the son of a dog!"

This was not the answer Elizabeth had expected. "Can you help me?" she asked, dismayed to hear a plaintive whine creep into her voice.

The white man looked at her consideringly. "I'm afraid you got me mixed up with someone else, ma'am," he said at last. "I'm not in the rescue business."

His words gave her an idea. "I'll pay you."

He laughed. "I'd be a fool to take your money. Or"—he paused and eyed her thoughtfully—"anything else you're offering. I'm not about to offend Isaac Thompson here. His father—nah, not just his father, his whole clan—would never trade with me again." He gave a chuckle.

The miserable chief smirked at her. So did his tall friend.

"Is that so?" she shouted impatiently. "I suppose your trading money is more important than rescuing a white woman from these heathens' clutches!" Hands on hips, she wanted to wade in and yank that young man out of his canoe.

"Yes, ma'am," he answered politely. "Sure is."

Then, to Elizabeth's chagrin, he continued to banter with the two Indians, leaving her feeling left out and forgotten. And unrescued.

When he paddled away, with a wave and a dip of his paddle, she wanted to scream. Muttering to herself, she marched back to her log and sat down, dejected.

The miserable chief appeared at her side. "He cannot help you," he said, and, to her surprise, for a moment she thought she heard kindness in his voice. "He is a trader at Fort Simpson, a white man's fort up near where we come from."

She stared at him moodily, wondering why he had suddenly decided to speak English. "I don't understand," she said at last. "He's white. He should have rescued me."

The treacherous, English-speaking villain shook his head. "He's Indian. He looks white because his father was a white man. But he's Indian in his heart."

Her own heart sank. How would she ever be able to tell who was who in this strange world she'd been cast into?

Disheartened, she sat with her head in her hands for a few minutes, and when she finally looked up, his tall friend had joined him. "What is your name?" she asked the friend, deciding to ignore the bane of her existence for a while.

"William Kelp," he answered.

Her glance caught the other Indians. "And what do you call that tattooed man who is kicking Jake?"

"Jake?"

"I named him that," she informed him. "The one with the messy hair."

"Oh." William Kelp appeared to be considering this. Then he said, "The one who is kicking is called Fisher. And over there is Marten Fur. They are both Tsimshian nobles. That means they are important chiefs."

"And him?" She pointed to each man in turn and

at last learned the English names of her forced companions. Besides Marten Fur and Fisher, the other Tsimshian was named Fin. The Haidas, besides the notorious Isaac Thompson and his friend William Kelp, were Killer Whale and Crab.

"Are all of you Haidas nobles?" she asked, curious.

"Isaac and I are nobles, but Killer Whale and Crab are commoners. They are people who are not nobles, and not slaves. Ordinary people."

"Free people," said Isaac. "No slaves. But the Tsimshians brought a slave. We Haidas bring only free men with us."

She ignored that.

"And what," she asked icily, "are you going to do with me? Am I to be a noble? A commoner? A slave?"

"You?" asked William Kelp.

They both looked uncomfortable suddenly.

"Yes," she answered, "me. After all, you plan to kill Mr. Burt. What do you plan to do with me?"

William Kelp said to Isaac Thompson, "You get to answer that question." He walked away, humming.

"Wait!" she called. "Come back!" But he kept walking.

"He didn't tell me the Indian woman's name. Who is she?" muttered Elizabeth.

"Her white name is Susan," said Isaac Thompson. "Susan Connor. She is a Haida woman."

"I do not wish to converse with you," said Elizabeth.

" 'Converse'? " He grinned. "You use words the traders at Fort Simpson do not use. What does 'converse' mean?"

He had a good ear for the language, she could tell, because he spoke the new word perfectly. "I am not here to teach English to heathens," she snapped.

"No," he agreed. "You are here because I steal you."

She glared at him. "Exactly," she said at last, chagrined at his audacity. "I demand," she said clearly, "that you let me go. You can take me to Fort Victoria, and I will get help from there."

"Cannot do," he said.

"Why not?" she demanded. "You seem to be in charge here. The others do what you say. Why can't you just free me at Fort Victoria?"

She thought he looked sad when he said, "Big trouble if I do that."

"Bigger trouble if you do not," she shot back.

He shook his head. "Not so big, I think. Better to keep you."

She wanted to shake some sense into him. "Listen to me," she said. "If you take me to Fort Victoria, I will not tell anyone how I got there. I will get help from the white people at the fort. I will not tell them about you and your men."

Actually she would. She would tell them to seize these miscreants and throw them in whatever jail they had at the fort for stealing her and Mr. Burt. But she tightened her lips. This heathen, this Isaac Thompson, with his wayward lock of black hair falling over his forehead in oh, such a dashing fashion, need not know a thing about what she planned to do. He'd find out soon enough.

"Just let me go to the fort," she pleaded when he didn't answer. He looked as if he was seriously considering what she said.

115

But he still did not answer her. Instead, he pulled out a package wrapped in checkered cloth.

She ignored the package, pressing her advantage. "You have Mr. Burt. He's the one you wanted. Not me. I just got in the way. Let me go and we'll pretend the whole thing never happened."

"You are important," he said at last.

"Not as important as Mr. Burt," she lied. "You have him. Let me go."

"You are the wife of John Butler. If we can't have John Butler, we take you."

She stared at him, askance. "The wife of whom?"

"John Butler."

"John Butler?" Her mind floundered. Whatever did he mean?

"That is what I said."

"Yes, yes, you did," she agreed readily, not wanting to offend him when there was a possibility of convincing him to let her go. "But you see, I am not the wife of John Butler."

Isaac Thompson stared at her, deep into her eyes as if willing her to tell the truth.

"You say you are not his wife?"

"Yes, that's what I am saying. I am not John Butler's wife."

"Who are you, then?"

"Elizabeth. Elizabeth Powell."

He looked puzzled. "Lis-uh-buth is the right name."

She frowned. "Whatever do you mean?"

"At the town of O-lymp-ya. We asked about John Butler. Some people told us he had a wife named Lis-uh-buth."

"Oh!" she exclaimed, understanding dawning. "You mean my aunt! Oh, yes! My aunt is named

Elizabeth Butler. She recently married John Butler. He is my new uncle."

Isaac Thompson frowned. "He is a very bad man."

"I really do not wish to argue with you about whether he's a good man or a bad man. Obviously, some terrible mistake has been made and you've stolen the wrong person. Not," she added hastily, "that I want you to go back and steal my aunt. But since I am not the person you thought I was, I want you to let me go."

When he didn't say anything, she said, "Just take me over to Fort Victoria. That is the best thing to do. Let me go and I'll forget everything. You can go on your way, take Mr. Burt . . ." She stopped to catch her breath. She was babbling, she knew it.

While she was wondering what to say next, he called over the other Indians. Speaking in their language, he explained the terrible mistake. Several exclamations greeted his news, and the tattooed chief, Fisher, looked furious. He looked ready to hit Elizabeth, so she took a few steps away from him and the other Indians. The slave, Jake, came alongside her and said, "Me think you in big trouble now."

"No, I am not," she snapped. "I told him to let me go. This is all a terrible mistake."

Jake shrugged. "Mistake or no, they not let you go."

"What will they do with me?" she hissed.

He shook his head. "Do not know," he said. "But you go with them now. Not go back to white people."

She stared at the matted-haired man. "Surely

that cannot be. Look," she pleaded, "you tell them. Tell them to let me go."

He snorted. "I slave, remember? They not do what slave says." With another snort, he walked away.

Mr. Burt was sitting on the log. She went over to him. Perhaps he could help her.

"So," he said. "What the hell was that all about?"

"I want them to set me free," she said. "They thought I was my aunt."

"Yeah? What they want with your aunt?"

Elizabeth shrugged. "I really do not know, but they thought I was Elizabeth Butler. I suspect, however, that they really wanted Uncle John."

"You don't say so?" said Mr. Burt insinuatingly.

"What does that mean?" she demanded. "*You* know why we're here. You tell *me!*"

He held up a hand. "Not I," he said. "I know nothing."

"Why are they going to kill you, then?"

"Because they're mean devils. Kill anyone who gets in their way."

"You weren't in their way. You were on my uncle's beach. They had to paddle out of their way to find you."

Mr. Burt's gaze flicked away.

When he didn't say any more, she said, "I think you know. I think you know why they want to kill you. And why they want my uncle. You just won't tell me."

"It's none o' your damn business."

She glared at him, rising dislike for the man filling her bosom. "You and I are the only white people on this miserable voyage," she said. "I expected we would help one another, you and I. But no. I

118

can see that you won't help me! Very well, do not.
But I will not aid you, either."

He whirled on her. "I'll help you," he said. "I'll
help you if you give me a little somethin' to make
it worth my while."

She stared at him, shocked into silence. He took
her silence for a rebuff. "Whatsa matter?" he
snarled. "I'm not good enough for you, is that it?"

"No," she said when she found her tongue. "No,
that is not it."

"What, then?" he demanded. "Do you think
you're too good for me, Miss High and Mighty, too
good for ol' Burt?"

She turned away, sickened. "You are facing
death, Mr. Burt! I would be more concerned about
that, if I were you!"

He fell silent at her words. She walked away, a
slight feeling of satisfaction running through her.
For all the trouble she was in, at least she did not
face certain death as he did. And, she suspected,
he probably deserved it. She wondered what he'd
done to make these Indians so angry at him. From
what she had seen of Mr. Burt, it was probably
something not very nice. Probably something very
bad. Probably something truly awful.

She sighed. Well, whatever it was, it was his
problem. She had other things to consider. Like
how she was going to get away from these stubborn Indians.

By now the Indians had said whatever they
wanted to say, and were spreading out their blankets near the fire. She retrieved her blanket from
the canoe and went over to lie down by the fire.

She couldn't help glancing at the Indian
woman—Susan, was it?—to see if Isaac Thomp-

son was going to lie with her. He hadn't said it, but she suspected they were husband and wife. Or perhaps lover and mistress.

A sudden thought crossed Elizabeth's mind. Wouldn't Miss Cowperth be shocked to know what her charge was thinking these days? She conducted an imaginary visit with the strict old woman. "You see, Miss Cowperth," she could see herself saying, "I really wanted him to lie down with me, as he had done for the past two nights, but this other woman was there. So, I was forced to tear out her hair. Handfuls of it. I'm sure you understand."

With a chuckle, Elizabeth lay down on her blanket. No, Miss Cowperth would not understand. Elizabeth was beginning to suspect that Miss Cowperth would never understand anything about this crazy voyage she had been forced to endure.

She looked up to see the object of her contemplation before her. She stared at him. In the firelight, his dark hair had reddish overtones, and that same little lock of hair dangled over his forehead. She sighed. It would be so much easier if he looked like that ugly tattooed chief, instead of the handsomest man she'd ever seen. She sat up slowly. "Yes? What is it?"

"For you," he said.

She looked at it. "That looks like a present," she observed. It was a checkered cloth package. She didn't want to take it, but her curiosity was getting the better of her. What could he, a heathen, possibly bring her for a present? She supposed she could tell him that if he truly wanted to give her a present, he could take her to Fort Victoria, but she was exhausted by the whole battle. Emotions could do that to her.

She took the package he held out to her and untied the string around it. She lifted the checked material, and underneath there was a dull gleam in the firelight. She gasped. It was a comb, inlaid with polished shell on the handle. "Why," she cried, "it is beautiful! Where—where did you get it?"

"At the fort."

"How did you know I wanted a comb?"

His eyes played over her face and hair, and she flushed. She must look an utter mess. She looked into his eyes but saw no censure there. Some amusement perhaps, but kindness, too. "Thank you," she said simply, feeling flustered. "Thank you," she said again. "I must use it." She reached up and undid the thick mass of her bun. Slowly she began combing the tangled strands.

She looked up to see him watching her, his eyes following every stroke of the comb, and she felt suddenly warm inside. She smiled shyly.

He leaned over and touched her lips with his in a gentle, sweet kiss. She leaned into the kiss, holding her breath in surprise. When the kiss was over, he pulled back a little. "You very good," he said. "I am glad you are not John Butler's wife."

She lifted an eyebrow. "Back to that, are we?" she said, but inside, she felt all warm. She really did not feel like arguing with him.

He reached over and ran his hand gently down her cheek, and she shivered at his touch. "I keep you with me, Lis-uh-buth." She shivered again at how he said her name. "I take you to my home."

She looked at his face, at those lips that had just

touched hers. She found herself leaning toward him.

Then reason intervened.

She shook her head. "I cannot go to your home," she said. "I must go back to Olympia. Back to my aunt and uncle."

He looked at her, and she saw the kindness mix with sadness. "No," he said. "You stay with me. I will treat you good."

She smiled. "No doubt you would, but we will never find out, will we?" She felt a little sad as she said it. How odd. How was it, she wondered, that a heathen would treat her kindly and a white man like Mr. Burt would turn his back on helping her?

She wrapped the blanket around herself and pulled it up until it covered most of her face. That way he couldn't kiss her again and drive all rational thought from her head. "Good night, Isaac," she said.

He smiled. "Good night, Lis-uh-buth," he said softly and went to his own blanket.

When she could hear his even breathing and knew him to be asleep, she touched her fingers to her lips where he'd kissed her. Then she smiled to herself and snuggled under the blanket.

She awoke the next morning to shrill cries and the sound of blows. The slave, Jake, staggered around camp, pursued by the furious tattooed chief. Jake yelled at the top of his lungs, waking the other men. When he stumbled past Elizabeth, he cried out, "Mister Burt has escaped!"

Chapter Eight

Elizabeth sat up groggily. "Wha—?"

"Mister Burt escaped!" yelled Jake as he ran past Elizabeth again. Fisher chased him and shook a big stick at him viciously. Elizabeth wondered how long it would take the tattooed chief to realize that hitting the slave would not bring the white man back.

She could not say she was really surprised at Mr. Burt's escape. A glance at the shoreline showed the black canoe was still there. So he must have escaped through the forest. She supposed she wished him well, but she couldn't help thinking that, wherever he was, he would just bring more trouble upon himself. Ah, well, it was not her business.

She glanced around sharply, suddenly realizing how very quiet it was now that all the Indians had run off into the forest to hunt for the white man. Her business was her own escape.

Carefully casting off her blanket, she gazed around once more, unable to believe that she was the only one left at the campsite. She spied the Indian woman, rolled in a dark gray blanket. But she lay very still and appeared to be asleep, so Elizabeth got slowly to her feet, as silently as she could.

Her black boots were useless for running through the woods, she realized, so she did not put them on. She spied the Indian woman's shoes and placed her own feet in them. The fit was a little tight, but Elizabeth decided the leather shoes were better than her flapping boots. She reached for the comb that Isaac had given her and grabbed up a piece of fish from last night's meal, then tiptoed off into the forest, hoping she was traveling in the opposite direction from the Indians.

She ran down a deer path, stumbling now and then on salal roots. The bushy undergrowth was thick and came almost to her knees, but the trees were farther apart, allowing her to run between them. When she was some distance from the camp, she began to hum to herself. She'd done it! She was free!

Smiling to herself, she slowed her pace to a walk. Wouldn't they be surprised to find her gone! She chuckled, imagining the yelling and shouting that would greet her absence. She hoped Fisher did not beat Jake for *her* escape.

As she walked along, she surveyed the forest. Her plan had been to start out in the opposite direction from the fort and circle around. She assumed Mr. Burt would head directly for the fort. The Indians, chasing after him on whatever trails led to the fort, would be crowding the woods. So if she stayed cautiously in the background, circling around, she should make it to the fort by nightfall, long after the Indians had found, or not found, Mr. Burt. She did not want to spend a night in the woods, but she would if she had to. Anything to keep from being recaptured!

She could hear ocean waves beating against rocks some distance away through the forest, on the side away from the fort. She was always careful to remain aware of where the fort must be. It was to the northwest, as best she could judge. The undergrowth got thinner, and soon she found herself walking through low grass. She could see trees lining a cliff; the sound of pounding waves was louder.

A white mist was gradually lifting, revealing blue sky. Curious, she walked down a long hill until she could look over the cliff. There, huge white waves crashed against black rocks. How pretty! she thought. Gray gulls flew lazily on gentle wind currents, and the blue water sparkled from the sun.

She smiled to herself, amazed at how beautiful everything looked when one was free.

Her good humor rose as she walked along the cliff. It was a lovely day, she was free, and in a little while she would be marching through the wooden gates of Fort Victoria. Life was wonderful!

Life began to get a little less wonderful when she realized she did not quite know any longer in which direction the fort was. She thought it was off to her left, but she'd been following the cliff for some time and she realized she had not strictly kept the fort's direction in mind.

Well, no help for it now. Her stomach was growling and she was thirsty, so she sat down on the grass, her legs dangling over the cliff, and pulled out the piece of fish she'd taken from the Indians' camp. It tasted good, but she would have liked some water to drink with it. She was getting thirsty, and in her haste to leave camp, she'd forgotten to bring water.

Since walking along the cliff, she'd seen a small creek that trickled over the cliffs to the water below like a dribbling waterfall. But the water had looked muddy, and she hadn't quite got her courage up to drink it. She recalled that Miss Cowperth had once cautioned the young ladies in her charge about unsanitary drinking water.

"Never drink dirty water," she seemed to remember Miss Cowperth saying, and, like all the advice Miss Cowperth gave, this was most helpful. Why, Elizabeth might die out here in the woods, all alone, if it were not for Miss Cowperth and her wise, timely advice.

Well rested after her simple meal, Elizabeth got to her feet and continued on. She was trying to keep herself calm, but she had to admit she was really quite worried about where the fort was located. After all, this was a big forest to her left. And cliffs were to her right, and water after that. All very big and vast, and she was beginning to feel quite lost. No, not lost, really, just small. That was it. Everything was big and vast, and she was small. She tried to summon another one of Miss Cowperth's sermons, words or quotes, whatever she could remember, but nothing came to mind except, "When strolling along the street, always be sure to use your parasol. That will keep your skin from burning."

Elizabeth's skin was feeling hot now, but sadly,

there was no parasol. . . . And her feet hurt. Shoes that had seemed only a trifle tight when she first stole them now felt painfully tight. She limped now and then. One heel was bleeding.

And it was starting to get darker. Oh, not *dark* dark, but darker. The sun was low in the sky. She'd thought that by now she would have found the fort, but here she was, still out on the cliffs, wondering when she should cut through the forest to reach the fort.

Best to do it now, she told herself. *Be of courage.* She didn't think Miss Cowperth had said those words, but someone had. Maybe her aunt. She wondered how dear Aunt Elizabeth was doing. Had she already given up and mourned her niece for dead?

Tears came to Elizabeth's eyes as she thought about her aunt. Aunt Elizabeth had done so much for her. She'd worked hard, making dresses and garments for rich folks so that Elizabeth could attend Miss Cowperth's school. She'd taken Elizabeth in when her mother had died. She'd been mother and father to Elizabeth, only wanting what was best for her beloved niece. Elizabeth even suspected that Aunt Elizabeth had married John Butler to provide a home for her, a home she'd been unable to provide when Elizabeth was younger. Sadly, she thought perhaps her aunt did not realize that Elizabeth was a young woman now, and would one day soon want a home of her own. She hoped that Aunt Elizabeth had made the right choice in John Butler; after all, she had not known him long. Now, after meeting Mr. Burt, who called himself a friend of John's, Elizabeth had very real fears that John Butler was not quite the fine man her aunt thought he was.

She stopped. All this reminiscing and thinking was getting her nowhere. It was time to strike into the forest, to go directly to the fort. The Indians by now would have either recaptured Mr. Burt or would be back at camp. The fort would be safe to approach.

Taking a deep breath, Elizabeth plunged into the forest.

It would have been better, she lamented quietly to herself, if she had not waited so long to go into the forest. In the forest it was dark; quite, quite dark. And there were noises.

Not animal howling noises, but noises nonetheless. Noises like crackling branches. Noises like squalling babies.

And then suddenly there came an unearthly piercing scream, like a woman crying out in pain. When she heard that scream, Elizabeth's heart did several flip-flops and, panic-stricken, she tore off down the trail. She ran for what seemed a very long time, gasping, looking over her shoulder, uncaring of the branches that scratched her face as she raced by. Finally, exhausted, she stumbled to a halt. Still shaking, she looked over her shoulder. Had she left the screaming woman behind? Only silence greeted her.

She was a coward. She really was. If she had any bravery in her whatsoever, she would go back and help that woman, not run like an idiot through the forest, her only thought of panicked escape. Perhaps together they could help one another to the fort. Even now, she should turn back and look for her.

But she didn't, and so, as she walked along, Elizabeth castigated herself for the coward that she was. Finally, she could stand it no longer. Her conscience bothered her too much. So she swung around and headed back the way she had come.

At first she called gently, "Hello? Are you there?" in a hoarse half whisper. She did not want to alarm the woman, nor did she want to alert any lurking Indians to her presence. The thought of Jake and his forest Indians suddenly entered her mind. But then she calmed herself. They were far, far behind, left back near the island where they'd sheltered from the storm. Relief flooded through her as she stumbled on. Where was that woman?

Getting no answer to her whispers, she grew bolder and called out a little louder. "Hello? Hello? Ma'am? Where are you?"

Still getting no answer, Elizabeth began to shout. "Hello? Ma'am? Are you there?"

Still no answer.

She rounded the corner of the trail and suddenly came face to face with a huge cougar. Its yellow-gold eyes glared at her. When it snarled at her, she put out her hands and began to back up, very, very slowly. Suddenly the great cat turned and ran, and Elizabeth, noting its rapid departure, whirled and ran in the opposite direction. She ran until she could run no longer. Exhausted, she threw herself down on a low bed of leaves, and lay there panting.

So much for the screaming woman, she thought with a shiver. Had the cougar eaten the poor soul? Another shiver ripped along her spine. Oh, what a terrible day her first day of freedom was turning out to be. And now it was getting darker. And that cougar was still out there somewhere. Looking for another woman to eat.

Still exhausted, Elizabeth crawled through the bushes on her hands and knees. Then she slowly rose up on her knees, then got up to her aching feet. Her shoes pinched terribly. Her limbs ached horribly. Her dress was now a ragged tatter about her waist. She cared little that her bedraggled petticoat was now her skirt. Her skin was scratched and bleeding from all the branches that had slapped at her in her mad dash through the woods. And her hair—well, her hair was utterly hopeless. She pulled the beautiful comb Isaac had given her out of her pocket and reached up to comb her hair.

She froze.

There, leaning against a tree, watching her, stood Isaac. He leaned casually, arms crossed, and his dark eyes held a little glow as he watched her. The lock of black hair was, of course, in its usual place, falling gracefully across his forehead. He looked good. Very, very good.

She couldn't stop herself from tottering over to him on shaking legs and throwing herself into his arms. Fortunately, he caught her. His arms closed around her, and she shut her eyes, drawing strength from him. He felt warm and strong, and she was as glad to see him as she'd ever been to see anyone in her life.

"Cougar," she managed to gasp at last. "It ate a woman."

"You see this happen?" he demanded. He looked alarmed and surprised at the same time, but she noticed he kept his grip on her. Not that she wanted to leave those powerful, protective arms.

"No." She shook her head to emphasize her words. "But I heard her scream."

"You heard a woman scream?"

"Yes! And I saw the cougar!"

He began to laugh. His shoulders were shaking.

"What," she said icily, drawing away from him, "are you laughing at? Is it funny to you that a woman was eaten?" She turned her back on him, furious that she should think a heathen would care, actually care, about a woman being eaten. What was wrong with her that she thought he would understand? He was not even civilized!

He shook his head, still laughing. He walked around her until they faced one another. When he'd subsided to a smirk, he said, "That's what a cougar sounds like. A screaming woman."

Mortified, she threw her hands up to cool her hot cheeks. "I—I thought—"

He shook his head, his face solemn, but his black eyes sparkled with suppressed laughter. "That cougar cried out, and you heard it."

She closed her eyes, trying to understand. For a long, tortured hour she had lived with the thought of that poor woman, had searched for her . . . and now to find out that there was no woman . . . only a huge cougar and its yowling cry.

Elizabeth opened her eyes slowly. "Very well," she said, and her chin lifted. "I understand." She swallowed and straightened her shoulders.

"I will continue on my way now," she said. She would not let him know that the thought of the cougar somewhere out there still frightened her.

He reached for her shoulders. "Now we go back to Indian camp."

She removed his hands from her shoulders. "No! Now we go to Fort Victoria."

He jerked his thumb over his shoulder, in the opposite direction from where she'd been headed. "Fort Victoria that way."

"No," she said, "it is not. It is *that* way."

He shrugged. "I think not. That way."

"My, but you can be stubborn," she said. She set off in the direction she thought the fort to be in, which was *not* the direction he had indicated. He walked along behind her, and she heard his breathing. He sounded angry. Too bad. He must think her a fool to fall for such an uncivilized, heathen trick as to point her in the wrong direction.

But after a while, as it grew darker, she had to admit that she was not quite so certain that the fort was ahead. And he seemed no help, merely following along behind her. So she stopped and asked, "Where are we?"

"In the woods," he answered.

"I know that," she snapped. "But is the fort over there?"

He shrugged. "You said so."

"I know I said so," she answered. "But I'm not so sure now. And it's dark."

"Very dark," he agreed. "Except for the moon." The moon was somewhere, giving off its pale light, but it hardly penetrated the depths of the forest.

"You're being no help," she said.

He looked at her. "Are you cold?" he asked. "Hungry?"

"Yes," she answered.

"Thirsty?"

"Yes."

"Good. We go this way." And he led her in a

132

slightly different direction. In a short while she heard pounding ocean waves. "Are we going to the cliffs?" she asked uncertainly.

"You see."

They kept walking. In a while they came to a stream. They drank for several minutes, and then, vastly refreshed, continued on. Later, they arrived at the cliffs. Out across the water, the moon was huge as it rose above the waves and cast its silver beauty on the foaming water below them. To Elizabeth's surprise, Isaac kept moving forward, right to the very edge of the cliff. Then he started down the side of it.

"Where are you going?" she asked in astonishment.

"I show you," he said. He reached out a hand to her and waited. After a minute, she walked up to him and she took his hand. The feel of his fingers closing firmly around hers gave her a feeling of relief. She wasn't alone in the dark forest any longer. Someone was with her. Someone, she hoped, who could keep cougars away.

They went down the little path, which gradually wound down the side of the cliff; the big moon over the water was their only light.

They arrived at a small beach where the waves lapped at the gravel several feet from the cliffs. "This is beautiful," she said with a shiver.

"Yes," he agreed.

"Have you been here before?" She turned to him. It seemed different now. It was just the two of them, on a little beach, the cliff surrounding them at the back, rocky arms reaching out to the sea at the sides, and the ocean in front of them. Logs thrown up by the winter tides lay at angles to the high-tide line.

He nodded, but his grip on her hand tightened. He led her to a little grassy spot, looking very dark gray under the moonlight, and sat down. Then, to her surprise, he took off his shirt and laid it on the grass. "You can sit here," he invited.

She went and sat down, inching just a little away from him. "It is so pretty here," she said.

"I have been here many times," he said.

She turned to him quickly. "With Indian maidens?" She fought to keep the jealousy out of her voice.

He stopped his movements and said, "With my men. On trips to Fort Victoria. And to O-lymp-ya."

"Oh." It was a favorite camping spot, then, she thought. She shivered slightly.

"You cold?" he asked.

"A little," she admitted.

While he made a fire, she watched him work. His muscled body moved with an easy grace, and she couldn't take her eyes off him. When he bent over the fire to blow on the wisps of flame, the little black lock of hair fell over his forehead. She smiled to herself. He looked so handsome.

"I suppose," she said after a little, "that we are going to spend the night here."

"Yes." He rose and gathered some more wood. She did not feel obliged to help him, oddly. She just wanted to watch him. She suddenly realized that she'd never seen him gather wood before; it had always been herself or Mr. Burt or Jake that did it. She wondered if it was beneath his chiefly dignity to gather wood, and smiled to herself at the thought.

"You hungry?" he asked at last, when he'd deposited a goodly amount of wood. Enough, she thought wryly, to keep the fire burning for a week.

"Yes," she answered. But there was no food. She had eaten the last of the fish earlier in the day, and she didn't think he was carrying any food with him. He did, however, carry a small leather bag at his waist, which he rummaged through. Whatever he was looking for, he found, because he said to her, "Be back. Stay here."

She was glad to stay by the fire. The light of the moon was strong enough that she could see him run lightly over the rocks and boulders piled on one side of the beach. He stopped at a spot on a large rock and knelt down. Then she understood: he was fishing. He wasn't gone long before he returned, a small gutted salmon dangling from one hand. Its silver skin glowed in the moonlight. He split a piece of driftwood, wove the salmon between the pieces and set it upright in the hot sand next to the fire. The searing coals soon cooked the orange flesh.

They ate salmon by moonlight, serenaded by the music of waves lapping against the shore. Elizabeth sighed with happiness. One could not ask for anything better, she thought. Good food, a peaceful evening, warm weather and someone to keep the cougars at bay. She smiled to herself. Life should always be so simple.

She leaned back on the grass and stared out at the white foam of the waves. The waves were especially glowing this night, with little trickles of white light racing across the ridges of the water.

Some conversation was in order, she thought.

While she was thinking about what to say, other

than her usual "Where are you taking me?" and "What are you going to do with me?" he said, "You miss O-lymp-ya?"

"Not really." The words slipped out before she could call them back. To her astonishment, she realized it was true. She did not miss Olympia. Not the town, nor the farm where she'd stayed for two months, nor Uncle John. She hadn't known many people there before she'd been abducted.

"I do miss my aunt."

"Ah, yes." Except for that agreement, he was silent. She tried to figure out what he was thinking. "Do—do you have an aunt?" she ventured.

He looked at her, surprised at her question, and she flushed. Obviously, he had not been thinking about Indian, or white, aunts or even families. She didn't know what he'd been thinking about. Probably about fish.

"Does your aunt fish?" she tried.

"Yes," he answered slowly. "Does yours?"

"No." She shook her head. She could not even imagine Aunt Elizabeth fishing. "She sews."

"So?"

"Make clothes," she said hastily. She made the motion of a needle going in and out. Surely Indians sewed clothes.

He nodded, and she relaxed. He understood about making clothes. "What does your aunt do?" she asked.

"My aunt dances and sings. She is a high-ranking woman and her songs are only sung at special feasts."

Now it was Elizabeth's turn to flounder. An entertainer for an aunt? "Does she sew her own costumes?" asked Elizabeth politely.

"She weaves them," he corrected. "Sometimes slaves make clothes for her."

"Oh." Elizabeth had forgotten about the slaves. It was a rather intrusive note in an otherwise calm evening.

She cast about for something else to say. Miss Cowperth's book on etiquette did not cover such topics as what to say to a man on a beach on a moonlit night. No, it did not.

"You sleepy?" he asked.

Suddenly she realized she was going to be sleeping here. Beside him. Alone. Just the two of them. "No," she lied. "I feel quite, quite awake, thank you."

He grinned. He didn't know she was lying, did he?

"I will sleep now," he said. "You, too."

He lay down, on half the shirt. He was leaving the other half for her to lie upon. She continued to sit, her chin resting on her knees. She stared out at the water. The fire sputtered and chirped and popped.

After a time, she wondered if he'd gone to sleep. She risked a glance over one shoulder and saw that he was leaning, head on one elbow, watching her. "You tired?" he asked softly.

Something in his voice, the gentleness, stirred her. "Yes," she said at last, sinking down beside him. "I am tired."

She lay on her back, staring up at the stars. They were clear white pinpoints on this summer night. She felt his arm go over her stomach, gently pinning her to the ground. She had known this moment would come. Had known ever since she'd first seen him. And now that it was here, her heart raced with excitement.

She reached up and stroked his face. He turned and kissed the palm of her hand. Shivers went through her at the touch of his lips. When he paused, she moved her hand up, up to his forehead and dared to touch the lock of hair that dangled there. "I have been wanting to do that for a long time," she whispered.

He kissed her then, and she knew he had been wanting to do more than that. He leaned over her, putting more of his weight on her now. She pulled his head down and they kissed, his lips warm on hers. She sighed happily, and her toes curled. His skin felt smooth and warm. She ran a hand down one of his arms, over the black tattoo of the raven.

He pulled her closer.

His legs rested on hers, and she felt him lifting her, helping her out of her ragged clothes. She shed them with ease and then her body was naked. A warm whisp of breeze drifted across her skin, giving her goosebumps. She moved closer to him.

She pressed herself against his naked chest, and now the lower part of him was naked, too. She felt him, aroused, against her leg. She peeked down to see what that part of him looked like, but it was too dark to see. This was her first time with a man, and she didn't want to miss anything.

Their skin touched everywhere, and she liked the warmth and smoothness of him. His weight on her felt comfortable. His mouth moved over her cheeks and chin, planting little kisses everywhere. She giggled. Then his mouth was back on hers and he was gently demanding entrance to her mouth with his tongue. She wanted to ask him what he was doing, but she couldn't get the words out and after a while she liked what he was doing, so she wiggled her tongue against his. When he moaned, she got excited and pulled him closer to her. Then he placed a knee between hers and inched her legs apart, and she gasped. He certainly was close to her, she thought. It would be hard to tell where one of them began and the other one left off.

Then there was something pressing at the door of her womanhood, and she got nervous, trying to push him away. He wouldn't go, however, and kept pressing into her. She gasped again as he penetrated her. He went very still and waited, as if for her to catch her breath.

"Oh, my goodness," she moaned.

Then he started to move inside her, back and forth. Her whole body moved with him, and she was startled. She tried to get away from him, but she was pinned beneath him. She was not going anywhere.

Her futile pushes swiftly changed to acceptance and she pulled him down, closer, ever closer. They were kissing again and she liked the feel of his mouth on hers. He ran his hands up and down the length of her body and she liked that too. Then his hand went down between them, and she could feel him touching her, down *there*. He was moving his hand against her and it felt warm and lovely. She felt a tenseness in her that she'd never felt before. She wanted—she wanted—something, but she did not know what.

Ah, but he was making her feel so good, so happy. She hugged him to her, kissing him in gratitude. Suddenly a wave of feeling crept over her, starting in her loins. It burst through her, exploding, and it was a feeling she had never known before. She arched her back and cried out until her cries were muffled by his kisses. "Hold me," she cried. Her body was doing things it had never done before . . . sweet, secret, wonderful things.

Later, she went very still. "What," she gasped, "was that?"

When he didn't answer, she thought maybe he didn't have a word for it. She certainly didn't. But, oh, it felt marvelous. She hugged him to her and noticed he was very still also. In fact, he lay heavily upon her. She pushed at him, and he rolled half off her.

"I'm cold," she muttered, realizing the breeze had turned a little cool. He wrapped an arm around her and let out a great sigh. He squeezed her and kissed her on the forehead. Then, to her surprise, he went to sleep.

How could he sleep after what they had just done? Everything had changed. For her. For him. For them.

She remembered the whispers she'd heard at the School for Young Ladies on those late nights when she and the other girls had stayed up, talking long into the night. Suddenly those whispers made exquisite sense. Elizabeth knew she had just been deflowered.

She lay there for a little while, staring up at the stars that had witnessed it all, her deflowering by this man she scarcely knew. Remorse set in. There was nothing in Miss Cowperth's book about this kind of thing. What they had just done was something married men and women did, not a woman and the man who had captured her. What, she wondered, had she done?

She sighed and snuggled against him. Whatever it was, her body liked it, even if her mind had a hard time accepting it.

She lay awake for a time. Then she, too, fell asleep, resting in the comfort of strong, protective arms wrapped around her.

In the morning when they woke up, she felt shy with him at first. But he treated her kindly, helping her put on her dress, combing her hair for her, and so she began to relax around him. They didn't start the fire but set out once again to find the fort. In the light of day, with her newfound knowledge, she realized that her ragged dress did little to cover her. But Isaac didn't seem to mind. She caught him eyeing her once or twice that morning and was even moved to smile at him.

When he smiled back, her heart flip-flopped.

They headed back into the forest, and after they had gone a little ways, she said, "I think the fort is that way."

"Why?" he asked.

"Because I smell smoke." She glanced at him. She had to admit she was surprised he was allowing her to go to the fort. He had seemed so against it, before. Perhaps making love had changed that for him. Perhaps now he was willing to let her go, though she found in herself a certain reluctance to let *him* go.

"Do you smell that smoke?" she said. "That is Fort Victoria," she announced triumphantly. She whirled to face him. This was it. It was time to say good-bye. She wished they had not shared so much last night. It made it so much harder to say good-bye this morning.

"Thank you," she said earnestly. "But now I must go into the fort."

He looked at her, arms crossed over his chest, a stubborn expression on his handsome face.

"Don't you understand?" she cried. "I must go to the fort. You must go back to the camp. I will be free now."

"Not free now," he said, his voice a growl.

"What do you mean?" she cried. "I will go there. And you will go back!" She pointed behind him.

"No."

"If you go into the fort," she said, trying to reason with him, "You will be in big trouble, very big trouble. However, because you helped me find this fort, I will give you a chance to get away." And because of last night, she thought to herself.

"Go now!" She pointed to the forest behind them. "I will walk into that fort. I will be safe. And so will you—if you go back into the forest. Now leave!"

He still looked stubborn.

"Well, are you going to go?" she demanded. "If I walk into that fort with you, *you* will be the one captured. The whites will throw you in jail!" Much as she tried, she could not keep the concern out of her voice. She walked over to him and ran a finger down one of his strong bare arms. "I would so hate to see you put in jail," she whispered, and part of her reeled in shock at her own boldness. But it was true. To cage a magnificent man like this would be an outrage. He had to leave; he had to understand she wanted to help him.

"You come with me," he said. And he no longer

looked like her gentle, kind lover. He looked angry. And he glowered at her.

"I will not!"

He took her wrist and gave a tug, and she was reminded of the first time she'd met him. When he'd carried her off. She stared at him, suddenly understanding.

They were different. Very different. And while he was attractive, he was also deceitful and—and a woman stealer. When he just glared at her and stood blocking her way to the fort, she realized he did not understand her.

He was, after all, a heathen. And she was civilized.

He was an Indian. And she was white.

He had been raised in some nondescript Indian village. His education had been from the sea and the forest and other heathens. *She* had been raised in San Francisco, and her education was from Miss Cowperth's Finishing School for Young Ladies.

She was better than he was.

She shrugged at his silence. She should have expected no more. "Have it your own way, then." She started down the trail toward the fort and stepped around him. To her surprise, he let her pass. He was big enough to stop her; she knew that already.

She looked at him over her shoulder. "If you go into that fort with me, I will not help you," she warned. "You captured me and stole me from my home. You deserve jail." Then she bared her teeth at him in a gritty smile. How good it felt to say exactly what she thought.

He grinned back at her, still not understanding.

She marched down the trail.

They had arrived just in time, she noted, for it was early morning and the fort's gates would be opening. She pushed aside a large green cedar branch and beheld—the Indian camp.

They ate a breakfast of smoked salmon and drank plenty of fresh, clear water with all the others. And Elizabeth still did not deign to talk to him.

To walk into camp, her back rigid, with him walking right behind her, no doubt looking as smug as a man could look, was just too, too much! Far too much for one civilized woman to endure.

Jake had glanced at her quizzically, but she shook her head, too angry to speak. And it did not help her mood that Mr. Burt was sitting there like a big lump on a slippery log. Evidently his escape attempt had gone awry. Like hers.

Mr. Burt grunted when he saw her.

She was too disheartened to say anything. After eating, she plopped down on the sand by the fire, trying to warm herself.

"Just as happy as a bluetick hound at a possum party, aren't we?" said Mr. Burt.

She ignored him.

"What were you doin' with that damn Indian?" snarled Mr. Burt. "I'm not good enough for you, but he is?" He glowered at her.

Her cheeks hot, she refused to let him goad her into speaking to him. After a while, he gave up and sank into his own reverie.

The Indian woman, Susan, came up to her and pointed at Elizabeth's feet. She said something in the Indian language, and Elizabeth could guess what it meant. Reluctantly, she slipped off the too-tight leather shoes and handed them sheepishly back to their outraged owner. Susan grabbed the shoes from her and flounced away. Then she called over her shoulder in English, "Do not do that again!"

Elizabeth frowned. Did every one of these Indians speak English?

Then her mind swiftly reverted to her own problems. How could this be happening to her? She had planned—no, expected—no, demanded! that she be freed. She had escaped, wandered in the woods, gone through the terror of a screaming cougar, been deflowered, and then—to return to the same dang Indian camp she'd left yesterday morning! It wasn't fair. And it was enough to make a grown woman cry.

She brushed away a tear, glancing around to make sure no one had seen. She sat in a miserable huddle beside the fire for a long time. After a while, she noticed that everyone else had gone down to the water. They were loading their things into the canoe. It was time to paddle on. To wherever they were going.

With a groan, Elizabeth got to her feet and walked over to where her blanket lay on a log. She folded it carefully, wondering what would happen now. She'd tried to escape. She'd failed.

As she finished with the blanket, she heard Isaac come up behind her and say, "I know you are sad about the fort."

She turned around and looked at him. In his dark eyes there was a little glow.

She shrugged away from him. "Yes," she said at last, "I am very sad about the fort." Then she closed her eyes, unable to look at the pity in his eyes as her disappointment welled up again.

145

"Come here, Lis-uh-buth," he said softly.

"No," she whispered back.

"Yes," he whispered.

"No."

But now he wasn't whispering. Instead he was reaching for her and dragging her unresisting body toward him, uncaring of what the others saw. He pulled her up against him, and she could feel his long, hard body against hers.

She closed her eyes, not wanting to look at him, not wanting the others to know what had passed between them. But they knew. And he knew. And *she* knew.

"It will be all right," Isaac said, kissing her.

"No," she answered sadly. "It will not be all right. Ever again."

She let him lead her down to the black canoe.

Chapter Nine

"Tell me," said William Kelp in the Haida language, speaking over his shoulder as they paddled. "I recall that your Tsimshian uncle, the great chief All Fear His Name, promised you a wife when you returned with the murderer. A Tsimshian wife."

Isaac Thompson glared at his friend's back. The Indians sat in rows, the Tsimshians on one side, the Haidas on the other, all facing forward as they paddled. It was an overcast day, and they were in open water. Gray sky, gray water, some swell to the sea, but not enough to stop paddling. There was no wind, so they expected no sudden storms.

Elizabeth sat huddled near the bow of the canoe, watching them. Isaac knew that William had spoken in Haida so that the Tsimshians could not easily understand them. Of course, the whites could not understand them either.

"What are you going to do with the white woman?"

Isaac frowned. He did not like his friend's prodding questions. And he was surprised at them. He hoped the others, especially the Tsimshians, had not noticed his new behavior toward the white woman. "I will take her with me to our Haida village."

"Oho," said William. "Your new Tsimshian wife will not like that."

"What do you mean?" Isaac wished his friend would keep his questions to himself.

"Let me see," mused William. "You must marry the woman that your uncle offers. We have been at war with the Tsimshians for a long time, and a wife will stop the wars. So you cannot say to your uncle, 'Keep the Tsimshian woman, I will marry someone else.' Oh, no. You cannot tell your uncle that. You will have to marry the Tsimshian woman. On the other hand—"

Isaac was getting thoroughly sick of his friend's musing. "Mind your own business."

"On the other hand," continued William, unperturbed, "your new white woman will want you all to herself. The white men marry only one woman at a time. She will expect that from you."

"Who," snapped Isaac, "says I will marry her?"

"You will make her your slave?"

Isaac winced.

William was watching him over his shoulder. "I thought not."

"Hmm," continued the wretched William, "you will not make her your slave. And she is a white. And unimportant. She has no clan, no family with wealth to help her give potlatches, and no family to give her important names to pass on to her children. She can bring nothing to the marriage. She has no brother to guide your sons and no sister to teach your daughters. She is a liability to you, is she not?"

By now Isaac was glowering.

"I think you should marry the Tsimshian," advised William. "She will bring you much wealth, and names and dances. She will be a very high-ranking woman and taught in the proper Tsimshian ways, some of which are our ways. Her family and clan will do everything they can to keep peace between the Haidas and the Tsimshians, because they will not want to go to war and fight against their daughter's children. But this woman—" He subtly indicated the watchful Elizabeth with his chin—did she know they were discussing her? "This white woman will bring you nothing but difficulty. Her people will want her back. There will be war with the whites over her. And for what? She owns no songs, no names, no dances, and knows nothing of Haida ways. Hunh!" His grunt indicated his extreme distaste for Isaac's predicament.

Isaac set his jaw grimly. It was too late to think about things like marriages and alliances now. He had already mated with the woman, and he knew he wanted to do so again. There must be some way to keep her.

He paddled in silence for the rest of the day as he thought about it and refused to speak to William.

They camped that night on a beach. They were in safer territory now and less likely to be attacked by other Indians. They could relax more. The fire was bigger, and they cooked salmon and cod. It was a feast of a dinner.

Isaac had noticed the Tsimshian chief, Fisher, glaring at him now and then. And sometimes Fisher glared at Elizabeth. Isaac was very wary around Fisher, and he realized that the Tsimshian chief still posed a threat to him. Had Fisher been the one to order the ambush that night, when Elizabeth had cried out and saved Isaac's life? Isaac strongly suspected Fisher had done so. He was no doubt waiting for another chance. It also bothered Isaac that Fisher watched Elizabeth with such ferocity. No good could come of that.

He decided he would take Elizabeth away from the others for the night. He could take her into the forest and they could sleep there, away from Fisher and his glares and William and his prying questions.

Isaac walked over to Fisher and told him to keep careful watch on James Burt. The Tsimshian readily agreed and ordered the slave to tie up the white man. Once that was done, James Burt was kicked to the ground where he would sleep within arm's reach of Fisher, who tonight would sleep with a knife in one hand. Fisher told Marten Fur to stay on guard all night to prevent any possible escape.

In that, at least, they were united, the Haidas and the Tsimshians, thought Isaac. They both wanted the murderer to be brought before All Fear His Name.

When the time came for everyone to roll into their blankets, Isaac took Elizabeth's blanket and her hand and led her down a deer path to a sheltered place he had found earlier. There was grass and low bushes to place their blankets upon so that it was a soft place to sleep. He thought she would like that.

He must decide soon what to do with Elizabeth, because tomorrow they would reach his uncle's Tsimshian village.

Elizabeth could not stop her wildly beating heart. They shouldn't be doing this, she warned herself. No traipsing down this woodland path with their blankets. She'd had plenty of time all day to think about last night. And to worry. And to tell herself that it should not happen again.

There was not a single chapter in Miss Cowperth's book about having sex with a man. Elizabeth had an excellent memory, and she knew Miss Cowperth had never addressed the topic. She wondered why. It seemed important enough.

But then, when she really thought about it, no one had *ever* told her about having sex. The half whispers of the girls at the school comprised her only knowledge on the subject. And dear Aunt Elizabeth had never said anything about being with a man, although Elizabeth did remember her aunt once promising her a long talk on Elizabeth's wedding night, whenever that was to be. Elizabeth wondered now if her aunt's talk might be just a little too late.

In between bouts of scolding herself as she and Isaac walked along, Elizabeth wondered if they were going to make love again.

Isaac was putting the blankets on the grass when she asked him, "Where are we going? I mean in the canoe. Where are you taking me to? Please tell me."

He glanced at her, and she wondered for a moment if he would even answer her. He could be very stubborn, this Indian lover of hers. She'd seen that in him. Of course, he had to be strong around the others; she understood that. The others looked like tough, possibly vicious men, and he had to be very strong to stand up to them. Like that one man, Chief Fisher. He sent chills down her spine, the way he stared at her.

But surprisingly, Isaac answered her. "Tomorrow we arrive at my uncle's village."

"Your uncle?" She waited, hoping he'd tell her more.

"Sit down," said Isaac, patting the blanket beside him. She did so.

"My uncle," began Isaac, "is a man who cries. You would say he grieves. Very much. For his dead nephew."

"That is sad," said Elizabeth. She knew how very hard it was to lose someone you loved. Her mother had been dead for a number of years, but Elizabeth still missed her. And her father? Who knew where he was? She had planned to search for him in the Northwest. Little chance of that now, since she'd been captured.

"My uncle's nephew was murdered," Isaac was saying. "So my uncle, who is a very wealthy man, you would call him rich, paid me to go and find the men who murdered his nephew."

A small feeling of dread pooled in Elizabeth's stomach. She didn't think she was going to like this story.

"James Burt is one of those men."

"And the other?" Elizabeth held her breath.

"John Butler."

She sagged. "Uncle John Butler."

"Your uncle, yes." Isaac crossed his arms as he stared at her. He did not look friendly.

"He is not my real uncle," protested Elizabeth. "He is only my uncle by marriage. My aunt married him."

Isaac shrugged. "He is a murderer."

She shivered. Her aunt spent every day with the man. She wondered if he would kill her.

"How—how did they kill the nephew?" she asked.

"Shot him. Dead."

He looked so grim and angry that she wondered that he did not shoot her. "You should give Mr. Burt to the authorities in Olympia," she said. "They will dispense justice. It is not up to your uncle to do so."

"No," said Isaac. "They will not. They set him free."

"Oh." She didn't know what to say to that. "Are you sure Mr. Burt actually killed the nephew?"

"Yes. Many people saw it."

"Oh." She pondered that. "At least you have Mr. Burt," she said at last as brightly as she could.

"Yes," he agreed. "My uncle will be pleased."

"What," asked Elizabeth delicately, "is your uncle planning to do with Mr. Burt?"

"Bury him."

"Oh." Elizabeth winced. She supposed this was Isaac's polite way of saying that his uncle was going to kill Mr. Burt. She thought about this for a while, then said hopefully, "Since you have the murderer, perhaps it will be all right to let *me* go."

"No," he answered. "You will stay." The finality in his voice brooked no argument.

"But you have no need of me," she protested.

"Your uncle wants the murderers, not a woman you accidentally captured at the same time!"

"No," said Isaac firmly. "I keep you. You come with me to my home."

"But I don't want to," wailed Elizabeth.

"It is the way of my people," said Isaac.

She frowned. "It is not my way."

"No," he agreed. "You learn."

She glared at him and crossed her arms. He was not the only stubborn person on this blanket.

She wasn't expecting him to reach for her and drag her across the blanket. Nor did she expect him to kiss her senseless. But that was what he did.

"How," she moaned, "can I think when you kiss me like that?"

His breathing came in thick gasps. "I do not know. I cannot think, either."

Somehow, his admission heartened her. This was all new to him, too.

"What is happening to us, Isaac?" she asked, looking into his eyes.

He shook his head. "I do not know. I only know I want you. I must have you." He drew her to him again.

They kissed for a long moment. Then, holding her with one hand, he began to peel off her clothes with the other. Soon she was kneeling naked on the blanket. She glanced around, suddenly fearful someone would see them. But there was no one. Only the trees. And they wouldn't tell.

Slowly he sank down beside her. He reached out and pulled her to him. She could feel the heat of his skin all the way along the length of her. "Wait!" she gasped, "This is going too fast for me!"

He leaned back and met her eyes. There was a twinkle in his. "We go slow for you, Lis-uh-buth," he said easily.

And they did. She felt like molten liquid in his hands; she had never known that a man could do such things to a woman and still make her cry out for more. She felt as if he knew every inch of her, intimately, and a time or two she tried to push him away when her innate modesty overcame her. But he smoothly made his way back to her, and she found she couldn't protest about something that felt so beautiful.

They strained together in a passionate embrace, and she felt him move inside her. She wanted him, and she found herself demanding his body, crying out and urging him on. Here, in the forest, where there was no one to see them or hear them, she felt free and unfettered. She could cry aloud her joy and passion. She felt so alive as she arched under him. There was nothing gentle or tender about their joining, but she wanted him as badly as he seemed to want her.

They clung together, crying out their ecstasy. Sweat dripped off her, and she could feel that the heated skin of his body was slick, too.

Later, as they lay with arms around one another, a light breeze dried the sheen of sweat that covered them. She turned to him. "What is between us, Isaac?"

He hugged her. "I want to keep you," he said. "Keep you for always."

She smiled and lowered her eyes. "I want that, too," she whispered, yielding to the feelings in her heart. They kissed, and she ran her fingers along his chin. She looked deep into his dark eyes.

"When I am with you, I want to stay with you," she said.

"I want that," he whispered, kissing the line of her jaw.

Her fingers gently touched his lips to stop the tiny kisses. "But I know I shouldn't stay with you," she said. "I know I should go back to my own people."

He shook his head. "I want you to stay with me," he whispered. "I do not want to let you go. But my people—" He shrugged. "They have other ways, ways that might be hard for you."

She sighed. "I think your people's ways would be very hard for me, Isaac."

"Yes," he said solemnly, taking her palm and kissing it.

She watched his dark head bend over her hand, and a wave of tenderness for him surged through her. He was a fascinating man to her, and she wondered if perhaps they could be together, his people and her people and their different ways notwithstanding.

And what would Miss Cowperth say?

Chapter Ten

It was late afternoon when they paddled into the bay of the village of All Fear His Name. Naked children played on the beach. When they saw the visitors' canoes, they ran shouting up to the longhouses. Soon the old chief and several of his retainers walked down to the beach to meet them.

Isaac smiled to himself. His old uncle would be well pleased at Mister Burt's capture.

The bottom of the black canoe ground against the gravel, and the commoners on shore jumped into the water, eager to help pull the canoe further ashore. When the craft was stable, Isaac helped Elizabeth out. Burt was dragged out of the boat by his captors. His hands were tied behind his back. He looked worried, Isaac noted in satisfaction. He should.

"Greetings," said All Fear His Name. "Welcome to the travelers who have returned from their distant voyage. You met with success!" He sang a welcoming song, and then the procession wound its way up the beach to the largest longhouse.

Burt was dragged through the main door of the longhouse, then thrown down onto the lowest floor, a drop the height of a tall man, where he landed, sprawling, a mere hand's breadth from the cooking fire. Many people streamed into the house, anxious to see what would happen.

Isaac and his visiting Haidas were given a special place to sit, and he saw that it was a place of honor. He smiled to himself.

All Fear His Name walked in a stately manner to the head of the great house and arranged himself carefully on his large carved wooden chair. He signaled for his talking stick. Two women, nobles by their dress, fussed over him, straightening his woven blanket cloak. Several well-dressed noblemen and women gathered around the old chief. When he was settled, he nodded to Isaac.

Isaac rose and walked forward, knowing that the bright black eyes of many Tsimshians watched him. He motioned to William Kelp and Fisher to bring Burt over to the chief. They dragged the bound captive to his feet and propelled him over to stand in front of All Fear His Name. Burt reeled slightly as though dizzy.

Fisher slammed him to the dirt floor. "You cringe at the great chief's feet," cried the nobleman. "You are a craven dog!"

Murmurs of satisfaction raced through the gathered crowd watching the proceedings.

All Fear His Name kept his face very still and unreadable, but Isaac sensed a satisfaction in him that the others no doubt felt as well.

"Who have you brought to me?" asked the great chief at last.

"We could not bring John Butler to you. We tried to find him but could not. But we captured Mister Burt, one of the murderers of your beloved nephew, Tsus-sy-uch," said Isaac formally. "We have brought Mister Burt to you so that you may build your memorial pole on his body and ease your grieving heart."

At the mention of his nephew, All Fear His Name did clutch his heart, then seemed to gather himself. "It is good," he said. "Bring him closer."

Fisher kicked Burt, then pushed the white man until he shuffled forward in the dust.

For a time All Fear His Name glared at the white man, caught up in his own thoughts. Then at last he nodded and said to Isaac, "You have done well. I am greatly pleased with your success."

His words warmed Isaac. A lifetime of shame began to fall away.

"Bring in the dancers," said All Fear His Name. Soon the clacking sound of deer hoof rattles announced the dancers' entrance. Ten men and eight women entered, all dressed in their finery of woven blankets and carved cedar masks. They danced and sang, and All Fear His Name nodded his head in time to the beat. When the dancers were finished, the great chief ordered that the food be brought out. Soon women with trays of berries and fish circulated among the crowd. Isaac offered some food to Elizabeth, who shook her head. "Go ahead," he urged. "Eat."

"I—I can't eat," she whispered. "I am afraid."

He looked at her. She appeared pale and slight in the presence of so many Haidas and Tsimshians.

He could understand how she might feel frightened. "I will keep you close to me," he promised. "No one will hurt you."

She nodded, and he thought she looked relieved.

"Isaac," muttered William in his ear, "you'd better listen to this."

"And now," All Fear His Name was saying, "I will show you the canoes I plan to give to Fights With Wealth, my Haida nephew. He has done a very good thing for me, and I am well pleased with him."

The people cheered, and Isaac sat stoically, though his heart warmed to hear the approval of the Tsimshians. He had longed for this moment. At last his name was cleared, and his mother's. Now the Tsimshians regarded him with respect.

Two beautifully carved canoes, each as long as three men, were carried by eighteen men past where the Haidas sat. The canoes were of exquisite workmanship, and Isaac was very pleased. His uncle had indeed, at long last, honored him in a proper way.

"And now," announced All Fear His Name, "I promised my nephew that I would give him a bride. I keep my word." He pointed to a wooden screen set to one side. "Bring forth the bride," he said with a flourish of his arm.

At this moment, Isaac was very glad that Elizabeth could not speak the Tsimshian language. He would have to think what to do about his Tsimshian wife—but he would think about that later, after the feast was over and he and his Haidas were headed back to their own territory. With Elizabeth. And, he thought wryly, with his new wife.

"Hmm," he heard William say. Isaac turned to

glance at the screen. From behind the screen came two Tsimshian noblemen leading a small woman. Her head was covered with a white woven blanket that displayed the Eagle crest. This was very proper, because Isaac belonged to the Raven clan and he could only marry an Eagle or one of the other clans, never a Raven.

His bride, her shoulders shaking slightly under the blanket, was brought forward.

Isaac suddenly noticed that one of the men leading her glared at him ferociously. He stared at the man, surprised by his hatred. Then he remembered. It was the petty chief whose face he had dragged across the gravel on the first day he had arrived in the Tsimshian village. And the petty chief clearly remembered the insult, judging by the furious scowl on his now scarred face.

"What was his name?" Isaac muttered to William Kelp.

"Blackfish," prompted William. "Chief Blackfish. Looks like you are marrying his kinswoman." William's voice indicated he did not anticipate great happiness in the marriage for Isaac.

The older nobleman stopped and lifted the blanket covering the woman. As he pulled the blanket back, her face was revealed. She had long dark hair brushed until it shone, and her face was swollen and reddened from the ravages of tears. "Looks like she does not want to marry you," observed William.

Isaac grunted, hoping Elizabeth did not understand any of the proceedings. His Tsimshian bride-to-be looked the very picture of unhappiness. And she bore a strong resemblance to Chief Blackfish. They were no doubt brother and sister.

William caught the resemblance, too. "It will be like being married to Blackfish," was his comment.

Isaac's heart sank. This was not the bride he wanted. But he could not refuse to marry her. To do so would gravely insult his uncle, the Tsimshians and all those guests present. The peace between the Haidas and the Tsimshians was too new, too fragile, for him to reject the bride. He had to accept her.

He sighed heavily.

"Isaac?"

He turned to Elizabeth. "Yes?"

"Why is that woman crying?" she whispered.

"Feels sad," he answered.

"My, yes, but she does," observed Elizabeth. "I hope they can help her."

William raised a brow at Isaac, but Isaac felt no compulsion to explain what was going on to Elizabeth. He would wait. William's frown told him his best friend did not agree with putting off the explanation.

The grieving bride was led over to her seated kinsmen and women. They placed her in the middle of a cedar mat. Many gifts were piled around her. She burst into loud sobs, and several of the women patted her and murmured to her, trying to console her.

Isaac fidgeted helplessly. William crossed his arms and snorted. The two Haidas behind Isaac muttered under their breath.

If All Fear His Name noticed the bride's reluctance, he forbore to mention it.

"And now," the great chief said to the silent audience, "I will announce my decision about how the murderer, Mister Burt, will die."

162

Everyone turned to listen to the chief's words.

"This is my decision. The craven dog will die by canoe!"

A gasp went up from the crowd, and several murmurs rippled through the crowded longhouse.

James Burt did not understand what was happening to him. He stood there, arms bound, and glared at the old chief, and once in a while craned his neck to look at the crowd. Once he spat on the floor, and Isaac suspected it was to show his contempt. Finally, Isaac walked over to the old chief. "Great Chief, would you like to tell this insignificant sea cucumber what plans you have for him, and why? It may make him regret his terrible actions."

"I do not care if he regrets them or not," said the great chief. "But I would like to see him suffer. I need someone who speaks this uneducated dog's language to speak up and tell him what I have said." He motioned to the slave who had accompanied them on their voyage. "Maggot will speak and tell this dog what I have decided." He waited for the slave to translate.

Although Isaac's command of English was better than Maggot's, he decided to let the slave translate. The chief expected it, and it would embarrass him in front of his Tsimshian people if Isaac stepped forward now.

Maggot swaggered over to where Burt stood. Isaac thought that the slave liked having an important role in the proceedings.

Burt waited, shoulders slumped, sweating from the heat in the crowded longhouse.

Maggot, his clothes tattered and worn, his black hair matted, looked at the white captive and announced, "This great chief says you die by canoe."

"What the hell does that mean?" sputtered Burt.

"You see," said the slave. "Very painful. You will not like."

"Look, you son of a bitch," snarled Burt. "I know I'm gonna die! You turds have told me that often enough on this voyage to hell. But I got a right to know *how* I'm gonna die!"

But Maggot's translation skills were not up to explaining, and Burt would have to wait until later to find out the manner of his death. He seemed to realize the slave could not tell him any more, and his angry blue gaze scorched slave and noblemen alike.

"Make the preparations," ordered All Fear His Name. Several Tsimshian noblemen and commoners started to leave. Before they could do so, the old chief called them back. "Wait. I want to hear something more."

Chief All Fear His Name's attention was suddenly upon Elizabeth. Isaac had kept her close to him during the walk up the beach. He had kept her close by his side when they sat down, and he realized that the old chief had not noticed her before. Isaac had wanted her beside him so he could protect her from Fisher and any other Tsimshians who got too curious. But now it was the old chief who focused his black, gimlet gaze on the white woman. Isaac tensed.

"Who is the white woman?" All Fear His Name asked and nodded at Maggot to translate.

Isaac spoke up before the slave could say anything. This situation must be handled carefully. "She is my captive," he said formally. "She will return with me to my home."

"Aaaaieeee!" cried the new bride. She burst into fresh sobs.

Isaac could hear William's intake of breath.

The old chief ignored the bride's wailing and appeared to be pondering. Then he nodded. "You will return to your home with two women, then." For the first time he showed some humor. "Take your Tsimshian wife that I promised you, and this white woman. You will be a very busy man. Heh-heh."

The audience tittered.

Isaac grimaced. He could not get out of marrying the Tsimshian woman if his uncle so decreed, but neither would he give up his Elizabeth. He thought the wife would accept that situation; after all, many wealthy chiefs had several wives. But he was not so sure Elizabeth would accept it. He would have to think of something . . .

Suddenly Burt yelled out and leapt toward the door. He had broken one of his bonds. He flailed around as the men near him grabbed him. Fisher rushed up with several men to restrain him.

Burt snarled at them, "Get away from me! Let me go! I'll kill you!" Fortunately, not many of the men understood him. Finally Fisher and the others had him tied up again. Panting, the enraged man glared around at the crowd. His malignant gaze fell upon Isaac—no, Isaac realized suddenly— upon Elizabeth. With a loud growl, Burt said, "Elizabeth Butler." Then he repeated many times, "Elizabeth Butler!"

"Why is he saying my aunt's name?" murmured Elizabeth, behind Isaac.

"I do not know," he answered. "But we have to keep him quiet." A frisson of unease raced up his spine. He got to his feet, intending to silence the captive.

But the white man's cries had caught the old chief's attention. "What is it he says?" All Fear His Name asked Maggot.

The slave shook his head as if he did not know. But Isaac thought perhaps he did know but was reluctant to cause trouble for Elizabeth. After all, she had given him an important name and treated him kindly on the voyage.

Burt was saying over and over, "Elizabeth Butler, Elizabeth Butler. This woman is the wife of John Butler!"

Grimly, Isaac marched over and clamped his hand over the man's mouth. By now the great chief was standing and demanding to know what his captive was saying. Isaac stuffed a rag in the man's mouth, then tied a rope over it.

Maggot shook his head, and Isaac was close enough to see the beads of sweat on the slave's brow. Isaac walked back to his place and sat down. He met Elizabeth's alarmed gaze with what he hoped was firm resolve.

All Fear His Name frowned at Isaac. Isaac shrugged as if he did not know what the white man said. "Why is Mr. Burt saying that?" whispered Elizabeth behind him. "I am not John Butler's wife."

"Shh," warned Isaac. "Mister Burt hopes to hurt you."

"Me? Why?"

"To hurt you. To hurt me. Who knows what is in his heart?"

The great chief's visage reddened in anger.

"Maggot! You tell me what this man says or your two sons will die!"

A gasp went up from the slaves lingering near the fringes of the audience. At the great chief's nod, one of the young Tsimshian noblemen seated near him left his side and walked to the fire. There he reached down and snatched up a young boy of about three winters from his mother's arms. The mother, a slave woman with matted black hair and ragged clothes, cried out in alarm and reached for her child, but the nobleman slapped her arms away. He carried the child over to the great chief and set him at his feet. The slave woman started crying.

Maggot, visibly cowed at seeing his son treated so, hurried over to bow in the dust before the great chief.

"O Great One," he said, "this miserable dog says that this white woman is the wife of John Butler."

All Fear His Name looked up. "Is this so?" he demanded of Isaac.

"No," said Isaac tersely. "Mister Burt may say that, but it is not true. He lies. This woman is not John Butler's wife."

All Fear His Name regarded Isaac, and as Isaac met the black gimlet eyes, he felt as though the old chief were staring into his soul.

"I do not know you," said the chief slowly. "I do not know to trust you."

"That is because you did not do your duty to me when I was young," pointed out Isaac, bitterness rising in him. "Had you taken me to live with you and taught me when I was a young boy, you would know that you could believe my word. Also," he continued, "you can see that I do what I set out to do. You sent me to find the murderers, and I have brought back one of them to you. That should tell you that I am a man of my word."

All Fear His Name glowered at Isaac and rose slowly from his chair. The child at his feet crawled away and no one stopped him. The sobbing mother ran up and snatched him away, carrying him to the far confines of the longhouse.

James Burt watched them, gloating satisfaction in his blue eyes.

"I," said the great chief slowly, "believe this white woman to be the wife of John Butler, the second murderer of my beloved nephew."

The whole longhouse went quiet.

"As such," stated the chief, "she will die in his place!"

Chapter Eleven

Loud cheers rang in Isaac's ears.

The old chief held up a hand. The crowd quieted. "Her death," announced the chief, "will also be by canoe."

More cheers.

Isaac's mouth went dry with fear. What had he done to Elizabeth? He should never have captured her, never brought her here to face this. She was going to die a terrible death, and it was because of him. How could he have let this happen?

He spoke up. "O Great Chief," he began, "please let me speak."

The old chief held up his hand for quiet, and everyone leaned forward, eager to hear the Haida. "Before you speak," said the old chief, "I will give an order." He turned to Fisher. "Tie up the white woman."

Fisher's grin was of pure delight. "I will," he said, and went to get rope.

"Now," said All Fear His Name to Isaac, "you may speak."

Isaac tried not to watch as the tattooed nobleman tied Elizabeth's hands behind her back. He had to look away when Fisher tied a piece of cloth around the lower part of Elizabeth's face, effectively cutting off speech. Her wild eyes convinced him he had to do something. But with only four Haidas against several hundred Tsimshians, what could he do?

It was all Isaac could do to breathe. Words failed to come out of his tortured, dry throat. At last, he was able to say, "I—I wish to repeat that this woman is not the wife of John Butler."

The old chief frowned. "You come here with your Haidas and think to lie to me. You think to pass off this woman as your captive, for your own pleasure. Little thought did you give to my heart, torn apart by the death of my beloved, obedient nephew. His murder must be avenged. Bah! I should have known better than to trust a Haida."

"You would rather trust the word of the murderer, James Burt?"

"What reason does he have to lie? He will die either way. I am just pleased that the truth has come out. Now I will have two bodies to set my memorial pole upon." He motioned to Fisher. "Take her to the back of the longhouse. We will kill Mister Burt first."

Isaac could see the tears running down Elizabeth's face. Beside himself, he shouted out, "Wait!"

"You address me?" demanded the old chief, affronted.

"I ask you, O Great Chief, to spare the woman. She is weak and pitiful and will do nothing to help your revenge."

"As the wife of John Butler, she will do much," corrected All Fear His Name. "John Butler will cry many tears when he learns of her death."

Isaac saw that his uncle was not to be moved. No words from Isaac would ever convince the Tsimshian chief that James Burt had lied.

Isaac took a deep breath. "I ask you, O Great Chief, let me die in place of the woman!"

All Fear His Name stared at Isaac. So did a number of noblemen who heard his request. "You would die in place of the woman?" asked the chief. A horrified look crossed his face before he could hide it.

"I will die in her place," said Isaac, even as despair filled his heart. He could not save Elizabeth from the anger of the chief. Therefore, let the chief vent his anger on him. It was all he could do for the woman he had placed in such danger, a woman he realized he had come to love. Isaac stood straighter. "I will die in her place. But I ask that you set her free."

All Fear His Name glanced at Elizabeth, then back at Isaac. "It shall be so," he said sadly. To Fisher he said, "Untie her." Disappointment flickered across the tattooed chief's face, but he did as bid. When Elizabeth was standing free of her bonds, Isaac held out his arms to be tied.

"Tie him up," ordered the old chief, and Isaac thought that his uncle spoke regretfully. Any sign of regret disappeared when his uncle became aware again of the watching audience. All Fear His Name said, "You will die a painful death by canoe.

171

I will bury your body at the foot of my nephew's memorial pole." His voice shook on the last words, and Isaac wondered if it had cost him something to pronounce Isaac's death.

"Isaac!" Elizabeth cried and held out her hands beseechingly to him. "What is happening? Why are they tying you up now?"

He looked into her beautiful blue eyes, eyes he would never see again, and wished he could tell her how much he loved her. But he could not. Instead he said, "I cannot save you anymore, Lis-uh-buth. You must leave here and go back to your people. That is the only way you will be safe." He would not tell her about his pending death.

To his relief, he saw William Kelp step to Elizabeth's side. William would take care of Elizabeth.

He watched as his best friend started to lead away the woman he loved, the woman he would die for.

Then Fisher stepped between them. "Not so quickly, Haida," spat the Tsimshian nobleman. "I will take care of this woman. The great chief has asked that she remain in my care." He sneered at William.

All Fear His Name nodded. "It is best she not see the rest of the ceremony." By that he meant Isaac's death. Isaac thanked his uncle for the small mercy. But he knew that Elizabeth had now been set into worse trouble with Fisher as her guardian.

"Watch her," Isaac said to William. "I give her care over to you. See that she returns to her people."

William nodded.

"My nobleman will see to it," interrupted All

Fear His Name. The tattooed Fisher smiled smugly.

Also smiling was Chief Blackfish, leading his sister and his father over to the great chief. While the father spoke with All Fear His Name, obviously breaking off the marriage to Isaac, Chief Blackfish strolled over to Isaac.

"It is a good day," he said, and his black eyes shone with anger. "It is a good day when I see you get the death you deserve."

Isaac stood straight and proud. "I go to my death a man," he answered. "You will always be the insignificant chief who licked my foot. Your people will never forget that."

A cry of rage erupted from the younger nobleman, and he struck Isaac a swift, hard blow to the cheek. Isaac reeled, his head thrown back from the force of the blow. He bent to the side from the pain, unable even to raise his bound hands to his face.

"You will stop!" cried an angry voice. All Fear His Name strode over. "Leave the captive alone! I gave you no permission to strike him!"

Chief Blackfish shook with his anger. "I go now," he said, and ran from the dwelling.

"O Great Chief," William Kelp's firm, deep voice broke in. "I tell you, do not do this. Do not kill this Haida chief. If you do so, his father, who is a mighty chief, will come and make war upon you."

All Fear His Name turned, and his voice was frigid. His pride as a Tsimshian was pricked. "Let the puny Haidas paddle their canoes to our shores. We await them eagerly. We will give them war!"

William's shoulders slumped and he turned away. Isaac tried to meet his friend's eyes, but William obviously felt he had failed Isaac and would not look at him. But Isaac cared little. He realized now how fortunate he was to have this friend who had loved him and tried to save him.

Then Isaac's gaze fell upon Elizabeth in her ragged dress, with her brown hair falling out of the lopsided bun on her head and her blue eyes brimming with tears as she watched him. She had never looked so beautiful. "Oh, Isaac," she whispered.

And he realized how greatly his life had been enriched by her presence. They had been together only a short time, but it had been a time he would never forget in the even shorter time left to him on earth.

Elizabeth was the most precious woman he had ever known. How fortunate he had been to find her. He could never regret loving her. Perhaps it was not such a bad thing to die knowing that loving someone was the most important thing in life.

He had that knowledge, at least.

"Come," said a Tsimshian nobleman, pulling Isaac's bound arm. He led him away. Isaac looked over his shoulder and met Elizabeth's blue eyes for one last moment. He wanted to yell out to her that he loved her, that he wished much happiness for her in her remaining years on earth. He wanted to cry out his love to the rafters of the longhouse.

But he kept silent. They held one another's eyes until he stumbled and the nobleman gave him a harsh push. "Watch where you are going, Haida dog!"

Isaac kept his back straight as he walked out of the dark longhouse into the blinding light.

He would love Elizabeth forever.

Chapter Twelve

Elizabeth could hear the yells and happy cries of the crowd outside the longhouse. She wondered what they were doing down on the beach to make such a noise. Inside the longhouse it was quiet and dark and hot. Everyone had gone. Fisher and two of his men had dragged her over to a corner of the house, pushed her down onto a cedar box to sit, and tied up her hands. Fisher had personally tightened the rope around her wrists. He had walked away with a grin. She had a feeling he would return, and she dreaded the prospect.

Fisher had left a man to guard her who was sitting sullenly in the corner, angry that he was missing all the excitement. But her guard's mood did not concern her; only Isaac did. What was happening to him? When they'd freed her, she'd been so relieved. She'd thought the danger was over—until they'd bound up Isaac and forced him to go with them. Now she feared the worst. She feared greatly that they were going to kill him.

She had plenty of time to sit and think. She tried to ignore the cries of the Indians down at the beach. She thought back to the first time she'd met Isaac, when he'd thrown her over his shoulder and carried her to his canoe. She remembered the time he'd saved her from falling overboard in the terrible storm. And her traitorous mind kept harking back to the times they'd made love, on the beach, in the forest.

If only they had not come to this awful village, she thought, they would both be together and alive. Miss Cowperth would certainly have much to say about Indian hospitality!

She could hear someone coming into the longhouse and sat up a little, hoping against hope that the Indians had changed their minds and were going to free her. When she saw it was Fisher, she slumped back on her seat.

In his wake he dragged Jake, the slave. Fisher and Jake drew near, and then Fisher threw the slave down onto the dirt floor and pointed at Elizabeth while he said something in his language.

How strange, she mused, that the Indian language sounded so musical in Isaac's deep voice, while from this man, Fisher, the words sounded garbled and dissonant.

Jake got slowly to his feet. "This chief"—he glanced at Fisher—"wants you know you be his slave. Great chief give you to him."

Elizabeth's lips tightened. She had nothing to say to Fisher, but inwardly she hated the thought of having anything to do with him. She thought, however, that if she spoke, he would hit her or do something cruel. She'd already seen such behavior from him too many times.

When she did not answer, Fisher said something else to Jake.

Jake translated, "He wants to know are you happy being slave?" Then quickly Jake said, "I will tell him you are honored this chief choose you. Otherwise he kill you."

"Do not tell him I'm honored to be his slave!" she hissed, all caution gone. "I think he is a cruel, horrible man and I hate him."

Fisher said something, and Jake answered him, bowing several times. Elizabeth guessed he did not accurately translate what she had said.

Fisher smiled and nodded, satisfied with Jake's lies. Elizabeth sneered at Fisher as much as she dared. He said something else and poked the slave in the stomach, a move that hastened Jake to translate.

"The great chief say he return after two captives are dead. Then he take you to his bed."

His first words confirmed her fear: Isaac was to be killed. Then the full meaning of what the chief had said became clear, and some of the nauseous distaste she felt must have crossed her face, for now Fisher spoke sharply.

Jake translated. "He say you are fortunate slave woman to have him for owner. He not make you work hard. Just gather firewood and dig clams. Maybe he let you pick berry sometime—if you good. Even let you sit by fire."

Fisher spoke once more, then waited, grinning.

"He say he keep you from his wife. She like to pull out your hair. His number one wife mean. Number two wife pretty good, though. She friend."

Elizabeth gaped at him. What kind of a life was in store for her? Did they think she was going to join them in one big family? "I," she said between gritted teeth, "will never be this man's mistress, or concubine, or slave or whatever he plans! Tell him that!"

Jake said, "I no fool. I tell him that, he kick me."

She frowned. "Well, tell him that I demand he set me free so I can go back to Fort Victoria!"

Jake said, "I tell him you happy slave." Before she could say anything, he began translating loudly and went on for some time. Fisher beamed. Then he and Jake walked back toward the long-house door. They passed the guard in the corner, who complained loudly, but Fisher only waved a hand dismissively at him.

Elizabeth wanted to cry. Isaac was a prisoner, possibly facing death. She might never see him again. And here she sat, forced to become Fisher's slave. Oh, what would become of her now?

She was jerked out of her reverie of worry and fear by loud shouts near the entrance to the longhouse. She sat up; it appeared she was to have more visitors, and if her hearing was accurate, they were of the drunken sort.

She squinted into the darkness, dread seizing her. Two figures lurched toward her. As they got closer, she could see by the light of the fire that they carried bottles with them, liquor bottles. Her lips moved in silent prayer. *Please don't let it be Fisher*, she prayed.

It was not Fisher. As they drew near, she saw to her surprise that it was William Kelp, and Susan, the Indian woman who had traveled with them from Fort Victoria. Both were drunk as lords.

Elizabeth gaped at them. Never had she thought to see the dignified William and the pretty Susan in such a state of inebriation. "Oh, no," she murmured to herself.

The two Indians ignored her and staggered over to where her sullen guard had parked himself. He sat up and reached out to them. Susan swayed on her feet and barely managed to hand him her bottle. The guard took a hefty swig and wiped his mouth with the back of his hand. Then he lifted the bottle and took another great swig. The bottle winked in the firelight.

The Indians talked back and forth in loud voices, in the Indian language, of course, so Elizabeth had no idea what they said. But she thought it very sad that William, Isaac's good friend, should be so inebriated when Isaac needed his help so desperately. Why wasn't William out on the beach trying to free Isaac? She wanted to scream her anger and disgust at him, but she knew that he and Susan were too drunk to understand a word she said.

Their voices grew quieter, and finally she heard snoring. She glanced over and saw that the guard had fallen asleep. Susan and William sat near him, also asleep.

Suddenly Susan arose and started walking toward Elizabeth, her gait even and straight. Behind her, William got up and started walking, also without staggering.

My goodness, thought Elizabeth. *They certainly recovered quickly from that drunken spree*.

They reached her, and William pulled out his knife and began sawing through Elizabeth's wrist bindings. "Wha—?" she began.

179

"Quiet," whispered William. "We must get you out of here. The guard should sleep for some time, but we have to hurry."

"Put these on," said Susan, handing Elizabeth her leather shoes. On her own feet, Susan wore another pair. Elizabeth's wrists ached from the tight rope, and she wanted to cry out when the blood started to flood back into her hands. But she tightened her lips and bent over, trying desperately to get the shoes on.

"Hurry," said Susan urgently.

Within minutes, they were sneaking out of the longhouse, using a small side entrance Elizabeth had not noticed.

They stayed well back from the beach, skirting along under the large spruce trees that edged the forest. Three huge bonfires burned down on the beach, shedding as much light as though it were daytime. She could see people standing around the fires and great crowds moving about between them. A cluster of people stood near one end of the beach. As Elizabeth watched, she saw a group of men tugging on a great rope and pulling a canoe slowly up out of the water.

As the canoe was dragged higher up the beach, several enthusiastic shouts went up. Then a blood-curdling scream rent the air.

"What was that?" cried Elizabeth, halting.

"Mister Burt," explained William tersely. "He die by canoe."

"But—but—how?" asked Elizabeth. Another scream tore through the night. She shuddered. "That isn't Isaac—" she cried as the terrible thought came to her. "My God, it is!" she started to scream.

William clapped his hand across her mouth, cutting short her cry. "Silence!" he said in her ear. "It is not Isaac! It is Mister Burt!"

Elizabeth almost fainted from relief. Then she scolded herself. She should not be rejoicing in Mr. Burt's death. It was just that—Isaac—he still lived! Then she shivered. But he would die, too. Like that.

"Weight of canoe kills," explained Susan. "Now you come." She took Elizabeth's hand.

"No," hissed Elizabeth, trying to pull her hand away from Susan, who held it in a viselike grip.

"Yes," growled Susan.

"What is it?" asked William. He glanced at the beach, obviously concerned that they would be seen.

"I can't leave," said Elizabeth. "I must go down and rescue Isaac." This time she succeeded in pulling her hand out of Susan's.

She walked toward the beach, only to be swept up from behind by William. Panting, he carried her back toward the forest and deposited her behind a large driftwood log. "You cannot go down there." His voice was firm.

"I understand your concern," said Elizabeth. "But I must. I will not stand by and allow them to kill Isaac!"

"Fool!" cried Susan. "You cannot stop it. They so many. We are three." She pointed at William. "He die. I die, if you go down."

"I'm very sorry for all that," said Elizabeth. "But I really must—"

Susan gripped her hands. "I not let you. I die!" Her fierce brown eyes held Elizabeth's, and it dawned on Elizabeth that this woman would do anything to prevent her from going to the beach.

"We risk lives to help you," said William. "Now you must come with us."

"But Isaac—"

"Isaac would want you to come."

Another scream echoed from the beach. Elizabeth froze. "Is that—?"

"No, I tell you. Not Isaac!"

Elizabeth could hear the anger in William's voice. She knew she was irritating him, but she could not just run off to save herself and leave Isaac behind to die. "I must go to him!"

Susan grabbed Elizabeth's hair and yanked her head back. "You listen," she snarled. "You come with us or I kill you!" She let go of Elizabeth's hair with a jerk.

Elizabeth saw the flash of steel and realized Susan held a knife.

William watched her. "We all die if you go to the beach. You, me, Susan. We all die. I cannot let you do this."

"You come or you die!" emphasized Susan, waving the knife. Susan was the more convincing of the two, decided Elizabeth.

Before Elizabeth could think of any other protest, Susan grabbed her hand and pulled her along. This time Elizabeth did not fight her. They raced down the forest path, William leading.

They ran until Elizabeth was panting and out of breath. Susan refused to release her grip and tugged a stumbling Elizabeth along.

"Please," gasped Elizabeth. "Please stop. I need to rest."

Susan looked over shoulder. "No," she said mercilessly. "We stop, we die."

Nothing could be plainer than that, thought

Elizabeth in her misery. She could no longer hear Mr. Burt's screams. They were either out of hearing range or—or—he had died.

They kept running, and by now Elizabeth had a pain in her side and her legs ached. Still they ran. She couldn't see where they were going. The only thing she knew was Susan's hand, pulling her through the darkness. At last she heard some waves breaking on rocks.

"Where are we?" she gasped.

"At a little cove," said William. "I hid a canoe here."

They ran a little farther and then their path descended. Soon they were on a beach, gravel crunching underfoot. Susan let go of Elizabeth's hand. They stood, panting, and Elizabeth took several deep drafts of night air. "What—what will they do with Isaac?" she found the courage to ask.

"After they kill him," said William, "they will throw his body into the sea."

Tears welled in her eyes at the thought of Isaac being crushed beneath the heavy canoe, then his broken, lifeless body being thrown into the water. She moaned.

"They do that to treat him like a slave," explained William. "Very bad."

"Yes," sobbed Elizabeth. "I do not want them to do that. He should be buried, at least." Somehow it was the thought of his body, lifeless, that brought up all her fear and grief. "Oh, William," she implored, "can't you do something? Can't you get his body and bury it? He should have a Christian burial." She sobbed again.

William answered stiffly, "I am no Christian. But

183

I, too, want him buried. He was my friend and I want a good burial for him."

"Please," begged Elizabeth, "please see that he is buried." She touched William's hand. "Please?"

He looked into her eyes and nodded. "I will do it," he said solemnly.

Somehow, knowing that Isaac would have a decent eternal rest lessened Elizabeth's terrible pain.

"Hurry," said Susan. "They might come."

No need to say who "they" were.

Elizabeth looked around for the hidden canoe. William led them over to some undergrowth above the high-tide mark. "Here," he said. "Help me."

All three of them pulled and tugged until they got the canoe onto the gravel. The Indians did most of the work. Together they dragged the craft down the beach, scraping the underside against the rocks. William said, "Lift it."

So they tried to keep the canoe up, but it was a heavy canoe for the three of them. At last, sweating, exhausted, they reached the water. William pushed the canoe into the water. Then he helped Elizabeth into it. He threw in two bags and a package. Then he handed Susan a paddle.

"Where's my paddle?" asked Elizabeth.

"Under the seat," said William.

He pushed the craft farther out, and Elizabeth wondered how he knew which direction to push it in. She could see nothing, but her ears strained to pick up any sounds that would help her get her bearings.

"Do you know where we are going?" she asked Susan.

The Indian woman snorted, and Elizabeth accepted that as a "yes."

William waded out into the water, pushing the canoe with the two women ahead of him. With a final push, he stood thigh-deep in the cold water.

"Good-bye," he said; then he said something in the Indian language to Susan. She nodded and picked up her paddle. She dipped it over the side and began paddling.

"Remember," cried Elizabeth. "Please get Isaac and bury him." She choked on the words and put her face in her hands. Her whole body shook with sobs. William raised his hand in assurance.

"Good-bye," called Elizabeth between sobs.

"We go in circles," said Susan, "if you do not paddle."

Elizabeth lifted her face. How could the woman think of paddling at a time like this? Then with a deep sigh, she reached for her own paddle and plunged it down into the water. The canoe swung round. Susan paddled on the other side. It took them a while, but working in unison, they were finally able to straighten out the craft and head in the right direction.

Elizabeth lifted her paddle and glanced back over her shoulder. She peered into the darkness. Perhaps William still stood on shore, though she could not see him. It felt as if he was watching them. "Do not forget," she called out to him blindly. "Please bury Isaac."

"Paddle!" William's voice drifted across the water.

Elizabeth turned back to her paddling; silent tears ran down her cheeks.

Susan paddled steadily. The two women paddled out of the cove and into the darkness of the open water.

Chapter Thirteen

They paddled alongside a rocky coastline to the east.

"You all the time cry," said Susan as she paddled. Now that it was not quite so dark, Elizabeth could at last see her companion and guide, even if through a blur of tears.

Elizabeth wiped at her eyes. She had tried to keep her grief quiet, but it had been most difficult. "So do you," she answered. She saw tears in Susan's eyes. "I miss Isaac," she whispered.

"Hmm," answered Susan. Elizabeth did not think her companion's answer was very encouraging; nonetheless, it was not outright censure. She straightened a little and resolved to do her crying in private. They had paddled for what seemed like days, but was probably only hours. Isaac would be dead by now. That thought brought fresh tears to Elizabeth's eyes. It was a true act of will, but she did not sob aloud.

"We stop now," said Susan. She guided the canoe toward the shore, some distance away. Elizabeth dutifully paddled, as she had done all night, when she had not fallen asleep at her place.

Elizabeth nervously noted that they were heading for sharp black rocks looming ahead. At the last moment, she saw a small sandy beach. She breathed a sigh of relief. The two women paddled the craft up to the beach, got out and dragged it higher. Only when the canoe lay above the high tide line did Susan stop pulling.

"We hide here. All day," said Susan. "Paddle at night."

Elizabeth understood. They were going to hide here, probably sleep—the good Lord knew she was exhausted—and then paddle some more that night. What kind of a grueling life did this woman normally live? she wondered, looking at the tall Indian woman. But Susan was already taking their scant supplies out of the canoe and obviously had no time for frivolous chit-chat.

"We go over there," said Susan. Without waiting for Elizabeth, she walked toward a small path that Elizabeth only now noticed. Elizabeth dutifully stumbled in Susan's wake.

They walked down the path until they were hidden from the beach by the trees. Anyone who happened to paddle past the beach would not know they were there, for the canoe was not visible from the water. "Go to sleep now." And the Indian woman lay down among the low green undergrowth and curled herself into a ball. Then she closed her eyes.

With a sigh, Elizabeth sat down on the low bushes too. Then she lowered herself carefully until she was prone on the cushioning plants. They were wet with dew.

She closed her eyes, wondering what Miss Cowperth would do in such a situation. Probably complain, she thought morosely. Then she thought nothing else as sleep claimed her.

William squinted into the fading darkness. A mist had settled over the water, making it difficult to see. Was that a floating log, or a body?

Pale streaks of dawn lit the early morning sky. He dipped the paddle again. He thought he could see something. He paddled the canoe closer. No, it was just a log.

Now and then he heard a faint drumbeat coming from the beach. The bonfires, seen through the mist, had burned down to orange blurs, and he could barely see the dark shapes of canoes and men lying scattered on the beach.

The frightening screams had ceased some time ago. Both James Burt and Isaac would be dead by now. William's only hope now was to find Isaac's body floating somewhere in the cold, dark waters off the rocky coastline. He thought the Tsimshians would deliver the worst insult to his friend by throwing his body into the sea, like a worthless slave's. He hoped they did not throw his body into the garbage pit, because he did not know how he would manage to find Isaac then. It was the sea or nothing, he thought dismally, remembering his dear friend and cousin. Any fishing or hunting or raiding William did would lack adventure now that Isaac was gone.

He stared at the green water as the swift current ran out to sea, carrying his canoe with it. By William's judgment, the sea would push any floating debris, or bodies, in this direction, away from the village.

He stood up carefully in the canoe, trying to see all he could. There was nothing but a few floating logs.

After he had said farewell to Susan and the white woman, he had returned to the village, following the overland path from the cove. Once at the village he had found his two faithful Haida retainers dead, their throats slit.

Realizing anew his danger, William had slipped away from the village under cover of darkness, stolen a two-man canoe and then paddled out to sea. He had badly wanted to paddle to Haida territory, but his agreement with the white woman held him here. He would find Isaac's body and take it home and give it a proper burial. However, if he lingered much longer, the Tsimshians would spy him and give chase in their canoes. And then no one would return to the Haida village to tell Many Salmon what had happened to his beloved son, Isaac.

But William could not find the body. And it was getting lighter. Soon the Tsimshians would awaken.

He gave one last paddle and was about to turn away when the fog lifted a little and he spied a lighter patch against a dark log. He paddled closer. Was it—? Yes, it was. It was a body. Not daring to breathe, William paddled swiftly toward the log. He could just make out a dark, black head propped on the log, and then, as he paddled closer, he caught a glimpse of powerful shoulders on top of the log. The rest of the body was under water.

Great sadness gripped William. If this was his friend, the very stillness told him everything. If he had held any hope that Isaac had somehow escaped, that hope was defeated now. With tears in his eyes, he paddled up to the log. He gripped a branch that grew out of the top of the log. "Isaac?" he whispered. "Cousin?"

No answer. The part he could see, the back, did resemble his friend's, and when he saw the Raven tattoo on the upper arm, he knew then. It was Isaac.

"Oh, Isaac," he sobbed. He gripped the body, and the head lolled back. William couldn't bear to look at his friend. He pulled the canoe alongside the log, holding onto the branch, and managed to get the head and then the shoulders of the body halfway into the canoe. The body was naked, and he could not get a good grip on the slick skin.

Strangely, it was warm. Great blue bruises bloomed under the tan skin. Had Isaac just died, then? wondered William. Had he somehow survived the canoe rolling over him, crushing him, only to expire in the water?

With great difficulty William got hold of a leg and lifted it, trying to treat his friend's body as respectfully as he could, even in death.

Finally, with much heaving and grunting William managed to get the body fully into the canoe and laid it out on the floor of the small craft. He rolled Isaac over gently, so he could see his friend's face one last time.

In death, Isaac was pale. Blood streaked down

his stomach and limbs where the canoe's weight had done such terrible damage. Mottled patches of blue bruises decorated his belly and chest.

Unable to look at his friend any longer, William swung the canoe around until the bow pointed for Haida territory. Home. He paddled slowly across the dark gray waters, his heart heavy at the burden he carried. Isaac was much loved and respected in the Haida village. His death would be a keen loss to his people. But his death was a greater loss to William. They had been inseparable since boyhood.

William paddled, lost in thought, wondering how he would tell Many Salmon of the terrible events and his son's death, when suddenly he heard a moan.

William went still. Was his friend's ghost speaking to him? His heart pounded with fear. He wanted to dive over the side of the canoe.

Another moan. William dared a glance at the body.

A shudder went through the body. Isaac was alive!

William leaned forward and shook his friend's shoulder lightly. "Cousin?" A look of pain crossed Isaac's features, and William quickly released his shoulder. His cousin had suffered much in the canoe rolling, and William would not add to his pain.

With renewed vigor, William dipped the paddle, pushing hard. Isaac was alive! He must get him to the Haida village. The healers there would help him!

Once, William stopped his frantic paddling long enough to give Isaac a drink of fresh water from a sea lion bladder. Isaac did not drink, but William

191

hoped that wetting his lips would be of some help. Though he had no food to feed him, William knew that in Isaac's condition food might cause more damage to Isaac's insides. Still, William could not deny him water in this summer heat.

With a last splash of water on Isaac's mouth, William set down the sea lion bladder and picked up his paddle. He set to paddling again, his mouth grim. He would get his cousin home, alive.

William shouted for help when he reached the beach of the Haida village, Place of the Sweet Berries. Several adults and children came running. Scattering the children aside, a tall noblewoman, her tattoos showing she was of the Eagle clan, strode forward. She gave a great exclamation when she saw her nephew lying half dead in William's arms; then she quickly called for more aid. With the help of several slaves and concerned women, they managed to get Isaac up to his longhouse. They entered the longhouse and carried him to his place of sleep. The aunt ordered a slave to run to her brother's longhouse, to tell Many Salmon his son had returned and was barely alive.

The sun was low in the sky when Elizabeth and Susan awoke. Dusk approached. Elizabeth slowly sat up, blinking, looking around, trying to remember where she was and how she had arrived there. When she saw Susan standing up, she got slowly to her feet.

"We go," said Susan. Elizabeth nodded and dutifully trotted after the Indian woman. They returned to the sandy beach.

"I catch fish," said the Indian woman, taking a

fishing line out of one of the packs that had been stored in the canoe. "You drink." She handed Elizabeth a skin bladder.

Elizabeth took it, wondering what the leather pouch was for. But she did not dare ask her hostess. So she stared at the strange thing.

With a snort, Susan reached for the leather pouch and raised it to her lips. She drank for a time, then handed the pouch back to Elizabeth. "Now you drink."

Elizabeth tipped it up and sipped gingerly. It was water. It tasted warm and awful, and she wrinkled her face in disgust. She handed the pouch back to Susan.

Susan shook her head, then set off, climbing over the rocks. Elizabeth sat down on the sand to watch her and ponder her own fate.

While Susan fished, Elizabeth worried.

The Indian woman returned, carrying a fat salmon. Elizabeth looked up, startled. She had not had enough time to worry about all that had happened to her.

While Susan built a fire, Elizabeth gathered scraps of wood. That, at least, she knew how to do. She fed the pieces to the fire, and soon a small blaze burned. Susan made a cedar rack to hold the salmon and cooked it beside the fire. Elizabeth's mouth watered at the enticing scents.

While they ate in silence, Elizabeth thought about Isaac and the horrible death he must have endured. She set aside the salmon, not wanting to eat any more. Susan finished her share of the fish, then got up and walked over to the fire, kicking sand on it. Then she wrapped the remaining salmon in broad leaves.

"We go."

They dragged the canoe back to the water, put their supplies and the salmon in it and pushed the craft into the water. Elizabeth walked steadfastly into the water, determined to prove herself of use on this voyage. Her shoes were soaked. Before going into the water, Susan took off her leather shoes and threw them into the canoe. Elizabeth resolved to do the same, next time.

"Where are we headed?" asked Elizabeth, settling onto her seat and taking up her paddle. She knew the routine.

"Fort Victoria," said Susan.

A little of Elizabeth's gloom lifted. She no longer had Isaac, but at least she was returning to her people.

They paddled for the remainder of the night. They rested for part of the next day, then set out in the afternoon. Elizabeth was heartily sick of fish and tepid water.

She was, however, very glad for her companion. Despite her quiet ways, Susan had become a friend, of sorts. Not the kind of friend one invited to one's salon, of course, or when one gave a dinner. Nor was she a friend to attend the theater with, but she was a friend nonetheless.

Susan caught the fish they ate, she found the fresh water they drank, and she kept them paddling in a steady southerly direction. Susan also decided when they would paddle, because one time a storm arose and they had to spend the night huddled in a cave. The cave smelled bad, and Susan took her paddle, holding it as a weapon, and walked to the back of the cave before she allowed them to camp there for the night. Elizabeth thought maybe she was looking for bears.

Elizabeth always did her best to help. She paddled as much as she could, despite her bleeding palms, and she gathered firewood every time they camped. Without her, Susan would have had so much more to do.

A time or two Elizabeth tried telling Susan about the School for Young Ladies and Miss Cowperth, but Susan did not seem to like those stories. She would shrug and urge Elizabeth to paddle harder. Sometimes Elizabeth asked Susan about Isaac and William and their life back in the Haida village, and Susan would actually tell her something. Apparently, the three had grown up together, playmates of sorts. As they became adults, the men would go off and fish and hunt. As an adult, Susan liked to go to Fort Victoria and stay for a time, then bring back presents for her family and friends. Elizabeth never found out exactly what Susan did at Fort Victoria, but she knew the Indian woman liked visiting there.

They paddled onward, and Elizabeth began to think that her whole life would be spent in this small canoe; she would grow old, wasting away from paddling.

One day, about noon, Susan lifted her paddle, pointed to the shoreline in the distance and said, "Fort Victoria."

Elizabeth let out a small cry of happiness. "At last!" she cried. "Oh, at last!"

Susan looked at her. "You happy?"

"Oh, yes," exclaimed Elizabeth.

"You forget Isaac?"

Elizabeth sobered instantly. "Of course not," she answered, stung by the implied criticism that she could so easily forget the man who had sacrificed his life for her. "I will always remember Isaac. I—I loved him." There. She'd said aloud what she'd come to believe in her heart. "I loved Isaac," she said again. "I will always love him."

Susan shook her head and dipped her paddle in the deep green waters off Fort Victoria.

"You do not believe me?" she asked Susan, surprised at the woman's reaction, and her own. Why should she concern herself with what an Indian woman thought of her?

Because, she answered herself, *that Indian woman saved your life.*

When Susan did not answer, Elizabeth asked her again, "Susan, do you not believe me? I tell you, I loved Isaac."

"I believe you," the Indian woman answered reluctantly after a time, "but I think you soon forget him."

"Never!" said Elizabeth. "I remember everything about him." And she did. She could picture his handsome face clearly. She could easily remember her last glance of him, when they'd looked into each other's eyes, before he was taken out of the longhouse to be killed. "You are wrong, Susan. I will always love him!"

Susan shrugged. "Maybe," she said.

They were pulling closer to the fort now, and Elizabeth could see canoes neatly lined up on the gravel beach. Susan headed their canoe toward the beach.

They reached the shore and got out, pulling the canoe into the shallowest water. It was all routine for Elizabeth now.

A shout from farther up the beach drew Elizabeth's attention. A white man stood staring at them, waving. Then he started walking toward them.

"You go now," said Susan. "That white man help you. I go find my friends."

The man walked up to Elizabeth. He was tall, well dressed, and quite out of place on the beach. "Where are you from, ma'am? Do you need some help?" He threw a suspicious glance at Susan, who was bending over the canoe, retrieving their supplies.

"Why, yes," answered Elizabeth. "I would like some help. I must speak to whomever is in charge here."

"That would be the governor, ma'am," he answered. "I can take you there, if you like." He held out his arm to her. She glanced down at the ragged remains of her garments, at her salt-encrusted leather shoes and at the raw calluses on her palms from paddling. All of a sudden, she felt embarrassed. "I would appreciate that, sir," she whispered.

He evidently expected her to take his arm, still holding it out, so she tentatively wrapped her fingers around his forearm. He felt solid, warm.

"This way, ma'am," he said briskly. And they started off.

They had gone a short distance when Elizabeth stopped. She must thank Susan for all her help. But when she turned to thank her, Susan was gone.

The canoe lay on the beach, neatly tied to a log. But no Susan. The small craft was the sole reminder of her time paddling down from the north.

"Something wrong, ma'am?"

"No," answered Elizabeth sadly. "Nothing. Nothing at all."

Chapter Fourteen

The Haida people of the village had done all they could to save Isaac's life. His father had provided plump halibut fish to make a nourishing broth. His aunt had had Isaac carried to the warm springs that pooled in the black rocks not far from the village. There, slaves had carefully laid him in the soothing, healing waters. But when long soaking in the sulphurous waters did not appear to do anything, they had carried Isaac back to his longhouse. The shaman, a sticklike man, his bushy, long hair sticking out all over his head, had come to help. He boiled and mashed fern roots and placed them on all the swellings of Isaac's body.

By the forth day it appeared that their efforts were failing. Isaac sank deeper and deeper into a coma, and his breathing was shallow. William was beside himself. He did not want to lose his cousin and best friend now, not after bringing him back alive from the Tsimshian village. After some thought, he went to talk with Many Salmon. Together, Isaac's father and William decided that they must ask the shaman to do more. Accordingly, the shaman was summoned.

In preparation, Isaac was laid out on a cedar mat near the fire pit where it was very warm. The shaman blew his breath on all the swollen parts of Isaac's body. Then he went to the door of the longhouse and blew the air out in a great gasp. He returned to tell the anxiously awaiting audience, "I have blown the poison out of the patient's body. He will now recover."

Unfortunately, the poison came back and Isaac grew even worse. His aunt rocked to and fro, crying, and her women and slaves cried with her. At last Many Salmon held up a hand and said, "My sister, please tell your women to stop their crying. My son is not yet dead. He can hear you, and your cries will convince him that he has died. There is still hope, and I ask that you refrain from giving up."

The aunt's sobs faded away, and she wiped her eyes and did as he asked. All her women wiped their eyes and ceased their keening.

Then Many Salmon asked the shaman to fetch Isaac's soul as it had obviously gone away from his body and was no doubt trying to find the land of the dead. Payment was negotiated, and Many Salmon agreed to pay a score of blankets. Then the shaman went into a deep trance. When the trance was over, he opened his eyes.

And so did Isaac.

"Your son is restored to you," the shaman told Many Salmon.

Many Salmon nodded and waved his hand at a retainer. The man hurried over, and Many Salmon spoke in low tones to him. Soon a mound of blankets was piled high in front of the shaman, far more than the twenty blankets promised. The shaman rose and took his payment and left the longhouse.

Isaac sat up. "What am I doing here?" he asked in a daze.

"You are in your home. You were returned to us, your family, by your cousin. He rescued you from the Tsimshians," answered his father.

William spoke up. "I found you resting on a log in the water. I think the Tsimshians thought you were dead and threw you in the water. I brought you back home."

Isaac looked at his friend and cousin. "Many thanks," he said quietly. Then he added, "Please give me some water." His aunt hurried over with fresh water and Isaac drank some; then he lay back down.

"Where is the white woman?" he asked William after a time. "Is she with the Tsimshians?"

William looked surprised at the question. "You must care for this woman, to ask about her so soon after waking up," he answered.

"Is she dead?"

"No, no," answered William hastily. "Susan and I led her to a cove, and I pushed them off in a canoe. Susan planned to take her to Fort Victoria, where she would get the help of her white people."

Isaac frowned thoughtfully at this news.

"You look much better, my son," said his father. "It is good that you are home." His aunt agreed, and all his watching family and friends and slaves heaved great sighs of relief.

Isaac looked at them, at his father, at his aunt, at all the people who loved him and cared about him. He looked at his friend who had saved his life. "It is good to be home," he answered at last. Then he added, "As soon as I am better, I am going to go and find my woman. I will take a party of men to help me."

"Oh, no," protested his father. "Leave the woman alone. Stay with your people."

"No," answered Isaac. "I will go and find her."

"My son," said his father patiently. "You have just returned from the dead. The shaman traveled to the land of the dead to bring you back to us. We thought you had gone away forever. Please stay with us for a time."

"Father," answered Isaac. "I am glad you helped me. I am glad I am getting better. But I must find her, even if I have to steal her back." Then he fell back, unconscious.

Many Salmon frowned.

"He is just like his father," observed the aunt.

Chapter Fifteen

Two months later

"I now pronounce you man and wife," said the Anglican minister. He wore black vestments with a wide white collar over his shoulders. The elderly man of the cloth beamed at them.

Elizabeth hoped her trembling lips did not betray her doubts. Beside her stood her new husband, Cyril B. Mandeville III. When he smiled at her, a possessive light in his blue eyes, she closed her own. She didn't want him to see that her thoughts were of another man, a man with long dark hair, with an unruly lock that fell across his forehead, a dead man, true, but nonetheless the man she loved. She was not in love with Cyril at all, she thought sadly. Her hand sought her stomach and rested quietly there. She was doing this for her baby's sake. And though Cyril knew that and had agreed to it, she knew he still hoped that, in time, she would come to love him.

And perhaps she would.

She glanced around the small church, barely one-quarter filled. There sat her dear Aunt Elizabeth. And—she grimaced—Uncle John. They had arrived at Fort Victoria shortly after Elizabeth did. They had been searching for her along the coast all the way up from Olympia and finally met with success when they arrived at the fort.

Behind them sat two elderly ladies, Marigold and Morninglory Fletcher, sisters who were mainstays of the church. They provided flowers from their large garden for all important occasions and included themselves in as many weddings—and funerals—as they could.

On the other side of the aisle sat Governor Douglas and his wife. The governor had been most kind to Elizabeth since her arrival, and she had sent a courteous invitation to him, not expecting that such a busy man would be able to attend her wedding. But he had found the time, and brought his gracious wife with him. With the governor was one of his deputies. Behind the deputy sat the janitor, waiting to clean up the church after the ceremony. At the very back of the church sat Susan, her long dark hair hanging down either side of her bosom, an impassive look upon her face. She slipped out of the church before the ceremony was over.

"You are the woman I love," whispered Cyril, bringing Elizabeth's attention back to him. "And I will love your child, too."

She smiled up at him, and this time her lips did tremble and tears welled in her eyes. "Thank you," she whispered, humbled by the love and sincerity that shone on his face.

When the brief ceremony was completed, they went out into the garden next to the church. Across the fence was the graveyard, home to the deceased pioneers of Fort Victoria.

The elderly Fletcher sisters served refreshments. Homemade bread with gooseberry jam, and hard-boiled eggs, courtesy of the Fletcher chickens, graced the church table set out in the garden. Everyone drank black tea, sweetened with honey and cow's milk, as a special gift from the governor.

Aunt Elizabeth said, "I am so pleased that you are married, dear. And to such a fine young man." She beamed as she sipped her tea. "Imagine. One of the San Francisco Mandevilles." Her little smile of pleasure lifted Elizabeth's spirits momentarily. Though Elizabeth thought her aunt exaggerated the social standing of the Mandevilles—they'd been one of the important families at the School for Young Ladies, but hardly of the city of San Francisco—Elizabeth felt grateful that *someone* was pleased with her hasty marriage.

Aunt Elizabeth had dressed elaborately for the ceremony. Her white gloves went well with her newly sewn flowered dress and matching hat. Elizabeth herself lacked white gloves and hat for the occasion. She had not had much time to prepare and had elected to wear her long brown hair hanging loose down her back. Small pink rosebuds, picked from the Fletchers' garden, adorned her hair.

Uncle John munched on a hard-boiled egg. Elizabeth watched him talking with his mouth full and turned away. Memories of Mr. Burt and what he and Uncle John had done would not leave her mind. Though she had told Aunt Elizabeth, the older woman remained with her husband. Elizabeth knew her aunt did not believe her, which was odd, because Elizabeth had always been truthful with her aunt.

After Elizabeth had arrived in Fort Victoria she had sought an audience with the governor, a kindly man of African heritage named James Douglas. Governor Douglas had assured her he would do everything he could to help her return to Olympia, even offering to provide a guide for her. But before she could leave, another summer storm had raged in the area, forcing her to remain at Fort Victoria. After the storm had passed and the necessary preparations had been made for her voyage, Elizabeth had discovered that her aunt and uncle had arrived at the fort, looking for her. And accompanying them was one of her old schoolmate's brothers, the highly estimable Cyril B. Mandeville III.

It was a most happy encounter, remembered Elizabeth. She and her aunt had shed many happy tears upon being reunited, especially because her aunt had confided that she had greatly feared Elizabeth was dead. Uncle John had hovered in the background, nodding now and then, and when the preliminary greetings were done, had sought his escape to one of the fort's public houses, where he'd proceeded, he told them later, to drink heartily to Elizabeth's good health.

Cyril had stayed. He liked Fort Victoria and wanted to start a business. Seeing him again had reminded Elizabeth vividly of her time at Miss Cowperth's. And when Cyril had begun courting her, Elizabeth had at first been flattered, then alarmed. She had no desire to marry the man she'd once had a schoolgirl's crush on.

Then Elizabeth had made the mistake of confiding in Aunt Elizabeth that she was pregnant. Nothing would stand in the way of that most determined of women. And so, somehow, uncertain of how it had all happened, Elizabeth found herself agreeing to marriage between Cyril and herself.

Ah, but there was one other small matter that had tipped the scales in favor of the marriage, she reminded herself. It was her second interview with the governor . . .

"Sir," she asked Governor Douglas, upon making another appointment to see him prior to leaving the fort, "may I be so bold as to ask if your man has learned of any information on the whereabouts of Mr. Theodore Powell?"

The governor answered, "Please sit down, Miss Powell." When she was seated, he continued, "As you requested, I did ask my man to make inquiries regarding one Theodore Powell—your father, I believe you said."

At her nod, he continued, "At first we received no information in answer to all our queries. But then we had a stroke of good fortune."

Seeing Elizabeth eagerly lean forward in her chair, he hastened to say "Miss Powell, I do not mean to mislead you. I fear my words were badly chosen. I meant good fortune in that we have news of your father, but alas, the news is not good. I greatly regret to inform you that your father is dead."

"Dead?" she started. "Why, that cannot be! I have only begun to look for him."

"I understand," said Governor Douglas, and she could hear the kindness in his voice. "But my man said there was no doubt. Mr. Theodore Powell was found dead in his cabin at the end of last winter. I am very sorry to have to be the one to impart such sorrowful news to you." He studied her out of compassionate dark eyes.

Her own welled with tears. "But—but—" She subsided into silence, trying to digest the terrible news.

While she strived to gain control over her feelings, he reached into his desk. "Perhaps this will help you," he said, handing her a ragged piece of paper. On it were scribbled words; she could not decipher them in her grief. She stared dully at the paper. "What—what does this mean?" she asked at last, looking at him helplessly.

"Allow me," he said gallantly, taking the paper from her lifeless hands. He placed his round wire spectacles on his nose.

He frowned and said, "It appears to be a mining claim. I believe it says 'For Miss Elizabeth Desiree Powell.' That would, no doubt, be you," he added, peering at her over his glasses like a wise owl. "It would seem, Miss Powell, that he has left you his gold mine."

At her surprised look, he added, "There is something else you should know. My man informed me that there were no workable mining claims in that area of the territory. He learned that there had been a run on claims, many men lost their savings, and alas, no gold was ever found. I again regret that it is I who must impart such sad tidings to you."

There was a little silence as she tried to collect her thoughts and stifle her feelings of sadness and despair. Finally, when she had some semblance of control, she reached with trembling fingers for the paper.

"My man told me this paper was found in Mr. Powell's hand. He was clutching it when he died. At least you can take comfort that your father's last thoughts were of you, Miss Powell."

She started, stricken, into the governor's kind dark eyes.

Suddenly she wanted to scream out her pain at the wrenching news. Her father, the man who had abandoned her and her mother when she was but a little girl, the man who had promised her mother he would return for them, the man who stayed away through her whole childhood and her lonely growth into young adulthood, this man, her father, had turned his last thoughts as he lay on his lonely deathbed in some little deserted cabin, to *her*?

The injustice of it all smote her, and she wanted to cry. But she did not. She bit her lip and nodded at the governor's words. She rose with as much dignity as she possessed, thanked him graciously for his time and stumbled out of his well appointed office. And she clutched the ragged little piece of paper to her chest as though it were gold.

My father, she thought, tears running down her cheeks as she walked down the darkened hall and out into the sunlight of a bright summer's day at Fort Victoria. *My father is dead, and now I will never, ever know him. All is lost. All is lost. I have no one . . .*

And so it was that a dazed Elizabeth had returned to the small house that her aunt had rented for their stay in Fort Victoria. And when her aunt had said one more time how desperately she hoped that Elizabeth would marry the kind and decent Cyril B. Mandeville III, for her own sake and for her child's sake, it was then that Elizabeth had said "yes."

Chapter Sixteen

"There is going to be a raid against the Tsimshians," said William.

Isaac glared at him. He knew he should be grateful to his friend for coming to visit, but the truth was, Isaac wanted to lie on his sleeping mat and do nothing. He had just received stunning news from Susan, newly arrived from Fort Victoria. Elizabeth had married.

Every part of his body hurt. He knew he had broken ribs and inside him somewhere, something else was broken. He could barely keep down a bowl of fish broth. Finally he became aware that William was still there, waiting. "You are going on the raid?" Isaac asked.

"Yes," said William. "I thought I would join the raid. The families of Crab and Killer Whale want to revenge the dead. They are angry at the loss of those good men; both of them had nephews to raise."

Isaac sighed. He felt guilty because he had taken the two men with him on the trip to the Tsimshian village in the first place. Though both men were commoners, they had been honorable, reliable, honest men. And now they were dead. Because of him.

Isaac turned his face to the wall. "I do not want to go."

William answered, "Perhaps when you feel better, you can join in on a revenge raid then."

"Perhaps," Isaac muttered. He knew he did not have any desire to go on a revenge raid. He just wanted to stay in his longhouse. The name of the longhouse, Much Food, Many People, had once meant that Isaac hospitably welcomed the village inhabitants to his home. Now, people seldom visited. Everyone in the village knew that Isaac just wanted to lie around.

His sore body made him short-tempered. In truth, he did not wish to visit with anyone. He just wanted to sleep so he could forget the pain.

And he certainly did not want to think about Elizabeth, the blue-eyed betrayer. No, he would stay on his mat.

"Uh-oh," said William.

Isaac opened his eyes.

"Here comes your father."

Isaac groaned.

Many Salmon marched through the house. Slaves and commoners alike scattered from his path. He was a great chief, chief over the whole village, and he wore his power like a valuable woolen mantle. He was a stout man and he walked proudly. Accompanying him were the usual assortment of slaves and noblemen and others who wanted favors. When Many Salmon reached Isaac's mat, the chief looked down and said, "So. This is where my son lies. Word is all over the village that you stay on your mats."

"You know it, Father," agreed Isaac. He put his arms behind his head, wincing slightly at the movement.

Nothing his father could say or do would get him up, he thought determinedly. He ignored the noblemen and slaves who stared down at him.

Many Salmon sat down heavily. The noblemen sat down with him, and the slaves, too.

"My son," said Many Salmon, "you have been like this ever since Susan arrived to give a potlatch."

Isaac did not say a word. He refused to tell his father anything.

"Are you angry because Susan did not give you enough gifts?" his father asked patiently.

"No."

His father pondered. "She comes from a good family. She gave many fine gifts that she got from Fort Victoria."

Isaac said nothing.

One of the noblemen leaned over and whispered in Many Salmon's ear.

"Do you want to marry her?" asked Many Salmon. "She would make a fine alliance for our family."

"No!" exploded Isaac.

His father waited. He looked at William. William shrugged.

"You do not want gifts, you do not want to marry

Susan," said Many Salmon. "What is the matter, then? You only started lying around the longhouse after she arrived."

Isaac turned his face to the wall, refusing to answer.

"You must get up," said Many Salmon. "I do not like my son to lie around. You should be fishing, helping with the canoes and being useful to me and to your people. Lying around this longhouse is not good. It sets a bad example for the village."

Isaac cringed inside at the contempt he heard in his father's voice. "I hurt."

"I am certain you do hurt, my son. Being almost crushed to death by a canoe will surely hurt anybody." He paused. "But I do not see why you need to lie around. You should be up and fishing. Only highborn women waiting to get married can afford to lie around the house. The rest of us have to work."

Isaac winced again. His father always said directly what he thought.

At last his father said, "I will go and speak with Susan."

Isaac said nothing.

"I will also bring the shaman to visit you. He has had much success with you in the past."

Still Isaac said nothing.

Finally Many Salmon and his retinue trooped out of the longhouse. William waited quietly.

"I have wondered why you lie here, too," he admitted. "When you first woke up from visiting the land of the dead, you said you wanted to go and find the white woman. Now you will do nothing."

"I do not want to talk about the white woman," said Isaac.

"Oho," said William. "It has something to do with her. Now I will be the one to go and talk with Susan."

"Do not," said Isaac angrily. "I am not a child, to be discussed by people. I am a grown man and I will handle my own difficulties."

"A difficulty is she?" asked William dryly. "Yes, I think that describes her."

"You never liked her," accused Isaac.

"I saved her life," answered William.

Isaac frowned. He was so angry at the white woman that he was picking fights with his best friend. "You are right," he answered heavily. "Leave me now. I would sleep."

"Very well," said William, getting to his feet. Isaac could hear the disappointment in his cousin's voice. William walked silently out of the longhouse.

Isaac relished the quiet, and the dark. When he lay still his body did not hurt so much. Soon he fell asleep.

"My son," said Many Salmon, shaking Isaac awake. "It is time to get up."

Isaac opened his eyes. He grimaced with pain. His head hurt, his stomach hurt, his limbs hurt. He just wanted to sleep. "Go away," he mumbled.

"Do not speak to your chief this way," reproached Many Salmon.

Isaac opened his eyes again. He turned his head to look at his father. "Where are all your noblemen and slaves?" he asked.

"I told them to go to their homes," said Many Salmon. "I wished to speak with you."

"Susan told you that the white woman is married," said Isaac bitterly.

"Yes, she did," answered his father.

Isaac turned his face to the wall. "Then I have nothing to say."

His father sighed. "It is not right that you should act this way," he said. "You are a man grown. Not a halfling boy."

"Please leave my house and let me lie here," said Isaac.

"It is not such a terrible thing," said his father, "that the white woman has married."

"It is," disagreed Isaac. "Please leave."

"A white woman needs to be with her people. It is good that she has married a white man. Then *you* can find a good Haida woman to marry."

Isaac snorted.

His father continued to sit there. Isaac sighed, but he refused to say any more. Why would people not leave him alone? All he wanted to do was sleep in his own longhouse.

"You wanted this white woman for your wife?" asked his father after a while.

"I do not have to tell you about this."

"No, you do not." His father appeared lost in thought for some time. "Well," he said finally, getting to his feet. "Now you have no reason to leave our village. You will stay with us instead of chasing after the white woman. You can get up off your sleeping mat and go fishing. Perhaps you can even go on the revenge raid against the Tsimshians. That is another thing I wanted to talk to you about."

Isaac sighed. "Does it have to be now?"

"Yes, it does. That is one of the things that happens when you lie around your longhouse. I can come and talk about your shortcomings with you."

"I do not want to talk about my shortcomings."

"Too bad," said his father. "I do not like it that we have to go to war against the Tsimshians. They are your mother's people. I told you I did not want war with them."

Isaac turned his head to look at his father. "I did not mean to start a war with them. It just happened."

"If you had brought back the man your uncle wanted, that would have been fine," corrected his father. "Bringing the white woman led to all this trouble. Now I will have to send my men—good, valuable, hardworking men who would be better off fishing and hunting and laying in stores of meat for the winter—now I have to send them to fight the Tsimshians. I am not happy about this, my son!"

Isaac lay there frowning. He was not happy about it either.

"And," continued his father, "I do not like what the Tsimshians say about you, and about our family. They think that because they killed you—they do not know you still live—that our family is no good. They think that they can talk about us. One of my noblemen—his brother married into a Tsimshian family—said the Tsimshians now talk insultingly about us Haida. They call us sea lion dung."

Isaac squirmed inside. He had caused his family, clan and people to lose face before the Tsimshians. His stomach churned with sick anxiety.

"I have potlatched many times to raise our name," continued his father relentlessly. "Before your visit to the Tsimshians, our family had the highest, most important name in Haida territory. You know that.

"Now we do not. You brought our name down, my son. I will have to potlatch many more times, give away many expensive presents, before I am able to walk proudly in front of my Haida people. I will have to call upon my old friends and, yes, some of my old enemies, to help me get enough canoes, slaves, blankets and salmon to give away. I will have to show that I am so rich I do not care what those Tsimshians say. I will be a very old man by that time. But I will tell you this. I do not intend to die with the name of Sea Lion Dung. I am not happy about this, my son!"

Humiliated, Isaac wanted to crawl out of his longhouse and hide in the forest. Unfortunately, his body could barely move.

Many Salmon got heavily to his feet, and Isaac breathed a quiet sigh of relief. He could not endure another heartbeat of his father's visit.

As Many Salmon walked away, he said over his shoulder, "I think it is very good that you stay in your longhouse. You stay right there. Do not get up. Then I do not have to worry about you starting any more wars with the Tsimshians or with the whites!"

Isaac stared at the rafters over his head and at the dried salmon and halibut hanging down. Lying in the longhouse certainly gave one time to think; too much time to think.

Later, his aunt walked in the front door, followed by two noblewomen and a woman slave. The slave carried a heavy bowl of something steaming. A curl of steam heavy with the scent of halibut stew reached Isaac's nostrils. He tried to sit up. Slowly, painfully, he succeeded. "You bring me something good to eat?" he said to his aunt.

She smiled at seeing him sit up. "My dear nephew, of course I bring you something good. I am an aunt who knows how to take good care of her only nephew."

He tried to smile back. He loved this aunt, Rain on the Sea. She had cared for him like a mother over the many years. And though she was his father's sister, she had little of the domineering ways of his father.

"I saw your father down at the beach," she said as she sat down. She spread her clamshell-colored woolen blanket neatly around herself. Her women took their places quietly.

"Did my father say anything to you?" asked Isaac with dread. He dropped the spoon he had just picked up. He feared he had little appetite after his father's visit.

"Oh," said his aunt, "do eat, nephew. You must get strong again."

Isaac shut his eyes, but he could still hear his father's words ringing in his ears. Gathering the things for another potlatch would be a hardship for the proud old man. By rights, Isaac should be the one to help get the potlatch goods together. He, not his father, had caused this new shame to come upon his family's name. He set the bowl of stew aside.

"Now," said his aunt, picking up the bowl and spoon. She fished around, spooning a chunk of white halibut meat out of the bowl. "Here. You must eat this."

Isaac shook his head. He lay back down. The humiliation of what his father had said to him had taken every bit of spirit from him. He wanted to roll over and die.

"Your father," said Rain on the Sea, "told me to feed you well." She smiled. "As if I needed to be told such a thing."

Isaac turned his face to the wall.

His aunt continued to sit there while Isaac ignored her. His father's words went round and round in his head. He had humiliated not only himself, but his father, his clan and his people!

"Come," coaxed his aunt. "Just take a little taste."

Isaac looked at her. An idea began to form in his mind. If he ate, and regained his strength, he could go and work for the white man's money. Then he would have enough to buy the potlatch goods he needed to give the biggest potlatch his people—and the Tsimshians—had ever seen!

With a groan, Isaac struggled to sit up. His aunt called to her women for help, and they were able to prop him up. With his aunt's help, Isaac was able to eat some of the halibut soup. He prayed it would stay down, so that his body could heal. Finally, his aunt set the empty bowl aside. She beamed at him. "You ate very well!"

He felt like a little boy again at her words. He flopped onto his back. "Thank you for bringing me this food. Now I can get better."

"Oh? I thought you wanted to lie in the long-house for the rest of your days."

He glanced at her sharply, but he saw she meant no rudeness. "I have changed my mind," he said.

"I know your father can be very convincing," she said.

Isaac snorted.

His aunt rose to her feet. "I must go and oversee some of the berrypickers," she said. "It is good that you stay here. When you stay in your longhouse, then everyone knows where you are and we never need fear that you are in danger."

He looked at his aunt sharply again, but again he saw that she was serious. Did she not realize that she made him sound like a whipped dog, hiding in his longhouse?

"I do not think I want to lie in my longhouse all day," he said. "I am not an old man to sit by the fire and nod off."

"What is wrong with that?" she asked. "When you get to be my age, such things appeal to one. And surely it does not bother you that the Tsimshians say that we Haidas are weaklings and fools."

His eyes widened in horror. His aunt expected him to accept such insults from the Tsimshians? Did she think it meant nothing to him that he, his father, their people were humiliated by such talk? What was wrong with her?

Or did she see him as so weak, so humbled, that he could not even act as a man should?

He wanted to yell at her for her lack of belief in him. Never had he thought his aunt would think he was such a fool, or so useless.

"I think those Tsimshians say they can kill you with their canoes and we can do nothing. Do not worry, my dear nephew. Somehow, your father will find a way to change that. He can potlatch them to gain our good name back.

"And today I can help you. Why, I myself am strong enough to go fishing. I will take some of my women and go out in the canoe and we will catch

221

fat halibut to bring back and cook for you. I can do this."

If his father's words had humiliated him, his aunt's words made him writhe sickly inside. An older, middle-aged woman like her, going fishing with her women in tippy canoes so that her nephew could lie around the longhouse? The shame of it made him want to vomit.

"You can stay in this house and be safe and warm. I will always bring you halibut broth."

He waved a hand at her. "Go. Please go," he said hoarsely, fearing he would vomit right then and further humiliate himself.

He could sense her rising to her feet. "Do you want me to bring you more stew?" she asked.

"Later," he ground out. "Tell William to come to me."

"Very well," she said. She and her women left him in the dark and quiet of the longhouse.

He lay there, thinking. He had to heal, he had to! And he had to get the white man's money so that he could purchase the potlatch gifts. He would go to Fort Victoria. He could find work there. And if he saw the white woman while he was there, well, it could not be helped. He must save his people. It did not matter to him anymore about her and her new husband. No longer would he lie around the longhouse, mourning her loss because she had married another man as soon as she thought he, Isaac, was dead. No longer would he think of her, of her betrayal of him by marrying another. No, that was not what would occupy his thoughts now.

He had once expected that she would remain faithful to his memory. It mattered little now. He had more important things to do. He had a potlatch to put on. And with William's help, he would grow stronger so he could do that.

"William!" yelled Isaac in frustration. What was keeping the man?

Chapter Seventeen

Isaac walked the streets of Fort Victoria. He had
risen early that morning, gone out in the pouring
rain in his canoe and returned to the fort. He had
sold two fat salmon to a Celestial man for his res-
taurant. Then Isaac had gone around to the places
of business asking for work. A logger told him to
come back later. A shopkeeper waved his arms and
yelled at him to get out of his shop. "Dirty Indian!"
Isaac stiffened his back at the insult. He hated being talked to by that man as if he were a dog.

Isaac pulled the white man's coat collar tighter
about his neck as protection from the pounding
winter rain. A cold wind blew, and the rain fell at
a goodly pace. The streets were muddy. Fortunately, he had boots to wear. His people were used
to going barefoot, even in winter. But in Fort Victoria the whites expected everyone to wear shoes.

William had stayed behind at the winter village,

Salmon Come Here. There were days when Isaac missed his cousin. It was lonely in Fort Victoria. But William had thought it better to stay and help their Raven clan gather fish to dry for the potlatch Isaac wanted to give. William had also hired some artisans to make bentwood boxes and some expert canoe makers to carve out the canoes that would be given away. It was Isaac's job to help pay the artisans and canoe makers. And Isaac's aunt, Rain on the Sea, had worked her berrypickers fiercely. Before he left, Isaac had seen huge baskets of dried fruit—all for his potlatch.

His father, Many Salmon, had barely spoken to Isaac before he left. Isaac could not tell if that was because his father was so busy amassing items for the potlatch or if he was still angry with Isaac. Probably still angry, thought Isaac despondently.

Even Susan was working to gather items for the potlatch, though she had chosen, like Isaac, to come to Fort Victoria to make money to buy the things needed.

Responsibility weighed heavily on Isaac. The potlatch had to be a success. He had to have more things to give than at any previous potlatch. He had to give a potlatch which even succeeding generations would talk about. And which the Tsimshians would respect.

He hunched his shoulders against the wind. He wished there was some way he could make a large amount of the white man's money. He had been in the town for almost seven days. Today, because it was the day the white people went to "church," he would take a little side trip he had been planning.

Isaac had seen "church" before because the white people at Fort Simpson had one. He had even been inside the church once. There he had heard stories about fishermen who caught netfuls of fish. He thought maybe they would have liked to fish in the waters around his Haida village, because he and his people caught netfuls of salmon, too.

Isaac walked along the narrow streets of Fort Victoria. He saw white people crowding into a little house when a bell rang. There were two Indian women with them. Not men. He waited outside, wondering if he should go in out of the rain. He could hear them singing songs. Now and then he could hear the white people's shaman speak. Sometimes, as at Fort Simpson, the whites' shaman yelled at the people, who all sat quietly on wooden seats and never spoke back to their shaman except to chant. Isaac did not want to go to church, because he thought it was not a very good ceremony. Not one gave out smoked salmon or dishes of delicacies.

But the rain was so strong he thought he might take shelter for a little while. The white man's shaman at Port Simpson had been a good man. He tried to help the Indian people. Perhaps this one would not mind if Isaac stood inside, out of the rain.

He opened the door quietly and walked inside. Candles glowed on a table set along one side of the building. A small wood stove burned in a corner at the back, and he edged closer to it. Steam rose from his woolen coat. On the other side of the church he noticed the dull light from outside coming through colored glass set in the walls. The colored light turned the white people into strange colors; some were blue, some red, some yellow. He frowned at their odd appearance.

He listened as the shaman, dressed in black and white robes, talked about forgiving one's enemies. The shaman even said one should love one's enemies. Isaac thought maybe this shaman did not know about the Tsimshians and the Haidas and all the fighting between them. Not one of them could forgive anyone. Everyone just kept fighting and raiding. This shaman certainly did not know what he was talking about. Especially when he said the hate had to stop sometime and that forgiveness was the only way to stop it. He said that otherwise the hate and cruelty would just keep on and on and people would keep getting hurt and crying.

Isaac thought about it. It would take a very unusual man to forgive the Tsimshians, he thought. He thought about all the pain he had suffered when they had rolled the canoe over him. He wondered if this shaman could forgive someone who rolled a canoe over him and shamed him before all his people.

With a thoughtful frown, Isaac glanced around the church. He looked up at the walls. There he saw a wooden carving of a man hanging on a cross. He wondered idly which was worse: death by cross or death by canoe.

Then he saw her. At least the back of her. He recognized that tangled topknot of brown hair on the back of her head. His Elizabeth. His heart pounded with excitement, and with fear. He stared at her, wanting to go to her and take her hand and pull her out of this place. But he could not do that. She did not even know he was alive.

He had to get out of here. He slipped back out

the door, wanting to race down the street. Instead, he forced himself to take several deep breaths and walk slowly down the steps. He would not flee. Not from Elizabeth, not from anyone. He walked down the street, not even noticing the mud and rain.

He walked for a time and then found himself in a part of the fort where there were houses. He remembered that Susan had described a house to him, a white one with red steps. It was where Elizabeth lived. With her new husband.

Isaac looked for this house, but promised himself he would just walk past it. He would not stop. He had important things to do in this town. He had to find work, and money. He did not have time to follow Elizabeth. No. She had done enough to destroy his life. She had married a man very soon after Isaac's "death." Obviously, she cared nothing for Isaac, or she would have stayed single all the rest of her days, mourning him. And he, Isaac, why, he had almost died for her. No, he would have nothing to do with her. He would marry a good Haida woman—later—when he could think about women again, and he would never miss the white woman, betrayer that she was.

He found the little white house with the red steps. Susan had forgotten to tell him that the window frames were painted yellow. As was the door. The roof was green. The house looked small and cramped. Not at all like a fine longhouse. There were no carved welcome figures with outstretched arms. No totem poles decorated the yard.

Only Elizabeth and her husband lived in the little house, Susan had told him. That was not very many people, Isaac thought. A good home was full of people: favorite relatives and their families. That made for a happy household, not a little, cramped, yellow-and-white house that only two people lived in. This was not a home, Isaac thought in disgust. Living in this house would be like living in a bent-wood box, a cedar box his people used for storage.

The windows were dark. It looked cold and unfriendly.

He had seen enough; he turned away. He would go back to where the businesses and stores were located and continue his search for a white man's job.

He walked away from the houses that neatly lined the street. Somehow his feet found their way to the church again. He was just passing by the church when the door opened and white people began streaming out. The rain had stopped. Isaac went across the street and stood beside a bedraggled oak tree, watching them. They seemed happy to get out of the little church. Perhaps if they had a bigger church, more like a longhouse, the people would want to stay, he thought. And if they served smoked salmon.

To his consternation, he saw Elizabeth again. But then, he had known he would, had he not? He dared not move for fear of drawing attention to himself. So he stayed, frozen, wet, watching her.

Of their own accord, his eyes went over her hungrily. He had missed her so. Beside her walked a tall man with reddish hair. He was talking to some men nearby and had turned away from Elizabeth.

Isaac's eyes swept over her. How long had it been since he had held her, talked to her? Loved her? A frisson of desire went through him. He still wanted her. Wanted her as his woman.

She turned a little to the side to talk to a woman

229

in a black woolen coat, and Isaac's eyes fastened on Elizabeth's stomach. It was very large. The shock of her pregnancy hit him like a blow from a Tsimshian war club. He had to grip the tree beside him, so disoriented was he. She was pregnant!

Sickened, he turned away. The woman he loved was bearing another man's child! She had truly made a mockery of his love for her, of his sacrifice.

But before he could move away, they were walking toward him. He could not move. He stood there, trapped, hunched against the cold, and watched her come closer. She dared to walk so proudly, he thought in contempt. She who had betrayed him, body and soul!

Elizabeth looked up—straight at him—at that moment. Their eyes met, and hers widened. She opened her mouth to say something, but he turned deliberately away. He would not speak with her. He would not see her. Not ever again.

He turned his back on her and strode away.

"Elizabeth?" said Cyril, gripping her elbow in concern. "Are you all right?"

She put her hand to her forehead. Surely she had not seen whom she thought she had seen. "Y-yes," she whispered. "I—I am fine."

"The baby—?"

"The baby is fine," she assured him. Bless Cyril. He took as good care of her and her baby-to-be as he would have if the child were his own. What woman could ask for more?

"Though I—I do think I should lie down when we get home, Cyril."

"Yes, dear. Let us leave now. Good-bye," he said

to the beaming Fletcher sisters. "Good-bye, Reverend Ayers.

"Good-bye," he said to several of the men and women who were standing around chatting on the church steps. "Good-bye, good-bye."

"There," he said, tucking her hand under his elbow. He patted her hand, and she thought again how fortunate she was to have him for a husband. He was so kind. "We will get you home in no time."

They soon walked up the front steps of their little home. He held the door open for her. Once inside, he lit the oil lamps and began building up the fire in the kitchen stove so that room would become warmer. Elizabeth settled into the rocking chair. He put a quilt over her. "There you are."

She smiled tremulously. She really should not be behaving so . . . so weakly, she thought. Yet seeing that Indian man—why, he had looked exactly like Isaac Thompson! Yet he couldn't be Isaac. Isaac was dead. She placed her hand on her belly and patted the little one therein reassuringly, reassuring herself in the process.

Cyril was boiling water in the kettle. Humming, he took down her teapot. Why, the dear man was going to make her a cup of tea. She looked at him, and her eyes brimmed with tears. If only she loved him. He was kind to her, he cared about her and her child—no, more than cared, he loved her. He had told her so on three separate occasions.

She cried at the drop of a handkerchief these days. It must have something to do with her pregnancy.

She dashed the tears away and smiled at him.

He smiled back. "Feeling better?" he asked solicitously.

"Yes," she answered, and it was true. She had been sadly mistaken. That Indian man was not Isaac. Isaac had died in that horrible Tsimshian village. She would never see him again, no matter how much her heart longed for him.

"I must go in to the office today," Cyril was saying apologetically. "The crew have to get the Monday edition of the newspaper ready, and I . . . well, I want to be there to look it over. It has to be very good."

Cyril was proud of his newspaper, the *Fort Victoria Trumpeter*, and Elizabeth was proud of him. It was a fine newspaper that people read and discussed. The letters to the editor always complimented the paper.

"You go ahead," she encouraged. "I will be fine. That cup of tea will restore me." She smiled. "Go on."

"Very good," he said. He went and got his hat and coat. "Are you sure?" he asked, pausing in putting on his coat. "I could stay."

"No, you go," she said. "The *Trumpeter* is very important."

He grinned. "It is. And this is going to be the best edition we've put out!"

She waved to him as he closed the door. When he was gone, she listened to the silence. It was lonely, being by herself. She rested her hands on her belly again. She had the little one, she had Cyril, and even her aunt would come to visit her again, should Elizabeth but ask. But there was a loneliness in her heart that would not go away. It ate at her, night and day.

She felt the tears welling again and wiped them

away. All she was doing through this pregnancy was crying. She had to stop feeling sorry for herself. Had to. And she had to stop imagining she had seen Isaac.

Chapter Eighteen

A fleeting twinge of guilt went through Isaac when he saw Elizabeth sitting at a table in the small kitchen of her house. He should not be peeking in her window. But he could not help himself. He knew that her husband was working late at the newspaper. And Elizabeth was home by herself.

It was dark, and one or two street lamps far down the street flickered. No one was around. It was the perfect time for him to steal her. For that was what he had decided to do. He could not get her out of his mind. Thoughts of her over-shadowed everything else: the potlatch, his father's stern admonitions, any training he had ever had about being an honorable man. He could not live his life without her. He knew that now. Therefore, it was time to steal her and take her back with him to his Haida village. She would be safe there, and none of these white people would know where to look for her.

He had watched her house for several days now, in between looking for a white man's job. He had noticed that there were few new houses being built in the fort; the building had been halted for lack of wood. When he got back to his village, he would speak to William. They could buy some of the land near Fort Victoria and log it. Then he could sell the logs to the white settlers at the fort for their homes. It was a good plan and would bring in money for his potlatch. It would be better than working for one of the whites here. None of them seemed to want to hire him. Several seemed to have been afraid of him because of his size. Well, let them be afraid.

The most important thing now was for him to capture Elizabeth and take her with him back to his village.

He had stowed a canoe; it was hidden down near one of the docks and had enough water and dried fish to last them for several days. Once they were closer to his country, he could catch fish to feed them. Yes, he thought in satisfaction, it was a good plan.

He was about to step from his hiding place at the side of the house when he heard some giggling. Three people were walking down the street. White people. A man and two women.

He slunk back into the shadows. He would wait until they passed by. But they did not pass by. Instead, they walked up the little muddy path to Elizabeth's house. He grimaced. Now what?

He heard them knock on the door and then Elizabeth's voice when she opened it. "The Fletcher sisters! And Reverend Ayers! How lovely to see you! Come in, come in! Let me get my white gloves . . ." There was more giggling, and then the door shut, cutting off her voice, a voice that he hungered to hear again.

Frustrated, he leaned back against the house. How long would they visit? And would the husband return while they were here? He knew that her husband always worked late at his shop, and he had counted upon that tonight.

He pondered what to do. Should he wait and hope that they would leave soon, or should he try again tomorrow night?

An owl cried out, and suddenly Isaac froze. What was an owl doing in the fort? In all his time here he had not heard an owl cry out. Why now?

He glanced around. The hairs on the back of his neck rose, though he could see nothing and no one. Someone, something was out there . . . watching.

He slid in closer to the building. Another owl cry. This time he was certain. It was a human, not an owl. But to unsuspecting ears, it sounded like an owl.

He judged the distance between the houses as a little more than the length of two men. He could sneak into the next yard and run behind the houses until he got to a busier part of the fort. Whoever was out there was up to no good.

He had reached the third house down from Elizabeth's when he saw them. Dark shadows following him. Someone was after him!

His mind raced as he darted to the next house, hoping the shadows had not seen him. But they had. Now they were running after him!

He raced out onto the muddy street, uncaring who would see him. Slogging through the mud slowed him, but he knew that if he reached a shop or a busier part of the fort, someone would see—

Too late: A hand clamped over his mouth, and a foot tripped him up. Three men, or more, piled onto him, and he found himself tasting mud. He tried to call out, but they cut off his shout with a well-placed blow to his throat, then to his head.

When he woke up, he was lying in the bottom of a war canoe, looking up into the grinning tattooed face of Fisher, the Tsimshian nobleman.

"So, Haida," said the grinning Tsimshian, "you escaped our village. But you will not escape us again."

Isaac shook his head, trying to clear his eyes of the hideous sight of four Tsimshians, all staring at him as they paddled. "Where—where are you taking me?"

He was surprised they had not killed him already.

"Back to our village. We will deliver you to our chief. This time the job will be done right. You will be killed."

"My uncle will not kill me," bluffed Isaac. "He will set me free. You are fools, every one of you." He spat mud out of his mouth as he said this.

They ignored his insulting manner and words.

"You will see, when we get to our village. And we will see how brave you are then, Haida dog."

Chapter Nineteen

Elizabeth sauntered past the Celestial, or Chinese, apothecary's shop and caught her reflection in the window. She wore a dark green coat with a black hat set jauntily on her brown hair, which was done in a bun. Her black umbrella was tucked under one arm, and her belly stuck out hardly at all. She smiled at her reflection, then peered at the dried herbs and little green, red and blue medicinal bottles that were set in the window. A Celestial man with a long queue of black hair opened the door and went in. A whiff of fragrant and exotic smells teased her nose before she turned away, not quite brave enough to enter the dim little shop, despite her curiosity.

Cyril worked all afternoon and evening at the newspaper and would not be home until just before midnight, so she had a great deal of time to herself. She enjoyed taking long walks through the town.

As she stepped into the muddy street, she thought about how good her life was. Her baby would be born in another few months, and Cyril was a kind husband. She had everything a woman could want, she insisted to herself.

A group of men talking loudly and walking boisterously caught her attention. They cut in front of her. She changed direction, anxious to stay away from them. She knew they had been drinking spirits in one of the public houses. Dodging drunk men was, unfortunately, one of the risks of walking through the streets of Fort Victoria.

A variety of shops lined the narrow street. People bustled along, going in and out of the small stores, talking with one another. The smells from a bakery mixed with the smells of a Celestial kitchen. She smiled to herself, liking the combination.

She had just walked past another shop and turned a corner when she suddenly halted. Three men were yelling and hitting someone down on the ground. One of the assailants wore a bulky brown coat and big boots. The other two wore blue jackets. They appeared to be workers of some sort, perhaps off one of the ships, or miners in town for a visit.

A closer look at the person on the ground revealed it was a woman. Without a second thought, Elizabeth raised her umbrella like a sword and swooped down upon the ruffians. "Get away," she cried, swinging the umbrella wildly until she heard a loud *thwack!* and a yelp as her umbrella connected sharply. "Leave her alone!"

Elizabeth cut a wide swath left and right, beating off the ruffians who dared attack a defenseless woman. Her umbrella struck two more of them. They scattered.

Never has an umbrella been used so effectively on so many men, Elizabeth thought in satisfaction. Though it was nothing she had learned in Miss Cowperth's school, it was effective.

"Are you all right?" Elizabeth reached down to help the poor woman up to her feet. "Those men!" she exclaimed indignantly. "They think they can—"

To her astonishment, she recognized the victim. "Susan! What—what happened? Why were those men hitting you?"

Susan stood on shaky legs. Her face was as muddy as her dress. She wiped at it. Mud was clumped in her long black hair. People stopped and stared at the two women.

Elizabeth suddenly felt self-conscious. Politely but determinedly, she pushed her way through the small crowd that had gathered round them. Susan followed. There were mutterings in the crowd, mutterings that Elizabeth turned a deaf ear to. "Whatever happened?" she repeated, ignoring the curious stares of those around them.

Susan looked at her. "Those men no like me."

"Filthy Indian." The ugly words drifted to Elizabeth's ears, and she glanced around to see who'd said it. Several men frowned at them. Two middle-aged women spoke behind their hands. But no one stepped forward to claim credit for the epithet.

"Why, Mrs. Mandeville!" exclaimed a woman's voice.

Elizabeth turned to see the elderly Fletcher sis-

ters. "Whatever are you doing, talking to that—
that Indian woman?" Both sisters looked shocked
at seeing her.

For a moment, Elizabeth felt shame rise in her
that she was somehow a bad person for talking
with Susan. Then reason asserted itself. Susan had
once saved her life. The least Elizabeth could do
was save Susan from those bullying villains. "I
know this woman," she answered with a shaky
voice. She swallowed and tried again. "I—I believe
she was set upon by those ruffians and I have but
come to her aid."

"That is all very well, miss," said a man briskly.
He wore a top hat and appeared to be one of the
richer citizens of the fort. "But you do not want to
encourage someone like her. She will either steal
from you or bring men to your door."

"I am sure I do not know what you mean," answered Elizabeth in her haughtiest, Miss-
Cowperth-like voice.

The man laughed. "You don't know what company you keep," he said. "That woman is a whore."

Elizabeth's eyes widened. "She is not! Get away,
all of you!" She swung her umbrella and this time
the small crowd backed away. The well-dressed
man walked away, muttering. The Fletcher sisters
clutched one another's arms as they tottered off.
Elizabeth had not meant to scare them off, only
the others. Nevertheless, she was not sorry to see
them go.

Elizabeth and Susan were left standing in the
street.

Elizabeth turned to Susan. "Come," she said as
firmly as she could. "We must go to my home. You

241

can have a bath and wash up." She was appalled to see Susan like this.

"Those people—" began Elizabeth. "They said terrible things about you."

Susan shrugged.

Susan was not a whore. Elizabeth *knew* Susan was not a whore. Elizabeth willed herself to dismiss the cutting, cruel remarks from her mind. "Come along," said Elizabeth. Susan did not appear too eager to accompany Elizabeth, but finally reluctantly agreed.

"Let's get you to my home," said Elizabeth briskly. They walked quickly along the streets, soon leaving the street with the crowded shops far behind. Elizabeth kept a sharp lookout for the three men, but they did not put in an appearance. Frightened out of their wits, she supposed.

Once at her house, Elizabeth offered Susan a chair in the kitchen and proceeded to make a cup of tea for her guest. Susan helped her lift two huge pots of water to the top of the stove. Then Elizabeth shoved some more wood into the stove so that it would heat the water intended for Susan's bath. "Here," she said to Susan. "Drink this."

Susan dutifully drank the tea.

"Now," said Elizabeth, "get out of those wet clothes and put this on." Susan handed over her muddy garments and put on the housedress that Elizabeth gave to her.

"There! Much better," said Elizabeth, pleased with her handiwork. With her long dark hair flowing over the pink flowered housedress, Susan looked very fetching indeed.

Elizabeth poured her own tea and sat down at the kitchen table to wait for the bath water to heat.

"What are you doing in Fort Victoria?" she asked Susan.

Susan took a cautious sip of her tea before answering. "I visit my friends."

The memory of the cruel words came back to Elizabeth. "What friends?" she asked. Perhaps Susan was in trouble.

"Friends," answered Susan. She took a sip of the tea.

"Men friends?" pressed Elizabeth.

Susan nodded. "Men give me gifts."

Elizabeth sucked in her breath and choked on her tea. "Susan," she said, setting down her teacup. "Why do the men give you gifts?" Dread was forming a sick knot in Elizabeth's stomach.

"I be their woman. For a little time. They pay me much money."

Her mouth agape, Elizabeth stared at Susan. This could not be. Susan, the woman who had saved Elizabeth's life was a—a—Elizabeth could not even say the word, not even to herself.

"I take money and buy gifts for my people," said Susan, watching Elizabeth intently. Her dark eyes showed no remorse. No shame.

Elizabeth swallowed. Could it be that Susan did not understand what she was doing?

"Susan," said Elizabeth, as gently as possible. "Those men, they can hurt you. They are bad men." She didn't know if she should tell Susan she was a bad woman for doing this thing. She finally decided to say nothing about that part.

"No, not bad men," said Susan. "They give me many gifts. Much money. I give gifts to my people. My people very happy. I very happy."

Elizabeth covered her face with her hands. Then

243

she slowly slid her hands down her face to see that Susan was watching her.

"You want to get gifts, too?" asked Susan.

"No!" Elizabeth jumped out of her chair. Susan was startled by her action. Elizabeth sat back down. "I mean, no. Thank you.

"Ooooh," moaned Elizabeth. What should she do? How could she help Susan? Susan should not be doing this.

"Susan," she began. "You must find some other way of getting money and gifts."

Susan frowned. "No. My friends do this. Many women do this. Many white men at fort. No wives. So they want Haida wives."

"You are—are wives?" asked Elizabeth.

"For a little while," said Susan. "The men give marriage gift. I take it. I am wife for a short time. Then man finds other Haida wife."

"Oooooh," moaned Elizabeth again. "What about your family? Do they know you do this?"

Susan smiled. "Yes. They like. Send my younger sister with me next time."

Elizabeth sucked in her breath. This was worse than she thought. Susan's family thought this was fine, nothing wrong with it. Oh, no!

"What—what about a Haida husband?" she ventured. "Would he like this?"

Susan shrugged. "Plenty Haida men married before, too."

Elizabeth wanted to cry. If Susan was thinking she was married to these men, then what she was doing was fine. It fit in with her people's beliefs.

"Susan," Elizabeth tried again. How could she make Susan understand she should not do this? "Susan. Do not do this. You will get sick." Eliza-

beth was desperate now, and she seemed to remember something about the unspeakable
diseases the prostitutes in San Francisco got from
men. And gave to them. "You will get sick and
maybe die."

"No," said Susan. "I take good herbs. I wash in
sea."

Elizabeth let out her breath. She realized now
she was not going to convince Susan of anything.
Susan was going to do whatever she wanted.

Troubled, Elizabeth also realized her own
choice was to accept Susan as she was or never
have anything to do with her again. She knew what
choice the Fletcher sisters would make.

And yet Elizabeth could not forget that, when
she was facing death at the hands of the Tsimshians, it had been Susan who had taken her hand
and forced her to run along the forest path to the
cove; she had saved Elizabeth's life. And on the
long canoe trip down from the north, it had been
Susan who had caught fish and dug clams for them
to eat. It had been Susan who knew which direction to travel. It had been Susan who paddled tire-
lessly. If it were not for Susan, Elizabeth bleakly
realized, then she, Elizabeth, would not be alive
and safe in Fort Victoria. So she tamped down her
concerns about what other people would think and
offered Susan another cup of tea.

Which was accepted.

They drank the tea while Elizabeth tried to get
used to the new idea that she was going to be a
friend to Susan despite what other people thought
and despite what Susan did to get her gifts. And
since Susan felt no shame and felt that what she
did was all right, perhaps Elizabeth could also ac-

cept what Susan did. It would help if she remembered that Susan believed she was married to the men each time . . .

"You like the fort?" Susan was asking.

"The fort? Oh, yes," answered Elizabeth, coming back to the present. "I like Fort Victoria very much."

"You like husband?" asked Susan.

Elizabeth nodded. "He is very kind to me."

"Good husband, then?" asked Susan, watching Elizabeth closely.

Elizabeth met the Haida woman's eyes. "Yes, he is a very good husband."

To Elizabeth's surprise, it was Susan who now looked troubled. Maybe Susan thought Elizabeth should be changing husbands frequently, as she did.

Seeing Susan sitting there reminded Elizabeth so much of Isaac that her throat ached with unshed tears. She wished she had the courage to ask about how the burial had gone, but she knew that if she asked Susan anything about Isaac, she would spend the rest of the day and night sobbing.

It was when Susan was leaving, wearing a spare, dry dress of Elizabeth's—a butter-colored one that looked very pretty against Susan's dark skin and hair—that Elizabeth allowed herself one tiny question. "Is—is Isaac's father well?" she asked, and she heard the trembling in her own voice.

At first Susan did not answer, but there was a question in her dark eyes. "You sure you like new husband?" she asked.

Elizabeth realized that Susan had not understood the question. "I like my new husband," she answered hastily, "very much. He is very kind." But she could not forget about Isaac. She hesitated, then plunged on. "Tell me about Isaac," said Elizabeth, half sheepishly, half defiantly. "It must have been very difficult for his father and his family when William brought his body back for burial." Her voice caught and she could not continue. She wiped at a tear.

Susan frowned. At last she answered, "Father well. William well."

Elizabeth nodded, wiping another tear surreptitiously. She could at least take some comfort in the knowledge that Isaac now rested among his people. "You know," she confessed with a shaky laugh, "I thought I saw Isaac—why, it was just the other day. After church." She gave another half-hearted laugh. "Of course, I know now I was mistaken. Still," she sighed, "he looked so much like Isaac . . ."

Susan waited on the doorstep, watching her through narrowed eyes.

"Oh, how thoughtless of me," said Elizabeth, realizing Susan was waiting. "Let me walk you down the steps to the street." She put on a black shawl to stay warm as the night closed around them. Once at the street, she said to Susan, "Come back in a day or so and your dress will be clean and dry."

Susan grunted.

"Good-bye," said Elizabeth.

Susan gave a little wave as she headed off toward the main part of the fort.

Elizabeth waved back. She had a new friend.

Chapter Twenty

"You know," said Cyril thoughtfully, "I have heard about your rescue of that Indian woman from several different people."

"Pshaw!" exclaimed Elizabeth with what she hoped was suitable modesty. After all, a woman did not flaunt a heroic performance to people so they could admire her. Miss Cowperth always stressed self-effacing, womanly behavior, which did not include boasting. "It was nothing." Elizabeth lifted the heavy iron off the stove. It should be suitably heated by now for pressing Susan's dress.

"Ah, but I wish that were so," answered Cyril. "It seems that the people who have mentioned it to me, and as I said there were several, did not like it that you helped that poor female."

"I beg your pardon?" Elizabeth stopped her ironing long enough to stare open-mouthed at her husband.

"It is true," said Cyril, meeting her shocked gaze with his pale blue one. "Indians are not well liked around here."

"Well," sputtered Elizabeth, "I suppose I knew that. But it made me so angry, Cyril, to see those bullies beating up my friend. Of course I didn't know she was my friend at the time—"

"Wait!" Cyril laughed, holding up a hand to stop the barrage of words. "I take it you rushed to her defense, knowing only that it was a woman."

"Yes, that is true," acknowledged Elizabeth. "I would have done the same for any woman. Or man, for that matter." She added, "An umbrella is a wonderful thing."

Cyril chuckled. Elizabeth had already told Cyril how she had beaten off the attackers with her black umbrella.

"I've been thinking about this," said Cyril slowly. Elizabeth paused in her ironing. Cyril had a formidable brain, one that was always thinking. She had come to admire him greatly in the short time they'd been married. Admire, yes, but still not love, she thought sadly.

"I have been thinking of writing an editorial for the newspaper," he continued. "One that will let the citizens of this fort know what it is like to be an Indian. They should know what it is like to have a host of invaders with strange ways come and settle down in one's midst. Do you think my readers would like that?"

Elizabeth tightened her lips as she ironed. No doubt the readers would not like it, but she hesitated to discourage Cyril. He was a caring, honest man, and she thought that if he wrote such an article, it would perhaps do some good. From what she'd learned of Cyril, he cared deeply about the rights of his fellow man. He wanted people to be treated fairly before the law and by each other. Which was not something everyone wanted, thought Elizabeth.

"Elizabeth?"

She came out of her reverie. "Oh. Cyril, I think it would be a very good thing to do," she encouraged. "There are so many more Indians here that live outside the fort. Would you say a thousand or so?"

"More like three thousand," answered Cyril. "That was the tally by Governor Douglas's man at the last head count."

"Three thousand," said Elizabeth thoughtfully. "And there must be about three hundred whites within the fort."

"Roughly that number."

"And of course, some Celestials and a few Africans," she said.

"Governor Douglas himself is of African heritage," said Cyril. "And I believe he would encourage a more tolerant view." His mind was obviously on his newspaper article.

Elizabeth liked the governor. He had been very helpful to her that day she'd first arrived at the fort, desperate and alone.

"I will work on it tonight," decided Cyril. He picked up his jacket. "Thank you for a delicious luncheon." He gave her a peck on the cheek. She leaned forward to receive his kiss.

"I expect I will be home after midnight again,"

he said ruefully. "I don't like to do that, but I have been thinking about this article. I do want to write it, because I believe I have something important to say."

"I know you do," said Elizabeth, her heart thumping with pride. He was a wonderful man, a caring husband and an excellent newspaperman. Several times she had heard comments from people about articles he had written. And while not everyone agreed with Cyril, he always wrote about timely topics in a thoughtful fashion. "It will be a wonderful article," she assured him.

He glanced at her. "Do you have the pistol?" he asked. She nodded. Cyril had insisted she carry a pistol in her reticule when she left the house. He had even taught her how to shoot. He was worried about the dangers of the fort.

He brushed her lips, patted her stomach where the baby nestled, and headed out the door. The preoccupied look on his pale, handsome face told her he was already composing the editorial in his mind.

"Don't wait up for me," he called over his shoulder as he walked down the little path to the street. "Go to bed early. You need your rest. For you and the baby."

She smiled at his thoughtfulness. Yes, she was a lucky woman to be married to Mr. Cyril B. Mandeville III.

Elizabeth opened her eyes in surprise to see sunlight streaming through the tiny glass square that was the bedroom window. She glanced around and yawned. Morning already!

Then she paused. Where was Cyril? His side of

the bed was flat and unruffled. His nightshirt showed he had not used it, so he had not come in late and risen early to go back to the office. He had not returned in the night. Not at all.

Slowly she rose out of bed and shrugged into a robe. How unusual. Cyril was always as good as his word. If he said he would return at a certain time, he did so. She reached for her comb, the one with the mother-of-pearl handle, her cherished gift from Isaac, and pulled it lightly through her hair.

Then, feeling slightly uneasy, she shuffled into the cold kitchen. The fire had gone out in the stove, and she spent the next twenty minutes trying to light the cedar kindling so that the woodstove would warm the kitchen. By the time she finally managed to start a fire, the kitchen was filled with smoke, and she staggered, coughing, to the front door to open it and let the smoke out.

Susan was coming down the path toward her, so Elizabeth opened the door wider. All hope of warming the small house quickly fled. She smiled to see the Haida woman.

"Susan!" she greeted her. "You have come for your dress?"

The Indian woman grunted and pushed past Elizabeth into the house. Befuddled by her friend's strange behavior and the smoke, Elizabeth closed the door and went back into the kitchen. Susan was already seated and had taken off her heavy winter coat.

"I will have some hot tea for you as soon as this stove heats up," Elizabeth promised her guest.

Susan nodded and remained in the chair, arms crossed. Her face had a closed look to it, as though she did not wish to be quite where she was.

"I have your dress ready," said Elizabeth, trying for a sprightly note in her voice. "It is all ironed. You can change into it if you wish."

Susan nodded, so Elizabeth went into her bedroom to fetch the dress. When she returned, she handed it to Susan and then Susan went into the bedroom to put on the dress. She closed the door, and Elizabeth wondered anew at the gesture of modesty. Then she decided that she liked Susan; Susan had proven herself to be a friend, and what the rest of the world said or did mattered not at all in this little white house in Fort Victoria.

Susan came out wearing the dark, dull blue dress. She also held Elizabeth's comb in her hand. She set it on the table. "That dress looks pretty on you," said Elizabeth politely. But truly, the butter-colored dress she'd lent to Susan fitted and looked better. "Why don't you keep the other dress, too?" she offered. Guilt stabbed at her. If Susan looked too pretty, more men would want to "marry" her. And that was not what Elizabeth wanted for Susan.

Susan grunted at the offer and stuffed the light dress beneath her coat. That settled that, thought Elizabeth, bidding a mental farewell to the dress.

The two of them sat, waiting for the water to boil. Elizabeth hoped the silence between them was what was called "companionable" in the novels she read, but she couldn't be sure. The silence might be called "uncomfortable" or even "bored." The Swiss clock, brought over from England by ship, ticked unnaturally loudly in the room.

At last the kettle whistled, and she jumped to her feet in relief to make the tea.

She had just placed Susan's cup of tea before her

when there was a heavy knock at the door. "Now who is that?" she wondered aloud.

Susan said nothing, only lifted one black brow.

Elizabeth opened the door to find a man standing there. An official-looking man, middle-aged and overweight, dressed in a dark blue woolen uniform of some sort. He took off his cap. "Mrs. Mandeville?"

Her hand flew to her throat. "Why, yes."

"I am from the governor's office," he said.

"Please," Elizabeth said, trying to remember her manners as alarm seeped through her, "won't you come in?"

He hesitated, then stepped inside. He nodded politely at Susan, for which Elizabeth silently thanked him, then stood, awkward, hat in hand.

Elizabeth went and sat down in the rocking chair, her stomach feeling huge this morning. The baby was kicking, and she was still tired; she had not rested as well as usual. And this man's presence was unsettling. Why was he here?

"Mrs. Mandeville?"

"Yes?"

"I'm afraid I have some bad news." In alarm Elizabeth glanced from him to Susan.

The Indian woman nodded. *She knows*, thought Elizabeth. *She knows something is wrong, and that's why she's here*. A frisson of gratitude went through Elizabeth at that moment. The Indian woman was here to help her. In her own way, she was offering friendship. But Elizabeth's gratitude was quickly overshadowed by a looming fear.

"What—what is it?"

"Mr. Mandeville—"

"Cyril!" Elizabeth jumped to her feet. "What has

happened?" Her hand clutched her throat. "Is he all right? For God's mercy, tell me!"

"I'm trying to, Mrs. Mandeville," he answered softly. "Mr. Mandeville passed away in the night."

Her hands flew to her cheeks, and her mouth dropped. "It cannot be!" she cried. "No! It cannot be! Why . . . why, he was here. Just last evening! Said good-bye. Kissed my cheek!"

"I'm sorry," said the man. His gaze shot to the door, and she thought he wanted to run out of the house. But she didn't care.

"There must be some mistake—"

"No mistake," the man said, turning his hat in his hands nervously.

Elizabeth looked helplessly at Susan. Susan slowly nodded. There was a sadness in her dark eyes that told Elizabeth he spoke the truth.

She sank down into the rocker. "It cannot be," she moaned. "It cannot be!"

The man shuffled his feet in one place. He glanced longingly at the door again.

"What happened?" asked Elizabeth, clutching her robe closed at the neck. This couldn't be happening to her.

"He was shot—"

"Shot?" Elizabeth stared at him, aghast.

The man cleared his throat. "He was uh, shot. Last night. By a gang of ruffians."

"Ruffians?"

"Drunken ruffians," explained the official. "Mr. Mandeville happened to be passing by a group of men. They were fighting on the street. One of them pulled out a gun. There was a shot. Your husband died."

She put her face in her hands. Such a short, succinct accounting of Cyril's last precious moments on this earth. She shook her head and moaned. This couldn't be happening.

"I am sorry," repeated the man. She heard in his voice that he truly was sorry. She started to cry then. Tears came, and she didn't know if they were for Cyril or Isaac or for herself. All three, maybe.

"Uh, Mrs. Mandeville," said the governor's man. "I have to be going . . ."

She nodded, waved a hand. She didn't look up, because she couldn't. The tears just kept coming.

She heard him walking toward the door.

"Wait!" she cried out. "Where—where is Cyril—the body?" She wiped at the tears. Fresh ones spurted out.

"At the church," he said. "You can find his body there. We—we thought that would be best."

Elizabeth nodded and hunched over in the chair. Cyril was gone. He was dead.

Isaac was dead. Her father was dead. Her mother was dead. Everyone was dead.

The door closed quietly. The sound of the ticking clock filled the room, a background noise to Elizabeth's sobs.

Elizabeth felt a hand squeeze her shoulder. Susan's compassionate gesture set off another round of tears.

Chapter Twenty-one

Elizabeth wiped tears from her eyes as she read the newspaper. It was Cyril's editorial. His words lived on after his death.

The Indians who live in this vast forested land are the sons and daughters of the Creator just as we are. They have harvested the fish and clams and deer and cut down cedar trees for thousands of years. It is we who are the new-comers here. Yet we treat them as if they are in our way, as if we own this land and they are the interlopers. We tell them where they may live and we keep the best land for ourselves. We take their forests and sell the logs.

We clog up their streams. We dig up their ground to find gold. We do all this so that we may have more and more wealth, ever more.

Theresa Scott

It started one hundred years ago, when we sent traders on ships to cheat them. We gave them spirits, powerful alcohol to drink that was new to them and clouded their thoughts. That way we could cheat them even more.

The only white person who seems to care about what happens to the Indian is the missionary. The missionary does his best to save their souls, while the rest of us are dedicated to stealing everything we can from their bodies.

It is not a proud record, readers.

The other day my wife was out walking and saw three (white) men beating up an Indian woman. My wife had the courage and bravery to effect a rescue of the Indian woman. But was she congratulated? Was she considered a brave person, a heroine who rushed to the aid of her dusky-skinned sister?

No, readers, she was not. She was reviled, yes, reviled. People said she should not have interfered. They said she should have stood by and allowed the Indian woman to be beaten, nay, even killed if those spiteful bullies so desired.

What is the matter with us? What is happening to our society that we protest the rescue of a poor, defenseless Indian woman? I will tell you that the true measure of a society is how it treats its weakest members. By that measure, our society is in trouble, readers, very big trouble, indeed.

*I fear that the ones who are in real need are not
the Indians, but ourselves. We are the ones who
need help for our souls. And what missionary
will rescue us?*

The words blurred through her tears and she
had to stop reading. Cyril's last words. The last
words he would be remembered for.

She sobbed for a long time. At last she wiped her
tears and slowly went into the bedroom to dress
for the funeral. This was the most difficult day of
her life. She had thought her life was going well.
She had a husband who loved her, a baby due.

And now her well-ordered existence was destroyed. By one stray bullet from a drunk's pistol.
Destroyed.

Life wasn't fair.

The minister had delivered a fine eulogy, but Elizabeth had listened in a daze. Dully she looked
around the small church as she followed the coffin
out the door. Who were all these people? Did she
know them? Were they friends of Cyril's?

Then, not caring, aware only of the dull ache inside her, she walked through the doors and out
into the churchyard. A man she'd never seen before
sprang to her aid as she walked down the two
church steps. She shrugged out of his touch once
her feet reached the bottom.

She did not want to be here. She did not want to
see these people, as caring as they appeared to be.
She wanted to hide in her little house and cry.

For the rest of her life.

She wanted to cry for a life that had taken all the
wrong turns.

Where was the young, happy, hopeful girl she'd been when she'd left San Francisco? All that was left now was the dull shell of a woman who had loved and lost one man, then had come to respect and trust another man. And now he was gone.

Was she destined to go through life alone? Was every man she ever loved to be killed? Where was God? What kind of a life had He planned for her? Whatever it was, she didn't want it. She just wanted to curl up in her bed and sleep and never come out of her house again.

Everyone was moving toward the small cemetery across from the church. Elizabeth followed blindly, not knowing or caring what she was supposed to do.

Reverend Ayers intoned some words over the deep, dark hole where Cyril would rest forever more. As Elizabeth looked into the maw of the grave, she thought of jumping in. But just then the baby kicked, and she was reminded that she was supposed to stay on this side of the grave.

"Did they catch the man who fired the gun?" asked a woman, standing nearby. The people stood in little knots near the edge of the grave. Elizabeth blinked. She thought she'd seen the woman before but could not summon a memory of where or when. The woman's question was distasteful, however.

"No." Elizabeth turned away. She was the widow. She would not stand for stupid questions on this day. Let the governor or whoever was supposed to catch murderers do it. She was too exhausted, too spiritless, too listless, too dull, too unhappy to care.

The dirt was poured over the grave, and people

began to drift away. She stood there, staring down at the rich black dirt and wondering when it would be her turn.

But she was not allowed to stand alone for long. The Fletcher sisters came by and offered their polite consolations. Elizabeth nodded and turned to the next mourner. She did not recognize most of the people who were attending Cyril's funeral, but she supposed that he was a man of consequence in the town, being the editor of the only newspaper.

"That was an interesting article your husband wrote," commented one man with a nod. He did not say whether he agreed or not, but at least he'd had the generosity to mention Cyril's last words. She found herself bestowing a shaky smile upon him.

Reverend Ayers somehow magically appeared at her elbow. "I liked what he said about missionaries," he joked. When Elizabeth only sighed, he quickly moved on to speak to other parishioners.

Throughout the remaining ordeal, Elizabeth nodded and sighed. People came up, said a few words, then left. She didn't see Susan. Perhaps attending funerals was not something her Indian friend did.

Elizabeth continued to stand at the black graveside. Who had invented funerals and made them the ordeal they were for the surviving family? she wondered. If she had her way, mourners would have a special dispensation to go home, draw all the curtains, lock all the doors and sit in the cold and dark until they either died or decided to come out and live. As for herself, she would probably elect to stay in her house until she withered up and died.

Finally, everyone had left the churchyard. Reverend Ayers had gone back into the church to do something or other, and the Fletcher sisters had carried away the last of the flowers. And still Elizabeth stood dully at the graveside, staring at the black dirt where Cyril lay.

It started to rain, and only then did she stir. She forced herself to walk, one foot in front of the other, back to her little white house with the yellow trim. A house she and Cyril had once been so proud of. Now it was a mere shell. A place to sleep. Not a home. How could it be a home with only one person in it?

She walked up the little path and up the red steps. She opened the door, stepped inside and closed it mechanically. The house was cold, but she didn't have the energy to put more wood in the stove.

She took off her coat, pulled her black shawl around her shoulders and sat down in her rocker. Then she bowed her head and cried.

Chapter Twenty-two

Isacc was surprised that it was the nobleman Marten Fur who gave him the piece of smoked fish. Isaac had been given little to eat since his capture, and he had expected that the Tsimshians would give him nothing. They had put him in the bottom of their canoe and paddled for their village. Whether he got to their village on a full stomach or an empty one was of no concern to them.

Marten Fur held out the piece of fish. It smelled good to Isaac. There was no animosity in the Tsimshian nobleman's brown eyes, no rancor. How had Isaac missed that before? During the trip north from O-lymp-ya, he had not particularly noticed Marten Fur except to note that he had a calming influence on the more volatile Fisher. Isaac did not recognize the two other men with Marten Fur and Fisher.

Isaac reached for the fish, half expecting it to be

snatched away as in a child's game, but Marten Fur held it steady. Isaac took it and reluctantly nodded his thanks to the Tsimshian. Isaac liked it better when he could believe that all Tsimshians were bad people. Why was Marten Fur doing this?

Isaac ate the fish slowly, taking the time to ponder his situation. And to overhear the Tsimshians speaking to one another. They had kidnapped him because they thought they could win All Fear His Name's favor, and an expensive prize, for returning Isaac to his uncle. They said All Fear His Name would want to finish the job he had started: Isaac's death by canoe.

And should Isaac ever forget what it was like to be crushed by a canoe, he had but to look down at the long red scar on his ribs to remind him.

In his heart, Isaac resolved he would not go willingly to the Tsimshian village. He distinctly remembered the weight of that canoe; he refused to go through such pain ever again.

Next, the nobleman passed around a water bladder. All four men drank, and Isaac licked his lips as he watched the movement of the bulging sack. It had been a long time since he had had a drink of water.

Marten Fur handed the bladder to him. Isaac took it, threw back his head and drank long and deep. He wiped his mouth with his arm. The water tasted good.

He handed the bladder back to the nobleman, and Marten Fur placed it between his feet. Isaac eyed it, wondering when he would get another drink, already thirsty again.

Several times during the course of the long day he leaned over and groaned. He held his stomach and moaned. The Tsimshians ignored him.

At dusk, they pulled into a small cove and paddled toward the sandy beach. Isaac knew of this place; he had camped here a time or two with his own men.

It was Isaac who was forced over the side of the canoe and made to pull the heavy craft in. He did so, groaning with every pull. Some of the Tsimshians helped pull the canoe up on the beach, but they let him carry most of the weight. Twice he fell onto the sand, much to the others' disgust. They told him to carry the paddles up to the beach, but when no one was watching, he tucked them under the seats of the canoe.

Now the Tsimshians told him to gather wood—like a slave, thought Isaac contemptuously. But he put on an outward appearance of doing whatever they ordered as he seethed with anger inside. He limped along the beach, picking up piece after piece of wood, and groaning now and then.

He walked along the beach, straying gradually away from the others. When he heard a half-hearted shout from one of the Tsimshians, he limped back toward them, then stooped to pick up another piece of wood.

The Tsimshians sat around the fire as it was growing dark. Because it was still winter, the nights grew cold. Fortunately, it was one of those rare winter nights when it was not raining and the sky was clear. He could see the stars.

The Tsimshians must have believed Isaac incapable of much movement, for they neglected to tie him up. He smiled to himself.

The Tsimshians wrapped themselves in blankets, neglecting to give Isaac one. He lay awake, shivering. After a time, he heard snoring. Then he felt a nudge on his foot. Marten Fur surreptitiously passed him an old blanket. Isaac took it gratefully. He wondered at the kindness of the nobleman. Perhaps there were some good Tsimshian people, after all.

When he was certain that Marten Fur, too, slept, Isaac quietly arose. He picked up the water bladder and a chunk of fish left over from the evening meal and walked with silent tread down to the canoe. He pushed at the big craft until he got the stern in the water. Just as he was pushing the bow into the water, one of the Tsimshians gave a loud shout of alarm.

Isaac waded out into the water, pushing the canoe ahead of him. He jumped into the canoe, showing none of his limping behavior. The cries of the Tsimshians grew louder; they were closer. He reached for a paddle and dug the pointed end into the water as strongly as he could. The canoe shot forward out of reach of his pursuers.

But now two of them were throwing themselves into the water and swimming after him. He turned around and saw that one was very close. He made another stroke of the paddle, then beat at the man with it. Struck, the man screamed and let the canoe go ahead. The other man swam toward him, but Isaac waved the paddle at him, and he displayed a sudden reluctance to come closer. He contented himself with hissing insults at Isaac.

With a chuckle, Isaac paddled hard and soon left his angry, shouting pursuers behind.

He pointed the bow of the canoe south, back to Fort Victoria—and Elizabeth.

Chapter Twenty-three

Isaac reached Fort Victoria the afternoon of the fourth day of paddling. The canoe was too large for one man to paddle, and he had proceeded slowly. A light mist fell as he made his way into the fort's harbor. He could see the open gates of the fort. Outside the walls, the fort was surrounded by the many tents of the Indians who lived there. Across the bay were more Indian dwellings. A blue smoke haze from the many campfires lingered in the air. It was a cold, wet day and he would be glad to find shelter.

He beached the canoe where he had first brought Elizabeth that long-ago day in the summer. He walked the forest trail until he reached the Fort. He did not have any white man's money or a coat or white man's boots with him. When the Tsimshians had captured him, they had stripped him of everything of value, including his knife and boots.

They left him with only an old pair of pants to wear. He could not go barefoot into the fort.

He decided to look for any Haida Indians who might be camped nearby.

He sauntered past the tents of the forest Indians and drew their glares. He shrugged. Haidas, easily recognizable by their tattoos and height, were feared by many of the local tribes. He saw some Tsimshians that he recognized from his unhappy time spent in their village. He quickly slid behind a group of Tlingit Indian tents before the Tsimshians could see him. He circled around past a cluster of Kwakiutl tents. The Kwakiutl were warlike, and he did not care to fight with them.

After a search, he found a small enclave of Haidas. They were camped to the north of the fort, on the other side of a grassy hill. The rest of the coast Indians preferred to avoid Haidas because of their reputation for raiding other tribes. Nor did the Haidas seek others out.

These Haidas, though strangers from a village called Sea Otter Cove, were friendly to Isaac. Their village was somewhat to the north of his own. The Haidas turned out to be of the Raven clan, as was Isaac. They were willing to share what they had. They gave him a warm coat, a white shirt and a pair of white man's boots. One of them even handed him a hunting knife in a leather sheath so that he was once more armed. Isaac accepted the clothes and weapon with heartfelt thanks. Then they fed him a generous portion of freshly roasted deer meat. He ate well with them and drank the water that ran in a nearby stream, but he refused the whisky they offered. He had seen the ravages of whisky and wanted no part of it.

When he told them he was thinking of buying some land and cutting the trees down to make logs to sell to the whites, several men said they would like to help him.

They told him about a white man who owned a small sawmill at some distance from the fort, but he did not hire Indians and he did not do very good work, they reported. He was known to "forget" to deliver logs for weeks at a time.

Isaac thought maybe if he were to open a sawmill it would be a good way to help Haida Indians who lived down in this area. He could sell the lumber to the whites. Then they could build some more little white houses like Elizabeth lived in.

Elizabeth. He had to go and find her. He wanted her, and a new idea had lodged in his mind. When the Tsimshians had kidnapped him, he'd had time to think. He hated being kidnapped. Elizabeth probably hated it, too. If he kidnapped her, she would not like it and she would hate him. He did not want that. There must be a better way for Isaac to get Elizabeth for his own.

It was time to leave the camp. He thanked the Sea Otter Haidas for their hospitality and promised he would return when he had need of their help.

They bade Isaac farewell, and he left, heading for the fort. He felt much better, now that he had some food in his stomach and he was dressed better. Now he could set about finding work again to carry out his new plans.

Elizabeth woke up sleepily from dozing in the rocking chair in her kitchen. It was dark in the room. No surprise there. Since Cyril's death she'd

Theresa Scott

favored the dark and had taken to lighting lamps only when she began bumping into things.

There was a slight movement, and her eyes turned in that direction. "Isaac!" she gasped. Disbelief pounded in her brain and her heart. But—but Isaac was dead! Fear sucked her into a yawning black chasm.

Then she fainted.

When she awoke, he was still there, sitting in the other kitchen chair at the table. Several of the lamps were lit, and the uncertain flames sent shadows wavering across the walls. "Isaac?" She sat up straight in her rocker and blinked several times. "Is that you? Am I dead, too?" She had wanted to die, these past few weeks. Had thought of it many times. But she hadn't known one could think oneself into death.

"It is me, Lis-uh-buth," came his gentle voice. "Isaac."

Her hand went to her throat. "But—but—"

It looked like him. Same handsome face with the nose a little hooked at the tip. Same lock of black hair falling across his broad forehead. Yes, it was Isaac.

"No, I am not dead," he said quietly, answering her. "Neither are you."

"But how—?" She floundered, trying to understand. What was he doing here? He was alive!

"William rescued me," he explained. He still hadn't moved. Just sat in the chair across from her. Truth be told, had he moved—even a muscle—she would have jumped up and run screaming out of her chair, pregnancy or no.

"William found me floating on a log in the water after the Tsimshians tried to kill me."

Elizabeth felt stricken. "Oh, Isaac! I wanted to be there to help you! I wanted to find you and help—"

"It is all right, Lis-uh-buth," he answered. "I told William to get you away from there. He and Susan did what was right."

There was an understanding note in his voice, and she relaxed a little. Evidently, he understood how dangerous it had been for her, for Susan and William, too.

"Isaac," she said, struggling to get out of the rocking chair. Only then did he rise and walk over to help her. She looked up at him towering over her, and she wanted to weep at seeing him. He was alive! She lifted a hand and ran it along his jaw. "Oh, Isaac," she whispered. "I can't believe you are alive!"

He turned his head into her hand and kissed it. Shivers went through her. "Oh, Isaac," she moaned, rising and lifting her arms. She encircled his neck and hugged him close. She could feel his heart beating, and hers.

Suddenly he lifted his head. His black eyes stared into hers, and she saw anger flare there. "Your husband," he said, his voice thick and unsteady. A part of her realized that she affected him as much as he affected her.

"My husband?" She frowned, trying to clear her spinning head, spinning from his kiss. "What about him?"

"When will he be back?" Isaac glanced around as if preparing to meet Cyril at any moment.

Her shoulders drooped. "Cyril is not coming back, Isaac. He will never come back."

Isaac frowned. "He left you?"

"In a way," she sighed. "He is dead. He was shot. He lies in the graveyard."

Isaac started, and a nerve in his jaw flickered. "He is dead, then."

She nodded sadly. "He was a good man."

"You love him?"

It seemed to her that tension suddenly swelled in the room. Isaac was watching her. His black eyes never wavered from her face.

"Love?" she mused. "Or *loved*?" she pondered to herself, finding to her surprise that the answer was important. "Did I love him?"

Isaac looked white about the lips.

She met Isaac's eyes squarely. "I cared about him," she said at last. "He was kind to me. But I don't know if I loved him. I admired him."

Isaac raised one eyebrow. "You marry very soon."

"Soon?" Now she felt as if they were playing a game. "Soon after what?" Softly she answered her own question. "Soon after your death."

He glared at her.

So he did not like it that she had married Cyril. "Isaac," she said. "I believed you to be dead."

When he said nothing, she continued, "I faced the rest of my life. Alone. And"—she glanced down at her belly—"I was pregnant."

"You carry his baby." It was a statement.

"Wait," she insisted. "You need to know this: *I carry your child!* Not Cyril's. Cyril married me so that he could help me raise my child. Mine and *yours*."

Isaac's eyes narrowed. Clearly he did not like what he was hearing. "Mine?"

She nodded and crossed her arms across her breasts. They stood, toe to toe, glaring at each other.

He crossed his arms, too. And frowned deeper. "My child?" He said it so softly she almost didn't hear the wistfulness in his words.

"Your child," she confirmed. She smiled tremulously. "I wanted your child, Isaac. I was happy that I carried your child. When I thought you were dead, our child was a part of you, the only part of you still left on this earth. I love our child."

He smiled, and she felt tears well in her eyes. He wanted the child, too; she could see it in his eyes.

Excited now, she burst out, "Let's get married! Let's raise our child together! He will have his father and mother to love him and teach him." She waited, holding her breath. Never would she have thought that she, Elizabeth Powell, could be so bold as to ask a man to marry her!

But this was Isaac. She threw herself into his arms. He caught her deftly and looked down at her. Then he turned his face away. "I cannot."

Her heart dropped. "You cannot?" she repeated in disbelief. "What do you mean, you cannot? You are here. I am here. We can marry. We can give our child a home—"

"No," he said and turned back to face her. His handsome face was grim. "I cannot marry you."

"But why?" she cried in bewilderment. "I am not married, I am a widow." Suddenly she hesitated. "Are you already married? Have you taken an Indian wife? Is that the problem?" Fear cut through her.

"No." He shook his head for emphasis. "I am not married to an Indian woman. But I cannot marry

273

you." He eased his head back and took her arms from around his neck. She wanted to crumple to the floor and cry. Somehow, though, she managed to stay upright.

"I have to clear my name," he said to her.

But it was too late. A wave of shame had already engulfed her. He did not want to marry her. He did not love her, or their child.

"I must give a potlatch," he continued. "Until I do that, any child I have will be dishonored and humiliated. *You* will be dishonored and humiliated, married to me."

She shook her head. "No, Isaac, no!"

He held up a hand to stop her feeble protests. "You do not understand our Haida ways. I must do this thing. I must give a great potlatch and invite many people. Only after that will my name be cleared."

"You are right!" she cried out. "I do not understand you—or your Haida ways!" She wept in great, gulping sobs. "I only know you do not want me! Or our baby!"

He put his arms around her, "Oh, Lis-uh-buth," he murmured, and she sank against him. "I do want you. But I cannot do this. To you or to our child. I know what it is like to be a child of a slave, of a humiliated person. I will not put our son or daughter through that. Never!"

She heard the vehemence in his voice . . . but it could not match the agony in her heart. "Our child needs its father," she urged. "You are that father. I ask you, in God's name, to be a father to my child. To marry me and be with our child!" She realized that everything about her, every hope and dream she held for herself and their child, throbbed in those words. She needed Isaac to marry her and help her with their child. If he could not do that, well, then she was alone. Alone. *Oh, God, not alone!*

"I will not marry you," he said, his tone calm, implacable.

They faced each other like ancient enemies, each knowing the other's weaknesses, giving no quarter.

"Very well," she said, "I will not ask you again. I do not need to beg a man to marry me." She held her head high. It was she and her child. They would survive. She would see to it.

But inside, she wanted to cry, she wanted to throw herself on the floor and kick and scream her frustration and fear. She wanted to die of despair.

Instead, she walked over to the front door and opened it. "Get out," she said, pointing to the dark night that awaited beyond the red steps. "Go!"

He walked over to the door, and it seemed to her that it took him a long time. Then he was poised on the threshold. He looked at her, about to say something; then he turned and plunged out into the night.

She slammed the door after him.

Chapter Twenty-four

Three days later

When he fell into step beside her, Elizabeth wanted to pretend she did not see him. But they had only walked a dozen steps before her voice betrayed her. "I do not see why you have to walk with me, Isaac. Can't a woman walk through the streets of Fort Victoria without being accosted?" She fiddled with her beaded, orange reticule. Anything to keep from looking at him.

Next, she peered into the Celestial herbalist's shop. Someday she would get up the courage to go in that strange shop and smell the herbs and pick up the dried plants. Yes, she would. Finally, she whirled to face him. "I do not want you walking with me, Isaac. I have nothing to say to you. You have nothing to say to me."

He stared at her, his jaw clenched stubbornly.

"Lis-uh-buth," he began, but she held up her hand to ward off his words.

"Stop! I will not listen to you. We have said everything we have to say to each other. Good day!"

She left him standing by the Celestial herbalist's. When she turned around to see what had become of him, she saw that he was going into the shop. With a flounce in her step and a muttered, "Well!" she continued on her way.

She had reached the outskirts of the fort when he caught up with her. She was a little surprised, because she thought he'd given up on finding her. At last she halted and stared at him, her eyes searching his. "What is it you want, Isaac?"

He frowned at this new tack. "You no run away this time?"

"No, Isaac," she sighed. "I have decided I must stay and fight my battle." She knew he would not understand her allusion, but she didn't care.

At his look of bafflement, she said, "Tell me what it is you have to say. I will listen." *Then I will run for the hills*, she added silently.

He held out a wretched, dried-up weed to her. It looked like a chicken's claw with a little white ribbon tied around it. "I give this to you," he said, and there was an amused gleam in his eye, which she wanted to ignore.

She took the weed, sniffed it and said, "What is it?"

"Love plant," he said.

"Hmmph, doesn't work," she said and handed it back to him.

He looked disappointed. "The man from China say it help us become friends."

277

She shook her head adamantly. "No, Isaac, we cannot be friends. We have never *been* friends, we will never *be* friends. And a weed won't make us friends." Uncaring that her verb tenses might confuse him, she added, "Are you quite finished?"

He studied her until her face flushed under the heat of his perusal. He tucked the weed back into his jacket pocket and mumbled something.

"What did you want to say?" She barely restrained herself from stamping her foot in impatience.

"You doing all right, Lis-uh-buth?"

How was it that his deep, soft voice had the power to melt her? Undone, she said, "No, Isaac, I am not all right. But I will be. Soon." She stared off into the distance. "One day. Maybe." She turned back to him. He looked good. He was wearing a leather coat and a warm pair of pants and boots on his feet. He looked, as usual, extremely handsome. "And you, Isaac. Are you doing all right?"

She wanted to ask more: Where are you staying? How are you managing? Is William here? Are your friends here? Does anybody who loves you stay with you? Are you healing well after your canoe ordeal? But she refrained. Silence would have to suffice. She was no longer a part of his life. He had made that clear.

"So-so," he answered.

Despite herself, she laughed. She wouldn't have thought he even knew the meaning of the expression. But she'd forgotten his facility with the English language and his ability to pick up new words. "Just so-so, Isaac?" she mocked.

He shrugged. "I work. I look for land."

278

She started to walk, and he fell into step. She asked, "What are you going to do with land?"

"My family and I will buy some land. Set up a sawmill."

She pondered that for a while. "Why will you set up a sawmill?" she asked cautiously. She really should not be asking, should not be showing any interest at all in him after the way he had treated her, but she *was* curious.

"I sell lumber to the whites. I give jobs to Haidas."

She continued to walk as she thought about that. "You want a business here? At the fort?"

He nodded. "I need to make money, Lis-uh-buth."

She halted and peered at him. "Why?" Her heart started to pound faster. Could it be that he recognized his responsibility to her and their child? Was he trying to help?

"Potlatch," he explained.

She resumed walking. "Oh, that." Disappointment flooded her. Why was it every time she talked to this man they misunderstood one another? "Well," she said flippantly, "good luck with your old potlatch."

"Thank you, Lis-uh-buth," he answered gravely.

She increased her pace, hoping he was finished with all his talk and would just go away. But he didn't.

"What plans do you have, Lis-uh-buth?" he asked politely, matching her steps.

She frowned. "I do not have to tell you, Isaac."

"No," he answered agreeably. "Just would like to know."

"Why?" she challenged, halting.

279

He shrugged. "Just to know how my friend Lis-uh-buth is doing." He held his hands out, palm up, as if he were a perfectly innocent "friend."

She swung her reticule back and forth idly as she pondered how to answer him. "Isaac," she said at last. "I am not your friend. I do not want you for a friend." *I want you for a husband*, she wanted to add, but didn't dare. She couldn't face another rejection of herself and their child.

"Go find Susan, or—or William. They are your *friends*." She spat the word out, so foul did it taste in her mouth.

"You angry, Lis-uh-buth?"

She increased her stride. She wished he would just go away.

They had been walking outside the gates of the fort for some time. There was a forested area off to the west and a grassy meadow to the east.

They had walked in a large circle and were coming back along near the forest. They had said nothing to each other, but she had tolerated his presence because at least she had someone to walk with, and to guard her.

They passed large spruces and cedars. Isaac still remained silent. So did she. She decided to try one last time. "Isaac," she began. "You know I care about you. More than that, Isaac. I love—"

She halted and gasped. A man staggered from the bush and lurched toward Isaac. At first Elizabeth thought he was drunk, but then she saw that his staggering was a ploy to get closer to Isaac. Then the man jammed a pistol against Isaac's temple.

Isaac froze.

Elizabeth fumbled in her reticule, trying to find

her own half-forgotten, pearl-handled pistol. Thank God Cyril had insisted she carry one!

Elizabeth stared at the assailant. He looked strangely familiar. He was Indian; his thick hair was matted. "You stop. I kill you!" he said to Isaac.

"Jake!" she cried. "Whatever are you doing?"

Isaac watched the slave warily.

The slave glanced at Elizabeth, obviously unhappy to see her. "I must kill him," he said with a pleading note in his voice. "Great chief say so."

She frowned. "The chief told you to kill Isaac?" She closed her fingers around the small handle of her pistol. Carefully she inched it higher until it was near the top of her reticule. All she had to do was lift and fire. "Why does he want Isaac killed?" If she could keep Jake talking, she sensed she would have the advantage.

Isaac spoke up. "My uncle wants you to kill me?" There was resignation in his voice. It must be terrible, thought Elizabeth, to have relatives who wanted to kill one.

"I do not want to!" wailed Jake. He sobbed and dashed tears from his eyes, but the hand with the gun remained amazingly steady.

She lifted her own gun and trained it on the sobbing slave.

"But he tell me I must. Or he kill my two boys."

"Your sons?" asked Elizabeth, frowning.

"Yes," cried Jake. "My two sons. That chief is so cruel. If I do not kill this man, the chief kill my boys."

Isaac and Elizabeth were silent at this. Though Elizabeth could sympathize with the slave, she did not agree that killing Isaac was the best way out of his dilemma.

281

"You put that gun down now, Jake," she said in a cold voice. "Or I will kill *you!*" By God, she was not going to lose another man. Cyril had been killed by drunks. She was *not* going to lose Isaac again!

Jake looked at her, trying to determine whether she was serious or not. Grimly she nudged the air with the pistol. "Drop your gun," she said, "or your boys will have no father at all."

The thought of his sons must have convinced Jake, because he dropped his pistol. It clattered to the ground.

Isaac bent down and picked it up. He peered at it. "What are these scratches on it?"

"Chief's name," answered Jake sullenly.

Isaac tucked the pistol in his waistband. Jake's eyes followed it.

"Now," said Elizabeth, "you back away from us, Jake. Go on." She waved the gun.

Reluctantly he took several steps back.

She let out her breath. Whether she really would have shot him, she didn't know. But she thought she would have. She'd been angry enough to.

"You kill me now, miss," said Jake.

She frowned. "No. I don't want to kill you, Jake. I just want to make sure you don't kill Isaac."

Jake shook his head slowly. "It not matter now. I be dead. My sons be dead. Chief kill us all when he find out I not kill Haida chief." He glanced sorrowfully at Isaac, the cause of his woes.

"Nonsense," said Elizabeth.

"It true," said Jake and there was such dullness in his voice that Elizabeth began to fear for him. "Chief kill my boys."

"Did All Fear His Name send you to kill me?" asked Isaac.

"Not that chief," answered Jake. "The other one."

"Which one is that?" asked Isaac in surprise.

"Chief Blackfish. He angry at you. You make him lick up spit."

Isaac's guarded glance met Elizabeth's. She wondered what that news meant, because Isaac looked a little surprised.

Isaac turned back to Jake. "Blackfish sent you down to Fort Victoria to kill me? He knows I survived, then."

Jake nodded. "He not happy to hear that. He send me to kill you. I did not want to, but—" He shrugged. "He have my boys. So I do it."

While Isaac pondered the slave's words, Elizabeth glanced around nervously. There was no one nearby and no one watching them from the fort. Now that the excitement was over, she was beginning to get nervous. What if other Indians came along to help Jake? "Isaac," she suggested, "let us return to the fort."

He nodded. "You too, Jake," he said.

The slave started sobbing. "It not matter now. Nothing matter. That chief kill my boys now. You give me gun so I shoot myself."

Isaac frowned thoughtfully. Then he said to Jake, "Do not talk of killing yourself. Who will help your boys? If you die, no one. Your wife cannot help them."

Jake stopped his sobbing and looked at Isaac. Slowly he nodded and said in the Indian language, "It is as you say, Haida chief."

"You go back to Tsimshian village," Isaac an-

283

swered in Indian. "You tell Chief Blackfish you could not find me."

Jake sniffed back a sob.

"Then I send for you. For your wife. For your boys. You come down and work for me. But do not tell chief that. Not yet."

For the first time, Jake looked hopeful. He sank to his knees on the ground and bowed in front of Isaac. "Thank you, thank you," he cried.

"Get up," ordered Isaac, looking embarrassed.

Jake scrambled to his feet, doing his best to oblige Isaac.

"Remember," said Isaac. "You tell Chief Blackfish you could not find me. You tried very hard to find me. You tell him that."

"Then you come for me and my boys?"

Isaac nodded. "When the time is right."

Jake smiled and bowed. "I thank you, Great Chief." Isaac nodded again, and Jake trotted off into the trees.

"Do you think he'll come back and try to kill you again?" asked Elizabeth, wondering what had been said.

"No. He will go back to Tsimshians. I help him. Later."

Elizabeth shook her head. What kind of man helped someone who'd tried to kill him? Isaac had depths she had never suspected. She lowered her pistol into the reticule.

Just then, Jake parted some branches of trees and called out to them. Elizabeth grabbed for her pistol.

"I need gun," said Jake, trotting toward them.

"He's going to try again," warned Elizabeth under her breath. "Do not trust him, Isaac. He's going to kill you!" Her hand shook as she held the gun. This time, she feared, she really would have to shoot him. But she would do it to save Isaac. Part of her mind registered how much Isaac truly meant to her.

"Don't come any closer, Jake!" she cried out, pulling her pistol out of her reticule and pointing it at him with a shaking hand.

Isaac crossed his arms across his chest and watched the oncoming slave stolidly.

Jake stopped and held out both hands, palms up to Isaac. "Please, Great Chief," he said. "I need pistol. It belongs to Chief Blackfish. When I go back to him, he will want his pistol."

"Isaac, don't give it to him," warned Elizabeth. "He'll shoot you with it."

Isaac and Jake stared at one another. Elizabeth could see the tension in Isaac's strong frame. Finally Isaac said, "I give you the pistol. But if you kill me, you kill any hope your boys go free."

Jake's head jerked upright at that. "I not kill you," he said at last, slowly. "But you help me. Now. I trust you."

Isaac smiled a half grin. "I have to trust you, too." He pulled the pistol out of his waistband and held it out to Jake, handle first.

Jake reached out and took the weapon. Elizabeth kept her own weapon trained on the slave. If he shot Isaac, she would—

Jake tucked the pistol in his ragged belt and patted the handle. "I go now. Back to Tsimshian village. I help my sons. You remember this: I no kill you. You help my sons." There was a pleading note mixed with a warning note in Jake's voice.

Isaac nodded. "I keep my word."

Elizabeth let out her breath, unaware she'd been holding it.

Jake trotted off. She watched him go. Then she glanced at Isaac.

He was watching her. His eyes dropped to her gun. "Maybe you like me. Maybe you want to be my friend, Lis-uh-buth," he drawled.

She tucked the pistol back into her reticule. "Pshaw!" she exclaimed. She wouldn't let him think she was actually protecting him. "I just don't like to see anyone killed." She wiped the sweat from her brow.

"I do not believe you," he said.

She tossed her head. "Believe what you want."

He grinned. "I think you my friend. I think you kill Jake to help me." He reached into his jacket and pulled out the little claw-shaped plant he'd found at the Celestial shop. He held it out to her. "Friends?"

She glanced at the thing. Then at him. She held out her hand and took it.

"Maybe," she said.

She didn't quite know how she found herself in bed with Isaac, but it felt different. Very different. The only other two times they had made love had been outdoors. But tonight they were in her bedroom, with fourteen lit candles to brighten the darkness and a bouquet of flowers to perfume the air. On her dresser, next to the comb that Isaac had given her, lay the little dried-up clawed plant from the Celestial apothecary's store. Over them was draped a lovely counterpane, a warm, blue and green and purple quilt, and under them were clean white sheets; crocheted white pillows propped up their heads. *Isaac is definitely more than a friend tonight*, she thought wryly.

She slanted a glance at his long brown frame, unfortunately mostly hidden by sheets and quilt. It was cold in the room, and she snuggled further down under the covers. Then she quickly lifted the top sheet, and her eyes widened.

"Isaac!" she cried.

He yanked the sheet back down. "Scars," he said patiently. "From my time with the Tsimshians."

Terrible scars, she thought. Huge purple welts ran along his ribs and stomach, welts that had yet to fully heal. Fear and pain tore through her. She ran a hand over his black, black hair, brushing it back from his craggy face. "Oh, Isaac, what they did to you."

He took her hand, turned it and kissed her palm, his lips soft against her skin. Her heart almost broke at thinking what he had gone through. For her. Then he lowered her hand to one of the scars on his ribs and patted it. "You heal it," he said, half jokingly. Then his black-fringed dark eyes met hers and he pulled her closer until their noses were touching.

"I lived because of you," he breathed. "The whole time, I thought only of you. That is what kept me alive."

She gasped at this. "Oh, Isaac," she moaned, pulling his head to her bosom. "I wish—I wish—" But she didn't know what words she could tell him as she hugged him to her. She couldn't speak of her fear for him, of her loss of him . . . "I wish it had never happened to you," she said at last.

He brought his head up and reached for her, putting his arms around her. Soon they were locked in an embrace, and she was holding him as tightly as she could; she would never let him go. Once she'd thought him dead, and today she'd almost lost him to an assassin's pistol. She would hold him to her, she would keep him with her and never let him go.

He was kissing her all over now, and she loosened her hold just a little. Their lips met, and his tongue entered her mouth, searching, calling to her. She answered, entwining her tongue with his. Soon it was their bodies that entwined; she rubbed her breasts against his chest and her bigger belly against his. They were alive. They had this day. Tonight they would love one another.

He entered her slowly, gently, as if she were a delicate flower. And she opened for him, wanting him inside her, wanting to feel the closeness of him, to breathe in his essence, to know that he was alive, that she was alive, that they were one. A sense of urgency swept over them as their loveplay deepened. "Oh, Isaac," she moaned. "I love you so much."

He did not answer, but she felt his muscles tense and felt him drive further into her. She welcomed him, yielding her heart and her body. This was Isaac, the man she wanted, the father of her child, the man she loved. She clung to him, and held on to him until their wild ride together subsided. Then he held her, and she looked into his eyes, fiery in the candlelight.

She wanted to tell him how much she loved him, how much his "death" had hurt her, but the words would not come. So she settled for cupping his face in her hands and closing her eyes and kissing him, softly, gently, lingering upon his forehead where his black lock of hair always fell.

This single kiss must tell him what her words could not: that she had feared greatly for him, that she had missed him deeply and that she thanked God that he was with her at last, safe and sound. And further, that she loved him and would always love him and that she was so happy he was the father of her child.

One little kiss must tell him all this, she thought. *One little wordless kiss.*

But he seemed to understand, for he wrapped her in his arms and then he fell quiet, until his even breathing told her he was asleep.

She lay there awake in the candlelight, wondering what turn her life would now take. And wondering, in her heart of hearts, if he could possibly love her as deeply and profoundly as she loved him.

Chapter Twenty-five

"Auntie!" cried Elizabeth, opening her arms wide.

Aunt Elizabeth fell into them, and the two women hugged. Elizabeth closed her eyes. Having her dear aunt here was bliss. "Oh, it is so good that you are here!" she cried, holding on tightly to the older woman.

Auntie patted her back. "There, there, dear," she soothed. "I came as quickly as I could."

Elizabeth buried her head on her aunt's shoulder. She wanted to cuddle in the old arms. All was well now that Auntie was here. She felt her aunt patting her head. The dear, dear soul.

Reluctantly Elizabeth raised her head and looked into her aunt's blue eyes. "Thank God you've come!"

"Hush now, child," said Auntie. "No need for strong language."

Elizabeth smiled and stepped back. "Come into

my house, Auntie," she said. Sometimes strong language was all that could express how she felt.

Her aunt picked up her valise and stepped across the threshold. Elizabeth glanced around outside. "No Uncle John this time?" Not that she wanted him here. But he was, after all, her aunt's husband.

"I have something to tell you, dear," said her aunt as she walked into the kitchen. She set her valise down and plopped down into a chair. She glanced around. "Ooh, my, but it's warm in here. And you are certainly burning the oil lamps."

"I like it that way, Auntie," said Elizabeth. "Now, what is it you have to tell me?"

Auntie straightened and took off her hat. She fidgeted with her coat and finally ended up standing and taking that off, too. Then she sat back down. Through it all, Elizabeth waited patiently. She guessed Aunt Elizabeth was a little upset.

Elizabeth sat slowly down in her rocking chair, giving her aunt time to settle.

"Well, dear, I came here as quickly as I could," said Auntie. "As soon as I found out about poor Cyril, why, I just had to come."

Elizabeth reached over and patted her aunt's hand. "I appreciate your coming to see me at this time, Auntie. It is a great comfort to me."

Her aunt smiled at her, pleased. "I would have come sooner, but . . . well, something got in the way."

Cyril had passed away two months earlier. Travel from Olympia would be slow, especially with the winter weather, but not *that* slow, mused Elizabeth.

Her aunt took a breath. "I have decided to leave your uncle."

Elizabeth stopped rocking.

"John Butler is not . . . er, he is not the man he represented himself to be."

Elizabeth waited. She had already told her aunt that he was a murderer. But her aunt had not believed her. Why the change?

"I find I can no longer live with the man. I am suing for divorce."

Elizabeth gasped. "This is very serious."

Her aunt nodded, a firm look on her sagging face.

"But I am glad for you, Auntie," said Elizabeth. "It is a wise thing to do."

Her aunt shuddered. "You do not know all there is to know about that man."

"I know some," said Elizabeth. "And what I know I do not like. I told you before—"

Her aunt held up a hand. "I do not want to hear it," she said.

No talk about the murder, then, thought Elizabeth. "What is it he did?" she asked cautiously.

Her aunt fell silent. "He has taken to drinking," she said at last.

Elizabeth nodded, afraid that if she said anything, her aunt would not confide in her.

"And when he drinks, he is . . . well, he is, er, he is cruel to me."

"Does he say mean things?"

"Yes."

The ticking of the clock sounded unnaturally loud. Elizabeth's fingers tightened on the wooden arms of the rocker.

"Did—did he do anything? Did he hit you?" She held her breath.

"I'd prefer not to say," said her aunt.

Elizabeth rocked furiously in her chair. She hated the thought of her dear aunt married to a cruel, violent man. When Elizabeth suddenly realized the rocker was inching up so close to the table that there was no room for her belly, she said, "You are welcome to stay here, Auntie. I need help, what with the baby coming. Would you be so kind as to stay and help me?"

"Why, yes, dear." Her aunt beamed. "I was going to suggest that very thing."

Elizabeth smiled. Now her aunt need not return to that terrible man. After the long years of her aunt helping Elizabeth and protecting her in San Francisco, Elizabeth could now offer the same protection to her. "I am taking in sewing to help support myself," Elizabeth said ruefully, pointing to a half-finished morning dress draped over a hanger. "I make enough to pay for the food I eat. And I find that teaching reading and writing supplements my income quite nicely."

"Well, *I* can certainly help with the sewing, dear." Aunt Elizabeth held up her two plump hands and smiled.

Elizabeth smiled back. They would do well together, she and her aunt.

"Welcome to Fort Victoria, Auntie!"

Two days later there was a knock at the door.

Elizabeth opened it and Isaac stood there, a long salmon dangling from one hand. She stepped aside to let him in. "Oh, how very nice," she exclaimed. During her time at the fort, she'd grown to relish the taste of the flavorful, orange fish.

He held it out to her and she took the fish eagerly. "My aunt and I shall enjoy that for dinner."

"Your aunt?"

"My aunt has come to stay with me," announced Elizabeth. He looked around. "She is at a fitting right now. She is sewing a dress for a neighbor."

He nodded. "I have come to tell you something."

She waited, watching him warily. "Yes?"

"I have the land now."

She frowned. "How did you get it?"

"My family. They help."

She did not quite know how that worked, but she nodded as if she did.

"I start my sawmill very soon."

"Well, I suppose that is wonderful news," she said flatly. But it did not make her feel happy. Nothing Isaac did made sense to her. And each day brought the birth of her child—their child—closer. And he was doing nothing, absolutely nothing, to help her. It was all on her shoulders. The sewing, the teaching. Where the next meal was coming from. All on her shoulders. Thank God for Auntie's arrival.

The front door opened again and her aunt stepped inside. "Brrr, that rain!" she exclaimed. She stopped short when she spotted Isaac. "Who—?"

Elizabeth introduced her aunt to Isaac. There was an awkward silence. Her aunt visibly straightened, and a cold look came into her eyes.

"I know I have not mentioned him to you before, Auntie—" she began.

"Is this the young man who stole you away from us?" Her aunt's voice was ice.

"Yes," squeaked Elizabeth.

"Is this the man who is the father of your child?" More ice.

"Yes." Elizabeth's answer was barely audible to her own ears.

Her aunt put her fists on her hips and glared at Isaac. "And what plans do you have for marrying my niece?" she demanded.

Isaac stared down at her. "None." His jaw was set grimly.

"Then leave this house. At once!" Her aunt pointed to the door.

Isaac walked over to the door and opened it.

Elizabeth said nothing. She had to admit that she was proud of her aunt. Not, of course, that she would say so. "Auntie—" she began.

Her aunt held up a stubborn hand. "In our family, we marry."

And we divorce. But Elizabeth did not quite have the courage to say so aloud.

Auntie turned to Isaac. "Go!" she blazed.

Isaac seemed about to say something. His face was dark with anger. But he turned and left, closing the door quietly behind him.

There was a long silence after he left.

"I know you think it wrong, dear," said her aunt. "But you will see that it is for the best. If that young man won't do the honorable thing and marry you, you do not want him. If he won't stay around and help raise his own child, you are better off without him."

"Yes, Auntie," she answered meekly.

"I suppose you know I cannot let you into the house."

It was the third time Isaac had come to the door in as many days. Both previous times Aunt Elizabeth had turned him away with the wrath of a

Greek Fury while Elizabeth watched secretly from her bedroom window. This time, however, Auntie was out, fitting a dress for another neighbor, and Elizabeth had been able to answer the door.

"My aunt tells me I should not see you or have anything to do with you."

Isaac's black eyes flashed. "What do I have to do? Kidnap you?"

She looked at him reproachfully. "Surely you know better. That did not work the last time."

"It worked better than this."

Isaac looked grim, she thought. And he looked tired. Had he been getting his rest? Where was he staying?

"Oh, Isaac," sighed Elizabeth. "My aunt is merely trying to protect me."

He frowned. "She does not have to protect you from me."

"Oh? She thinks she does." *And so do I.* "After all, you have said you will not marry me. You know I carry your child, yet you do not want me as a wife."

He glared at her, his jaw set stubbornly. "There is good reason," he said at last. "I must give the potlatch—"

She held up a hand. "I know, I know, the potlatch." She sighed. This discussion was not getting anywhere. She glanced behind him. It had stopped raining, and it would be a while before Auntie returned. "Let us go for a walk," she suggested. "I'll get my coat."

They walked through the muddy streets, staying to one side to keep the mud off Elizabeth's shoes.

"How is your sawmill coming along?" she asked politely.

"It is started. I have some of the frame up, but it will take more work." He glanced at her. "There are two men interested in buying wood from me. One wants to build a hotel."

"Customers already?" she murmured. "My, how fortunate for you."

He didn't answer, and she slanted a glance at him. The sheen of the sun on his black hair intrigued her. She wanted to reach up and touch it but she did not dare. After all, he did not love her, and wanted little to do with her. She would keep her distance.

"It is good about the sawmill," he conceded at last.

"Are you so certain that your sawmill will make money?" she asked.

He shrugged. "I try. I hope it will make money. I need the white man's money."

She laughed, and her voice sounded brittle even to her own ears. "Just because you need money doesn't mean your business will do well, Isaac."

He glanced at her. "You care, Lis-uh-buth? You care if I make money?"

She shot him an angry glance. "Of course I care. I want you to succeed. I want your sawmill to do well." *I want you to give that damn potlatch and get it over with!* "It's just that people have tried to do things before and failed."

He looked surprised. "You know someone tried a sawmill?"

"Not a sawmill," she confessed reluctantly. "A— a gold mine."

He looked bewildered. "I am not finding a gold mine. I make a sawmill, Lis-uh-buth. No gold around here, anyway."

She flushed. "I know you are not looking for a gold mine, Isaac. It's just that . . . well, my father—" She hesitated. She had told no one what she'd learned about her father, nor about his worthless gold mine. She certainly had not told Auntie. Aunt Elizabeth hated any mention of Theodore Powell.

"My—my father had a gold mine," she said at last.

Isaac looked interested. "He do well?"

She shook her head. "No. There was no gold. And he died."

Isaac frowned. "He is dead? Your father is dead?"

She nodded.

She heard his intake of breath. "Your father is dead. Your mother is dead. Your Cyril is dead. You thought I was dead. Death is a big part of your life, Lis-uh-buth."

"Yes," she agreed sadly.

"You have your auntie," he continued. "Do you have anyone else?"

She pondered, then shook her head. "Only my auntie."

He frowned. "I have a big family," he said. "I have my father, my aunt, my cousins, my clan. Then I have my village. Then all the Haidas."

"You do have a lot of family," she agreed sadly, feeling more like an orphan than ever.

"Tell me about your father. His gold mine."

"Not much to tell," she admitted and briefly explained the whole sad story about her search for her father, about Governor Douglas's help and about the mining claim found in her dead father's hand.

"He think of you, Lis-uh-buth," said Isaac when

she'd finished. "When he dies. That is a good thing, I think."

"Yes," she admitted softly. There were unshed tears blocking her throat and she found she could say no more.

After they had walked in silence for a time, he said, "In Indian way, if it was from my father, I would go there."

"Go to the mining claim, you mean?" she asked in surprise.

"Yes. A gift like that from your father is valuable."

"No," she corrected him sadly. "It is worth nothing. The governor told me the claim was useless."

"Maybe so," said Isaac, and she heard a stubborn note in his voice, "but it is a gift. From your father. Go and see it. See where he worked. Where he died. That is the Indian way."

When she said nothing, he added, "I will go with you. That will help you. Too much death in your life, Lis-uh-buth."

She was touched by his kindness and silently marveled at his compassion toward her. To her surprise, she found herself saying aloud, "Very well, Isaac. We will do that."

After a week's travel they arrived at the cabin.

Aunt Elizabeth had vehemently disagreed that Elizabeth should travel alone with Isaac. And when she heard it was to the place where Theodore Powell had spent his last days, Elizabeth thought her aunt would have an apoplectic fit. To Elizabeth's eternal mortification, Auntie had insisted upon coming along with them, to protect Elizabeth's reputation.

Now the three of them, Isaac, Elizabeth and Auntie, stood staring at the cabin. Budding aspens waved in the early spring breeze. A creek, swollen from spring rains, dashed madly past them at some distance. Two big Haida men, friends of Isaac's, fished in the creek.

"So this is the cabin where Father died," murmured Elizabeth sadly.

"Hmmph," said Auntie. "Just what I expected. A fitting end to a wandering fool."

When she saw Elizabeth's hurt look, she said, "Sorry."

Isaac frowned. He and Auntie had not gotten along well at all during the whole trip, and Elizabeth was about ready to throw both of them in the creek. However, she took a breath and said, "I know you did not approve of him, Auntie. But he was my father, all the same."

"He did not do well by you or your mother," answered her aunt stoutly. "My sister died early because of him."

Elizabeth stared at her.

"It is true," insisted Aunt Elizabeth. "Your mother would still be alive if that man had not run off."

"He wrote to us," said Elizabeth loyally. "He was going to send for us. Mama showed me the letter, written in his own hand."

"Hmph, well, he didn't send for you, did he?" needled her aunt. "Just like everything else that Theodore did. Never quite happened the way he said it would. Couldn't depend on that man for anything."

Elizabeth gritted her teeth and stared in silence at the cabin.

"We go in," said Isaac at her side.

"No, we don't," said Auntie. "I'm not going near that place."

"You wait," agreed Isaac. He started forward.

Elizabeth hurried after him, leaving her aunt to wait, arms crossed and glaring ferociously at the cabin.

"Did your father kidnap your mother?" asked Isaac cautiously.

Elizabeth glanced at him in surprise. "Kidnap? No. Why do you ask?"

He eyed her. "Aunt sound like she is angry at dead father. Same way family acts when someone is kidnapped."

"Hmm," said Elizabeth thoughtfully. Now, why would he know about such things? "No, my father did not kidnap my mother. But my aunt did not like him. He told her and my mother that he would return for us, but he never did. We received only that one letter. He promised us," said Elizabeth in a dreamy voice, "but we never heard from him again."

Isaac shook his head. "Too bad."

It was said compassionately.

They walked up to the door. The cabin was dilapidated, made of peeling logs with a lean-to shed on one side. The shake roof was littered with branches and debris shaken down by winter storms.

Isaac pushed; the door creaked open.

He stepped back to let her look inside.

Heart beating, she peered into the darkened interior and saw—nothing. Only an old wooden bed with rotted, crisscrossed rope for a mattress. A table and a chair. A half-gone sack of flour that the mice had chewed open. Little white mice tracks led everywhere. There was no sign of Theodore.

Of course, they must have buried his body, Elizabeth scolded herself. Once they'd found him, they would have buried him.

Still, it hurt to look at the cabin where he had stayed. His last days on Earth had been spent here, and her throat ached again. She wished she had known him, her father. Been able to talk with him, visit with him. Now it would never happen. He was gone, and she was alone . . .

She stood inside the cabin, looking around the tiny dwelling. There was nothing on the walls, no curtains, nothing of a homey nature. Her heart sank at the loneliness the room indicated. No beauty, no warmth, nothing but bare spare, utilitarian necessity. How sad that her father should meet death in such a spartan place.

She thought of the mining claim. She'd brought it with her and she reached into her reticule and pulled it out. In the dim light she could barely see the faint pencil lines, her father's handwriting, deeding the mine to her.

She sighed.

"What is that?" Isaac's voice startled her. She'd completely forgotten about him and Auntie, so intent was she on her father and her great sense of loss.

She folded the paper and tucked it back into the reticule. "Just my father's claim."

Isaac glanced around. "Not much here," he said.

"No. Not much," she agreed. If she let it, she knew the pain of her father's loss could crash in on her and strike her to her knees, so much longing did she have for him. And then it slowly passed and she could breathe again.

She moved a step closer to Isaac. "He lived here. Died here." She swallowed. "My father."

Isaac took her hand, and she felt the warmth of his hand close around hers. "He would be proud of you, Lis-uh-buth," said Isaac. "If he knew you, he would have been proud."

She shrugged. "Nothing to be proud of, Isaac," she said sadly. "I haven't done anything with my life. Just kind of drifted from San Francisco to Olympia, then to Fort Victoria. With your help," she added wryly. "But not really very much."

"Hmmph," said Isaac. "You go to white man's school to learn. You travel with aunt. You take care of her. You help your friends when they about to be shot. That is all good."

She looked at him. Maybe her father would have been proud of her. . . . Well, she'd never know now, would she?

Heart heavy, she turned away. "Auntie is waiting," she mumbled and walked out the door and stepped into the weak sunshine.

Isaac followed her. Elizabeth stood silently, watching the two Haida men fishing and feeling the brisk breeze on her cheek. Her father's last resting place. At least it was tranquil.

"Can we go now?" demanded Auntie. "I don't want to be caught in the mountains when the sun goes down."

Elizabeth started and glanced at the sun. It was low in the sky. Her aunt was right. If they did not leave soon, they would be trapped overnight on the trail somewhere. "Of course," Elizabeth agreed. "We can leave now."

Her aunt promptly started back along the path they'd traveled. With a shout to the Haidas, Isaac started after her. Elizabeth thoughtfully followed.

They reached the little town of Blakeville just as the sun was setting and slowly made their way to the hotel where they'd stayed the previous night. Elizabeth and her aunt took one of the rooms, and the Haidas left to camp on the outskirts of the little town. Her aunt and Elizabeth were getting ready for bed—Elizabeth was already in her night rail— when there was a loud pounding on the door. With a look of alarm, her aunt sprang to the door like a guard dog. "Who is it?" she cried through the door.

"It is Isaac. Open up," came the voice from the other side.

Auntie glanced at Elizabeth, then snapped, "No!"

"Please, Auntie," begged Elizabeth, feeling mortified. No doubt every guest in the hotel could hear Isaac bellowing.

"No!" hissed her aunt. "You are in your night garments. He shall not see you like that!"

"I'll get dressed," Elizabeth offered, between poundings on the door.

"No!" Her aunt shook her head stubbornly. "He mustn't see you like that!"

Elizabeth dared not remind her aunt that Isaac had seen more of her than showed in her night rail.

More banging on the door.

"Go away!" shouted Auntie.

"Auntie!" huffed Elizabeth. "How can you?"

"I do not want him here. It is late. Why, it is ten P.M.!"

"If you do not let him in, he'll keep shouting and pounding," warned Elizabeth.

"Let him."

Obviously, her aunt was uncaring of the effect upon the neighbors. Elizabeth paced back and forth before the door. "Please, Auntie!" But her pleas were futile.

Finally Isaac stopped pounding and silence fell upon the floor. Elizabeth tiptoed over and placed her ear next to the wall. She could hear nothing.

"He's gone," said Auntie with a note of satisfaction in her voice.

Elizabeth met her aunt's gray glance. "Yes, he is. I wonder what he wanted."

Her aunt shrugged. "Nothing important, I'm sure."

Elizabeth raised an eyebrow at this, but she said nothing. She staggered over to the bed, suddenly tired from the travels of the day. She got into her bed and waited patiently for her aunt to blow out the lamp.

Snuggling into the quilts, Elizabeth yawned and again mused drowsily, "I wonder what he wanted."

Her aunt's snoring was her only answer.

Elizabeth awoke to the morning sunlight pouring in through the thin yellow curtains. Something had awakened her—there it was again. More pounding on the door.

"Go away," muttered Auntie, pulling her pillow over her head. Seizing her chance, Elizabeth got to her feet, padded to the door and threw it open.

"Isaac!" Her hand clutched her throat, drawing her night rail close about her.

"Lis-uh-buth!" His hair was askew, but my, he looked handsome.

"What—what is it, Isaac?"

"I find out something important. I talked to Indian man from here. He say your mine claim is not worthless! Much gold!"

Chapter Twenty-six

Elizabeth sauntered along the narrow street of Fort Victoria, carefully stepping around a pothole. The sun was out, she felt cheerful—except when she contemplated Isaac and his potlatch—and it was a good day in her life, she told herself.

As she strolled past the shops, she happened to glance across the street. And halted in her tracks.

She blinked, thinking perhaps her eyes had deceived her. But they had not.

It was the old Indian chief from the village where she'd gone with Isaac—the man who was his uncle, Chief All Fear His Name. At his elbow walked Jake, the slave.

Several other Indian men, all dressed in unique combinations of white man's clothes mixed with Indian blankets, walked with the chief.

She frowned. She felt her face flush with anger. It was all his fault, this chief who had given the

Theresa Scott

order to kill Isaac. His fault that she'd had to flee. His fault that she had thought Isaac was dead and then married Cyril. His fault, his fault!

Raging, she crossed the street, ignoring the mud and potholes as she marched up to him. "It is all your fault!" she cried. "If you hadn't ordered Isaac's death, we'd be married by now!"

The old Indian chief turned piercing black eyes upon her, as did the Indian men with him. But Elizabeth was in no mood to let a few sets of piercing black eyes upset her. Jake's eyes rounded in surprise.

She swung to face him. "Tell him," she ordered. "Tell this chief that it is all his fault. He ordered Isaac's death. Everything bad that has happened to me ever since has been *his* fault!"

All her anger at the turn of events in her life came rushing over her. Nothing, *nothing* was going as she wanted, and it was all this man's fault! He had ordered Isaac to find Mr. Burt and Uncle John, which had started the whole mess. Why, even her kidnapping could be laid directly at his door!

"And now Isaac has to give a potlatch—an expensive potlatch—to clear his name! And it's all your fault!"

Jake said something in the Indian language to the chief, but every now and then he looked warily back at Elizabeth.

"Tell him!" she demanded anew.

When Jake finished translating, the old chief drew himself up to his full but short height. He spoke at some length, gesticulating in the air. Several of the men with him nodded in agreement.

When he finished, he waited for Jake to translate.

But Jake was reluctant.

"Tell me," she ordered. "Tell me what he said."

Jake had a sheepish look on his face. "He say he did not know Isaac still alive. He go and get him now. Isaac be in big trouble," added Jake reproachfully, and Elizabeth doubted that the chief had said *that*.

Elizabeth glared suspiciously at the old chief. He looked back at her, his black eyes bright.

Guilt crept into her anger. "Bah!" she exclaimed. "He won't find Isaac." Isaac was working at his sawmill. *She* would not tell these men where he was.

"Do not be so sure," warned Jake.

She stared at Jake. "But that other chief knew . . . that one who sent you to kill Isaac, he knew that Isaac was alive—"

"You not talk about that," interrupted Jake hastily, glancing at the old chief. "This chief tell the truth. He not know Isaac still alive. Other chief not tell him. Other chief only want to kill Isaac."

Elizabeth frowned. "Well, I am angry at *this* chief! He started all the problems I have. And me with a baby on the way."

"Old chief do that too?" asked Jake in astonishment.

Elizabeth stared at him, mortified. "No, no, he did not. Don't tell him I said that."

Jake relaxed a little. "He say that you very angry. Should not yell at great chief like that in front of his middle chiefs and little chiefs. He not like. You have to give him many canoes for insult."

Feeling chastened, Elizabeth suddenly found herself staring at her shoes for a moment. Then she lifted her head defiantly. "But he is to blame for my predicament." She glared at the old chief. "And I won't give him any canoes."

"Maybe he just testing, see if you give canoes easily." Jake watched her, then glanced nervously at the chief. "Do not tell Isaac that I here with old chief. Isaac told me to stay in village and wait."

Elizabeth sighed. "I suppose this chief forced you to come to Fort Victoria with him."

"To talk white man's talk, yes."

The life of a slave was a precarious one, she thought. To Jake she said, "You tell him this: it is all his fault that Isaac has to gather possessions for the potlatch. It was this chief who humiliated Isaac. And now Isaac has to potlatch to overcome that. You tell him he has to give *me* canoes!" Perhaps she could get the canoes for Isaac to help with his potlatch.

Jake dutifully translated. When the old chief was done speaking his answer, Jake said, "He say he not give you canoes. You get your own canoes. He say, too, that he not want you to marry Isaac. Now he know Isaac alive, he want him for his nephew again. He give good wife to Isaac." Jake shrugged unhappily, indicating he was only the bearer of bad news.

Now Elizabeth was really angry. "Well, that is just too bad!" she cried. "I am not going to stand by and let him marry Isaac off!" The very idea! This old chief was decidedly not a helpful man.

There was a burst of Indian language as the old chief, his black eyes spitting fury, spoke directly at Elizabeth. When he was done, she said to Jake, "What did he say?"

"He say if you want to help Isaac, you give Isaac money. Give him money in front of everyone."

Speaking in an even voice, Jake added, "You not take this old chief's advice. If you give money to Isaac in front of people, then you humiliate him. He will never marry you, believe me. Old chief knows this. He angry at you."

Elizabeth stared open-mouthed at the old chief. Her brain worked frantically as she tried to come up with something to reply, but all she could think was that this old chief, this cunning old chief, right here in the streets of Fort Victoria, was working to destroy her standing with Isaac. The very nerve of him. And oh, the cunning!

"You close mouth," advised Jake.

She snapped her mouth shut. Then she said abruptly, "You tell him, tell him . . ." She pondered. "You tell him that I will take his very good advice. Tell him many thanks for such wise advice."

Jake looked at her askance. "You sure? You fool to take it."

"Jake!" she exclaimed, glaring at him. "You tell him what I said. I will take care of myself! This old chief is not going to outwit me."

"Maybe," said Jake. "He might. He pretty smart."

"Tell him," gritted Elizabeth.

Jake spoke in the Indian language to the old chief, and finally the old chief nodded his head with great dignity.

"He believe you. He think you fool woman. I tell him you go and give Isaac money for potlatch."

The old chief actually cracked a mocking smile.

Elizabeth breathed a sigh of relief. He did think her a fool, didn't he? Well, now that she knew what his plan was, she had better find Isaac. And she had

311

better make sure that this old chief had no influence on him at all!

"Please give my polite thanks to this chief," she told Jake. "Tell him . . . oh, tell him good-bye for me. And I never want to see him again!"

"I not tell him that part," said Jake with a grin.

She hurried off to find Isaac, leaving the great chief and his retainers standing in the street, Jake still translating.

Chapter Twenty-seven

"Isaac, I tell you, I have received money from my gold mine. Quite a significant amount of money. I give it to you. You use it. Go ahead and use my money for your potlatch."

When she saw the anger cross his face, she held her breath. His lips tightened, but he only shook his head and said nothing. However, she knew him well enough to know that he was very, very angry.

So, she thought. *That crafty old chief knew this. Whatever I've said has greatly angered Isaac. I'd better not try this tactic any longer.*

Fortunately, she had taken Jake's advice and was offering the money to Isaac in private, not in front of other Indians as the old chief had suggested.

"Never mind," she soothed. "I see you do not want to do this. We will think of something else." Indeed she would! The longer it took him to give his danged potlatch, the longer she would have to wait to see what he would do afterwards. She hoped he would marry her. She was getting bigger by the day. But she couldn't say any of this aloud to him, or to Auntie, who was listening from the kitchen.

Isaac shook his head once, very stubbornly, as he stood on her front porch. As usual, Auntie refused to let him into the house.

It was a black, rainy night, and Elizabeth's front porch gave Isaac little protection from the constant downpour. And it was long past the dinner hour. Isaac had come to her house after his sawmill closed down for the evening, and she wished she could at least invite him in and feed him some dinner. She had not found Isaac at the sawmill when she'd left Jake and the old chief, so she was relieved that he'd come to her house. But unfortunately, Elizabeth lived with one stubborn aunt, and no matter what she said, her aunt absolutely refused to let Isaac into their home. Many times Auntie had reminded Elizabeth that he had no intention of marrying her, and so Aunt Elizabeth did everything in her power to keep him away.

Sometimes Elizabeth felt like a rebellious child instead of a woman grown and widowed. She was capable of making her own choices about men, thank you. But somehow Auntie always had the last word.

"No, Lis-uh-buth," Isaac said in that deep voice of his. "I will provide for the potlatch. It is not right to take money from you. I have saved money for the potlatch. One hundred dollars."

One hundred dollars. She sighed. It would take him *years* to save for the potlatch. At times she wished he wasn't so honorable.

"Elizabeth?" came her aunt's voice. "Who is it, dear?"

"It is Isaac, Auntie," said Elizabeth demurely, hoping her aunt would stay sewing quietly at the table and not come rushing up to the door to yell at Isaac as she had done three times in the past week.

But Elizabeth's hope was futile. Auntie thrust her sewing onto the table and marched over to the door, her shoes clicking briskly on the wooden floor.

"What do you mean by coming here, young man?"

Elizabeth closed her eyes in embarrassment. Why, oh why, did her aunt have to be so . . . so . . . protective?

When Elizabeth opened her eyes, she could see Isaac's grimly set jaw. She wanted to shrink into the parlor and hide from both of them.

"It is time for you to leave—" began her aunt.

"I come to invite you to my home," said Isaac with dignity.

"Your home?" sputtered her aunt, clearly caught off guard. "Your home?"

Elizabeth stifled a shudder. She suspected he was living in a tent at the back of the sawmill. Auntie would not appreciate visiting *there*.

"Yes," said Isaac. "I go visit my village. Up north. I want to bring Lis-uh-buth with me. And you, too."

Her aunt looked down her nose at him. "To your home, young man?"

Isaac waited patiently while Auntie pondered. Her eyes narrowed suspiciously. "And just why do

315

you want my niece to go to your village? So you can steal her again, I suppose!"

"Auntie!"

"If I steal Lis-uh-buth, I would not bring you, too," he said.

Auntie's mouth turned down. She actually looked affronted. "And just where is your village?" she demanded, sticking out her jaw.

He pointed in a direction that Elizabeth supposed was north. Her heartbeat quickened. For Isaac to invite her to his village, why, that might mean he wanted her to meet his family! And . . . if he wanted her to meet his family. . . . Just how were things done among the Indians when it came to marriages? Hope kindled in her breast.

From the dawning light in her aunt's eye, she was thinking the same thing. "Just when do you plan to leave?" demanded Auntie.

"Tomorrow."

"What?" shrieked Auntie. "Why, that gives me no time to pack!"

A small smile curved Isaac's firm mouth.

Elizabeth met his midnight eyes. "We would be honored to visit your village," she answered in her best Miss Cowperth-like voice.

"Yes," echoed Auntie. "But no tricks, now. And just how are we getting there, young man?"

"Canoe. We paddle all day. Sleep on beach at night."

Auntie's mouth turned down.

"You traveled that way coming up from Olympia," Elizabeth reminded her aunt coaxingly.

"Hmmmph. I suppose I'd better get packing," said Auntie with just a trace of a smile at Elizabeth. She hurried into the back bedroom.

Elizabeth turned to Isaac. "Thank you for your invitation," she said gravely.

"It is all right," answered Isaac. "I would like to bring only you, but your auntie is very fierce. If I take only you, she would paddle after me and bring you back."

Elizabeth nodded. "She would."

"Probably turn over the canoe and spill all my men into the water," added Isaac.

"Probably," agreed Elizabeth.

"And try to drown me," said Isaac.

"Yes, no doubt," answered Elizabeth.

He smiled. "Very fierce. Tell you what. We bring her along to keep the cougars away, too."

They paddled into the Haida village. From the beach many Indian people watched them. Elizabeth shivered. It had been a long voyage and she was tired. She glanced over at Auntie, who was starting to stand up in the canoe, the better to see.

"Ho," said Isaac. "Please sit down, old auntie. You stand when we get closer to shore. You can be like a visiting chief."

By now Elizabeth knew that when one went to visit another village, the highest ranking member in the canoe stood in the bow, dressed in his or her finery and waited for the canoe to land—gently.

Her aunt plopped down on the canoe seat.

There were two other paddlers in the canoe, the same two Haida Indians that Isaac had met in Fort Victoria, who had come with them to her father's gold mine. They were silent men who had paddled uncomplainingly the many miles it took to reach Isaac's village.

Elizabeth stared at a long row of gray, weathered

houses that lined the beach, above the high-tide line. She counted fourteen houses, some of them over one hundred feet long. Tall carved poles, painted colorfully, stood at the corners of several dwellings. This was Elizabeth's first glimpse of totem poles. Canoes were pulled up on the beach, and naked children played in the sand. Groups of women dug clams. But every one of them stopped what they were doing and stared at the arriving canoe. Several sauntered over to where the canoe would beach.

The canoe ground gently into the beach gravel.

Feeling many eyes upon her, Elizabeth waited until Isaac could help her out of the craft. One of the men then unloaded Auntie, who splashed awkwardly in the water, wetting her shoes. Then Indian people began taking out of the canoe the many items Isaac had brought from Fort Victoria: blankets, pots, pans, dishes, knives and more items of every description.

Isaac led Elizabeth and her aunt up the beach to the largest longhouse in the center of the village. The sides were made of great slabs of graying cedar, and the roof gently sloped from a center pitch. Large rocks dotted the roof, to keep the roof slabs of cedar from blowing off in a storm. "This is my father's house," said Isaac. "We will tell him we are here to visit. Please come with me."

Elizabeth nervously straightened her dress, and her aunt did likewise. Both women followed Isaac through the oval door into the darkened interior of the house. A fire burned in the center, on the lowest of the two levels. Dried, brown fish carcasses hung from the rafters. Indian men and women sat on mats on the higher level along the sides of the house. Children chased one another, racing among the wooden boxes and jumping over benches.

Isaac led the way to a place at the far end of the house. They walked past several families' quarters.

A large gray-haired man watched as Isaac made his way through the longhouse. When Isaac was ten feet away, the man rose slowly to his feet. The man glanced at Elizabeth, and there was a calculated shrewdness in his gaze. He said something in the Indian language, which Isaac answered in kind.

Then Isaac turned to Elizabeth and her aunt, explaining, "My father welcomes you visitors from a distant land. He will feed you and entertain you and hopes you will have a pleasant visit."

Elizabeth smiled and nodded; her aunt did the same. Since they'd arrived in the Indian village, her aunt had been surprisingly quiet.

A woman with thick, black, matted hair brought Elizabeth and her aunt wooden bowls of soup. Fishy smells emanated from the bowl. "Please," said Isaac politely, "go ahead and eat."

Elizabeth and her aunt sat down on woven cedar mats set out for them. Elizabeth picked up a carved wooden spoon and scooped up a sample of the broth. "Mmm," she said to her aunt, "Very tasty." And it was. Different from anything she'd ever eaten, but tasty.

Her aunt tried some, then set down her spoon, a tight grimace on her face. "I'll eat later," she assured Elizabeth. Elizabeth looked at the expectant faces of the men and women who came over to watch them. Isaac and his father were also looking in their direction.

"Uh, Auntie," whispered Elizabeth. "I think we will offend them if we don't eat some more. Please try."

Her aunt glanced around, saw all the faces watching her and gingerly took another sip of the broth.

"Very good," murmured Elizabeth encouragingly, taking another sip and being careful not to slurp.

They sat for some time, Elizabeth and her aunt dipping their spoons into the broth now and then until a woman came and took the bowls away. Next, a woman brought over a wooden platter piled with smoked salmon. Elizabeth and her aunt could not hope to eat all of it, but she found the fish even more appealing to her palate, so she ate two pieces.

Isaac and his father talked together for some time. At last Isaac walked over to where the two women waited. A tall, thin, gray-haired woman followed him. She wore a conical hat on her head and an elaborately woven blanket in black, yellow and white over her shoulders.

"This is my aunt, Rain on the Sea," said Isaac. "She will help you find a place to put your things."

He said something in Indian to his aunt, and the woman nodded imperially. Elizabeth looked in vain for a welcoming smile.

"She is full of herself, isn't she?" snorted Auntie.

"Hush," cautioned Elizabeth. "Don't be rude, Auntie."

"She's the one being rude," insisted Auntie, glaring at the woman. The woman glared back.

Elizabeth thought she caught a glimpse of amusement in Isaac's dark eyes. "I will come back for you at the evening meal. I must discuss many things with my father."

"Hummph," said Auntie. "He brings us here and then deserts us."

"Hush, Auntie," said Elizabeth. "He brought his aunt over to help us."

"Some help."

"She is our hostess," reminded Elizabeth. "Let us be polite." They followed the straight-backed woman as she wove her way through the long-house. Children and slaves alike scattered out of her way like leaves before a storm. She led them to a dark corner. Two empty cedar boxes sat in the corner, and there were cedar benches along the walls. She pointed to the benches and boxes and gave a long speech in her language.

"I think she's telling us this is where we are to stay," said Elizabeth.

"I don't like her," said Auntie. "I don't like this house. I don't like the food."

"Please, Auntie," begged Elizabeth. "Let us give them a chance. After all, we are guests. Let us behave well." She nodded at the older Indian woman and thanked her, even though neither of them could understand the other.

The woman raised one brow, glared at Auntie, then turned to a skinny, matted-haired woman beside her and said something. The slave woman nodded and glanced at Elizabeth and her aunt. When the aunt walked away, the matted-haired woman remained.

Elizabeth glanced around. "Let us get our things from the canoe and put them here," she said. They left the longhouse, the matted-haired woman trotting behind them.

"What is she doing?" asked Auntie, jerking a thumb over her shoulder in the direction of the matted-haired woman. "Why is she following us?"

"I think she's our servant," answered Elizabeth. She didn't want to use the word "slave."

They started down the beach toward the canoe. As they walked along the beach, a small crowd gathered and followed them. By the time they reached the canoe, there was a knot of about thirty people sauntering along behind them.

Elizabeth and her aunt took out of the canoe everything they had brought from Fort Victoria. The matted-haired woman took one of the heavier bags from Auntie. Auntie grabbed the bag back from her. "That has all my clothes!"

The woman tried again, reaching for the bag, but she was too slow for Auntie, who snatched it out of her way. Then the matted-haired woman lunged for the bag. There was a vigorous tug of war between them before Elizabeth said calmly, "I believe she is trying to help you, Auntie. She wants to carry it for you."

Auntie stopped in mid-pull, grimaced at the woman, then reluctantly let go. The woman carried off the bag in triumph, running toward the longhouses.

Auntie, a determined look on her face, marched up the beach after her. There were chuckles from the watching throng. Elizabeth hastened after them. Murmurs echoed in her wake.

"I feel like I'm in a circus," called Auntie over her shoulder.

So did Elizabeth, but she refused to encourage her aunt in further rudeness, so she said nothing and smiled shakily at the Indians, none of whom smiled back.

Over the next several days, Elizabeth and her aunt settled into a routine of sorts. In the morning they would arise, stretching and yawning, from their sleeping mats. A woman would deliver a bowl of soup or some berries to break their fast. They would then walk around the village and, if the tide was out, saunter along the beach down by the water. Sometimes they would see women digging clams at the sandy part of the beach, sometimes they saw them picking berries on a hillside, but always there was activity. Once they came across a woman butchering a deer, and both Elizabeth and Auntie turned away, gagging.

Elizabeth liked to sit on a log on the beach and stare out at the water. Behind her, the village was set against great towering trees, while in front, the open bay provided a different scene every day. One day the water sparkled green and light played on the crests of little wavelets. The next day the water was dark gray with slow rolls of foaming waves breaking against the gravel beach. The day after that, the sea might be as still as a green mirror. Elizabeth thought she had never seen such a beautiful place in her whole life.

During their time at the Haida village, Susan arrived and was able to explain some of the Indian ways to the two women. Elizabeth was glad to see her but not too interested in the Indians' customs. It was Isaac she was interested in, but, unfortunately, she rarely saw him.

"I have had enough," she announced one morning to her aunt after their morning bowl of fish soup.

Auntie looked up in astonishment. "Enough of what? Soup for breakfast?"

"I have seen Isaac only once in the last two days. When he brought me here I thought . . . I thought . . ."

"Yes?" answered her aunt. "You thought what?" She leaned forward.

"I thought he wanted to marry me," said Elizabeth in a small voice.

"That's what I thought, too," acknowledged her aunt. Both women fell silent. Elizabeth felt foolish after her outburst. She got to her feet. "I am going for a walk."

"Wait for me and I'll join you," offered her aunt.

"No," said Elizabeth. "This is something I must do by myself."

"A walk?" asked her aunt in astonishment.

Elizabeth sighed and hurried out of the longhouse. She wanted to talk with Isaac. She and her aunt had been in the village for several days. She wanted to know why they had been invited here. Evidently, her assumption that it was to meet his family was incorrect. Other than that one time, Isaac had not included her in any visits to his father.

She walked over to Isaac's longhouse. No Isaac. Finally a slave pointed at the beach. A group of men were down on the beach, standing around a newly carved canoe. Elizabeth set off.

When she reached the beach, she saw Isaac pointing at the canoe and speaking with William. Evidently, they were discussing the beautiful craft. Two Indian men were bent over the bow, shaving bits off it. Cedar curls lay everywhere on the beach, and the scent of cedar hung in the air.

She stood watching, uncertain of how to approach him. He seemed different here. Unapproachable. She had seen his people defer to him. Many did his bidding. Why, one would think he was an important person here.

After a while, he saw her and came over to speak with her. "You like the canoe?" he asked.

"It is very beautiful," she answered. And indeed it was. Its reddish brown sides were sleek from the smooth carvings of the master craftsmen who worked on it.

"It is for my potlatch," he assured her.

She smiled tremulously. His potlatch. Was that why they were here? "Isaac," she said finally, "can we go for a little walk? I need to speak with you."

He glanced at the workmen and saw that they were working diligently. He nodded at William; then he and Elizabeth strolled down toward the far end of the beach, where there were no people and they would be at some distance from the longhouses. This pleased Elizabeth, who wanted Isaac all to herself.

She slid a glance at him as they walked. He looked handsome as he strolled beside her. His little lock of hair dangled over his forehead, and he looked strong and proud. She thought maybe it was a good thing for him that he'd decided to visit his village. She thought he felt welcome and at home here, far more than he had appeared to be in Fort Victoria.

Finally she decided to delay no longer with her questions. "Isaac, why did you bring me to your village?"

"Got tired of your aunt keeping you away from me at the fort."

She pondered that. "But you don't even come to visit me while we're *here*."

He glanced at her, and she felt a shiver when she looked into those brown eyes. "I am busy here, Lis-uh-buth," he said. "I have the potlatch to get ready."

The potlatch, the potlatch, always the potlatch, she thought impatiently. "But what about me?" she demanded. "What about us?"

He frowned. "You have enough food, Lis-uh-buth?"

"Why, yes," she answered in surprise.

"You sleep in a dry place when it rains?"

"Yes."

"You have plenty of water when you are thirsty?"

"Yes, yes, I am fine with that—"

"Your auntie has food, sleeps well, has plenty of water?"

"Well, yes, my auntie is fine, too, but—"

"Everyone good to you? No one hurt you?"

"Why, no, of course no one has hurt me—"

"Then you doing very well," he observed.

She frowned. It appeared that she and Isaac had very different ideas as to what was "fine." "I would like to know why you invited us to your home, Isaac," she continued determinedly.

"Thought you would like to see the houses, the trees, go for a canoe trip."

Her heart fell at the thought. She had traveled by canoe for several tiring days, slept on cold, hard beaches for several nights in a row, made her poor old aunt do the same, all so that he could show her some houses and trees?

She moaned and put her hand to her forehead. Whatever was the matter with her? Why, oh why, had she not demanded an explanation from him *before* she'd left Fort Victoria? All this time she'd thought he wanted to introduce her to his family, in preparation for marrying her and being a father to the child in her burgeoning belly.

"I talked with Susan," he said.

"Oh." She squirmed inside a little at that. She would prefer he had not actually talked with Susan, but she should have known that word would get out eventually.

"She tells me you have a new mother."

"Why, yes," said Elizabeth as pleasantly as though one got a new mother every day. "I had to do something while I was here." *And you neglected me for so long*, she wanted to add. Maybe if he had not left her alone so much, she would not have been forced to act on her own.

"My aunt be very good mother to you."

She smiled again. He would be surprised to know that Auntie did not think so. In fact, Auntie had had quite a bit to say, had almost raved actually, when Elizabeth had told her the news. But Auntie was just jealous. After all, it was she who had been like a mother to Elizabeth for so long, and now Elizabeth was becoming daughter to someone else, to Rain on the Sea.

Elizabeth hadn't actually planned it that way; it had just . . . well, just somehow happened when she was discussing Indian village life with Susan and Susan had mentioned that in order for two people to marry, they must be from different clans. There was the Raven clan and the Eagle clan. Elizabeth had quickly learned that Isaac was a Raven.

Therefore, his bride must come from the Eagle clan. After that, it had been short work to convince Susan to help her convince Rain on the Sea that she, an Eagle woman of very high standing, needed a new daughter. Although the older Indian woman had not seemed delighted at the thought, she had at last agreed to it. The adoption ceremony had taken place yesterday evening. Many people had arrived and gifts had been given. Isaac had stayed at a distance from her during the ceremony, and she had been surprised at that, but then, maybe he was angry that she'd been adopted. Too bad. She was glad she'd been adopted.

The fact that Elizabeth and her new mother could not speak a single word that the other could understand did not bother Elizabeth. She was doing it so she could marry Isaac once his potlatch was given. And as an adopted Indian, she could give him money and speed things along so that he could give his potlatch much sooner. The sooner he gave the potlatch, the sooner she could pressure him to marry her.

Elizabeth smiled smugly, pleased with her planning. Everything was turning out well, she told herself. Isaac would have his potlatch, he would then marry her, and she would have a father for her child.

She wondered a little at the desperation driving her. Desperation and fear. Growing up without a father did that to a girl, she thought bitterly. She would never, ever subject her child to life without a father. Never.

Her thoughts drifted to her own father, the man she'd never known, the man who'd died in a lonely cabin, clutching a torn piece of paper with her name on it. He'd promised to return to her and her mother; he'd promised. But he never returned. The truly sad thing was that she would rather have had him than his gold mine.

Surreptitiously she wiped a tear from her eye.

"Are you cold?" asked Isaac, catching the action.

She shook her head and pressed her lips tightly together to try to gain some control over her emotions. She would use her father's legacy, the gold mine, to gain a father for her child. Her child would never know the loneliness she'd known. The hunger that had gnawed at her heart. Never.

She halted and dug her fingernails into the palms of her hands until they hurt. "Isaac," she said, tossing her head, "I have something to tell you."

He lifted an eyebrow. "You have more surprises for me?"

"More surprises?" Her eyes narrowed.

"Your new mother was a surprise."

She smiled. "Yes. Well, I wanted a mother."

He frowned. "Your auntie is not enough?"

She smiled coldly. "No."

He stared at her, his eyes roving over her face. "My aunt is an Eagle. Now you are an Eagle, too."

She nodded. "I like that." She did not add that it was part of her plan so that she could marry him.

He was silent. At last he said, "You have a new surprise?"

"Yes." She pulled out a fat roll of bills, hundred-dollar bills. Money she had brought all the way from Fort Victoria just for this purpose. "As an Eagle I can give this to you for your potlatch." She unrolled the bills, straightening them. "You can use this money to buy gifts for your potlatch, or whatever it is you need." She smiled and held out the money. "Here."

His face was ashen. When she looked into his eyes, she saw he was horrified. Then angry. Her hand faltered. "What—what is wrong?"

"I will not take your money. I told you this before! It is not right for me to accept money from you for my potlatch. You are an Eagle. I cannot accept the money!"

She was stunned. "What do you mean?" she cried, not caring that her voice rose on a shriek. "I was adopted so I could be an Eagle Indian. I want to marry you. I have to be an Eagle to marry you. If I'm an Eagle Indian, I can help you with money, too!" Her heart pounded. Something was wrong, terribly wrong.

"A Raven can only marry an Eagle," he said. "You are correct about that. But I cannot accept money from an Eagle for my potlatch. Only from Ravens. Only Ravens can help me give my potlatch."

"What?" She could not believe her ears. "No! It can't be!" She whirled on him, glaring into his dark eyes, willing him to understand her—and her desperation. "You *have* to marry me! I want to give you this money so you can give your potlatch . . . that's the only way you'll marry me!"

He frowned. "I cannot marry you. I told you that. My potlatch comes first."

His words were hard and cold and fell like black boulders between them, building an impenetrable rock wall. "I will not let my child be born to a father who has no standing with the Haida People. Or the Tsimshian People. It is better for my child to have no father than to have a father who can only humiliate him."

"No!" she cried. "No!"

"Be silent," he cried. "You do not know what you talk about."

"I do know!" she howled. "My father was gone—all through my childhood! My child needs his father! You must marry me! Our child needs his father!" Fear gnawed at her innards like a ravaging wolf. She was trying to force him to marry her, but she didn't care. It was either force him or subject her child to constant loneliness. And she would *not* put her child through that.

He gripped her upper arms. His grip was tight, his breath came in short panting sounds. "You listen! I not give my child a life of slavery. Of humiliation! You know nothing!" He cast her aside, and she stumbled, then recovered her footing on the rough beach. "You know nothing about my people. Nothing about potlatches! Potlatch will set me free. Set my child free! You know nothing!" And with a last angry glare, he turned his back on her and marched back up the beach.

She felt the tears running down her cheeks. Amazed, she touched one, wondering where the wetness had come from. The tear glistened on her finger and she stared at it.

More tears welled in her eyes.

Her life lay shattered before her. No husband for her. No father for her child.

She stumbled down the beach after him.

Chapter Twenty-eight

Elizabeth sat on a huge black rock overlooking the swirling dark green water. Each time, the waves withdrew back out to sea and then attacked the rocks again, pounding and bellowing, sending white foam spraying over her.

Behind her, far up on a hillside, her aunt, her adoptive mother and several other women picked berries. But Elizabeth did not want to pick berries. She did not want to do anything. She just wanted to sit, slumped, and stare at the water as it surged in and out of the rocks.

How had her life come to this? she wondered.

She had made a fool of herself over a man who did not want to marry her. She had followed him to his village and demanded he marry her, and he had rejected her. So now here she was, seven months pregnant, sitting on a boulder overlooking the foaming waves that pounded the rocks below.

Outwardly she appeared quite calm, dull and quiet, really, if her aunt were to look at her. But inwardly she was in turmoil, just like the water. She wanted to pound and splash and surge and push. She liked the loud, deafening, sucking and surging sounds of the water. It lashed and splashed and pushed and rolled. She stared, fascinated.

Now was the time to look at the state of her soul. If she was ever going to have the courage to face the truth about herself, it was now. She had run away from her problems in San Francisco. She had married a man in Fort Victoria to avoid her problems. She had manipulated two Haida Indian clans in an attempt to get Isaac to do what she wanted.

She had run about as far as she could go—to an Indian village whose name she could not pronounce, up in a land she had never even known existed. And now she faced the turmoil of emotions and frustrations that roiled inside herself.

What was so important about marriage? she asked herself. She had been desperate for Isaac to marry her. Why? For society's approval because of the coming baby? She had been educated by Miss Cowperth. But the teachings at the Finishing School for Young Ladies seemed far behind her now. She could survive in Fort Victoria as an unmarried mother.

What about financial support? She had her own money now. From the gold mine. She didn't need him to support her. She and her aunt could manage very well, just the two of them, raising her child. They would have the funds necessary to feed and clothe and educate her child.

So why, then, this frantic craving for a man? And

for a man who was just as desperately running away from her, to problems of his own, which he hoped to solve by giving a potlatch?

Was it fear for her child? Was that her deep concern?

She squinted at the plunging white water. She wanted to run away from the question, but she dragged herself back to look at it. There was a glimmer of truth in the question. She wanted her child to have a father. To her, a father meant a caring man who stayed around and helped raise the child. A man who would talk with the child, play with him or her, and guide and help the child through the years to adulthood. A man who would love that child with all his heart. No halfhearted measures for the man who would be father of *her* child. He would be committed, lifelong.

She wondered why she hadn't thought of all this *before* she had slept with Isaac.

But was her fear for her child masking a deeper concern? What about her own needs for *her* father?

She covered both eyes with her hands to shut out her thoughts. This was getting a little too close to the pain.

Time to look at the water. She peeked through her fingers at the raging, boiling water. The surging and foaming was hypnotic. She could sit here all day and watch the water and never have to ask herself any difficult questions.

But if she wanted to know what drove her, if she wanted to know why she had chased Isaac all the way to his longhouse, only to be told, politely but firmly, that he had to talk to some men about his potlatch, then she had better sit here and think until she was clear within herself.

She wanted to be free. She knew that. Freedom for her meant being able to make her own decisions and choices because she was acting in a rational manner, and not because she was fearful of something or lacking something. Especially something that had happened a long time ago. If she wanted to be truly free, then she knew she had to plow a little deeper into her motives and thoughts. And now, she thought as she took a deep breath, was as good a time as any.

Elizabeth had grown up without a father. She had lived with that knowledge ever since she was a small child. It had permeated her to the very marrow of her bones. No father to pick her up and hug her, no father to ask how she was doing, no father to teach her things, to walk with her. No father to love her.

Her mother had loved her. And her aunt. And she knew she'd had more love than some people. But the gaping hole where a father's love should be reached all the way down into her soul. She was only now beginning to realize the depth of her father-wound. It was a huge, gaping hole that she wanted to fill. And she wanted, she realized, to fill it with Isaac.

She had longed for, nay, yearned for her father all of her life. Was that what was at the bottom of all her feelings? The hungering of a girl-child for a father? Was that what had made her chase this man to the ends of the earth? Feelings of aloneness filtered over her and through her. Then they became a roaring element inside her like the plunging waves below. She found herself crying, tears streaming down her face as she sat on the rock and sobbed with her face on her arms. She shook with the sobs, clenching her fists over her mouth to keep from crying out. She thought she would die from crying. . . . She hadn't known it was possible to feel so bereft, so alone, so needy.

She cried for what felt like a long, long time. When she at last lifted her head, she wondered how it came to be that she was still here, on this black rock, and with the sun still shining. The gulls still rode the air currents overhead. The waves still splashed.

Yet everything had changed. Inside her, *everything* had changed.

She had been trying to give her child the father she had never had. Somehow it made strong emotional sense to her. Her loneliness was so deep, so painful, that she'd thought only a father's love could save her. And she had wanted to spare her child the loss that she'd known her whole life. She felt as though she'd just gone through a battle and was still reeling from the knowledge of the depth of her pain and loneliness.

At that moment, surrounded by trees and rocks and pounding water, she said a prayer to God. She had never been a religious woman, but deep inside her she sensed she must turn to something greater than herself for help at this very important moment in her life. She prayed for God to fill the hungering in her heart. Nothing, *nothing* else could fill her unless God helped her first.

Her prayer finished, she felt a sense of calm.

She took a deep breath, inhaling the salty sea air into her lungs, down into the depths of her being. So now that she knew this about herself, that she had this great, deep loneliness, what was she going to do?

She closed her eyes. She had to think. She didn't want to chase Isaac anymore, she knew that. While he was a fine man with many good characteristics, he had his own battles to fight. She wouldn't burden him with herself. Nor with their child. If he wanted to be a part of his child's life, she would welcome that. But if he chose to pursue his potlatch work with his people, well, she would accept that, too. He had helped make this child. If he valued his child, he would find a way to love and be with their child.

As for herself, she was done chasing him. It had turned her into a desperate wretch who thought only of herself, of her neediness for a husband. Such neediness was unfair to her, and unfair to Isaac. He couldn't fulfill that need in her. No one could. No one.

She let her breath out, slowly and carefully and deeply. It felt as if a heavy burden had been lifted from her breast.

Self-realization was a terrible thing, she thought. It did set you free, but at a very high price. And for her, the price was recognizing the loss of her father. And feeling the utter loneliness of that loss. She would never have him in her life. Ever. He was gone. He had made choices that kept him away from her. And that was real in her life.

And it led to an even higher price. For she knew that she loved Isaac. Cared for him in a way she had never loved any other man. But she could not force him to love her. Nor would she want him under such terms. He, too, must be free. Free in his own way. And that meant he had to give his potlatch. Had to reclaim whatever it was *he'd* lost.

For she suspected that, maybe, great loss was something they'd both had in common for a long, long time.

And when he had reclaimed his losses, when he'd found that part of himself that he searched for so desperately, then, and only then, would she and Isaac be free to love one another fully.

She sat on the rock for a long time. Finally she rose slowly to her feet, picked up a pebble from the top of the rock and tossed it down into the swirling water. It disappeared, making no mark in the foaming waters. How strange, she thought, when this place had marked *her* so strongly.

Then she turned and walked slowly back to the village.

Chapter Twenty-nine

"Look," said Elizabeth. "There is William."

"Who is William?" asked Auntie, looking in the direction Elizabeth pointed.

"Isaac's friend. I think he's a cousin. And a member of the Raven clan." Elizabeth had been spending some of her time at the village quizzing Susan about the inhabitants and their customs. She found it all very interesting and sometimes asked questions that even Susan could not answer.

Elizabeth pointed to the tall man who was walking down the beach. He carried some rope and was heading for one of the canoes that lay near the water. "I must get something for him. I'll be right back," said Elizabeth eagerly, a plan forming in her mind.

She left her aunt staring open-mouthed at her as she hurried to the longhouse where they were staying. She ducked inside the darkened interior and then rummaged through her possessions, which she kept in one of the carved cedar boxes. Finding what she sought, she hurried back to her aunt.

"Let's go and speak to him." Elizabeth wanted to run to get to William, but she found she had to slow down because of her belly. Also, her aunt could not move as quickly on the beach gravel as Elizabeth could. She waited while her puffing aunt caught up with her.

"Just what is so important about seeing this man?" demanded her aunt.

"You'll see," said Elizabeth serenely.

She reached the canoe that William was lifting into the water. "Going fishing?" she asked.

"Yes," he said. "I heard the salmon are biting over near that island." He pointed in the direction of a tiny island some distance north of the village.

"Before you go," said Elizabeth, "I want to give you something."

William looked at her curiously. When she pulled out the roll of hundred-dollar bills, William said, "Oho. I have heard about you and your money." Isaac must have told him about her unsuccessful offer of the money. Elizabeth would have blushed if she could, but she felt no shame for trying to help Isaac. Before, when she'd offered him money, she'd been doing it to help herself—to force him to marry her. Now, after her time spent thinking on the rock, she realized that she still wanted to help him. But she wanted to help him so that he would be free. She would give selflessly to him out of her love for him.

"I want to help Isaac," she said. "I want to give you this money to help Isaac give his potlatch."

William looked at the money, then at Elizabeth,

then back at the money. When he didn't take the money, Elizabeth said, "I learned that if I give the money to someone in his clan, then that person can use the money to help Isaac."

"Yes, that is correct," admitted William. "But white man's ways are different . . . especially with money."

Elizabeth smiled. "Very different," she agreed. "I know how important it is to Isaac to give this potlatch." Indeed, she'd asked Susan several questions about potlatches. Elizabeth had a new understanding of them as an important way to announce to the Haida society any changes in a person's status. She knew now that Isaac could wipe out the social humiliations he'd suffered from the Tsimshians and increase his prestige by giving this potlatch. His whole family and clan would benefit from a successful potlatch. And so would his son or daughter.

"I want Isaac to be able to give a fine potlatch," continued Elizabeth. "Perhaps he can even give it sooner with this money."

"Perhaps," agreed William, eyeing the money dubiously. "We give the potlatch next year, maybe the year after. We have plenty to do."

Elizabeth's heart fell. "Next year?" she murmured in dismay.

"Or the year after," said William.

"Elizabeth." Auntie was tugging on Elizabeth's sleeve. "Are you sure you know what you're doing? That is a very large sum of money."

William glanced at Auntie but said nothing. Auntie was emboldened by his silence. "Where did you get so much money?" she asked Elizabeth.

"Some of the money is from the sale of Cyril's

newspaper." She had sold the newspaper business to Cyril's friend, Marvin Slater, who had been eager to buy it. "The rest of the money came from my goldmine. It pays very well. You know that."

"I do, dear. I didn't realize you'd brought so much of your money with you. But Elizabeth," Auntie stared at the bills. "Will—will Isaac pay you back? I don't think he has much money, dear. I don't think you should lend him this money." Auntie was sounding firmer now that she was, as usual, taking a stand against Isaac.

But Auntie had not been the one asking Susan questions. "I am going to *give* it to Isaac. It will come back when another high-ranking person gives another potlatch and invites the Ravens."

Auntie gasped. "*Give it*? Are you sure you want to do this, dear? I'm sure your father would not want you throwing away good money that he worked so hard for."

To have Auntie, who had always hated even the mention of Theodore Powell, now telling Elizabeth what he would have wanted was ludicrous.

"My father is dead, Auntie," reminded Elizabeth. "He won't know."

Auntie's mouth worked but she was unable to come up with an answer. She clucked helplessly.

"Furthermore," said Elizabeth evenly, "he wouldn't care." She drew herself up to her full height. "But I care. I care that Isaac is able to give the biggest and best potlatch that has ever been given."

"You do?" marveled Auntie. "Whatever is wrong with you, dear? Did you eat something that didn't agree with you?" She looked worried.

"No," answered Elizabeth, and she patted her

aunt's hand. "Auntie, I *want* to give this." And she truly did not care what her aunt thought, or William, for that matter. Self-knowledge was indeed a powerful thing.

"Very well," said William. "I will take the money and give it to the Raven clan." He reached for the money that Elizabeth readily handed over. Without counting it, he tucked it inside his shirt. Then he pushed the canoe out into the water.

"William," she said before he paddled away, "count the money. Tell me when the potlatch will be held."

Good-naturedly, William reached inside his shirt and pulled out the money. He counted it and then stared at her thoughtfully. "Isaac can give his potlatch now," he said quietly.

Elizabeth smiled. "Thank you, William," she said. He gave a wave, tucked the money back in his shirt and paddled off toward the island.

Elizabeth and her aunt walked up the beach toward the longhouses. Now Isaac would have the chance to give his potlatch. And Elizabeth would have the satisfaction of seeing that he could have it soon. Her father's gold-mine money was proving its usefulness.

"I just don't understand young people these days," grumbled her aunt.

"So you don't think I should have given that money to Isaac?" mused Elizabeth as they sauntered along.

"No, I don't," said Auntie. "That money would have kept you very well for a very long time. You don't know if there will be more."

"No, I don't know," she admitted. She smiled ruefully at her aunt. "Auntie, you forget something. I wouldn't even have *had* that money if it hadn't been for Isaac," she said. "It was his idea that we go to the goldmine to see where my father died. Remember?"

For once her aunt was silent.

Chapter Thirty

The next day Elizabeth and her aunt were walking through the village, dutifully following behind Elizabeth's new mother. Rain on the Sea was dressed in her best blanket and dress and was taking them to visit some old Indian women. Normally Elizabeth would be bored. But she had asked Susan about the old women and discovered that they were highly respected and held much knowledge about Haida ways. And one of them was a shaman woman. So Elizabeth was eager to meet them.

Auntie, however, at her side, offered a little different perspective. "I don't see why we have to go and visit these people. We don't know them; we can't even speak their language. And I hate fish."

"We'll meet them and they may turn out to be wonderful people. We're learning their language. And I suggest you eat the berries they offer instead of the fish." Elizabeth was beginning to have little patience with her aunt's complaining. In her own world of Fort Victoria, or Olympia, or even San Francisco, her aunt was confident and no-nonsense. Here, all she did was complain.

A man was walking through the village, crying out loudly.

"Who's that?" demanded Auntie. "Why is he yelling." She put her hands over her ears.

Rain on the Sea stopped, however, and appeared to be listening intently to what the man had to say. When he'd finished, she glanced at Elizabeth and smiled. Elizabeth smiled back, puzzled, and they continued on their way.

It wasn't until Susan joined them several hours later that Elizabeth got an explanation about who the man was and what he had said. "He is our town crier," she told Elizabeth. "Like your newspaper. He tells news."

"What did he tell today?" pressed Elizabeth curiously.

Susan smiled. "Nothing you want to know."

Elizabeth pondered.

Susan took mercy on her. "He say potlatch begin very soon. Guests invited to come."

"A potlatch?" Hope rose in Elizabeth. "Is it Isaac's?"

Susan smiled. "Yes. He say some other things. I not say."

And try as she might Elizabeth could not get Susan to reveal what else the man had said. Not knowing the language was frustrating, she thought.

That evening, Elizabeth requested her first lesson in the Haida language, and Susan was happy to oblige. Elizabeth paid particular attention, trying to get the pronunciation right. The more she learned of the language, the more she would understand about these generous and unusual people.

Auntie snored through the lesson.

Isaac walked over to where Elizabeth sat by the fire. "Would you like to walk out under the stars?" he offered, looking impossibly handsome.

Her breath caught in her throat as she looked up at him. Slowly she got to her feet and followed him out of the longhouse. They left Auntie dozing by the fire, tired after a long day of berry picking.

Elizabeth liked walking along with Isaac. They strolled in a peaceful mood down to the beach. The full moon shone round and yellow in the black sky and left a pathway of gold on the water. Little waves licked the shoreline.

They dipped their bare feet in the water as they walked. "I have much to tell you," said Isaac.

She glanced at him in surprise, and her heart beat faster. "What is it?"

"I am going to give my potlatch," he said. "Very soon. I am sending paddlers out to all the villages to invite many guests." He sounded very pleased and proud. "I thank you for money you gave to help my potlatch."

Elizabeth felt warm inside. Her money was doing some good.

Then his craggy face grew solemn, and she suddenly wanted to reach up to his cheek and wipe away the concern she saw there. "What is it, Isaac?" she asked softly.

"You should not give money away, Elizabeth."

She thought about that. "I love you, Isaac. I want to help you. If you have your potlatch, then we can . . ."

She almost said "marry" but her courage faltered at the last. She remembered the desperation that had driven her, the fear that she must have a husband and a father for her child. Desperation did not make a good start to a marriage. She had been wrong to get pregnant, but she would not compound her problems by marrying a man who had other commitments on his mind.

She took a shaky breath. It might turn out that she must raise her child alone; she might have to grow old alone. If so, then so be it. She would be brave. Marriage to Isaac would trap them both in lives neither one wanted. She smiled. "You can give your potlatch."

"I thought about refusing the money," he said, glancing at her.

"Why did you accept, then?" She was curious to know what he thought. She realized that she seldom knew what he thought and they did not talk much about it. The language differences made things more complicated, too.

"I can give the potlatch and be free. I have money coming from the sawmill. It does well. I will give you sawmill. Pay you back."

"I don't want your sawmill," she answered, alarmed.

"You want to own me, Lis-uh-buth?"

She looked at him, shocked anew. "No, I don't want to own you! How can you say such a thing?"

"You give me money, I take it. You own me. You own me until I pay it back. That is the white man's way."

She frowned. "It isn't supposed to be like that."

"You want to help me, I understand that. I like that. I take the money because it come from a good heart. You have a good heart."

She nodded, relieved that he understood. "Yes, I do want to help."

"But a good heart still wonders sometimes if it will get the money back."

He had her there. She probably would wonder.

"I give you my sawmill. Pay back the money. Then you can sell the sawmill back to me, if you want."

She thought about it. He was a proud man, and she realized deep down inside that she wouldn't have wanted him if he'd just taken her money. "Very well, I will own your sawmill." What an amazing business life she had, she thought. A gold mine from her dead father and a sawmill from Isaac. She, who had arrived in Fort Victoria penniless, now had two successful businesses.

She smiled. "When are you giving your potlatch? Next week?"

"When everyone gets here," he answered.

She knew she would get no more out of him about when it would take place. She had noticed that the Haida people viewed time differently than she did. Nothing took place at an exact time the way she was used to.

It was so peaceful walking with Isaac. And no matter what happened in the future, she had this beautiful moment with him. She became very aware of every breath she took, every star that twinkled down on them. Aware of the salty smell in the air, the rough sand under her feet, the warm water that lapped at her feet when she walked through the waves, the moonlight that bathed their skin to a golden color. The smoky man-scent of him carried to her on the gentle breeze. The crisp lapping of the waves echoed in her ears. There was a peace between them that she had never felt before. She loved him. She wished they could always walk under the moon on this beautiful beach and be at peace. She wanted to hold the moment forever. She closed her eyes and inhaled deeply, impressing this place, this time, on her memory. Even when she was an old, old lady she would have this moment.

"What are you thinking?" he asked softly, cocking his head at her. His black lock of hair dangled over his forehead. He looked so handsome.

"Just happy," she murmured. And she was. After all she had been through, the move from San Francisco, the kidnapping, the time in Fort Victoria, the paddling and camping, tonight she was genuinely happy. All the way through to her soul.

"I am happy, too," he answered. She reached for his hand and he took hers in his. They squeezed hands. She almost didn't want to speak, afraid to shatter the beauty of the moment.

So they walked along and when they came to the far end of the beach where the creek flowed down the beach and into the sea, he halted and pulled her close. They kissed there, under the moon, and she thought she could happily die.

His lips moved on hers. She felt his tongue move into her mouth, and she groaned. He caught her closer to him, moving against her until she could feel his manhood. They clung to one another. "I want to have you," he whispered.

"I want you, too," she whispered back.

He led her to a place up the beach where no one could see them. They sat down on the sand, and he began taking off his shirt. Then his pants.

"What are you doing?" she whispered.

He looked at her in surprise. "I want to have you," he repeated.

"Yes, but not here. Not now."

"I thought you wanted—"

"Well, I did say that, I suppose. But I'm pregnant. We're on the beach. I can't just—"

"Yes, you can," he said.

"No, I cannot," she answered. She patted her belly. "I think it is too late, Isaac. We must be careful about the little one." Auntie had said something to that effect one day not so long ago.

Isaac looked disappointed. Very disappointed. He put his shirt back on, slowly, and his pants, too. "I hold you," he said at last, pulling her back into his arms.

She leaned against him, her back to his chest. They sat for a time like that, watching the beach and the moon and the water. He rested his hands on her belly. Her belly was firm. He patted it gently. "I think about our child," he whispered, and shivers went through her.

"So do I," she murmured.

"This important child," he said.

"Yes," she agreed. She already loved this baby, would do anything for her child. She wondered if he felt the same way. Probably not, she decided. It was different for a man.

Again and again, the waves rolled in to the beach, making a soft swishing sound. "I wish we could always be like this," she said wistfully.

"No," he said.

"No?" She squirmed around to look at him in surprise.

"No," he shook his head. "We can be like this. But I want to hold you. I want to be inside you."

"Isaac!" she reprimanded, slightly shocked at his words.

"I do," he said stubbornly.

She softened toward him. "I want it, too," she admitted. "But we have to wait until after the baby." Curious, she added, "Will you wait?" She held her breath.

He glanced at her, his midnight eyes unreadable in the moonlight. "I wait."

It was a simple answer, but she hoped he meant it. She patted his hand. "I will wait, too."

She felt him kiss the hair on the back of her head. She sighed happily. Time would tell if they would be together. For now it was enough to have this moment.

Chapter Thirty-one

Throughout the past week there had been frequent visitors to the village, arriving in three or four canoes at a time. Elizabeth watched one morning as two long canoes pulled up to the beach, followed by three smaller ones. The Indians in the canoes, men and women and children, began unloading their things and stacking them on the beach.

"That is strange," muttered Susan.

"What do you mean?" answered Elizabeth. She was trying to understand the Indians' customs and frequently relied upon Susan for information.

"Tsimshian chief arrive. Not in big group. Just a few canoes."

Elizabeth stared at the canoes. "Five seems like a goodly number," she observed.

"Not for a middle chief," said Susan. "Should be many, many canoes. He is important chief."

"Maybe he did not want to travel with the main

group," suggested Elizabeth. "Or maybe they set out with the main group and got separated by winds, or a small storm."

Susan shrugged. "Maybe."

The two women watched as the small parade of Tsimshians passed them on their way to one of the smaller longhouses. It was a female retainer of Elizabeth's adoptive mother who led the visitors to a place to stay.

Elizabeth would have forgotten the small incident had not something else happened later that day.

She was sitting on a log down at the beach watching women dig in the sand for clams, when a Tsimshian chief sauntered over to her. She knew he must be a Tsimshian chief because he was dressed very well, his clothes and hat were not in the Haida style, and he looked vaguely familiar. She thought perhaps she had seen him at the Tsimshian village the one time she'd had the misfortune to stay there.

"You like it here?" he asked. He put one bare foot on the log where she sat and waited, leaning a little on his leg.

She was surprised he'd dare to speak to her. Most of the Indian men and women she'd met preferred to keep their distance from her. She was too different from them, she supposed, being from a different place and society and thus far too strange for them to feel comfortable with her.

"Why, yes, I do," she answered, glancing at him. He was of medium height, fairly young, and had a recent scar on his cheek, the pink swath standing out against his swarthy skin. He had small dark eyes that watched her closely. She felt a little uneasy, but what could he possibly do, here on the beach, with Indian men and women she could call upon just a little distance away?

"Good," he said, and nodded his head vigorously. He, too, appeared to be glancing around, and she wondered if he felt uncomfortable talking to her. "You marry Haida chief?" he asked.

How could he know she hoped to do that? For a moment, words failed her. Then she realized that word must have spread in the Indian villages about her presence here, and he must be curious. "I might," she answered. Not that it was any of his concern.

"Good," he said, and his dark eyes lit with satisfaction. "I tell you something," he said, leaning slightly toward her. Now she was the curious one, and she couldn't help leaning forward to hear what he had to say.

"Big celebration here," he said in a low voice.

Where was the secret in that? She already knew about the potlatch. She slumped back on her log.

"Chief you marry going to give away many things," he said.

"Yes," she agreed politely, "he is." So this Tsimshian chief had no news. He just wanted to talk. Disappointed, she stared out at the sea.

"He give away canoes, blankets, bowls . . ."

"Oh, yes," she answered. "He will do that."

"Give away many things."

"He will," she said, her politeness a little more forced. She wished he would just leave.

"He buys many slaves," he said.

"Yes."

"He was at my village, buying many, many slaves."

355

She nodded. Isaac had made several trips to villages, buying cedar boxes and fine baskets for his potlatch. She had seen some of them, and they were beautiful. She supposed he would visit a Tsimshian village for potlatch items. She was a little surprised, though, that he would buy slaves . . .

The dark eyes of the Tsimshian chief held hers. "He going to kill slaves. Kill many, many slaves. You like?"

Her mouth dropped open. "Kill—? Many slaves—?" Whatever was this chief talking about? She tried to gain some semblance of control. "What do you mean, kill them?"

"It is true," he said. "To be a big chief, he will kill all his slaves. Then Indian people very proud of him." The chief smiled, revealing a gap between his front teeth.

She did not like him.

"Many chiefs do this," he continued. "It is the old way. Very old. Your chief very proud."

She did not like his grin. She did not like what he had to say. She wished he'd leave.

"I go now," he said and took his foot off the log. He sauntered off.

She watched him go. She did not like one thing about him. But she could not pretend to ignore his words. If what he said was true, Isaac was planning a dreadful slaughter.

She caught herself. Isaac would not do such a thing. Isaac was a good man. He was kind, and caring.

But, she continued thoughtfully, he *had* kidnapped her. He *had* killed a man. There was a ruthless side to him.

She got up from the log. She would find William and talk to him about it.

But she was not reassured when she spoke to William. Rather than ask William outright if Isaac was planning to kill his slaves, Elizabeth tried to probe delicately. She discovered that Isaac had, in fact, been buying slaves and that he had been to a Tsimshian village. And William did not know what Isaac planned to do with the slaves. He admitted, under Elizabeth's questioning, that in the past, great chiefs *had* killed slaves to enhance their social standing.

Elizabeth knew that Isaac was desperate to raise his social standing. But surely he would not kill people to do it. Would he?

Her heart sank further when William said that such a thing had been done at a potlatch when he was a little boy. A slave had been dragged to the fire and quickly killed and his body buried at the corner of a longhouse. Then a totem pole was raised over the spot.

Elizabeth turned away, feeling sickened. She did not want to be party to whatever Isaac planned. And now it was too late.

Chapter Thirty-two

"You do not know, do you?" Susan asked.

Elizabeth paused just as she was reaching for a plump blueberry. "Know what?" She plucked the blueberry and popped it into her mouth. It was sweet and juicy. She glanced over at Auntie, who was putting berry after berry into a twined woven cedar basket on the grass beside her.

"Know what?" prodded Elizabeth again when Susan did not answer.

"About the potlatch."

Elizabeth stopped picking and swung around to gaze at her friend. "What should I know about the potlatch?" she asked cautiously. Something in Susan's voice puzzled her.

"Big announcement soon," said Susan.

Elizabeth relaxed. "Oh, that. You mean about the canoe?" Isaac had recently purchased a third beautiful canoe from a Haida craftsman in a northern village. It was to arrive "soon."

"No, not canoe. More Tsimshians are coming."

Elizabeth felt her heart drop, but fortunately her hands kept plucking berries and she didn't think Susan had noticed the effect of her words.

Not more Tsimshians, thought Elizabeth. *How will I keep from running and hiding in fear?* She would never forget creeping away from the Tsimshian village and hearing James Burt's horrible cries. "When are they coming?"

"Soon," answered Susan.

Elizabeth chastised herself for asking a time question. She tried again. "Who will be coming?"

"Great chief that you saw at village."

"That must mean All Fear His Name."

"Yes. All his middle and little chiefs, too. Many of the people. Some slaves." Susan did not look too concerned as she ate a berry. Perhaps Elizabeth should not be concerned either.

"I don't want to see the Tsimshians. What if they start a fight?"

"Isaac and the other men make sure they not fight," answered Susan calmly, popping another berry into her mouth. Her lips looked dark blue.

That did not sound too bad, thought Elizabeth. She relaxed and picked a particularly plump berry.

"Isaac buy blankets and pots and pans at Fort Simpson."

"He is certainly adding to his potlatch supplies," said Elizabeth cheerily.

"Isaac buy up all Haida slaves."

"Oh?" Elizabeth's hand paused just as she was reaching into the bush for a handful of berries.

"He buy Tsimshian slaves."

"How nice," said Elizabeth. She wrapped her fingers around the berries and pulled a few off the branch. They squished in her hand.

"Not good way to pick berries," observed Susan.

"No," agreed Elizabeth ruefully.

They picked quietly for a while. Elizabeth tried to distract herself from what Susan had told her about the slaves. She could see Auntie over on the other hillside. She was picking berries with Elizabeth's adopted mother. The two older women occasionally did things together, and Elizabeth hoped that some of Auntie's jealousy was wearing off. After all, Rain on the Sea was a kind, regal woman, but Auntie was . . . well, she was Auntie, actually the only mother Elizabeth had ever known.

It was getting dark as they walked back to the village. Elizabeth felt tired but pleased with her work. It was very satisfying to be carrying the baskets of berries and to know she'd helped pick so many of them. Also, they would make a very tasty addition to the potlatch menu.

"What did you say about the slaves?" asked Elizabeth evenly as they walked along.

Susan glanced at her and shifted the heavy basket she carried to her other hip.

"Isaac buy up Haida slaves. Tsimshian slaves. All slaves he can find."

As always, Elizabeth felt uncomfortable at the mention of slaves. Slaves were a part of the Haida and Tsimshian life, but she did not feel it was right to enslave people.

"Does he need so many servants, then?" she asked cautiously, trying to forget that the other chief had said Isaac would kill his new slaves. And she preferred to call them servants. It did not sound as bad as "slaves." But she had to confess that seeing the matted-haired creatures hurrying about the village on a multitude of tasks was discomfiting. She estimated that about one-quarter of the village population were slaves, most stolen in raids from other tribes. She supposed they were kept so busy they did not have time even to comb their hair. Or sew up the holes in their clothes. Or find decent footwear. They all went barefoot. Still, she was hesitant to say anything, because she was a guest in the Haida village. But she did not like to see people enslaved.

"In past, slaves thrown away at potlatches," Susan said. She then said a Haida word that meant "throw away."

"Where do they throw them?" asked Elizabeth.

" 'Throw away,' " said Susan delicately, "sometimes mean 'kill.' "

"What?" cried Elizabeth, stopping dead in her tracks.

"Very great chiefs throw away slaves at potlatch. Shows how great chiefs are. Visitors very amazed."

"Amazed?" Elizabeth stared at Susan as Susan unwittingly confirmed her worst fears. "You mean the chiefs kill the slaves to show the guests how important they are?"

"Yes," nodded Susan. "Only very great chiefs can afford to buy slaves, then throw away."

"I suppose," gritted Elizabeth as she trudged determinedly forward again, "that Isaac intends to 'throw away' these slaves he is buying?" She repeated the Haida word Susan had used.

"They not cheap," said Susan. "He want visitors amazed."

"I see," said Elizabeth through clenched teeth.

She did indeed see. She saw very well. Isaac *was* going to kill slaves to enhance his own prestige. Just as the other chief had told her. There were a few little potlatch details she should have inquired about; she saw that now.

"I will not have anything to do with killing people," Elizabeth told Susan. She was getting more and more alarmed about the potlatch. Isaac—kill people? What had happened to the man she thought she knew? How could he do such a thing?

By the time they reached the trail to the village, Elizabeth was practically running, despite the load of berries she carried. "Wait," puffed Susan. "No run. Walk."

"I can't help it," Elizabeth called over her shoulder. "I must speak with Isaac!"

She hurried ahead.

When she reached the longhouse, she set aside the baskets. She asked a slave if he'd seen Isaac and hurried in the direction he pointed.

She found him visiting his father. "Isaac?" she said politely. He came over to her.

"Lis-uh-buth! Good to see you," he said enthusiastically.

Ever since their moonlit walk, they had been so happy together. Until now.

"I must speak with you, Isaac."

"What is it?"

She led him to a quiet corner of the dark house, not too far from the hearth fire.

"Are you buying up slaves?"

"Yes." He grinned. "Many, many slaves."

"Isaac," she said, gazing into his dark eyes. "I must insist that you not throw these slaves away!"

He frowned. "What you mean?"

362

"I know what you plan to do, Isaac."

"Many slaves."

"And you plan to throw them away?" She used the Haida word Susan had taught her.

"Yes."

Her eyes rounded in fear and horror. She gripped his arm. "Isaac, you can't! You mustn't do that!"

He straightened and removed her hand. With great dignity and pride he said, "I give best potlatch. I throw away slaves. You come to potlatch."

"I'm afraid that I must refuse your invitation," she said in her best Miss-Cowperth-like manner. "I find that I shall be unavoidably busy."

Now it was Isaac who gripped her arm. "You will not be busy. You come to my potlatch!"

"No!"

"Yes!"

"No!"

"Yes!"

"Isaac, we are getting nowhere. I do not wish to come and see you throw away those slaves!" She shuddered. The very thought of the carnage and blood made her want to vomit.

"You come," said Isaac. "And after potlatch, we marry!"

Chapter Thirty-three

Elizabeth counted fourteen canoes paddling into the bay in front of the Haida village.

"Where are they from?" she asked Susan.

Rain on the Sea answered and Susan translated. "Your mother say they from Tsimshian village. You know them. Great chief and all his little chiefs."

Elizabeth wanted to run and hide in the longhouse. Of all the guests who had been arriving for the potlatch, she'd been dreading the arrival of the Tsimshians the most. She actually did not want to see any guests, truth be told, since she had learned that Isaac was going to kill all the slaves he'd bought.

She'd retired to her longhouse the day after she'd discovered this terrible information, but it had done her not one whit of good to hide out. Isaac had visited her now and then, always being pleasant and polite. But she was not fooled. A man who could cold-bloodedly plan the killing of defenseless slaves was not the man she wanted for a husband. Ever.

And he thought they were getting married! The village crier had gone through the village telling the people the news that there was to be a great wedding feast after the potlatch. Susan had kindly translated.

Elizabeth felt sick just thinking about it.

Auntie had rallied somewhat and stopped complaining about the food and the beds and the fish and started complaining about all the Indians arriving. Elizabeth was growing tired of her complaints, and she had put off telling her aunt about Isaac's intention to kill slaves. Somehow she just couldn't upset her aunt further. As for Rain on the Sea, Elizabeth suspected that her adoptive mother understood more of the English language than she let on, but even so, her mother could do little to stop the coming carnage. Also, Rain on the Sea seemed to approve of her nephew's actions. That comes of growing up in this society, thought Elizabeth miserably to herself. The prestige became more important than anything, especially more important than lowly slaves.

Realizing that hiding in her longhouse was not the action of a mature adult woman who was going to have a baby in a few months, Elizabeth forced herself out of the longhouse and down to the beach. Susan went with her, and they decided to take a closer look at the new arrivals.

All Fear His Name stood in the first canoe, splendidly dressed in hat and woven cloak. The men and women in all the canoes sang songs, and then, just off shore from the beach, the great chief's canoe stopped and he sang a song, gesturing with his arms and stamping his feet. The canoe moved slowly toward the beach, and he debarked, very carefully, from it. Several watchers sauntered down to the beach.

Isaac, his father and several of his father's retainers appeared from their homes and walked down to the beach, each one elaborately dressed. Many Salmon scattered white down on the beach. The puffy little feathers descended like snow.

"Peace," said Susan. "White feathers tell Tsimshians we feel peaceful."

Elizabeth hoped the Tsimshians felt peaceful, too.

A melodic welcoming song was sung to the newcomers. Elizabeth was pleased that she could understand several words in the song.

She glanced over at Isaac. He looked very handsome in his Haida costume. Her throat tightened.

He wore a woven blanket over his shoulders. It depicted a black raven with its wings outstretched. On his head he wore a squarish hat. Round shell earrings dangled from his ears and his black hair was combed neatly down over his shoulders. His strong legs were bare. He and several men did a dance, and she found she could not take her eyes off him. How could a man who looked so vital and strong and handsome harbor such murderous intent? The pain in her throat intensified. She couldn't cry here, not with everyone around her. She tightened her lips, trying desperately not to give in to the despair she felt.

The Tsimshians were walking past her in a fine parade of color and movement. All Fear His Name led the procession. He was beautifully dressed, as was every member of his tribe. Elizabeth counted about forty people, several of them in very elaborate dress; no doubt all were chiefs. They chatted animatedly with one another, pausing now and then to nod or briefly greet a Haida acquaintance.

Susan made a low growl in her throat.

"What is it?" asked Elizabeth, drawn out of her sadness by curiosity.

"They say bad things." Susan frowned.

"What are they saying?"

Susan shook her head, obviously not wanting to tell Elizabeth what she'd heard.

Elizabeth repeated her question.

Reluctantly, Susan answered, "They say Haidas give cheap potlatches. They say they will laugh at foolish Haida dancing. They say they will laugh at our poor possessions. Throw them in the water."

Elizabeth sucked in her breath. Isaac had been one of the dancers. She thought he'd done a fine performance. What right did these people—guests, yet!—have to arrive and insult their hosts?

"If anyone throw in water, it be Haidas throw in Tsimshian," said Susan staunchly.

"Is the great chief saying this, too?" asked Elizabeth.

Susan glanced at All Fear His Name, who stolidly led his group. His back was straight and proud; Elizabeth saw nothing in his behavior to convey an insult.

"No, he say nothing."

Elizabeth privately felt relieved. She did not want to think that Isaac's own uncle would join in the insults.

Trailing behind the Tsimshian dignitaries came

a less dignified party. Slaves, Elizabeth realized, judging from their ragged clothes and matted hair. About twenty men, women and children plodded along. Some of the children were singing, only to be hushed by their mothers.

"Slaves," explained Susan. "Isaac buy."

So these were his victims, thought Elizabeth. Then her heart lurched. One of the male slaves, arm in arm with a matted-haired woman, and preceded by two little boys, suddenly came abreast of her. She gasped. The man caught her eye and nodded; then he smiled.

"Oh, no," moaned Elizabeth. "Not Jake, too."

"Jake, too," agreed Susan quietly.

Elizabeth had to turn away, lest Susan see her fear and anger. She was so angry she was shaking. How could Isaac do this? *How could he?*

It was obvious to Elizabeth that Jake had no inkling of the terrible fate awaiting him and his little family. Guilt flooded through her that she should even be a part of such a terrible event. She knew what lay in wait for Jake and his wife and sons, yet she felt helpless.

What could she do?

Throughout the afternoon more guests arrived. At dusk, when Elizabeth last counted the number of canoes on the beach, there were over forty-five. The longhouses were crammed with people, there was singing and dancing here and there, and she learned that the main potlatch, Isaac's big potlatch—the one he intended to clear his name— would begin sometime on the morrow. Though he intended that the potlatch would clear his name, for her it would only sully it. Blacken it. She could never look at him the same way again.

She was walking slowly along the beach when she heard footsteps behind her. She recognized those footfalls. She turned. "Isaac." The words came out dully, an echo of what was in her heart for him. Nothing.

"Lis-uh-buth." He walked beside her. "You happy about my potlatch?"

She felt no need to lie. "No, I am not happy," she said. "I am very angry."

"Angry?" He appeared startled.

"You are going to throw away all those slaves, Isaac. I know what that means." She glanced at him, hoping to change his mind.

But his firm jaw was set. "I give my potlatch, Lis-uh-buth. It very important. Then I can be a free man. Free of being called bad names by people."

So he did not want people speaking ill of him, did he? What about after word of the murders got out? No one would think him important then! Certainly no white people would!

He halted and reached for her, pulling her into his arms. Once, she would have wanted this. Once she would have cherished the feel of his strong arms encircling her. Now it was as though he were a tree, so little did she feel. He had killed her feelings for him. They had died when she'd learned of his true barbaric nature.

"I beg you, Isaac, do not do this thing," she whispered. She held her breath. Would he listen to her? Was there any hope that they could become man and wife, as she had once so deeply desired?

But his next words dashed all hope. "I must do this, Lis-uh-buth. For me, for my family, for my clan. For you and my child."

"Very well," she said, slowly extricating herself

from his arms. "I understand, Isaac." She bowed regally. She understood now. He was bent on doing this terrible thing. She must not appear to fight him, for a man who was ruthless enough to kill unarmed slaves would think nothing of harming a defenseless, pregnant woman. "I will see you soon." Let him wonder about when, she thought as she hurried away.

"Lis-uh-buth," he called after her. "Come back!"

She waved away the concern that she heard in his voice. "I will see you soon!" she called over her shoulder even as her feet hastened along the beach. She must get away from him.

And she must make some plans.

She found her aunt sitting by the hearth fire. Susan had disappeared, and Rain on the Sea was nowhere to be seen. In the rest of the longhouse there were people talking and laughing and shouting. Only in her own little corner was there any quiet.

She plopped herself down by her aunt. For some reason she could not explain, when things were bad, she found herself turning to her aunt. Complaints or no, she knew her aunt loved her and would help her.

Auntie was sipping something steaming out of a cup. She glanced up at Elizabeth's entrance. "Care to try this new tea?" she invited. "Rain on the Sea gathered some of the leaves when we were out picking berries. It's supposed to help me sleep better." Her aunt made a face. "With all the noise in the longhouse, I thought I would never get to sleep, but Rain on the Sea kindly produced these leaves." She took another sip. "Try it; it tastes very good." There was actually approval in Auntie's voice, and somewhere it registered in Elizabeth that her aunt and her "mother" were starting to get along well.

But Elizabeth had other things on her mind. "Auntie," she began. "I am very concerned."

"Oh?" asked Auntie. "I thought you might be. I heard from Susan that you are getting married." She giggled.

Elizabeth grimaced. She'd prefer to forget the plans Isaac had made. Well, she had made other plans.

"Auntie"—she lowered her voice—"listen. I have something very important to tell you." She glanced around to make certain they were not overheard. "We have to leave this place."

"Leave? So soon? I thought you were getting married!"

"No, I am not. Isaac is very mistaken."

"How can he be mistaken about something like that?" asked Auntie, puzzled.

"There's not much time to explain," said Elizabeth. "Trust me."

Slowly her aunt looked at her. "I don't want to leave, Elizabeth." She shuddered and gripped Elizabeth's hand. "I thought this was what you wanted."

"No! We're leaving."

"I'll never understand you, dear," Auntie said meekly. "But if you want to go . . ."

Elizabeth gave her aunt a brief hug. All her impatience with Auntie's complaining fled.

"But how?"

"We're to meet Susan on the beach after things quiet down. We're stealing a canoe and we're leaving this place. Susan knows the way!" Heavens, it felt as though Susan and she were always sneaking away from villages in the middle of the night. She attempted a smile to reassure Auntie. "You must gather up everything you wish to take with you. In the meanwhile, there is something I must do. At midnight we will leave!"

"So soon?" Her aunt looked frightened, and Elizabeth was reminded suddenly that her aunt was an old woman. An old woman, a pregnant woman and an Indian woman, all about to set out on a voyage of escape. What had her life become? But there was no time to think about such things. Time only to act. "I must go," she told her aunt.

Her aunt nodded. She was trying to be brave, Elizabeth could see that. She patted her aunt's arm. "Be ready." Then she heaved herself to her feet and hurried away. There was one more thing she had to do before she left this village.

Chapter Thirty-four

"Quiet, Auntie," whispered Elizabeth. It was the fourth time she'd cautioned her aunt. Why *did* Auntie persist in yawning so loudly?

"It's the tea," muttered Auntie, answering Elizabeth's unspoken question. "I should not have taken so much of it. Feeling tired. . . ." She started to nod off where she sat on a patch of dry sand.

"Wake up, Auntie," hissed Elizabeth. "I think I hear Susan."

Her aunt blinked several times and then sat up straighter, leaning against the log that Elizabeth sat on. Elizabeth jumped up and walked a little way into the darkness. "Susan?" she whispered hoarsely, hoping her friend could hear her.

On the beach it was silent, while up at the longhouses there was dancing and singing and drumming and music. The loud sounds wafted across the beach on gusts of wind.

Elizabeth and Auntie had already waited what felt like a long time. So far they'd waited about twenty minutes for Susan to show up. Twenty long minutes.

Elizabeth peered into the darkness. No Susan.

She glanced around nervously at the trees edging the beach before she went back and sat down on the log. "We wait," she told her aunt, hoping her voice did not betray her concern. The longer they waited, the riskier it became. If someone came along and spotted them out here sitting on the log, it would look suspicious.

This time Elizabeth let her aunt nod off to sleep. What difference did it make?

She gasped.

Susan appeared out of the darkness, barely visible. She wore dark clothing and carried two bags. Elizabeth picked up her own bag and nodded at her aunt. "We could let her sleep a little longer. Jake and his family are not here yet."

Susan looked at her sharply. "You say they be here soon."

"I thought they'd be here by now," Elizabeth explained unhappily. She glanced around. Loud sounds still drifted from the longhouses. The dark trees along the beach and to the side were silent sentinels.

"We can wait a few more minutes," she said. "Jake should be here any time."

They waited. Elizabeth fidgeted nervously with the leather drawstring of the bag she held. She realized suddenly that it was a gift from her adoptive mother, and a bolt of guilt shot through her. She would never see Rain on the Sea again. Regret went through her.

374

Ten more slow minutes passed and still no Jake.

"We go," said Susan. Elizabeth could hear the nervousness in the Indian woman's voice. Susan was risking far more than Elizabeth to leave this village. She was fleeing family and clan. Elizabeth was only fleeing an unwanted bridegroom.

She vowed to herself that she would make it up to Susan. Susan could live with her at Fort Victoria and they would be as sisters. Elizabeth found she no longer cared what the white people at the fort thought. Susan was her friend, and she was once more risking her life for Elizabeth. Elizabeth would not take such true friendship lightly.

They heard a noise over by the trees.

"They're here," whispered Elizabeth excitedly. All she wanted was to get Jake and his wife and children into the canoe. "Wake up, Auntie."

Elizabeth gently shook Aunt Elizabeth while Susan peered into the darkness where the trees were. "I hear them," Susan told her. "They're here."

Jake came out of the darkness toward the log. And behind him walked several men.

"Where is your wife? Your sons?" Elizabeth stared at Jake in astonishment. Then she realized . . . "Jake!

"Run!" she screamed at Susan. "We've been betrayed! Run!"

But before Susan could get to her feet, before Elizabeth could awaken Auntie, the men swept down on them. Jake looked sadly at Elizabeth and shrugged. He'd told them, Elizabeth realized bitterly. "You fool," she hissed at Jake. "You betrayed us! All of us! Now you'll die! You and your children!" Helplessness washed over her.

"Hush!" said a stern-faced Isaac. He walked up

to Elizabeth. He glared down at her while his men helped Auntie to her feet. Two men, one on each side of Susan, were there to make sure she did not escape.

Elizabeth lifted her chin. "You will not win," she said. "I will not marry you."

"I will marry you," he told her, and his voice sounded like angry thunder to her. "I want my child. I want you for my wife! I will tie you up if I have to."

Elizabeth suddenly remembered how she had first met this man. How could their time together have ended in any other way? She'd been such a fool to think otherwise.

She held out her hands straight before her, and he motioned to a man. The Haida tied her hands together. When he'd tied the last knot, she said to Isaac. "I will escape as soon as I can."

"Thank you for warning me of your plan," he said, and she wished she'd kept her mouth shut.

Recklessly, now that he knew everything, she added, "I will escape you and I will bring all the whites I can to destroy you!"

He raised an eyebrow at this. "I do not think so. You will never get away."

He said it so confidently that for a moment her courage faltered. Then she recovered herself. "Do not hurt my aunt," she cautioned.

Isaac waved at the two men helping the older woman. "Take her to the longhouse," he said in English.

"Don't hurt Susan either," said Elizabeth nervously as it dawned on her what a dangerous position Susan was in. She'd been caught helping someone escape her own people. A ruthless man like Isaac would no doubt kill her. Probably when he killed the slaves.

Isaac glared at Susan, and said something to her in a rapid burst of the Haida language. Susan glanced down at her feet. Susan had to act quiet and appear subdued, Elizabeth realized. Or else she would be killed.

She watched as Susan's hands were tied up, too. William was with the crowd of men and he said something particularly scathing to Susan. Or so it appeared from Susan's reaction. Now she was completely quiet. She even hung her head and bowed her shoulders.

Elizabeth wanted to encourage her friend, but she knew that to do so could prove deadly for them both, so she held her silence.

Grimly, the little party marched back up to the longhouses. Susan was taken away to another longhouse while Elizabeth was led to her own longhouse. Auntie already lay on her sleeping mat, snoring.

The men untied Elizabeth, then left her there, with only Isaac and her snoring aunt for company. "You escape now, you in trouble," said Isaac. With one last warning glare, he pointed to the two men who had taken up guard positions near Elizabeth's corner. So she would have company to prevent her escape, would she?

She lifted her chin proudly to show she did not fear him.

He frowned and shook his head. "I do not know why you do this."

She glared at him. "We've said everything there is to say, Isaac." She turned from him. She could no longer bear to look upon that handsome, de-

377

monic face and form. She crossed her arms over her jutting stomach and steadfastly kept her back to him. Only after she heard him leave did she go to her sleeping mat.

She tossed and turned restlessly all night, pursued by dark visions of Isaac chasing her through Fort Victoria. She awoke at dawn after a terrible dream in which he'd thrown her over his shoulder and taken her to his canoe. She would never escape him.

She sat up groggily. The two guards watched her alertly.

This day the potlatch would begin.

Chapter Thirty-five

It was midday when the speeches started. Elizabeth and her aunt were escorted from their living quarters to the longhouse of Many Salmon. Inside the house it was crowded with humanity. Every important chief and his retinue were sitting there. Slaves, all owned by Isaac, all destined to be thrown away, bore wooden trays heavily laden with berries or fish or clams and they circulated among the hungry guests with their offerings.

Elizabeth was not hungry. She turned away several offers of food, only to earn glares from Isaac.

"He is insulted because you will not eat his food," whispered Susan behind her.

The two sat on special mats placed for them next to Rain on the Sea's retinue of women. To outsiders it would look like Elizabeth and Susan enjoyed high-ranking places of honor. To Elizabeth, who knew better, their placement was to prevent their escape.

She was glad to see that her friend did not look harmed in any way nor appeared to be suffering. She would have asked Susan about her treatment had not Isaac been watching her so closely.

Auntie had slept late. Elizabeth wondered at the tea her aunt had sipped the night before. Whatever it was, it certainly helped people sleep. Her aunt smiled as she was brought in, led by the two men who had guarded them through the night. "Isaac said you are going to marry him," whispered her aunt as she sat down next to Elizabeth. "I am so glad you came to your senses. He will make you a fine husband."

Elizabeth snorted rudely. Wouldn't it surprise her aunt to know that her niece was sitting with her hands tied together under the blanket draped over her shoulders?

Her aunt looked at her. "A better husband than some," she said. "You're doing better than I did. I married John Butler. The rodent!"

Elizabeth almost choked. Comparing Isaac Thompson to John Butler was like comparing a cougar to a mouse. She wanted to say something, but she knew that, once started, she would be shrieking at her aunt, so she held her tongue.

Soon the dancers entered and performed for the crowd. Elizabeth stole a glance at the Tsimshians. To a guest, they appeared to be enjoying the dancing. She noticed the small mountain of berries and fish and meats piled in front of All Fear His Name. She doubted such a thin old man could eat that much, but she noticed he did not wave away the food. Several of his "little chiefs" were eating the proffered berries and smoked fish. There was no sign that they wanted to drag the dancers out of the longhouse and throw them into the sea as they had boasted.

Elizabeth turned her attention back to the dancers. After they had finished, a group of singers came in. A young boy sang a song, his voice very melodic. Elizabeth tried to understand the words, but she was so upset from all that had happened that she could not do so.

After the singers there were speeches. Then Isaac and his men and women of the Raven clan began handing out blankets. Not just one or two blankets to each guest, but a pile of blankets grew in front of each guest. Some of them could hardly watch the proceedings, so high were their piles.

After the blankets, plates and dishes were handed out. There were oohs and aaahs from many of the guests at such largesse. But the Tsimshian delegation remained silent. Only All Fear His Name appeared pleased with the gifts.

Now and then Elizabeth watched Isaac. This was his day. This was the culmination of all he'd strived for and worked for over the past several months. She saw the pride and happiness on his face, and her heart softened for a moment. But only for a moment. If she had not known what he'd planned, she would have been happy for him. But she knew. And she was not happy.

His father looked proud, too, and she saw that he was speaking often to Isaac. She'd always detected an estrangement between them, and she found herself wondering if this potlatch was overcoming the distance between the two men. Then she decided it was none of her concern. She would sit through this event, and then she would leave. Somehow.

As she sat watching, Elizabeth had plenty of time to bitterly regret her involvement with Isaac. As items were given away, she drifted off in her mind to the times she should have told him to leave her and her aunt alone. If only she had listened to Auntie. But now it was too late. Elizabeth should have known that he was barbaric and cruel. Why, oh why, had she not listened to others?

She came out of her reverie and glanced around. The guests would be staggering home under a full load of gifts this day, she saw. In addition to the blankets and plates being given out, there had been furs and shirts and woven cedar hats and knives. Three fortunate chiefs had received a beautiful canoe each. A beaming All Fear His Name was one of them.

Elizabeth had lost count of all the possessions that had exchanged hands. Everywhere she looked she saw potlatch items. Men and women chatted and complimented one another upon receiving the gifts.

The Tsimshian chiefs were beginning to look pleased. All except one of the younger chiefs. He looked vaguely familiar to Elizabeth. Then she realized he was the one who'd told her about Isaac's plan to kill the slaves. No doubt he, too, was unhappy at the pending murders because every time she happened to glance in his direction she saw that he was glowering—at Isaac.

Once she caught Isaac glaring back. She wished she knew more about the Haida customs so she could understand what was going on.

The food had been served, the gifts given out, and people were sitting in small groups talking and laughing. Jake was sitting with his family. He looked relaxed and happy as he played with his two sons. A wave of pity for him flowed over Elizabeth. She hoped he was enjoying this time with his family, because soon he would be dead. If only he had not been so foolish as to tell Isaac about their escape plans. She shrugged inwardly; she'd tried to help him.

The hearth fire in the center of the longhouse was built up, and buckets of grease were poured on the fire until flames shot high in the air. Elizabeth wondered how the chiefs and their followers sitting closer to the fire could stand the heat, but none of them got up and moved away, even though she could see beads of sweat glistening on many foreheads. After the fire display, things quieted down, and she was wondering if the potlatch was over when Isaac walked out and made an announcement.

Susan, seated behind Elizabeth, translated in a whisper: " 'Welcome, honored chiefs and esteemed guests.' " Here she named All Fear His Name and every other chief who was attending. Apparently, the chiefs were all seated in proper order of status around the longhouse.

She continued, " 'We pleased to invite you to fine Haida potlatch. You have expensive gifts from our Raven clan. You cannot give us better. We give better gifts than you. From now on, everyone say Fights with Wealth—that is Isaac—is good man, powerful man, rich man. No one can say different. No one can say bad things about me. Only good things. Anyone say bad things, they pay.' "

She continued on in this vein for a time. Elizabeth's ears perked up when she heard mention of the slaves. She tried frantically to undo her tied wrists under the blanket, but no matter which way she moved her wrists, they remained securely bound.

" 'We so rich, so powerful, we not need slaves,' " translated Susan. Now the matted-haired people were being urged to get to their feet and go down to the center of the longhouse. Several large Haida warriors dressed in their best finery guarded them.

Elizabeth's stomach clenched. This was the time she'd dreaded.

The unwary slaves walked willingly down to the fire. All of them had serious looks upon their faces, and she wondered suddenly if some of them suspected what was about to happen.

She could barely look at Isaac in all his finery as he ordered the slaves about. She wanted to shield her eyes, but she could not.

Finally, after all forty slaves had gathered by the fire, he said—and Susan translated—" 'Now we do something great. We throw away slaves. Our Haida village so rich, our Raven clan so rich, I am so rich, I can throw away slaves. You cannot. You have to watch. You see me throw away slaves.' "

Elizabeth closed her eyes in fear of the brutal deaths she was about to witness. Bile rose in her throat, and for a moment she thought she would throw up in fear, but she did not.

Behind her Susan explained, "Now William leads each slave to fire."

Eyes still closed, Elizabeth's stomach roiled. He

was going to burn them! Oh, my Lord! she thought in horror.

There was a commotion, but Elizabeth managed to refrain from opening her eyes. She had no desire to see defenseless men and women murdered before her eyes. Her hands clenched together. She prayed avidly for God's help for the slaves. For herself. For all the heathen souls who thought this was right and proper.

She was so busy praying that she didn't realize Susan had stopped translating until she heard her friend gasp. "They free!" cried Susan. "He free them!" Rapidly she began translating. Elizabeth's eyes shot open.

" 'In old days we throw away slaves. We kill. New times now. We no kill. We free them.' "

"Free? But how—?" Elizabeth's eyes widened. Her heart pounded. "Oh, my Lord," she shrieked. "He's freeing them!"

Several Indians glanced at her, plainly irritated by her outburst, but Elizabeth didn't care. "He's freeing them!" she kept repeating over and over to Susan and her aunt and anyone who would listen. Rain on the Sea leaned over and patted her kindly on her blanketed shoulder.

She'd been mistaken! Susan had been mistaken! The chief who'd told her had been mistaken! They'd all been mistaken! Isaac had not intended to kill the slaves, he'd intended to free them! All along he'd intended to free them!

Elizabeth shuddered in relief. While everyone was admiring the freed slaves, Isaac slipped over to her and with a quick slice of his knife, undid the bindings on Elizabeth's wrists. He helped her to her feet. He was beaming, and she smiled at him.

385

"You—you freed them," she breathed.

He frowned. "Yes."

"But . . . but I thought . . ."

"Yes?"

"I thought you were going to kill them."

"I would not kill slaves. My mother was a slave. I know the shame. I free them."

The depths of her misunderstanding hit Elizabeth with the full force of a blow. How badly she had misjudged Isaac. Badly, very badly indeed. He had cared enough about slaves to buy them, at great expense, and then set them free. Never had she known a man who would do such a generous thing. Never.

"I set you free, too," he said. "Not force you to marry. I was very angry."

"Not marry?" She swallowed.

He shook his head. "No need. I am free now, too. Free of the past. Free of the bad things people said about me. Free of bad things the Tsimshian do."

She stared at him, stricken. As she gazed at him, at his proud bearing, his handsome face, his kind dark eyes, she realized suddenly that he *was* truly free. In the same way she'd become free of the pain of her lost father, so Isaac had rooted out the pain of social humiliation. He had just done it in a different way than she had.

He wasn't going to marry her. The full enormity of her loss hit her, and she almost sagged to the floor, but he caught her.

"I love my child," he was saying urgently. "I help you with my child."

Oh, no. He was already planning a life apart from her. One that included their child, thank God, but one that did not include her. Oh, misery!

386

Her mouth worked, but no words came. What could she do? He had rejected her, rejected marrying her. He had made his decision. Oh, my Lord, what could she do?

She was frantically trying to think of what to do when William came over. "Time for marriage ceremony," he said with a smile at Elizabeth.

As Isaac opened his mouth to speak, Elizabeth laid her hand on his arm. "We are ready," she said boldly. "I am happy to marry Isaac."

William looked at her a little oddly, as if her answer was not what he'd expected, but it was Isaac's dark eyes that she focused on. "I love you, Isaac," she said firmly. "I want to marry you. Now is as fine a time as any." And then she smiled with what she hoped was a confident smile.

His eyes met hers. Looking into their dark depths, she saw her love reflected there. He loved her, too. Her heart soared. This was the man she loved. This generous, great, good man was the one she wanted to share her life with—forever.

Isaac grinned back at her. He lifted her hand and squeezed it gently. "I marry you now, too," he said.

Her heart beat faster, and she laughed up at him. "Oh, Isaac, I'm so happy!"

"You marry in the Haida way?" he asked.

"Oh, yes," she agreed. "We can marry in the white way down at Fort Victoria."

He nodded. "We marry two times." He chuckled. "We live in love all our lives."

"Yes, oh, yes, Isaac," she agreed. "Always!"

The Haida and Tsimshian people gathered around them. The ceremony began.

Epilogue

Six months later
Fort Victoria

"What are you doing?" asked Isaac.

Elizabeth glanced up from where she sat in her rocker. There was a box on the kitchen table and she was piling books into it. "I am giving away some books," she explained as she lifted her well-thumbed copy of Miss Cowperth's *Authoritative Guide to Modern Etiquette*. She read the title a second time, then slowly put the book in the box. She sighed. Miss Cowperth's advice was no longer of use to her. Elizabeth's life had changed so drastically since she'd left San Francisco that it no longer seemed important to wear white gloves or to know which dress to wear on which occasion. She didn't really care about which plate to use for serving cookies, either.

Her aunt was going to take the box of books to the Women's Auxiliary meeting tomorrow afternoon. Perhaps the Fletcher sisters would enjoy Miss Cowperth's teachings.

A cry came from the back bedroom. "Oh, Ian is awake," said Elizabeth. "Do you want to pick him up, or shall I?"

"I will pick up my son," said Isaac, walking into the bedroom. He returned with a cherubic-looking, black-haired baby in his arms. Elizabeth rose from her rocker and walked over to the gurgling baby. "Hello, sweetheart," she said, kissing Ian on the nose. His headful of black hair stuck out straight in all directions, and she ran her hand gently over his head. "He's got his father's hair," she teased.

Isaac grinned and bounced the four-month-old baby gently in his arms. "And he will be a strong Eagle, like his mother," said Isaac proudly. Among the Haida, a son took after his mother's clan.

The proud parents cooed over the baby for a time until Ian fell back asleep.

Isaac laid the baby down gently, then returned to the kitchen.

"I am giving the sawmill back to you," she said.

He looked at her in surprise. "It is all paid off?"

She nodded. "It was paid off last month. You've paid me back every dollar I gave you."

He grinned. "So why did I not receive my sawmill back last month?"

She smiled. "Just making sure we covered all the costs." She added, "I think your sawmill will continue to do very well. We had two new orders yesterday."

He nodded. "Jake and the other freed men have

worked very hard. They do good work, and I think that is becoming well known around the fort. Soon I will open another sawmill. Susan will help. She is very good at organizing things."

Elizabeth smiled proudly at her handsome husband. "Well, then, everything is in good order. What shall we feed your uncle when he visits tonight? Should it be deer meat or smoked fish?"

"All Fear His Name likes fish. All the people with him like fish."

"Fish it is, then," she said. "I think I'll get out my white gloves to serve it. What do you think?"

He looked at her in puzzlement. "White gloves? Did my aunt teach you that?"

"No, Isaac. Your aunt taught me how to weave baskets, how to smoke fish, how to dance properly, and a host of other useful things, but she did not teach me what to wear when I serve smoked fish."

Isaac smiled. "Ah, it is not important, then."

"No." She grinned. "Not at all."

REFERENCES

Bragg, L. E. *More Than Petticoats: Remarkable Washington Women.* Helena: Falcon Publishing Inc., 1998.

Cole, Douglas and Bradley Lockner, Ed. *To the Charlottes: George Dawson's 1878 Survey of the Queen Charlotte Islands.* Vancouver: UBC Press, University of British Columbia, 1993.

Crooks, Drew W. "Murder at Butler Cove: The Death of Tsu-sy-uch and Its Violent Consequences" in *Occurrences: The Journal of Activities at Fort Nisqually Historic Site.* Vol. XIV, No. 4. pp. 3-12. Winter 1996/97.

Dawson, George M. "The Haidas," Extract from *Harper's Magazine.* Seattle: The Shorey Book Store, 1882. Facsimile Reproduction, 1965.

Donald, Leland. *Aboriginal Slavery on the Northwest Coast of North America.* Berkeley and Los Angeles: University of California Press, 1997.

Garfield, Viola E. n.d. "The Tsimshian Indians and Their Neighbors" in the *Tsimshian Indians and Their Arts.* Seattle: University of Washington Press.

Lillard, Charles. *Warriors of the North Pacific: Missionary Accounts of the North West Coast, the Skeena and Stikine Rivers and the Klondike, 1829-1900.* Victoria: Sono Nis Press, ed. 1984.

McFeat, Tom *Indians of the North Pacific Coast.* Seattle: University of Washington Press. ed. 1996.

Miller, Jay and Carol M. Eastman. *The Tsimshian and Their Neighbors of the North Pacific Coast.* Seattle: University of Washington Press, ed. 1984.

Rosman, Abraham and Paula G. Rubel. *Feasting with Mine Enemy: Rank and Exchange Among North West Coast Societies.* New York: Columbia University Press, 1971.

Seguin, Margaret. *The Tsimshian: Images of the Past; Views for the Present.* Vancouver: UBC Press, University of British Columbia, ed. 1984.

Stearns, Mary Lee. *Haida Culture in Custody: The Massett Band.* Seattle: University of Washington Press, 1981.

Stewart, Hilary. *Cedar: Tree of Life to the Northwest Coast Indians.* Vancouver: Douglas & McIntyre Ltd., 1984.

Sturtevant, William C., *Handbook of North American Indians: Northwest Coast, Vol. 7.* Washington, D.C.: Smithsonian Institution, General Ed. 1990.

Vastokas, Joan Marie. *Architecture of the North West Coast Indians of America.* Ann Arbor: PhD thesis, Columbia University. Microfilm 1997 by University Microfilms International, 1966.

Captive Legacy

THERESA SCOTT

Heading west to the Oregon Territory and an arranged marriage, Dorie Primfield never dreams that a virile stranger will kidnap her and claim her as his wife. Part Indian, part white, Dorie's abductor is everything she's ever desired in a man, yet she isn't about to submit to his white-hot passion without a fight. Then by a twist of fate, she has her captor naked and at gunpoint, and she finds herself torn between escaping into the wilderness—and turning a captive legacy into endless love.

___4654-7 $5.99 US/$6.99 CAN

·Montana·
Angel

Theresa Scott

Amberson Hawley can't bring herself to tell the man she loves that she is carrying his child. She has heard stories of women abandoned by men who never really loved them. But one day Justin Harbinger rides into the Triple R Ranch, and Amberson has to pretend that their one night together never happened. Soon, the two find themselves fighting an all-too-familiar attraction. And she wonders if she has been given a second chance at love.

___4392-0 $5.99 US/$6.99 CAN

Dorchester Publishing Co., Inc.
P.O. Box 6640
Wayne, PA 19087-8640

Please add $1.75 for shipping and handling for the first book and $.50 for each book thereafter. NY, NYC, and PA residents, please add appropriate sales tax. No cash, stamps, or C.O.D.s. All orders shipped within 6 weeks via postal service book rate. Canadian orders require $2.00 extra postage and must be paid in U.S. dollars through a U.S. banking facility.

Name_____
Address_____
City_____State_____Zip_____
I have enclosed $_____ in payment for the checked book(s).
Payment <u>must</u> accompany all orders. ☐ Please send a free catalog.
    CHECK OUT OUR WEBSITE! www.dorchesterpub.com

Savage Revenge

BRIDE OF DESIRE

THERESA SCOTT

To beautiful, ebony-haired Winsome, the tall blond stranger who has taken her captive seems an entirely different breed of male from the men of her tribe. And although she has been taught that a man and a maiden might not join together until a wedding ceremony is performed, she finds herself longing to surrender to his hard-muscled body.

___4474-9 $5.99 US/$6.99 CAN

Dorchester Publishing Co., Inc.
P.O. Box 6640
Wayne, PA 19087-8640

Please add $1.75 for shipping and handling for the first book and $.50 for each book thereafter. NY, NYC, and PA residents, please add appropriate sales tax. No cash, stamps, or C.O.D.s. All orders shipped within 6 weeks via postal service book rate. Canadian orders require $2.00 extra postage and must be paid in U.S. dollars through a U.S. banking facility.

Name_____
Address_____
City_____State_____Zip_____
I have enclosed $_____ in payment for the checked book(s).
Payment <u>must</u> accompany all orders. ❑ Please send a free catalog.
CHECK OUT OUR WEBSITE! www.dorchesterpub.com

NIGHT RAVEN
Elaine Barbieri

With his fierce golden eyes, Night Raven sees a vision of the future that torments him, drives him to seek vengeance against the white man. Famed for his fearless exploits, sought after by the women of his tribe, he has sworn to show no mercy to the enemies of the Apache.

He sees her first in a dream, a woman with hair of shimmering gold and eyes of brilliant blue. Captured in battle, he is stunned when she appears to doctor his wounds, even more shocked by the traitorous longing she rouses in him. But when he manages to escape the fort, sweeping her onto his horse as hostage, he refuses to give in to his wildfire yearning. She, too, will know the torment of unfulfilled passion, he vows, for she is his enemy. But with each tender touch of her lips to his, Night Raven finds his resolve slipping, until captor becomes hostage and vengeance changes to mercy with the triumph of love.

TYKOTA'S WOMAN

CONSTANCE O'BANYON

Tykota Silverhorn has lived among the white man long enough. It is time to return to his people. Time to fulfill his destiny as the legendary tribal chieftain he was born to become. So what need has he for the pretty white woman riding beside him in the stagecoach, trembling beneath his dark gaze? Yet when Apaches attack the travelers, when one of his own betrays him, Tykota has to rescue soft, innocent Makinna Hillyard, teach her to survive the savage wilderness . . . and his own savage heart. For, shorn of the veneer of civilization, raw emotions rock Tykota. And suddenly, against his will, blue-eyed Makinna is his woman to protect, to command . . . to possess.

___4715-2 $5.99 US/$6.99 CAN

Dorchester Publishing Co., Inc.
P.O. Box 6640
Wayne, PA 19087-8640

Please add $1.75 for shipping and handling for the first book and $.50 for each book thereafter. NY, NYC, and PA residents, please add appropriate sales tax. No cash, stamps, or C.O.D.s. All orders shipped within 6 weeks via postal service book rate. Canadian orders require $2.00 extra postage and must be paid in U.S. dollars through a U.S. banking facility.

Name_____
Address_____
City_____ State_____ Zip_____
I have enclosed $_____ in payment for the checked book(s).
Payment <u>must</u> accompany all orders. ☐ Please send a free catalog.

The OUTLAWS: Rafe

Connie Mason

He is going to hang. Rafe Gentry has committed plenty of sins, but not the robbery and murder that has landed him in jail. Now, with a lynch mob out for his blood, he is staring death in the face . . . until a blond beauty with the voice of an angel steps in to redeem him.

She is going to wed. There is only one way to rescue the dark and dangerous outlaw from the hanging tree—by claiming him as the fictitious fiancé she is to meet in Pueblo. But Sister Angela Abbot never anticipates that she will have to make good on her claim and actually marry the rogue. Railroaded into a hasty wedding, reeling from the raw, seductive power of Rafe's kiss, she wonders whether she has made the biggest mistake of her life, or the most exciting leap of faith.

___4702-0 $5.99 US/$6.99 CAN